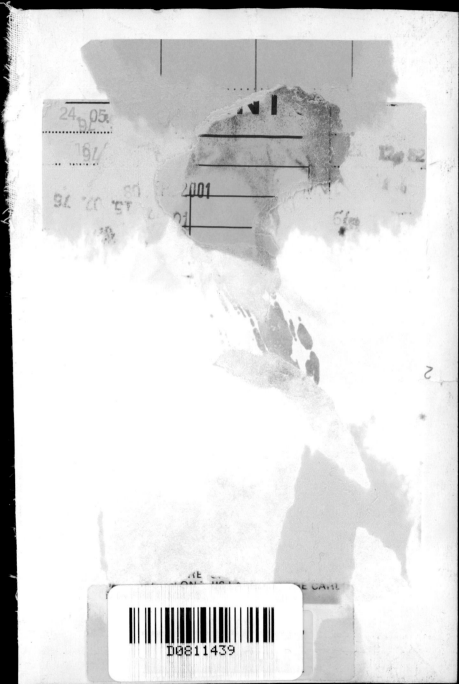

The Trap

Dan Billany

CEDRIC CHIVERS
PORTWAY
BATH

First published 1952
by
Faber & Faber Ltd
This edition published
by
Cedric Chivers Ltd
by arrangement with the copyright holder
at the request of
The London & Home Counties Branch
of
The Library Association
<u>1974</u>

<u>ISBN 0 85594 975 9</u>

74-16253 ✓

F BIL

D620D27

200063896

Printed in Great Britain by
Redwood Press Ltd, Trowbridge, Wiltshire
Bound by Cedric Chivers Ltd, Bath

PART ONE

PART ONE

Chapter One

There I stood, looking at the letter.

I don't believe I ever before in my life felt quite the same. I cannot describe my state. The postmark shook my very heart with confused emotions. It was 'Helston, Cornwall: 11.30 a.m., 15th December, 1942'.

[One has to give the history of an emotion: but not in any fashionable way. It's a question of what one wants to do, and there I fail, in a sense. I can't say in words what my object is, but that is not to say I don't know. I know precisely, in the sense that I reject the wrong impressions when I record the past: but I don't know what makes them wrong. A sense of falseness—'*that's* not it.'

Begin as you mean to go on.

What I want to convey is just truth: reality. Not the *effect* which results from truth, encountered by surprise on a gravestone, or on the wall of a public lavatory: but the simple bulk reality of events. I don't feel that any new technique is demanded, but I know myself: I know how delicate my balance must be if I'm not to be swayed to one side by the Sense of the Dramatic, or to another by the savour of words: or another by outrageous indignation, or another by its converse, humility resulting from fear. So for me at any rate there is the question of a sober, strong attitude to my writing, yet a sensitiveness: I must beat out my own way to the truth which lies behind my eyes and no others. There are as many truths as men, but there are so many reasons for not telling them. And above all this, is the fact that I shall be paid by the page, so to speak, for this, and I need the money. And yet I will honestly try.

So I don't want the running commentary of Hemingway, indeed I'm scared to fall into that style, because it's so near to what I do want to do, and yet it will betray my purpose completely. I don't want to leave you out as a spectator of my picaresque adventures, and yet I don't want to take you with me on an odyssey in the manner of Stevenson: I'm sorry to be so incoherent, but if you think, you'll see that neither way gives complete truth: there's something missing in both, perhaps it's the undertone of all my reflections, reactions, associations. Once that play of shadow is thrown in, the story will stand forth, as if you'd put on stereo-scopic glasses, in its living truth. In a sense it's the immedi-acy of William Saroyan that must be in with the story. But not quite the same personality, which after all is stagey in its simplicity—the Chaplin naiveté.

When I sit back from writing, and seriously consider what task I am setting out to do, I am afraid, I have the panicky fluttering of the heart that a portrait-painter has when he has put in the main lines of his subject, and, having done, say, the detail of an eye, sees that eye peering out at him from the paper with a cryptic, unanalysable beauty and resemblance to the model, as if the likeness is there, latent in the lines; and the artist catches his breath, afraid—can he bring that out, the speaking likeness? He trembles, feel-ing inside himself potentialities both for success and failure. He trembles on a narrow line; immense achievement is there, waiting on the stretch of his fingers, and the balance of all his being, if he can poise so nicely. And so I am afraid, be-cause I know how readily I can fail, but the success, if I can achieve it, will be beyond the earth and life. I am a por-trait painter: let me draw Truth, so that every grown man, who sees the picture, sees it with blinding recognition: that is Truth!

Here, before I begin, is my prayer for steadiness, and poise not to slip into the facile or the dramatic, not to laugh cheaply: whatever powers affect human accomplishment, make me constant throughout all the pages I am to cover: first, from literary falsenesses, from the temptation to slick-ness and meretricious lures in the opening pages, to entice the choosing reader at the station bookstall: from false sentiment which may develop in the middle section of my story: and from spurious rages and bitterness, and even worse, false pathos, in the conclusion.

O deliver me.

From false humility and the abdication of my own judgment, which are really due to fear, so that I should bow before authorities whom I did not in my heart acknowledge,

O deliver me.

From rhetoric and the deliberate writing of purple prose, with all their corollaries of false morals and lack of honesty with the reader,

O deliver me.

From all those various obstacles of vision and sobriety which intervene between the truth and the various schools of present-day writers,

O deliver me.

Make me myself alone: let me not echo the words of others, lest I also echo their thoughts in the belief that I am expressing my own.

This prayer is not addressed to God, since I do not believe in him, nor to any other Powers of the Air. If it were addressed to anything precise, I daresay it would be addressed to my Unconscious. But I haven't said so, because the notion of a man saying a prayer to his Unconscious seems ridiculous to me. Anyway, the Unconscious, like God, is deaf. Most people are really praying to their Unconscious when they think they're praying to God. But it makes no odds, there's never any answer.

Is it possible for a man to see what is before his eyes? Does he always see what is behind them? This is not obscurantism: I can put certain disconnected lines on paper, and you will see them as letters of the alphabet: your eye will fill in the gaps. But the material your eye puts in—isn't there. Your reading of the lines is a demonstration that you are seeing more than is before your eyes. You are reading—in a metaphysical sense—between the lines. Similarly, at Helston, which I propose to describe as objectively as I can, Lord Tennyson visited the Loe Pool, and, according to his published works, saw there 'an arm, clothed in white samite, mystic, wonderful'. Lord Tennyson also observed about the Loe Pool a landscape of jutting crags and iron cliffs. In fact, as can be verified by any metropolitan who cares to take a ticket on the Cornish Riviera Limited, these features observed by Lord Tennyson are not there. His description of Helston is highly dramatic, but he has eliminated much that is, to replace it with much that is not. Not that I'm saying his description is less accurate than mine. It is to his purpose, and his purpose included King Arthur and Bedivere, etc. My purpose is different, but I've no doubt at all that it will distort my vision. Emotional Relativity.

This is how I see Helston (and all those who have seen the town, passed through it, visited it for the Furry Dance, stayed in it, and last of all, those who live there, please add your own comments *between the lines*—you will in any case).

It is a small agricultural and market town in South-West Cornwall, within two and a half miles of the sea: the people there all speak in the most beautiful of English dialects, a low-pitched resonant burr which has the musical sonority of American without its nasal bleat; a manly accent, like Paul Robeson's in a way: they also transpose nominatives and accusatives with a freedom I find fascinating—'Us be after 'ee'.

Helston is in a valley, so that if you want to leave the town, you have to climb: all the roads climb out of Helston, except one which winds out by the Loe Pool, under the hill, to Penrose, and eventually to Porthleven: but as I remember it, that road is closed, you can't go further than Penrose. You have to go by the main Porthleven road, over the hill.

The Loe Pool is very charming: a smooth shallow sheet of water. Tennyson said:—

'And lo! the level lake, and the long glories of the winter moon.'

It is really the estuary of the river, silted up till it is divided from the sea by the Loe Bar. In the Valley, by the Loe Pool, I have often heard the quiet sighing of the sea on the Bar, a mile or so away.

You see, you can be quiet in Helston. God forgive me if I should talk of a 'sleepy old Cornish town': it isn't that. There is a quietness, I admit, which is proper to an organism that's half asleep, or half dead, but there's also the quiet of a man who is more interested in hearing and seeing than

14

in being heard or seen. That is the kind of quiet I found there. One could be at ease: not stealthy, but peacefully aware of the metabolism of existence. One had time to hear the sea and see the sky.

Nothing in that part of Cornwall makes a bid for your attention. Thank God for that. Thank God for unambitious things. Because frankly I've been brought to such a rawness of nerves by now, that the mere thought that Cornwall still is there, that the road slopes up out of Porthleven as it did when I walked there—those thoughts alone hurt me in a way that I don't care to encourage. I want to look at some solid Cornish cliff, and square stone houses for a time, till I get back my emotional balance.

It's grey and featureless when it rains, but when I look up at the unbroken blue above me now, how I long for the hissing rain of a September afternoon at Helston to be trickling behind my ears and under my collar again, while the town soaks in its basin of dark hills, and the dark sky streams down on it.

All this flood of recollections for a postmark.

Here is one more. The scene is not Helston, but Polpryn, more or less midway between Helston and Falmouth. I am in a drawingroom which now does not exist, anywhere in the universe—no, I'm not dreaming, merely writing the sober fact—and Elizabeth is playing the piano: I see the music sheet on the rest, *Sonntag* by Brahms (and the English word 'Sunday' above it), and I see Elizabeth's confident, quick fingers on the keys: we are both singing:

> 'The Sun gleamed from the golden skies
> And Heaven was bright within her eyes.
> How I long, how I long to be there by her side,
> How I long, how I long to be there by her side'.]*

There was a time when I wore barathea, brown shoes, a Sam Browne, peaked felt cap, and kid gloves, and carried a cane in the manner prescribed by my commanding officer. That was when I first came to West Cornwall. I got out of the train at Helston station, which is high up on the edge of the

* The passage between square brackets was crossed out in the original.

town. I had my respirator over my shoulder, and carried a big suitcase in one hand: with the other hand I dragged from the luggage van my valise, carefully, because my typewriter was inside it.

There was a popular phrase about England, right through the war—'You wouldn't know there was a war on'. But if you were in uniform, you carried the war about with you.

The road down from the station—typically wet, since in Cornwall either the rain has just stopped or is just about to start—was metalled with small stones in a tessellated pattern, which I later found very treacherous for nailed military boots. Down the side, between the narrow pavement and the road, ran what Elizabeth and all the Cornish people called a 'kennel'. In the north, where I was born, we should call it a 'gutter' I think, but if 'kennel' derives from 'channel', it is a better word. It was a stone channel, probably a foot wide and a foot deep; every so often it was bridged by paving-stones which connected the pavement and the road.

And down this channel ran water from the hills that stand all round Helston. It was gurgling in the kennels when I first saw the town, and it was the last sound I heard when I pedalled David's cycle for the last time up Coinagehall Street. Even in the driest weeks of August there is an inch of water, ribbing in the sunshine the bottom of the clean channel: once I saw a dog, panting from the heat, lie down on its belly in the kennel, facing upstream, breasting the water. In the rainy weather, the kennel confines a torrent of clear, hurrying, gurgling water which rises almost to the road. The sound of running water is to Helston what the sough of the wind is to Haworth. Even in August and September, after the brown dry corn has been taken in from the fields, you hear the brisk water at every corner where the kennels meet. In April it fairly raves along the kennel. I wouldn't be surprised to learn that Tennyson borrowed—so to speak—the water from the kennel at Helston to put it in the land of the lotus—'A land of streams. . . .'

Coinagehall Street is the backbone of Helston. It drops steadily to the South-West, through the centre of the town, till suddenly it is halted by the gates of the bowling-green.

The gates are square across the road: a newcomer, as I was, has the impression that, as a result of civic miscalculation, the main road has come to a dead end, and life is vain. But this is to blame unjustly. It happens that the hill down which Coinagehall Street runs, grows ever steeper, and finally breaks down to the market square in a precipice fifty feet down: so that the abrupt gates of the bowling-green have the purpose of preventing you from throwing yourself into perdition and a cow-pen. Nor does the road stop there, after all: investigation shows that it branches to the right and to the left, like a letter T, and here may I warn you to take the left fork, since the right is narrow and drops steeply. Both will lead you to Penzance, anyway.

On either side of Coinagehall Street are large and prosperous inns. One time or another I have been in most of them. The Blue Anchor brews its own beer, which is famous. Just now, though, I think with special tenderness of the Alpha: it is not licensed: coffee and tea there have sometimes been very good, and food is fresh, home-made and liberal. Such is memory, I can almost smell that coffee, and see the sunlight reflected on a window over the way.

If on foot, you may go through the gates of the bowling-green, on, and down the slippery stone steps which span the cliff-face. It was here that I first looked over the little park and the swings, the tennis-courts and the boating lake. Half to the left lay the valley where the Loe Pool lies, under the hump of Castle Wary: to the front rose another green hill, with a tree-hidden lane climbing its flank. I went down the steps, finding at the bottom a further confirmation of the civic prudence which I had already noticed,—a cast-iron urinal, painted an unobtrusive green, so sited that it may be perpetually flushed by the descending waters, suitably confined in pipes, at no cost to the citizens. I utilized this amenity, and went on towards the park: but you need come with me neither here nor there.

Chapter Two

The first time I entered Elizabeth's home, I was excited as if I were finding an extension of her personality. It was a singular home, but the precise nature of its singularity cannot be put into a few words. You will understand it later, when you know Elizabeth and David and their parents. At any rate, when I first went in, and Bonzo had finished licking me, I felt a delightful recognition, that this was in fact the only possible background for Elizabeth.

Damn it—enthusiastic: that is a word that helps in describing the Pascoe house. It was the house of a family that worked hard for a living, and valued every aspect of its home. There was no money in it, but the home was a conscious work of art: the planners had enjoyed the planning, and their home life was a happy savouring of the result.

By the thumping of my heart, and the heady elation and tide of emotions that went with it when I first went into her home, I was assured that in growing up one does not discard one's childhood, one merely adds to it. For I had known it all before. My breast, at nine years old, had shaken to very similar impulses. Oh yes. I had known them all already, known them all. It was but the repeating of a situation natural to my life, only this time with a clearer recognition that this was what I was born for.

When I was nine or ten, I fell in love with a little brown-haired girl in a blue dress, who lived in the next street but one. My love for her was a ravishing ache in my heart, never remitting. I know that I thought principally of her all the time I was awake, and I know that I wanted to dream of her, and sometimes I did. This is not phenomenal memory-work on my part, I am a man who remembers his childhood. For a long time every night, in bed, before I went to sleep, I thought of her—thought is too mild a word, I concentrated all my being upon her: for those delicious fantasies I used actually to hurry off early to bed—it amazed my father: my mother was dead then. My fantasies were like this: I would lead a band of boys from our street to make war upon the street she lived in. She, a Boadicea, would command the opposing force, and great hand to hand fighting would occur, broomhandles, bottles, half-bricks and wooden swords figuring. Finally my men would break and fly, and I, fighting desperately, but gashed across the forehead with a brick, would be made prisoner by the soldiers of the girl in blue. They, and she, would torture me, and I would faint: and, as I lay semi-conscious, she would bend over and stroke my forehead, and her lips would be near mine—after this my fantasy became vague, I had in my breast a labouring sense that a mighty satisfaction lay somewhere hid there, what it might be I could not realize: and my fantasies continually returned to this point and yearned there, with an unquenchable thirst.

I don't know that it's important to say it—perhaps it is: in actual warlike games, as a boy, I was not ever in the lead. My part was vatic: I stood in the rear and shouted my comrades on to victory. A misgiving still haunts me, that such is my nature still; in fact, I know it is.

I next fell in love when I was thirteen, with the boy who shared my desk at school. His name was Joey (I must not give his surname, and don't care to invent a name for him). Again this was an absorbing emotion. One of the great epochs of my life. He had very fair hair, clear blue eyes, a broad forehead, and was very good and kind. I remember plenty about my love for Joey, but it would not seem much in the writing, and anyway I have an inward reluctance to drag out details which probably wouldn't be understood, and wouldn't seem significant even to me if I put them in black and white. As an example, once during the hot weather, when Joey and I were walking home from school, he put his arm round my shoulders. It was a common enough gesture with him, in fact most schoolboys do it, without thinking: but I have remembered to this day the leaping of my heart, and all that incident is printed on my mind so that it will be clear when I'm an old man. Well, I said you wouldn't understand.

Joey died of tuberculosis when he was twenty. I happened to hear of it, but without grief, for I had not seen him since we were fourteen. I think the part he had to play in my life was completed and permanent. Something of him lives with me, and always will, arbitrating all I know of love and beauty and kindness.

It occurred to me not long ago to consider what had happened to the four of us who were boys together in Beaky's class. This was how it worked out: Fred was drowned in the North Sea seven years ago, which was three years after he left school: George went into the mines, and was killed in an explosion before he was twenty: and Joey was the last to die. I find it a queer, inscrutable thought that out of those four boys who played together, so short a time ago, I alone remain to represent us to the world. What sort of differences would it have made, if we had known how the future was arranged, and that those three boys were never to be much more than boys? Would I have felt, as I swapped cigarette-cards or rolled marbles with them, that I was playing with ghosts, boys with no future? Would Beaky have treated them with less cane and more kindness?

Having concluded the last two paragraphs with the same word, I had better return unobtrusively to Polpryn.

They did not, at any rate, stick me in a corner with the family photograph album on my lap, and talk to me over its pages, about Royalty or the weather. In fact, I did not find the photograph album till long after: it was a generous, stout book which Elizabeth had made herself, as an exercise in book-binding, but had never quite finished. Typical of her, the essential work was done, but the straw-boards were uncovered. Whereas the tidy, completed, gummed-cornered and indexed products of more systematic minds are not necessarily better. People who have tidiness and system often have little else.

'They use the snaffle and the curb all right,
But where's the bloody horse?'

Some of the photographs were fixed neatly in position

according to a scheme of David's, but the gum supply or David's application having failed, this series lasted only three pages. There were also some put in by Elizabeth, with some attempt at dating, but most of the pictures were identified by remarkable allusions—'The Hag' showed Mrs. Pascoe looking *eldritch* through the celluloid windscreen of a sidecar. Another was described in a way which recalled to me an auctioneer's catalogue—'Picture showing Mam and Dad on the A.J.S. the day the sidecar came away from the bike near Bodmin'.

Not affixed to a page, but loose in the book, was a small picture which drew me more than later ones. It was one of those oval pictures which were fashionable years ago, and showed John and Marion Pascoe at the time of their marriage. The date when it was taken, and the name of the photographer, were written on the back in ink which had aged to an unhappy brown as if in sympathy with the ageing of the hand that wrote it.

Which is the reality, the young photo, or the ageing exemplar? Behind his new wrinkles the young creature still stands, with increasing fetters and bonds, a great prince in prison. It might be worth while to cultivate that eye of discernment that can see through the crinkling, opaque flesh, to that truth which, by the evidence of the camera, once was, and therefore still is and ever shall be.

Dad (I called Elizabeth's parents Mam and Dad) had then only the incipient shade of those three horizontal furrows which now barred his forehead—merely the fine shades of reflection and a trace of perplexity suggested on the smooth unscarred face of a boy. His hair then was crisp and curly, as indeed it remained, but in the photo it had a self-conscious length, and pride, even vanity, in the way it waved back from his forehead. On his face was the young man's pleasure and shyness in being well groomed for this occasion: the eyes looked out, perhaps just a little doubtfully, on a life that was in the future. Young eyes are lit with the future, old eyes shadowed by the past. The thing that goes deepest to our hearts is to see old eyes that sometimes still shine, like children's, with projects for the future. But the eyes of Dad were in other respects the same, those dear, honest, kind blue eyes, hopeful, but a trifle unsure. The face was fuller, the cheek smooth, the smile nervous because of the camera.

'Mam' too was different. The photograph was of a girl changing to womanhood, a daughter, not a wife, a sister, not a mother. There was great beauty in her picture, but not so much an individual beauty, as the beauty of all girls who are growing to full life, the tender, innocent, kind beauty of an adolescent girl. Her thick black hair, worn very long, was parted in the middle and drawn down over her ears, to tie at the back of her neck, an old-fashioned but quite beautiful style. She wore a white silk blouse with a lace frill at the neck and down the front. There was little expression on her face, except the camera-smile and a certain air of questioning: of wanting to know what came next—yet I thought, looking hard at the beautiful girl-face, a tremulous confidence that whatever came would be good. Her teeth were white, and showed well in the smiling picture. She was very like Elizabeth at that time, but thinner in face, and rather older in expression. Yet somehow I thought I found an indefinable innocence or ignorance in the expression, perhaps emphasized by the arm which was linked under that of her future husband. She felt unsure about life I suppose, but she confidently hoped to find out, if she went on seeking. Meanwhile John would understand and look after things.

But did she ever really find the answer to that hopeful question on the face of years ago? From the picture I turned to the person, and looked at her as she cleared the table, now, more than twenty-five years after: I thought not; and a sense of sadness came to me. I promised myself very gravely that Elizabeth should not come to any disappointment or lack in life or love, and that to all her unconscious hopes and questions I would find a full and satisfactory answer. I prayed and promised that she should not wait all her life for intangible gladness that did not come.

There are three treacherous sisters whom I do not trust as far as I can see them, and their names are Faith, Hope, and Charity. Faith keeps doubtful company, and is often found in houses of iniquity: Hope takes it on herself to fob man off with promises which have no basis in reality: and Charity sells cheap salves for sore consciences.

Our civilization is a triumphant success, and no doubt a luminous epoch in the history of Man, but one can't help wondering if ever before in our earthly story we have done so much Wishing that things were not as they are, or so much Hoping they would change. Is it too unkind to see our civilization, at its present prime, as an endless procession of couples like the Pascoes, who come onto the stage with an uncertain hope in their eyes, expecting they don't know quite what, but at any rate a certain satisfaction, the answer to a certain hunger: who turn sometimes to the footlights on their busy way across the stage, and still have that unease and perplexity in their eyes; and who finally pass from the stage into darkness, eternal darkness, still with that question, that tantalized, perplexed hope, never again to have the opportunity of satisfactions, not knowing what they sought, not knowing what was amiss, not knowing where peace might have lain, neither knowing the question of their lives nor its answer, but knowing this clearly at least—that life failed them. The plant of the spirit did not flower: the body, waiting and wondering, died unblessed and unfulfilled.

How hard it is to say what I mean. The blight and failure is the common stuff of today: because it is in every face, we cannot see it in any. Invert the Evangelist's motto, and you get the statement itself—'There are millions now dying who have never lived', but the rot is so deep in us, it reaches the bottom of our souls. Centuries after us, saner men will see the dreadful sterility stamped on our pictured faces, but we will not see it: we are too surrounded by emptiness ever to conceive of fullness. But our eyes. They will reveal our blight to the future—Unfulfilled Hope. Eternal Hope. Unrealized Hope. We only live in Hope: in hope that tomorrow will give us that unknown satisfaction which, yesterday, Hope expected today.

Since they, Marion and John Pascoe, walked into the

studio twenty-five years ago to sit for that picture, what changes. The faithful picture still showed the image it had caught, a second's glance across a July day now gone for ever: a boy and a girl planning marriage, and going to the photographer to fix the impression of their state. And now that instant of time, frozen and unchanging by the magic of the camera, lived its own separate existence, while they had continued on their changing way. I could almost see her, patting her hair before a big, dusty, gilt-framed mirror: and then the photographer fixed, in black and white, something which had ceased to be true even while his shutter clicked. Two people had gone into the studio, four came out, two to live in everlasting youth and love like the figures on the Grecian urn:

'Oh happy love! Thrice happy, happy love,
For ever warm and still to be enjoyed.'

And two to wear away down the unsatisfactory years, till they were at last worn out with waiting for an unknown answer to an unformulated question, waiting for the spark from Heaven to fall. On the photograph, only a little fading or shadow into light, and the rusting of ink: on the flesh, what prints of change: what storms, what panics, what triumphs and what blows, what struggles, agonies, what ambitions crushed by the soft accumulation of days and years, what dear wishes unfulfilled, what dear hopes slaughtered, what tears, what joy, what grief—above and through all, what change, both in themselves and in the world around them: but after it all there remained one thing in common to the picture and the flesh: the eyes still looking for the fulfilment of a promise, that could not understand that life had broken the promise.

Chapter Three

Once, long ago, when our fathers and mothers were young, and making endless plans, and life stretched before them like a land of dreams, so various, so beautiful and new: when they were the New Generation, the wave-crest sweeping upon the beach, and not the wrinkled, ebbing water sucked back with a long, withdrawing breath under the wave that follows after, when the greater part of life was before them as it now is before us—for they too once ran forward and laid hold on life with just the same resolution and the same anxiety as we do now—there was a young Cornishman whose family, for reasons beyond this book, had moved to the industrial North of England, and lived in a town whose name need not be written.

At the age of fourteen, this young man had gone out to earn his bread, a matter which demands early and long attention in this world of ours, and apparently occupying a more important place now than ever before: for whereas at one time it was possible for a younger son to ponder such alternatives as literature, adventure, alchemy or divine philosophy, or even to throw in his lot with an itinerant Nazarene, he now, in a world whose productivity has increased more than a thousandfold, finds himself so stoutly harnessed to the Industrial Turntable, that he never for one moment faces any situation than the bridle and the bit; and to obtain a very poor living he must give away his life, toiling from boyhood to old age, in the wealthiest civilization in the world, to earn very little bread and less butter.

That was the situation of John Pascoe when he was fourteen, a young member of the slave class, or working class, which is another way of saying the same thing. In his last month at school he did not plan his future career, or analyse himself to find which way his inclinations lay: the working-class do not take this approach to life, except in a spirit of imaginative recreation, which therefore isn't an approach to life, but an escape from it. They are too closely in contact with bread and butter reality; the world has already planned their careers in the most fundamental way possible, and their progress through the world will be dictated by the immediate necessity of filling their bellies. Nice notions of honour and propriety, fastidious tastes, are luxuries beyond working-class purses. I write, oh Posterity (should you read these lines) in the middle of the twentieth century, and I write with a bitterness which will not die till I do.

Literature has made the working class a convention—literature, which needs leisure, and therefore has been written for the leisured classes, with always—irrespective of the merits of the author—a standpoint above five hundred a year. Or nearly always. One hardly knows how to write simply and straightforwardly, now, about the normal circumstances of ninety per cent of humanity. God, what a decadence!

It used to be the fashion to see the working class always from a little distance—if not through bars, at least through an impervious psychological screen, so that their actions and emotions were as irrelevant to the gentle Writer and the gentle Reader as those of flatfish on the floor of their aquarium, on the other side of their thick glass and in their own bottle-green element. Seen thus, as it were, from the pleasant islands where Real Human Beings lived (such as the Gentle W. and the Gentle R.), from the windows of Rugby Chapel or Eton, from Oxford or from Park Lane, or from the saddle of one's hunter, riding to hounds, the working-class, those droll, non-literary, non-ablutionary, non-intelligent, non-creative masses, made a pleasant background of racy, smelly, ludicrous movement for the activities of the normal non-working world. Seen thus from the back windows of Pall Mall and Piccadilly, the working class was an aggregate of smeary individuals who apparently carried their sustenance with them in spotted red handkerchiefs and billy-cans; the female of which might sometimes be encountered by the observer whose business took him into its haunts, wearing a flat masculine cap, padding (or 'shuffling') along gas-lit streets, carrying a jug of stout in one hand, and with a paper of fish and chips rolled up in her apron. And what fun, what delicious fun to read about the quaint activities of these creatures, and the odd things they said; what guffaws of hearty Christian laughter at those of our human brothers and sisters who were so debased and sullied and fouled by a lifetime's starvation and waiting at our offal-tubs that the mere conception of them was irresistibly comic! These singular beings might from time to time be introduced into serious literature, usually as 'comic relief', but sometimes with the stern salutary aim of contrasting their humble worthiness with the frivolity of some of their betters—as examples of Humble Worth, the working class at one time challenged the dog: and when this is described in literature, it was important that the working class be drawn with as ignorant and clumsy a pen as might be, for obviously the Gentle Writer—being a Real Person, resident not far from Park Lane—would not be expected to have real knowledge of this sub-human species. A Few Bold Strokes would suggest them.

That convention is now practically dead: only Dorothy Sayers, with her Lord Peter Wimsey:—

'His primrose-coloured hair was so exquisite a work of art that to eclipse it with its glossy hat, was like shutting up the sun in a shrine of polished jet: his spats, light trousers, and exquisitely-polished shoes formed a tone-symphony in monochrome.'

—oh Attie! 'exquisite'! Only Dorothy, whose mark of a man is that he can tell a wine by its taste; Dorothy, whose quotes of Quarles, Vaughan and Donne prove her Artistic Integrity and Nobility of Aim; Dorothy who, with the classic perception elevated by her profound Oxford meditations, handles modern art-conceptions with a sensitive certainty of touch—'a tone-symphony in monochrome'—Dorothy who has made art articulate—'. . . however much an artist will put up with in the ordinary way, he is bound to be sincere with his art. That's the only thing a genuine artist won't muck about with'—only Dorothy among us yet remains faithful to the old attitudes. How her Lord compromises within himself the delicate wit, the erudition, the calm, the intelligence and all the rest of the virtues natural to the non-working world! How skilfully and with how few words, he corrects the Common Persons he meets in 'bus, train or street! How the vulgar, 'flashy', 'horsey', persons of the Lower Orders, the bobbies, the sergeants, the plumbers, the butchers and the bellringers become the hilarious laughing-stocks of Lord Peter's, and Dorothy's, wit—that wit so subtle and so sensitive, so delicate and so adroit. (That I may not be misunderstood, my epithets are used in an ironic sense only. I do not find Dorothy Sayers' wit to be possessed of any of these qualities).

But Dorothy is in that respect a relic from a different age: there came one day to Park Lane and the world of Dinner-at-Eight an astonishing discovery, the discovery that it was outnumbered by the sub-human working-class in the ratio of nine to one—that, in fact, Park Lane wasn't the real world at all, but only a most unrepresentative corner of it: that Reality was nine tenths the Black Country. And further-more, if Piccadilly was looking out of its ivory tower, Wigan was looking in. A new attitude to the working class seemed to be necessary, their importance must be acknowledged. So long as no increase in wage rates was contemplated, there was no reason at all why the Upper Classes shouldn't go completely Proletarian: it was cheap, thrilling, and awfully good for the Ego. So the Intelligence, Good Taste, and Social Con-science of the Upper Classes formed itself into groups for the study of the Communist Manifesto ('unexpurgated, my dear: *so* devastating'): investigated the contents of the red spotted handkerchief; sipped at the stout in the old woman's jug: ate fish-and-chips from papers in Hebrew fish saloons; and wore red ties. Nor did they stop there: the pluto-plebeians, hypnotized by the violence of their own Oedipus complex, which set them psychologically in opposition to their own class—I'm speaking of a rising generation—per-suaded themselves that this rebellion gave them identity of interest with the working-class, believed they had actually become working-class by sheer force of will—unaware, completely, that the thing which divides the Working Class from the Upper Class is, quite simply, not a difference of ideals but a difference of income. They poured out the Soul of the Masses in odes, paintings and symphonic poems which were, they swore, made up entirely of authentic proletarian yearnings—the throb of beautiful machinery, the knocking-off whistle, the beer off-shop at the corner, the fish and chips, the smoking chimneys, the garbage, the dust bins, the dead cats, the snotty-nosed kids, the flies around the empty salmon tin, the Pit Head, the blast-furnace, and the Red Flag. There; no break in the chain from Galsworthy to Auden, and you can roll in a great deal of pictorial and musical make-believe as well; they may look down their noses at each other, talk contemptuously of the Liberal-bourgeois, but they're all twisted twigs from the old tree, they all belong between Piccadilly and Park Lane, they're none of them working-class, they can run how they like but they won't get far. Proletarian Art? There it was, on the Arty-Crafty walls, proletarian Art, all produced by the younger sons and daughters of the world that dines at eight. Naturally the whole world, everybody who was anybody, came to see it, this new, this daring, this Progressive, this Functional, this Futuristic, this Realist Proletarian Art—everybody, that is to say, except the Proletariat, which had not heard the news of its emancipation, and imagined it was still outside the Real World of Park Lane and so on.

Oh yes, yes, yes, yes! I know I'm holding up the story, and I don't care a damn. I've wanted to say this for years. Rancorous? By God I'm Rancorous. I'd be ashamed to the very depths of my soul if I could write about my class without heat.

But I weaken my argument, you say, by my class-prejudice and bitterness. Very good then, I weaken my argument, and what does that matter, since I haven't the least desire on earth to convince my enemies of the justice of my case? I don't value their agreement, and I don't believe I could gain it though I spake with tongues of men and angels. I am Working Class. I was born of workers amongst workers, and therefore I am a native of their country. I know how

29

they order their lives, because my own has always been ordered in the same way. I know what their prime secular ambition is, because it is also mine—not to be compelled to work by the threat of starvation. I am not thrilled by the rhythmic clank of pistons: to me it is worse than a bloody noise—it is a bloody noise in which some poor devils must spend half their waking lives in order to feed themselves and those they love. When Proletarian Art sets out the beauty of Labour, I begin to consider it's high time the Proletarian Artist did some. Bluntly, I happen to know that the Working Class is by far the greater part of humanity, and by far the better part. All that part of our society which I have labelled Park Lane is to me a vulgar tower of insincerities, an unreal world which, the higher the ideals it professes, the more it reveals that its one overwhelming law is that of self-preservation—an ivory tower which I shall help to pull down, I hope. I don't know how to address a Peer: I don't propose to learn: I don't know Veuve Clicquot from Amontillado, Dorothy! I've never tasted caviare or venison, I don't understand the Stock Exchange; and the mentality of a business man going into the City by the ten o'clock and lunching out at the Savoy is to me a profound mystery, interesting because inscrutable.

If in this book I should chance to deal at length with the detailed life of the wealthy, read then in high excitement: anything might happen: you are reading Romance.

If you had asked John Pascoe, when he was eighteen or so, and dissatisfied with his apprentice's pay, and his long hours of work, what sort of man he was, and if he had spoken his most intimate thoughts, he would have said something like this: —'I am not a mug. I am well-read, self-educated, broadminded and intelligent. As a working man, I believe in Trades Unions and Socialism. I like to read history, and popular science, and I am a good debater. Unlike many of my fellow-workers, I am a realist. I am not to be taken in by propaganda. I am fair-minded, and am the master of my fate. I take life to be a very exciting business, and propose to live it in the conviction that I shall not pass this way again. My realism extends as far as the moral certainty that there is no God, and no life after death. All things considered, I think I know myself, and I approve.'

Now all that just shows how little a man knows himself. His self-portrait would be so far from correspondence with objective measurements as to be unrecognizable. Those things he plumed himself on, his reading, his acuteness and his self-education, were the least outstanding of his qualities. For his reading, he only knew Shakespeare by the chunks of blank verse he had been compelled to learn at school— Mark Antony's oration, the Quality of Mercy is not strained, etc. He had never seen a page of Chaucer, Spenser, Marlowe, Milton, Jonson, Richardson, Bunyan, or Fielding: he had only the slightest familiarity with Wordsworth, Keats, Browning, or even Paine, Rousseau, Darwin, who might be supposed to be in his line. True, he had read *The way of all flesh*. He knows of only two poems, in the whole of English Verse, which meant anything to him—Gray's Elegy, and Omar Khayyam, and in his opinion, his firm and stubborn opinion, these two poems represented the zenith of the world's poetic achievement. As for his self-education, his awareness of Man as a unit in the cosmographic scheme— he could throw about words like Neolithic, Paleozoic, Protozoic, Paleolithic, to impress himself and his listeners in Trades Union discussions, but in his heart, he was hazy about which came first: and though he liked to bolster up his arguments with the Theory of Natural Selection, he couldn't have put that theory into words—in any exact sense he didn't know what it was. But he wasn't a bluffer: he honestly thought he knew something, he honestly believed that the difference, which he sensed well enough, between him and his fellows was one of superior knowledge: but in fact, it wasn't so at all: the difference was, that he actually valued and sought such attitudes and thoughts, that he was, in type, the poet, daydreamer and philosopher, and though he was such only in embryo, yet there was a difference in kind, which both he and his companions sensed. 'John's got a rare head on his shoulders', was how they put it. But he deceived himself nowhere so much as about his acuteness, since he hadn't any at all, so far as the quality can be estimated in terms of cash return. As a lad, if he and his friends were trespassing, and one of them was caught—that one was John Pascoe. At work, if anyone was unpopular with foreman or manager, through speaking too plainly, it was John, and he would be the first in bad times, to be dismissed. If there was a rush for anything free, or unexpected, he would always be at the wrong end of the queue, and if he contrived by mere tenaciousness to get his share, he would as like as not lose it, be swindled out of it, or give it away. In short, he hadn't at all enough of the quality which, if we are to survive and prosper, we must be born with—self-interest. He didn't grab: he was more interested in the rights of man than in his daily bread, which might be taken from under his nose, without his noticing, or not noticing in time. His character was this, that everyone was his friend: but friendship is a hobby beyond a poor man's means, on that scale at any rate. John Pascoe had too much heart and not enough stomach: he used his mouth for talking, while others couldn't talk with their mouths full. I reckon all the same that he got the best of life's bargain, though he never earned four pounds a week in his life, and never once, from birth to death, had money enough and to spare: yet he kept one thing the blind mouths lost—his childhood's eyes, his naïve generosity, his volubility, his external identification of himself with his fellow-workers (who let him down day after day, but he never believed it), his belief in good, a belief which he didn't know he had: he kept his kind, sincere foolish soul, and by God there he won, though he lost the whole world, for what shall it profit a man if he gain the whole world, if he lose his own soul?

That being his character, I won't take up time with his early history: we all had mothers and fathers, and most of us left school when we were fourteen, and grabbed some blind-alley job for a few shillings a week. We have a rough idea, according to our own personal experience, of the roads by which a lad gets 'the nonsense knocked out of him', learns to smoke and drink and swear, and copulate in passages after the cinema or a dance; wears overalls, leaves work

32

at half-past five each night, quarrels more often with his father than he likes to remember afterwards—and so on.

When he was twenty he was an apprentice pattern-maker: he was engaged to Marion Shaw, a north-country girl. During the war of 1914-18 he broke his apprenticeship and ran away to sea, ostensibly for better money. It was the first and last revolt of the poet and vagabond in him, the last assertion of the boy who could not grow up: he played truant from his apprenticeship and his girl and his life, and ran like a trapped deer for the open sea. There he found himself, and there finally he lost himself. There, like the Scholar Gipsy, he understood the prime secret of life, and that it is one alone, and evermore shall be so: but unlike the Scholar Gipsy he returned after a few years to the world of men. He was a junior engineer. He studied a little, but he was at once too wise and too foolish to lay down his life for advancement. Without knowing it, he had eyes that could read in books not made with paper and ink.

Marion couldn't entirely understand her lover. She admired, and even worshipped his intelligence, his political awareness, his magnificent phrase-making, his God's eye view of history and humanity: she was touched by his tenderness: she was exasperated and humiliated by his coarse jokes and language, yet often had to laugh in spite of herself. She sensed a certain bigness, generosity, in him: yet she couldn't help noticing that he had no tact, that he was often slow-witted, that he never made the best worldly use of opportunities, that his generosity ran to thriftlessness, that while he was enlarging on his own smartness he would never notice anybody stealing his watch: spiritually his eyes were never off himself, he was always planning to shine and show off, and be a peacock, and he often told the same stories twice to the same people. 'He'll never get on' she sometimes thought with apprehension. He assumed without question that he was the brains of the partnership, and for years Marion believed it. But she herself had an instinct for living, for winning her way, for getting her share, for soft-soaping the right people, for pulling a home together, which he completely lacked. Both of them were impressed, over-impressed, by money and pretensions. John, for all his revolutionary hot air, felt an inward sinking when he came in contact with bosses, or people with cars, expensive fountain-pens, and solid gold watches. Before pompous, gilded monkeys, he abased himself as before God. Marion, all her life, feared and venerated doctors, who were to her a species above human. A rooted inferiority complex was in them both.

The engagement, though John had gone to sea, was not broken, but the war broke up all other plans. John, in the merchant navy, was swept all over the surface of the earth. Marion followed his course in the shipping information which she was able to pick up from time to time from local sources. She never had much more knowledge of his where-abouts than an intelligent guess. He was home for three weeks in 1917, during the summer: the war had a catalytic effect on their emotions, they married in the first week and honeymooned (at Marion's home, and without money) in the remaining two; fourteen days after the wedding, John rejoined his ship and put to sea. They had consummated the wedding, Marion was pregnant.

These two human beings who had united their lives were very different from each other: perhaps they had little more in common than the tender passion which makes youth the loveliest of all things the heart can know, and the ability to see each other as they were not. Marion had, as you and I have, two lives, an external, real one, and an interior life of dreams and wishes. But she was not a sentimentalist, at least not after John's naïve style. Her real life now was a transitional stage between girlhood and wifehood. It was an affair of changing relationships with her parents, in whose house she conceived and bore her first child: it was an affair of scheming to do more than money allowed, of watching the windows of second-hand shops. It was a matter of the household tasks she had done from her girlhood, washing and drying crockery, cleaning brasses, till her pregnancy became too advanced for these. Meanwhile her wish-life was very closely related to this reality; she saw herself and John happy in a 'small, comfortable modern house', with electric light and hot and cold water. John should earn five, or even

34

six pounds a week. There would be a garden, with a patch of lawn, and a lilac tree, and there would be a front room, very nicely furnished, where guests could be taken to play the piano and sing or talk or play cards. There would be no brasswork in the house, but there should be very good china, and cutlery. In summer they would have salads in a cut glass bowl she had seen in Shillitoe's window, or one very like it. She, Marion, would wear pleasant, neat dresses, dark because she looked slight and graceful in a dark dress. John must be taught to comb his hair straight back, and *not* to pick his nose. When they could afford it, they would buy a little car, or at least a motor-cycle and sidecar. And the children would go to a good school. She would stand at the gate each morning and wave to them as they went off on their way to school. (And so she did, but it was not all as she had imagined.)

Her child was a girl, born in the spring of 1918, when the Germans launched their last great, confident offensive: no one realized then that all the misery would be over before the end of the year, except for tears that none could wipe away. John, away in Chinese waters, wondered if somewhere in that unreal island on the other side of the world a new life had flowered, sprung from his youth. It was a very difficult and painful birth; Marion suffered shocking agonies, worse than she had ever dreamed of. A trained nurse had to be engaged. Marion's family helped, so far as they could, to meet the cost, the remainder came out of the tiny sum which John had banked in both their names, for the future home. John's own family kept their distance at this time, which afforded an initial reason for the rift which later developed, and lasted a lifetime, between Marion and her husband's people. Marion, in the years that came, forced John on to her side, though his sympathies were always divided: the children too, in the future, only saw Marion's side of the question.

John also had his two lives, corresponding more closely to the conventional division of body and soul. His body entered into the normal relations with reality, worked for a living, etc., drank, and slept, and committed itself to marriage and

35

all the interlocking social contracts that tie an individual in the repressive structure of civilization. His soul was doubtful, and watched this progress anxiously. It seemed a soul that had not entirely shed its wings: wild impulses of escape throbbed in it as it watched the fetters accumulate. John had long day-dreams about a different, freer sort of life altogether; he dreamed of being a carefree, moneyless vagabond, taking his way gladly and easily through life and through the world, wandering in hot, beautiful countries beyond Gibraltar, beyond Singapore. He longed to brush away on one side all the petty claims of civilization, even the claims of love, and be just himself, alone, no doubt,—hungry, probably—but undomesticated, unbroken, still keeping his happy wonder at the novelty and beauty of life, obeying no laws because he had no impulse to disobey—to wander till he died, having gladly and deliberately given up much comfort, in return for which he had had life. His eyes were always about him, whether on the round blue sea or on the tropical ports whose stink did not make them any less celestial and brilliant. His soul lived avidly, its lips were thirsty for free living: his soul would even have forgone love for freedom. Sometimes when his ship touched port he went ashore with the other engineers and got drunk with them: but in the overture to drunkenness, though he laughed and was as obscene as any, and told the best story of the night, his soul sat somewhat doubtfully on the outside edge of things, wondering. And often that dubious soul took him ashore alone, and led him, wondering, through fantastic, vivid tropical streets, turned his eyes to the rickshaw-boys, and the strange mementoes of old ways very different from those of the West; and he wandered, fascinated, teased out of thought by the marvel of these different lives, and longed to live them all, to be the smart native policeman, the cadging shoe-black, the old wrinkled woman selling pomegranates, and even the lean yellow dog stretched sleeping in the sun. Odd lines of Kipling's remained unforgettably in his mind.

On board ship, he delighted in the smartness of his cabin, a little world all his own; it was the cleanest, brightest, most ship-shape cabin on board. He made also a one-stringed fiddle, and taught himself to play, usually sentimental tunes of the late nineteenth century—but sometimes an impulse to creation blazed up in his heart, and his nervous fingers fumbling, improvising, along the string—some tune that should be the very voice of his heart, he knew not what, would come forth—only it never did. That heart was not articulate. It never contrived to put its urgent message into music, and the improvisation died away or lost itself in some clumsy pastiche of tunes he knew.

But he was glad to get home: Kitty, his little daughter, was nearly a year old when he first saw her. She had been weaned, and had several teeth.

When their dreams were reduced to reality, there were discrepancies, Marion's 'comfortable modern home' was what they called a 'sham four'. You know the term: a kitchen and a scullery downstairs, and two small bedrooms upstairs. The ceilings were stained with damp, or faulty plaster. Elizabeth told me that one of the great mysteries of her young life was connected with stains on the ceiling—she had heard Mother surmise that the stains on the *downstairs* ceilings might have been caused by the previous tenants upsetting their chamber pots: but Elizabeth did not fully grasp the theory, thought it referred to the *bedroom* ceilings, and used to ponder, night after night as she lay in bed looking at the ceiling, how the stuff got *up there*: she imagined wild acrobatic frenzies.

And in the sham-four was neither electric light nor hot water.

The world after the war was not kind to John's inferiority complex. Wherever he went, there seemed to be people with a better right than he to be there. He had forfeited his priority at his trade, by breaking his apprenticeship, and there was nothing else he knew. He would even have gone back to the sea (in spite of Marion's opposition) but there was no ship for him. The local engineering shops were filled with men who had stuck to their jobs throughout the war. Further, among his competitors for jobs were men who had joined the Army, and had been through Ypres, Mons, Vimy and Passchendaele: if society felt any obligation at all (one doubts it) it was to these. Finally, for all his considerable aptitude, John was not so good at any particular job as the man who had stuck steadily to it. His father told him once that Jack of All Trades was master of none: which everybody knows, but it doesn't help much.

So all the time the little household of John, Marion and Kitty Pascoe flourished as a flower flourishes whose roots are in sawdust. It was a lean, stringy, pale household, where it was hard merely to find pennies for the gas-meter. Their furniture, little as they had, was to the last degree cheap and shoddy, and even so, it wasn't paid for. No need to dwell on it, as it is the common case of half the population of England. Fifty per cent of us can't really afford to live nowadays: with every breath we are living beyond our means. And, trapped down there in the cellar of civilization, dog eats dog and rat eats rat.

I mean, for example, that the benevolent people who supplied the Pascoes with furniture on a system of deferred payments, were waiting every week for their money. These philanthropists—one doesn't blame them, they had to live, no doubt—seeing in John and Marion two inexperienced seafarers steering their flimsy craft over the ocean of life, had hastened to show them what tackle was necessary, and to supply it, asking no more than two or three times its value for their services, and the privilege of paying weekly. There was a high chair and a pram for fair-haired little Kitty, and of course a tiny wooden chair with a hole in the seat—indispensable where there are babies, Mrs. Pascoe. And while Marion still thrilled to be Mrs. Pascoe instead of Miss Shaw, the tradesman added ten per cent for luck. His luck. There was a carpet which the salesman persuaded Marion was just what she had always wanted, and when she got it home—carried the damned thing herself—she did not dare to admit to herself that it was shoddy, and the flowered pattern hideous: to her, till it wore right out, it had to be the 'lovely carpet' which the counter-rat had called it. However, it wasn't long wearing out. Paying for it took much more time. The bed (one only), the table and chairs, the curtains, which all had to be the cheapest in the shop because the couple were so poor, were shoddy and flashy and frail: and

38

yet, before the paying was done they had cost far more than good articles. But there was no alternative.

Work grew scarcer. John got odd days here and there, labouring, and one day went to a wealthy landowner's estate trimming overgrown trees. Odd catchwork with nothing permanent about it. Every day the Pascoes sank deeper into extreme poverty.

At last, in sheer desperation, John walked—he could not afford 'bus fares—from one town to another, between Bradford, Leeds, Keighley, Doncaster, Thorne and Goole, seeking work. Where he was lucky enough to get a few days' work, he sent the money home to Marion, who bought necessities for Kitty and nothing for herself—but paid the rent. While John was away, the philanthropist who had supplied the high chair came and took it back, there having been no payment on it for five weeks: and he swore at the defaulting customer, for her breach of faith, and for the wear and tear which Kitty had inflicted on it. He had already had something like twice the value of the chair, which might have eased his pain. When John returned home again, Marion told him the story with even more colour than life, for even so early she had a tendency to pep up the truth. ('Mam doesn't romance: she improves the facts' John used to say, long after: Marion hated the phrase). John, driven beyond control by the cruelty and injustice of it, and that Marion had been molested behind his back, called on the philanthropist, and knocked him down in the front of his shop. The police took notice of the incident, but the philanthropist was not anxious for that kind of advertisement, and would not proceed with the case.

John next persuaded the local greengrocer to give him a couple of bacon-boxes, ostensibly for fuel, and he made Kitty a high chair himself. This was the first bit of bacon-box furniture the Pascoes possessed. Later they had much more, and John developed special technique for tea-chests. He considered it a failure on his part if he had to buy wood, but if this must be done—for ornamental furniture—he loved to buy mahogany, or to disguise deal as mahogany with permanganate of potash). Kitty's bacon-box chair was better than the one the philanthropist had reclaimed. In style, if anything, it was Baroque, perhaps with the intention of disguising the origin of the material. There was a deal of elaborate, flamboyant detail. John believed firmly, to the end of his life, that beauty was synonymous with ornament.

Her name was inlaid in letters of sycamore on the tray which was to support her food: no-one would have dreamed that the whole contraption was a bacon-box. The lettering was the most ornate John could devise, but was really not beautiful—

KITTY

or something of the kind, I forget the individual flourishes. But she never read it.

Shortly after Christmas (they bought a Christmas-tree for ninepence, a lopsided thing with about four branches: it was for Kitty. No presents on it, but some slightly tarnished ornaments from Marion's home, where they were kept in a cracker-box all the year round) John heard of a ship leaving Grimsby, with an old acquaintance of his as Chief Engineer. He went there immediately, was signed on as fourth engineer, wired goodbye to Marion, and sailed the same night.

A week later, Kitty took diphtheria, and died in the local sanatorium. Marion was thus, very suddenly, alone in the house. John's chair, and the high-chair, were both vacant when she sat down at table to eat. However, she did this rarely. She spent her time between her mother's home and her own, which she would not give up for all the urging. When she came back in the evening to her own empty house, she used to stand for a long time touching the high-chair which had been made by John for Kitty. In that way, amongst others, Marion Shaw became Mrs. Pascoe.

All her life she never lost the vivid memory of her first child. Kitty was the pattern with which she compared her later children. At all their baby actions her mind flew back to Kitty. Years after, when David was a baby, she used to lean over his cradle and call John's attention—'Look how he's screwing his little eyes up at me, just like Kitty used to do'. John forgot his first child, but Marion never did. She had always three children, not two. Though Kitty had only visited them, as it were, for two-and-a-half years, her mother never forgot. Kitty grew no older, but could never die. Hence Elizabeth ate her baby food, her milk and rusks, sitting in a high chair with the name 'Kitty' inlaid in the tray.

Chapter Four

At the time of Kitty's death, Marion was already pregnant, though she did not know it till a week after the funeral. Elizabeth was born in July 1921, on one of the hottest days of the year. Dr. Mackridge delivered the child, and warned John, who was home again, that it would be dangerous for Marion to have any more children, at any rate for a long time. During her pregnancy Marion had not been well fed, so that from that time onward her teeth became carious. Elizabeth's teeth also suffered: though they were not malformed, they needed constant attention when she grew up, as they were readily subject to decay.

From Elizabeth's birth, John never went to sea again. He was harnessed for life. But the sea, where he had passed his young, free, happy days, stayed in his mind. His body might be standing, years after, in the kitchen at Polpryn, washing the dishes—his soul (and this was why the dish water grew cold) was stepping off the gangway at Durban, or Cape Town, or visiting Civita Vecchia, Archangel, San Francisco, Alexandria, Bombay, Le Havre, or Suez. He had seen them all, and many, many more—Hong Kong, Sydney, Freetown, Calcutta, but he never saw them again. He went no more a-roving.

For a long time Marion was too weak to leave her bed, or to nurse Elizabeth. John's life became domestic, when he was in the house. He took any work he could get, bill-posting, chimney-sweeping, occasional gardening, but still was out of work more than half the time. Elizabeth could remember the time when John and two or three collaborators scraped up money enough to start a small joiner's and cabinet-maker's shop, and John took her to see the lathe and the fine machinery, and smell the sawdust and shavings. John talked cheerfully about being one's own master. But that failed, like most other things. There seemed years of failure, from Elizabeth's birth till she was nine or ten.

In the house John was always busy, particularly after Elizabeth's birth. At sea he always had a book ready for his leisure, but now he had no leisure, not even to read his daily paper. Perhaps he was cooking over the gas-ring, or mixing Elizabeth's baby-food; if not that, washing dishes, or repairing his boots with odd bits of leather bought 'cheap-like'; or at his bacon-orange-box, tea-chest joinery, planing up a bit of wood to be set aside as part of a cot for Elizabeth.

Days of poverty and hunger were not as dark as they sound. The home was, at any rate, a little universe, self-complete. There was a hearth and a fire, there was a door to close against the wind and the world: there was a baby, and its mother and father. Even the most ostentatious establishments don't amount to much more.

Marion's mother visited them every day. She thought the world of John, because he was like herself, honest, kind, and the sort of man 'who would never get on'. She looked after the baby—not to Marion's satisfaction—instructions continually flowed from the bedroom. She was very fond of beer, and used to bring a drink in every night for John and herself. She also brought potatoes, eggs, butter, etc., when she could get them. Two dainties which appealed to her particularly were a cowheel, and a pig's nose. Sounds curious, but true.

'Marion', John used to say, 'your Ma's been an angel to us'; Marion would wince, because she hated the sound of 'Ma'.

When John got home in the evening, generally his mother-in-law had something on the table for him to eat, and a glass of beer to go with it: and she would be by the fire, with little Elizabeth on her knees, dusting the baby's bottom with Fuller's Earth. There were a few things to be done, the table to clear after the evening meal, and the crockery to wash. These done, and Elizabeth given her bottle, the two would sit by the fire, enjoying the warmth, peace, and relaxation, the room lit only by the firelight. Usually, John went to the cupboard, some time during the evening, and took down from the top shelf a long, narrow bag, laced at one end, and made of strong green cloth which had once been a port hole curtain.

Opening the laces, he would slide from the bag his home-made one-string fiddle, which came forth, box end first, like a cobra sloughing its skin. In the bag was also a bow, and a lump of resin.

It's no use saying the tone of the thing was pleasant, except to a trained ear. The fiddle had none of the sonority of a violin: it had, in fact, a thin, piping wail. To John's ear it was rich, plaintive and evocative. After a stroke or so of the bow, to savour the tone, he would begin to play, his left hand sliding and quivering the whole length of the finger-board. He gripped the box-apparatus between his knees, rested the head of the shaft on his shoulder, and bowed it like a 'cello. The voice of the fiddle was unutterably, unbearably sad—sadder, the gayer the tune. It was so damned thin and keening. It was a comment on the aspect of life. It was like that Banjo of Kipling's: —

'And the tunes that mean so much to you alone
Common tunes that make you choke and blow your
nose,
Vulgar tunes that bring the laugh that brings the
groan,
I can rip your very heartstrings out with those.'

He used to play quietly, so as not to wake Elizabeth: that thin, heartbreaking little voice would sing through the four rooms, sometimes loud enough to call Marion's attention to her husband's skill, and please her with the music. John could not hear the worlds of sadness in the voice of the thing. His mother-in-law sat opposite him, in the uncertain fire-light which gleamed on the rim of her glasses, gazing at him with supreme content as he played. Her wrinkled hands were folded in her lap.

And the fiddle, whether he knew it or not, told the story of his heart: all the long-forgotten childhood yearnings, the hopes that died of disappointment, the griefs that wept themselves to sleep, the tears that were not wiped away, the important questions that simply were not answered. His

44

eyes on the fire, and an absorbed frown on his face, with sometimes a fake note, and generally a slur, with the quivering throb which he later loved in a Wurlitzer organ, John the Rover ceased from roving, played himself over the sea and over the years. Not sad tunes, but often songs which had been popular, and which he and Marion had sung in their earlier days:

'Down in Virginia', 'Beautiful Ohio', 'Asleep in the Deep', 'Golden Dreamboat', 'By the Blue Lagoon', 'Little Dolly Daydream', 'Bedouin Love Song', 'Thy Sentinel am I', 'The Bandolero', 'The Star of Bethlehem', 'Daddy', 'Lily of Laguna', 'Barcarolle' (Hoffmann). And then he put away his fiddle in its green bag, shared with his mother-in-law whatever beer was left in the bottle, and went with her 'as far as the 'bus stop'. She wore a little black coat which she seemed to have had all her life, and a black hat with a spray of cherries in the band—she pinned it to her thick white hair with a dangerous hatpin. Happy those early days, no matter that food and money and coal were scarce.

The cot where Elizabeth slept was intended to rock, or swing on two pivots, and thus lull her to sleep; but every time it rocked, it squeaked loudly, so finally it had to be fixed so that it couldn't swing. John was short of material when he made it, and this scarcity imposed an austerity on his design which was entirely good. But in one respect he would not be denied; he soaked it with Permanganate of Potash, and disguised it as mahogany. The cot stood beside the parents' bed for some months, till Marion had completely recovered, and then—with misgivings, but Dr. Mackridge advised it—was moved into the empty bedroom. Elizabeth, from the first, gave evidence of having inherited her father's wanderlust; from little more than two years of age she was very migratory, particularly when she had been put to bed; at any time up to midnight she was more or less ubiquitous. To restrain this tendency John devised a net of stout cords, which was fastened down over the cot and tied down at the corners every night. It was certainly one way of dealing with the problem, but I doubt if it was the best. Because of the unspeakable distress which Elizabeth expressed each night

45

when John thus reticulated her, the net was known as the 'Howling Net'. But after some experiment, Elizabeth found that nature had anticipated the emergency, and she could eat her way out by biting the net: she celebrated the discovery by appearing nocturnally on the darkling landing at the top of the stairs (wearing her nightgown and her mother's hat) suggesting a 'ta-ta'.

At her best (John used to say) Elizabeth was capable of biting through any existing cord-net within seven-and-a-half minutes. The logical answer, I suppose, would have been wire netting: Elizabeth and I agree it would be as well if parents were always clear about whether they want to keep children or chickens.

A black box used to stand by the cot. Elizabeth, after biting a hole large enough for her body, rolled out of the cot onto the box, and thence to the floor. The only sounds involved in the manoeuvre were two decisive thumps. Marion learned to detect these sounds above chatter, music, or any noise that might be going on downstairs.

During her long illness, Marion had formulated some standards of the home she wanted, differing entirely from the one she had got. To her, the most complete means of self-expression was in the making of a home: she had the building instinct of a beaver.

Both she and John were a little inhibited sexually, and kept their ecstasies for night and the bedroom. They didn't base their lives on their orgasms, as I would, and were not entirely in sympathy by day. They didn't trust their love far enough. By day, John day-dreamed of Trinidad or Honolulu, Marion of willow-pattern plates. Which brings me back to what I meant to say two paragraphs ago.

Marion's creed was something like this:

There shall be no brass in my house: it takes too much cleaning.

My furniture shall be solid: if too heavy to move, it shall be such as can be swept under.

There shall be no crevices, mouldings, or embossings to collect dust.

46

Carpets and wallpapers shall have a small pattern or no pattern at all.

Everything shall be simple, solid, plain and clean.

Useless articles shall not (because they may look pretty) be tolerated.

Unfortunately, by the time Marion had reached these conclusions, John and her mother, shaping the home while she lay in bed, had developed it in the opposite direction. For example, John had found in a lumber room in his parents' home an old clock, more than a century old: it had brass weights and pendulum, brass chain and hands, and a yellowed vellum face. He dismantled and cleaned it, and made it go, and when Marion came downstairs it was tick-tocking on the wall, the reflected sunlight dancing from the pendulum-bob. He had also found some brasswork for the hearth, and on the mantelpiece he had set a remarkably ornate brass candlestick which, one bibulous night years ago, he had stolen from a cabaret in Marseilles. And he had made a mahogany (genuine mahogany) table, a tiny, slight thing with slender arched legs, and on this table stood a healthy aspidistra. Marion's resolutions were checked. Even apart from hurting John's feelings, you couldn't throw everything out into the yard, the house would be as bare as a barn— or a cupboard, rather, considering its scale.

Work became better. Till Elizabeth was six or seven, John followed his trade, working fairly regularly for about two pounds ten a week. The Pascoes did not feel poor: Elizabeth had no unwelcome recollections of that period. Marion's mother, who never could give them enough, sent them her piano; a stack of tattered music accumulated, all at a certain level of taste: 'Le Poète Mourant', 'Rustle of Spring', 'The Robin's Return', 'Narcissus', 'Warblings of Eve', 'Sobre Las Olas', and 'Blaze Away'. While Marion played these, John felt his way into the tune and played the melody earnestly on his one-string fiddle. He never got the time quite right, or else it was Marion who didn't accord—from time to time they would stop to contest this point, but no improvement ever occurred. Elizabeth, having been trained to this sort of thing, had an instinctive faculty of accommodation adjustment, and in fact, felt it to be natural for fiddle and piano to be slightly at odds.

The fiddle was heard less and less as she grew older, till at last it became just a childhood memory, associated with a grown-up world which she didn't understand, and with many often-played tunes whose names she didn't know. The thought of the fiddle, when she was grown-up, brought back also the vibrations of the piano, dulled by the intervening ceiling and the pillow on which her ear was pressed. It brought back also that adult world which went on long after bed time, and was still bright, warm and cheerful when she, Elizabeth, had been asleep for hours. Creeping disobediently out of bed, she had on several occasions glimpsed that adult world, from the foot of the stairs, and once even been brought up, in her nightgown, to the supper table; so she knew just what the living room looked like when Mam and Dad 'had friends in', and there was tobacco-smoke, a bright fire, a clean table-cloth, music, talk, deep voices, laughter, and the scrape of chairs being pulled up to the table.

When Elizabeth was six or seven, the Pascoes left the North and went back to John's own country, West Cornwall, where John had obtained work as a 'bus conductor in West Cornwall Services. They took a small house at Polpryn, and the furniture followed them at intervals across England, according to how much carriage they could pay. It took the piano two years to make the distance.

We come to Elizabeth's schooldays. The first year at school left nothing on her conscious mind except a rocking-horse on which she should have had a ride but didn't, and a stout, white-haired female teacher who sprayed saliva when she spoke. But Mother remembered quite a lot about those years. Elizabeth did not play much with the children next door or the children from over the way, because Mother had (and passed it on to her children) a mistrust of the outside world, which led her to insist on early bedtimes, and on Elizabeth's being 'where I can see her'. This was a pity in many ways, and was surely due to that inferiority complex. Right from the first, therefore, Elizabeth's most familiar playmates were Pascoe reflections—Spud, the red wooden doll which Dad had made for her second birthday (stained with permanganate of potash): Bogy (also home made), the train whose wooden wheel now worn elliptical gave it a syncopated and thrilling gait like that of a camel: and other figures from the coloured pictures in the Jumbo Book, the Moon Baby, and Light for Little Footsteps.

Light for Little Footsteps was a digest for children of the New Testament story. Elizabeth called it 'the Jesus Book', and first loved it because she learned of a weakness of Mam's: by begging a story from the Jesus Book, Elizabeth was able to postpone her bedtime. Mother would take her on her knee, in the armchair and in front of the hot fire, and tell her about the Good Samaritan. But there were many delights about the Jesus Book. There was, on the front, a picture of a golden-haired little girl, in a spotless nightgown, about to ascend a flight of stairs—heading presumably for bed or Heaven. Elizabeth felt there was confusion here. The little girl held in her right hand a lighted candle, no doubt the light of Faith, but Elizabeth skilled not in these metaphysics. She simply identified the little girl as herself, going to bed, and attributed any discrepancies to the artist's ignorance. As for the candle, she pleaded powerfully with Mam to be allowed to conform in that particular: vainly. There were pictures equally rich and stirring within the Jesus book: one of them impressed itself very firmly on Elizabeth's mind, though the Jesus book was lent and lost when she was five, and twelve years later, when she first saw the original of Holman Hunt's picture, she reproduced from the darkness of the forgotten past, the phrase 'I am the Light of the World'.

We are ungrateful, we adults, to the books and pictures which were so much to us in our childhood. We owe them a better remembrance; they shaped us, and helped to draw the patterns in which life's experiences were to come to us. Perhaps we can't save the books, anyway we have usually ripped the pictures out by the time we are four or five: or at least we have drawn moustaches on the cherubim and seraphim. I have an old Browning, in which 'The Statue and the Bust' appears as 'The Statue on the Bust', but this is a more sophisticated emendation. But we might treasure the memory of those old, loved books, and in an occasional quiet moment set ourselves to careful recollection and reconstruction: so may we, now and again, find our way back to the children we once were, and by the vivid recreation of a picture in a book—The Moon Baby gliding to earth in his mother's shoe, or Mr. Jumbo holding a wheelbarrow full of assorted struggling animals and birds—we may regain for a second something which lies twenty, thirty, forty years behind us, the mood of wonder and delight in which we saw these books when we were very young. To be entirely engrossed with today, with meals and motor-cars and work and play, is a short-sighted selfishness. Have time to remember the child you were, give him a deep thought now and then, be sensitive to all you can of the past, and it will reward you with bright shoots of everlastingness. To live in the present moment is easy, any animal does it: to live in eternity is really to live.

The Present is a room; the Past furnishes it, the Future lights it.

Mind you, the stuff we provide for childish apprehensions would give us pause if we met it *à l'improviste* in later life: we absorb and swallow its contradictions whole, at a time when our throats are elastic. Only a child could spin that straw into gold. I have in mind the Jesus book again: it tended towards Sweetness and Light with considerable fervour, but how seriously do we, any of us, take the suggestion that Jesus Christ was a well-washed young man with a golden beard and blue eyes, who went about Palestine wearing a white nightgown, stylish sandals, and a melon behind his head, and carried a nightlight pretty well always? It needs a child to accept that, because a child has, above us, the ability to a conception in toto, whilst making all reservations in detail. A child believes that adults tell the truth, but knows that certain facts don't fit; very well, it admits the total scheme, and leaves all the questions, as it were, hooked up on their question-marks, awaiting the answer of the future. A child is puzzled, but not incredulous. That's why we grow up with such crazy beliefs—the immaculate conception, for instance: and thousands more. The halo, which Elizabeth always took for a melon, she did not contest: symbolically she swallowed the melon whole, and kept a vacant pigeon-hole in her mind for the explanation, when it came. Though, of course, the explanations never do come. Yes, we give children some queer stuff when we hand over to them, as the accumulated sagacity of the centuries, all the junk and lumber behind which we grown-ups try to hide from our own meanings.

All dolls, for instance, are presumably feminine, since I never yet saw in any toyshop a doll with a penis. Puzzling at first for children, I daresay. Perhaps that's why, to younger children, the most interesting part of a doll is not its face. Frankly, it seems to be an imposition to foist on to the good faith of childhood this maimed simulacrum of our contemptible inhibitions.

Another example. I once heard a woman teacher telling a class that they were Members of Christ. Now, this particular woman teacher was one of the most brutal, vulgar persons I have ever met; she had no thoughts worth the name, and she was utterly without tenderness. Yet she was talking about Christ, Christ who said 'Suffer little children to come unto me: of such is the Kingdom of Heaven': who took a child, set it in the midst of the talkers, and said 'except ye be as one of these, ye shall not enter my father's kingdom.' Well, this woman was taking that name into her mouth and spitting it at the children. 'We are all Members of Christ,' she said, panting in what I supposed was an effort to make her meaning plain—(Cowper might have told her, 'He is his *own* interpreter, and *He* will make it plain')—'We are all of us Members of Christ's *body*. Now I want you all to say after me "I am a Member of Christ".' Which accordingly they did, all except one little boy who was soundly slapped for inattention. So there you were. I had not the remotest idea what she meant by 'Membership of Christ', and I assume she was no clearer. But God alone knows what the children understood by the words they repeated.

Chapter Five

Mam had a phobia about candles, that was why she didn't let Elizabeth carry a lighted candle, like the little girl on the cover of the Jesus book. 'Dirty messy things they are', she would say. What she really meant was, she was afraid Elizabeth would burn herself to death. There was among Elizabeth's small and heterogeneous collection of toys an apparatus called a panorama. It was made of cardboard, and represented the proscenium of a theatre. A spindle stood upright at either end of the stage, and a long roll of white paper was attached at either end to one of these spindles. You turned a handle, and the screen of white paper moved across the proscenium. Now on this white paper were silhouettes of Dick Whittington: they showed the entire story, from the boy with the bundle who first moved across the stage, to the Lord Mayor of London: and by turning the other handle you could reverse his progress. Behind the screen was a socket for a candle, but Mam never allowed Elizabeth to have a candle in it. So Elizabeth used to sit rather pathetically for hours turning the handles backwards and forwards, gazing at the show, and trying to imagine what it would be like with a candle in it.

Mam was always like that. Nothing seemed to be used quite in the way it was meant to be. Things weren't *trusted* sufficiently. When they had more money she bought a dinner-wagon, because it was the sort of thing she'd always wanted to have: and, for better or for worse, it got itself used as a table for newspapers, music and odds and ends.

The sort of discrepancy Elizabeth noticed was that Mam didn't do the traditional things. Christmas puddings, in books, were round like footballs: Mam made them in a basin: wrong shape. Similarly Hot Cross Buns: when Mam made them, they hadn't a cross and were not hot. And candles again: there were two paper lanterns, expanding things, which were hung up regularly every Christmas, but they never had candles in them—except once, when Dad put candles in and lit them, to satisfy Elizabeth: everybody watched them for five minutes, and Elizabeth shouted with excitement. Then Mam blew them out. And again, candles on a birthday cake: Elizabeth never had candles on a birthday cake. Mam said it would spoil the cake. Elizabeth doubted this. Mam thought all these things were nonsense, but Elizabeth privately thought Mam spoiled things—made them all grown-up and unexciting.

When Mam made pancakes, she didn't toss them. She bought a jelly-mould, but continued to make jellies in a basin. The mould was used to keep nutmegs and odd things in.

One thing that did work was the revolving piano-stool which had come across England a year before the piano. In time it grew dull and uninteresting when you knew just how high it was safe to unscrew it: but when you spun round the other way, there was always a satisfying jerk at the end: and though the thing became monotonous, it was better than practising scales, and spelling out G.B.D.F.A. from the large-type Tutor. Dad, of course, might be in bed with a book if he was working late: in that case it was necessary now and again to attempt a couple of bars of HER VERY FIRST WALTZ, or some five-finger exercises: but between these, a steady meditative rotation helped to beguile time.

The rotating stool had suggested to Elizabeth some considerations regarding Relativity: unknown to each other she and Einstein were working on parallel lines. Her aim was, while spinning, to get a new perspective on Reality by postulating that she was stationary, and the world was spinning round her. In the profundity of her contemplation of this, she sometimes fell off the piano-stool. Here she was, immobile in a rotary egocentric universe. The house was going round her with a velocity which could be regarded as constant. Certain points of reference were to be observed. Here came the door, with mauve curtain—here the calendar and the hair-tidy—the window—the yellow curtains—the plant-table and aspidistra—the piano (deep notes first—

thump 'em with fist—BUNGG!)—high notes (thump 'em
—PLING!)—the fireplace, with kettle singing—the brass
dogs on the hearth—the cupboard, one door open, showing
cups and sugar—the armchair, and picture of bluebells on
the wall above—the scullery-door, with curtain—the sewing-
machine, with a great stack of newspapers on the treadle—
the clock, shining brass, swinging steadily—the table, with
red cloth—the couch, the picture of daffodils—the book-case
—the other armchair—the door again—the calendar—Ha!
Spud's leg sticking out from under the plant-table—the yellow curtains—deep notes—middle notes—thump 'em—
BONG!

Elizabeth in those days was a very pretty child, with a
turned-up nose and dancing brown eyes; according to the
photographs in the album she was one of the prettiest children ever seen. Her hair was thick and curly, and was cut
just short enough to show her neck, but hide her ears. One
long wriggling lock of hair often hung down over her face:
she would dash it back impatiently with her hand. She never
wore a hat. Mam dressed her in simple, cheap clothes, usually
made at home.

She had a good deal of her father's character in her, she
was very honest and naïve, delighted in applause, and was
easily taken in: but she also inherited some of her mother's
nervous sensitiveness, and as a child she was apt to fly into
indescribable passions if she considered herself unjustly
treated. Then she would do one of two things: either she
would set her teeth, close her eyes, and scream at the top of
her voice, sometimes for ten minutes together, stamping all
the time and dancing with rage: or she would 'run away for
ever', which meant that she went down to the end of the
garden and hid herself, sobbing, after first declaring that she
would run away and never come back again. (This second
threat was once actually used by Mam, in much later years,
when she had a 'scene' with Dad, Elizabeth, and David; and
she put on her coat, ran out of the house, and took the 'bus
to Falmouth, where Elizabeth overtook her, consoled her and
brought her back: which shows how far grown-ups remain
children.) When Elizabeth went into one of these 'tantrums',

54

Mam and Dad decided she wanted to be noticed, consoled, apologized to; and to be missed, and sought high and low; and therefore they took no notice of her, ignored her absence, and put her to the necessity of coming back into the family without consolation or sympathy. Why they should determine that whatever Elizabeth wanted was precisely the thing she shouldn't have, I don't know. I am perfectly certain her tempers and sulks and brooding would have vanished if they'd given her the love she was literally screaming for: as it was, when I loved her, and she was twenty, I knew she was liable to dark moods of depression, during which she spoke little and was very easily hurt: when I saw one of these clouds forming, I knew always that it had as its nucleus the fear that she was not loved—not a logical fear, but the ghost of an unconsoled child—and I always knew that at those times she needed more love and more understanding from me.

Mam was from the first very excitable. What was typical of her, and I found it also of Elizabeth, was the tendency to exaggerate—not merely to exaggerate incidents in a story she was retelling, but to exaggerate the emotional significance of things. She was hyper-sensitive. Sometimes she was capable of fury because quite a minor domestic operation had been done wrongly, a pudding burned, or even a kettle left empty. As a child, Elizabeth regarded the spilling of a cup of tea on the tablecloth as a serious disaster. Everybody would have to scatter in all directions for cloths, paper, one thing or another, Mam saying all the time 'My best tablecloth! it's every time alike. . . . .'

There was even a time after the birth of David, when Mam's nerves had become much worse through ill-health, when she threw a table-fork at Elizabeth, and cut her ankle. Elizabeth, who was then fourteen, was stupefied with horror, shock and grief, though the cut wasn't enough to hurt much: but to see blood on her ankle and to realize that Mam had *thrown a fork at her!* Mam, who was cooking at the gas-stove, didn't realize at first that the fork had struck her, though stricken to the heart at Elizabeth's scream of shock and dismay. She tried to justify herself in her own eyes, and said 'serves you right'. Elizabeth, in the other room, sat on the couch weeping brokenheartedly. David, who was seven, came into the kitchen and gazed at Mam with amazed accusation. 'You've made Elizabeth's ankle bleed, you Mam.' Mam tried once more to bluff it out, then broke down and ran in to Elizabeth—'Oh my bairn, my bairn, what have I done—what have I done? I'm not fit to look after you—' and so on, both Elizabeth and Mam weeping in each other's arms, David hopefully patting them both and saying 'Don't cry', and the bacon burning on the stove.

In short, Mam developed a tendency to hysteria. She exaggerated dangers and fears. She never allowed David to have a pocket-knife, or to go alone on the Falmouth 'bus, even when he was thirteen. And she was uneasy when the children were out of her sight: this contributed to the Pascoe exclusiveness. Elizabeth mustn't play in the street, certainly not after dark. Things might happen to her. If the children fell and hurt themselves while playing, and were brought in bleeding from minor grazes, Mam turned pale, clutched at her heart, and said 'My God!' This was not a good thing for the children, because it encouraged them to regard any bodily injury as a very serious matter: but there was a good side to it, because both David and Elizabeth, when hurt, tried to minimize the damage and not to show pain, 'so's not to frighten Mam'. When Elizabeth was seven, she was playing tug-o'-war: about a dozen children were on the rope, which, as they swayed backwards and forwards, pulled hard round the corner of a wall. Elizabeth's fingers were trapped between the rope and the wall; the nail of her little finger being torn out. She ran home, but refused to show Mam the finger till Dad had bathed and bandaged it.

Dad had not been so attached to Kitty as he was to Elizabeth. In fact, he had really taken much less interest in Kitty until just before her death. This was one of the unspoken, almost unthought things which Mam held against him in the depth of her heart, which rankled somehow, painfully but not quite consciously, between the two as they grew older. Mam was always seeing Kitty in Elizabeth—'she's just what our Kitty would have been if she'd lived'. And Dad didn't respond properly. He couldn't. His recollections of Kitty were by now pretty well conventionalized. Mam felt this deeply without quite understanding it. It hurt her, as if a living child had been ignored. The two of them loved Elizabeth, but in quite different ways: Dad's love meant that he had forgotten Kitty, Mam's meant that she remembered.

Mam and Dad by now had each a second-hand bicycle, and Dad fixed on his crossbar a small saddle for Elizabeth. Every Sunday, unless Dad was working—this was before David was born—they used to go out on their cycles, probably to some place on the coast, which was only eight miles from Polpryn. This was the first settled and peaceful period in their lives. They were still young, Dad was only thirty, and they still had every hope of a decent, comfortable existence, better food, better clothes, a bigger house, more money: but for the moment there was no hurry. Dad had regular, dependable work, and Cornwall was pleasant. So every Sunday they rode out from Polpryn, Mam and Dad, side by side, with Elizabeth sitting in sublime ecstasy on the saddle on Dad's crossbar. Every Sunday they pedalled away at a steady pace, smiling, laughing, enjoying the sunshine. They would eat their sandwiches in the garden of an inn, at a rustic table, with a glass of beer each, and lemonade for Elizabeth. Simple souls, still not unlike the John and Marion of the photograph.

Winter, 1928. You would know the Pascoe cottage from the others in the street, by its plain yellow linen curtains hanging straight down at each side of the windows. The other houses had lace curtains, looped in the centre, or heavy velvet which shut out curiosity and daylight, but Mam, with that same instinct which made her insist on Dad's and David's hair being brushed well back from the forehead, drew the curtains well to the side. Centrally between the curtains stood Dad's plant-table and aspidistra. At night the yellow curtains were drawn across the window, transforming it, with the gaslight, into a warm yellow square hung in the cold night, welcoming Dad home from work, and suggesting to him hot muffins, tea, warm slippers, and a glowing fire. There was sleeting rain all through the last weeks of November and the first ones of December. It was a fireside season, cheered by a better promise for Christmas than ever before; for as the Pascoes became more secure, so their Christmas-trees grew taller, the presents more exciting, and the marzipan on the cake grew thicker.

The Pascoe home had at last emerged, crystallized out of the years of uncertainty. It wasn't by any means all that they desired, though to Dad it was a real and sufficient refuge, and he wanted no better. Leisure came back into his life, he built a radio, played now and then his fiddle, and bought one or two books—'The Ragged-trousered Philanthropist', 'Looking Backward', and a second-hand 'Outline of History'.

Elizabeth loved 'dressing-up'—not, repeat NOT, dressing in her best clothes to go for a walk on Sunday, but dressing in some old concert-party togs of Dad's. Dad bought a second-hand gramophone about this time: one of the records was a banjo solo called 'Darkies' Holiday'. Elizabeth would creep slyly upstairs after tea, and remain there for some time, then shout down the stairs for 'Darkies' Holiday' to be played on the gramophone. No sooner did the banjo clang, than Elizabeth shot downstairs dressed from head to foot in the clothes of a nigger minstrel four times her size, her brown eyes shining in a black face, her gold curls covered by a black wig—the most comical, grin-provoking object imaginable—and danced, wriggled, pranced, strutted, rolled, bowed to the music till the record was ended, when she demanded it again. She took this dance pretty seriously, it gave her immense pleasure, and indeed it was uninhibited art.

Dad was off work on Christmas Eve, with a severe cough, but was well enough to do his half-shift of four hours on Christmas Day. Mam and Elizabeth delayed their Christmas dinner till he came back. Because of Mam's habit of acquiring things and putting them away in cupboards, boxes, and bottom drawers, such celebrations as Christmas were full of surprises. New crockery, a glossy new tablecloth, dinner-napkins, cut-glass bowls and decanters whose existence had been unknown, made the table quite different, exciting, and dangerous in case one spilt port, or black-currant wine. The cutlery, including a set of fish-knives which Mam had long concealed in a remote corner of her wardrobe, was polished and shining; so were the plates and glasses; so was the flagon of Tarragona in the centre of the table; so was the bottle of Jamaica rum which Dad had brought home in his pocket a week before; even the tangerines, even the walnuts were shining on a nickel-silver fruit dish which had only been seen three times since it had been a wedding-present. There were two Christmas crackers beside each plate, and a wineglass. Elizabeth had written 'Merry Christmas' on the mirror with a piece of soap. The fire, freshly stoked, was pouring thick yellow-grey smoke up the chimney, and little spurts of yellow flame burst out and hissed among the coals, sometimes igniting the gases in the smoke with quick, rosy flickers. The room was decorated with paper garlands, lanterns, holly and mistletoe. The strong, clean, piny smell of the Christmas tree was the first thing you noticed when you opened the door. (Mam swore each Christmas that she would never have another Christmas tree, the needles were such a bloody nuisance.) It stood on the sewing-machine, more or less hiding the clock: nothing was more beautiful or more thrilling to Elizabeth than a Christmas tree, or smelt so sweet and redolent. She used to put her face in amongst the piny branches and sniff. It was Heaven. The tinsel and the silver and the toys, and the dark, cool, earthy fragrance. Other delicious smells came in from the kitchen and mingled with the smell of the Christmas tree—the sharp sweetness of apple-sauce, the mouth-watering smell of roast chicken, the warm tang of rum, and a deep, rich, dark, fruity incense which could only be Christmas pudding. Then Mam carried in the chicken smoking hot, tiny sizzling crepitations popping all over its brown crisp skin, its chopped legs pointing at the ceiling, and Dad took up the carving-fork and knife which had, apparently, been hidden for six months in the tin chest in Elizabeth's room: the meal was on!

Soon after Christmas Dad received the most severe shock of his adult life. His cough, though the weather was mild, would not yield to honey, paregoric and glycerine. He slept ill, perspiring as he shifted in bed; the bad smell of his breath made Mam turn away from him. At last, coughing one day, he found blood on his handkerchief. He had tuberculosis. A fortnight after this he entered Tregannath Sanatorium.

Dad had little natural courage. He could force himself through an unpleasant business, but only by immense repression of his fears. He could not tread confidently and firmly through his dangers, with an easy, businesslike acceptance of risks. When the doctor told him he had tuberculosis, he collapsed inwardly, but, adopting a life-long formula, he put a bold face on it. He talked to Mam and his friends of 'going into Tregannath for a quiet holiday,' and the friends thought he was taking it splendidly, and admired his courage. Mam knew better. Behind his bluff, he was broken. He believed he would never come home again. He gave himself up. His life was finished. In a sense he was right. Though he recovered, the disease had struck him in the prime of his life, and with one blow had slammed and bolted the door on youth and energy. His *expanding* life was finished. When he came out of Tregannath, he was a shrinking man, forbidden to cycle or play games or run, forbidden to swim, and from that time he attempted nothing. The spine of his life was broken.

His despair, before he went into the Sanatorium, infected Mam. They thought their days together were numbered. In this crisis of sorrow their last child, David, was conceived.

In this pleasant mercantile world of ours, everything has its price. In the professional classes, the new-married couples discuss whether they shall have a baby or a small car. It is a question of upkeep. David was a luxury beyond his parents' means. David was a wanton extravagance. Oh God most High, do you see it that way, too? Shall the best of us consult our bankers before it is said, there is a man-child conceived? This is not intended for wit. The consideration of such a fact checks all laughter. If any man can read what I have written, and understand all it implies, *and laugh,* he should cut his throat.

But it was a more reckless extravagance in Dad to have tuberculosis. He couldn't afford it. While he was in Tregannath fighting the expensive enemy in his lungs, Mam, in her fourth month of pregnancy, was queueing two mornings every week for Poor Relief. It did not help for Dad to see, on visiting days, that Mam was starving.

You see, the organization of our world is such that those are best able to get a good living, who would be no loss to their fellows if they were dead. The good, the true, the generous, and the just, are easily trodden under. To be tender is to be vulnerable. You've got to be as hard as glass, and to have neither faith nor interest outside yourself, to survive and flourish.

The scum always comes to the top.

Dad improved whilst he was in the sanatorium. The doctor there told him that in six months he would be cured, but after four months Dad could endure the thought of Mam's hardship no longer, and he returned home. He was practically cured. His own doctor told him he was very lucky, the sanatorium treatment had come in time, and if he took reasonable care he was out of danger. But apparently his heart was affected. He was to do no more running, climbing or cycling. These prohibitions made him very unhappy at first, and always tended to fall across his mind like a shadow: not that he particularly wanted to do these things, but it was pretty dreadful to remember from time to time that he couldn't. He sold his cycle, and as usual he put a brave face on it: 'it was always an old crock,' he said, 'and now I'm an old crock too.' He was thirty-five.

The 'bus company he worked for found him work in the office, where he drew the same pay, but had easier work and better hours than before. This solved the principal problem. Mam was able to settle down and prepare herself for the nightmare of birth.

After David was born, Mam went into Polpryn Hospital, and underwent an operation. She suffered great pain, and recovered slowly. The doctors told her she was henceforth—in consequence of the operation which had been necessary—incapable of bearing children. Had it occurred to her, she could also, like Dad, have declared herself an old crock, for she was to 'rest whenever possible, always to go to bed early, keep the bowels open, take plenty of milk, cream, butter, eggs, fruit, liver and fish, and on no account to do anything at all strenuous.'

But *somebody* had to do the laundry; *somebody* must clean the windows: *somebody* had to scrub the floors and tables: *somebody* had to clear the ashes and make the fire: *somebody* had to swill the yard: *somebody* had to push the carpet-sweeper: *somebody* had to make the beds. That was why Mam became fretful, irritable and hysterical and Dad's expression became dumb resignation.

Before David was a year old, Mam was back in the hospital again, for a further operation: the consequence of disobeying instructions to rest. Her teeth were now in very bad condition, and the doctors decided to extract them all to prevent chronic poisoning. This was done at home, and when Elizabeth came home from school she found the doctor and the dentist packing up their instruments. Mam lay on the couch, her face bluish, blood at the corners of her mouth. She smiled at Elizabeth, a quiet, childlike smile with her sunken lips and hollow cheeks. She looked as if they had hurt her and pulled her about, but she mumbled that she had had no pain. Elizabeth felt a sorrow and pity that went to the depths of her heart. She kissed her mother's forehead. Then David began crying from his cot upstairs, and Elizabeth went up to him.

There were other operations after that: David, never breast-fed, and never enjoying his mother's secure presence because of her recurrent illnesses, was a nervous baby, subject to night terrors which paralysed his body with intense anxiety. He grew out of them when he was seven or eight.

Chapter Six

The most severe of Mam's illnesses was when David was six, and Elizabeth fourteen. After that, Elizabeth and Dad took great care not to let Mam do any hard work. But their ideas, particularly Dad's, were not Mam's, so a domestic situation developed in which Mam kept popping up from her chair or couch with objections and remonstrations—'No, don't put the tablecloth in the cupboard, John: we've been married for eighteen years, I'd 'a' thought by now you'd know where the tablecloth goes', or 'for Christ's sake don't make such a dust with the ashes—here, let me do it, that's no damned use' or 'let me do it Elizabeth, I'd rather do it myself, then I know it's right.'

Three years of this compulsory rest, as might be expected, did a great deal of good to Mam physically, and made her more irritable and fretful than ever. She became strong enough to take over most of the housework again, and she insisted on doing so: but there were immense changes to be made before she could be satisfied. For three years impotently she had watched things being done the wrong way: for that matter, she had such a proprietary attitude towards the home that almost any manner of doing the work was wrong if she didn't do it herself.

Mam's return to duty did not entirely, then, make for happiness. It made for greater comfort generally, because in the main her ideas on housekeeping were sound, and at first it was very pleasant indeed for Dad and the children to come home each night to some further surprise in the better arrangement of furniture or organizing of meals, or some corner of the house looking brighter and cleaner than they ever remembered it. It was good for Mother too, she looked forward to the family's return, one by one, and their exclamations of delight—'you Mam, what *lovely* curtains!' etc. Elizabeth was always the first to notice these changes and improvements; Dad always the last, often in fact he didn't notice at all, and this caused difficulties.

But having once established a new routine, Mam had to have co-operation from the family in following it: family habits are hard to change, if it's even so small a detail as failing to hang up a towel after washing, or putting one's working boots under the table after tea, instead of taking them into the scullery. Mam could not reorganize further, and at the same time correct the family's failures to carry out the first steps. In eighteen years of married life she had not prevented Dad from picking his nose, or from spitting into the fire (even when visitors were present). So she nagged. Every day she seemed to nag more, not at Elizabeth, who was always helping her, but at Dad and David. Poor David had little allowance made for his natural boyishness, the mud he brought into the house on his boots, his protracted loud imitations of such gramophone personalities as Gracie Fields, Peter Dawson and Caruso, his dirty knees, his clock-work train set spread out all over the floor, his cigarette-card album, his marbles rolling about under every chair, his miniature tool-kit with which (alone in the house) he carved his name on the piano, his caterpillars in matchboxes which stank filthily, his newts in a jam jar in the yard.

Then, also, the parents seemed such a long time making up their minds whether they were John and Marion, or Mam and Dad. It's a decision one has to make completely. You can't just let children happen to you. But John and Marion couldn't fully realize that, because of one damned thing or another, they had missed the happiness they had married for missed it completely and irrevocably, and that now they should proceed to whatever came next. It was a fault in their awareness of life. They still half-awaited the pleasures they had married to share. They still half-unconsciously wanted each other only, wanted a private world without the children in it. There were so many things one didn't tell the children, so many places you couldn't take the children. And now that they were reasonably well again, both, and had a little more money, they instinctively tried to enjoy together the dances and cinemas and little tête-à-tête pleasures they had been

64

mutely wanting ever since they married. But of course it didn't work. They couldn't split their home in two, even if they'd attempted it with their eyes open, much less unknowingly. It was like a wakened man trying to get back into a dream broken off just before its most delightful moment. But there persisted always an invisible separation between Mam and Dad on the one hand, and David and Elizabeth on the other.

Once a week Mam and Dad liked to go to the cinema. David had to be in the house, and (at first) in bed, before they could go—Mam's ordinance ('I'm not going to the pictures and leave our David roving the streets'—typical expression of Mam's point of view). Naturally enough, David was hard to find any night at bed-time, and even harder to find when it was required to advance bed-time by half-an-hour because of the cinema. Mam and Dad, clinging pathetically to the remnants of their private universe, magnified David's defection to a crime. ('Why the hell can't you come in when you're told?—Forgot? It's every time alike. . . .') David learned, because of these cinema-nights, to dread his father and mother when they came, *all dressed up to go out*, seeking him through the streets. It usually meant he would be smacked, and he would have to run home to avoid being smacked publicly. David formed the conclusion, from occasions when he stood weeping and washing his hands and knees at the sink—the backs of his legs tingling from blows —that Mam favoured Elizabeth. 'Our Elizabeth c'n do anything. She c'd get away with *Murder!*'

The Pascoes were at length getting a home together, after all their setbacks and struggles; new furniture, pleasant carpets, clean and pleasant things such as Mam loved, which made her home so different from every other, and it was just those things which David most damaged.

It didn't get better as he grew older, either, because there was in him a fiery sense of injustice, and if he were wronged he resented it beyond measure. An unjustified punishment stayed for weeks in his memory. He would reproach Mam with things she had long forgotten, and her forgetting was as bitter a thing to him as his remembering was to her.

As you would expect, the frequent intense friction between David and Mam was only one expression of a passionate attachment. He loved Dad with unquestioning reverence,
because he was so strong and clever and permanent, but in
his love for Mam there was an element of fear that she
might die, and of sympathy for her nervous impulsiveness.
He recognized himself in Mam, and loved her for the very
weaknesses which hurt him, because he understood those
weaknesses and felt them himself. Her type of kindness and
love, too, were his own: like him, she delighted to give
presents and pleasant surprises, like him she was cut to the
heart when her surprises didn't please, like him she was less
grown-up and confident than Dad. There was a song which
Dad played on his fiddle sometimes, and sang. It was called
'Daddy': the words were something like this:

'Lay your head on my shoulder, Daddy,
Turn your face to the West.
'Tis just the hour when the sky turns gold,
The hour that Mother loved best.

And now you're tired of your work, Daddy,
And I am tired of my play:
I wonder if Mother is thinking of us,
Dear Mother so far away.'

I forget the rest. The implication was that Mother was
dead. As soon as the fiddle played the slow descending notes
of the first line, agony and grief caught at David's heart, and
shame also because of the tears which he knew he could not
withhold; standing ashamedly in the darkest part of the
room, he would weep his heart away, unable to escape the
hypnotic music. 'I wonder if Mother is thinking of us, Dear
Mother so far away', so far away in the great, shining western
sky, so unutterably alone and far, Mother, dear Mother!
For mixed reasons, Mam and Dad laughed at this grief—
partly at the direct flattery implied, partly to reassure David
that it couldn't happen (in which they were wrong, David's
apprehension of the grief of life was accurate), partly from
an obscure embarrassment. But a particularly cruel Philis-
tinism was to tell their neighbours the Parkins about it, so

that when the Parkins were with them for the evening, and David came in, Dad winked at the visitors and began to play 'Daddy'. David had not seen the wink, but felt the suppressed—and not *really* friendly humour in the air—and determined not to be shown up. So as they laughed at the punk words of the song, he laughed too, forced himself to laugh at something as deep as his soul: and so it went on till the music reached the line 'The hour that Mother loved best', where suddenly his control snapped, sobs burst from him amidst his laughter—for he still was trying to laugh—tears sprang up into his eyes, and he ran from the room, leaving the grown-ups roaring with laughter but Mam, at any rate, feeling a little uncomfortable, embarrassed, even guilty under her laughter.

It was either love or hate always between Mam and David, and always passionate. Mam would flare into a fury on the least, most unintended provocation, she was at least as sensitive when her 'home' suffered as when David trod on her toes (she had painful corns). Then this situation would develop—

Mam: 'It's every time alike, as fast as I clean up, you tread muck all over. I might as well be a skivvy for what consideration I get. There's going to be an alteration, you David, before you're many days older. You don't mind how long you keep me at it. It isn't carelessness, it's downright badness, that's what it is———'

David (looks up coldly and vindictively from book about aeroplanes, stares Mam in the eyes, and looks back to his book).

Mam (in a sudden yell): 'And don't look at me as if I've done you an injury, either. All I'm here for is to wait on you hand and foot, and go round on my hands and knees cleaning up after you, while you get yourself stuck in a chair with your head in a book———'

David (deliberately and bitterly): 'Shut up, woman, for the love of God. You never stop nagging. Give your tongue a rest, will you?'

Mam immediately flies into action, but David, for all the negligence of his attitude in the armchair, has been watching

67

her alertly from under his eyebrows, and he is off like a rocket, knowing how dangerous it is to let Mam come to close quarters. He makes for the table and puts it between himself and Mother. Mother circles the table rapidly, usually in an anti-clockwise direction, David flies round in front of her, just out of reach: both grimly silent, saving their breath. Three times round the table, then one of them would giggle. Immediately the chase was over, they would stand facing each other across the table, roaring with laughter: David would laugh till he got a stitch in his side, Mother would laugh so hard that she had to sit on the couch.

David usually referred to Elizabeth as 'Spud', except when he wished to be gravely confidential or polite. The name had somehow got itself transferred from Elizabeth's doll to Elizabeth when David was very young.

Chapter Seven

The Pascoes were increasingly prosperous after the birth of David, but it was nine years, almost, before they moved into a larger house. When they did move, they had formed some ideas about what their new home should be. Elizabeth had matriculated and had won an Art scholarship which took her to study in Bristol, where I first met her. Dad's wages had been increased from time to time. Some furniture had been bought and stored ready for the new house, even before they knew where or what it was to be, and there was a little money, seventy or eighty pounds in the bank.

The house they eventually took was on the west side of Polpryn, on the crest of a gentle hill. It had a garden some fifty feet long, with six poplars at the end. In winter and spring, when the leaves were off the trees, you could generally see from the living-room window the distant shoulder of Tregonning Hill, perhaps ten miles away to the west. It was not a large house: downstairs, a brickwalled kitchen, a living-room, a tiny drawing-room, and a hall: upstairs, three bedrooms and a bathroom. It had electric lights and a hot water system; Mam's dream come true, twenty years too late.

Dad would have been content to live in the house just as it was. The others thought very differently. What, five thicknesses of filthy wallpaper or distemper on every wall, and every ceiling *caked* with whitewash? And just look at the garden—

Dad: 'Well, what's wrong with the garden?'

There was a cinder path down the middle, and on either side the sour clay was full of potatoes, Michaelmas daisies, cabbages, tangled vegetable haulms, marigolds, yellowed stalks of chrysanthemums, stumps of lettuce, rotting boards, an old bucket, and a heap of strawy manure among which rats had been seen to move.

'For God's sake let's have a clear go at it,' said Mother.

Dad and David began on the garden. Elizabeth helped at weekends and holidays. It was to become all lawn, with two steps down to it from the back of the house (influence of Mother perceptible—like the curtains pulled back to the sides of the window, and David's hair brushed clear from his forehead). The poplars were no longer to be docked and chopped about as they had been by the Pascoes' predecessors, but were to grow up like trees, to be a screen from wind and the outside world (again an exclusiveness which the children had from Mother, but Dad had not). Sweet peas and roses —for lack of time to devote to the garden—were the only flowers to be grown at first, but some lavender had to be planted: the flowers to be in the nearest part of the garden, just outside the living-room window, which would almost always be open, and in June, July and August there would be bowls of sweet peas in all the rooms. The garden was to be entirely surrounded by a privet hedge which should ulti-mately be seven feet high. (Dad made objections to this, for the unspoken reason that he looked forward to gossiping with the neighbours over the fence, but he was overruled: his family were not neighbourly.)

Three years later the privet hedge was practically con-tinuous, and was five feet high. The lawn was fairly well covered, apart from a central patch in the line of the steps, where everybody walked, and this patch David constantly watered and sprinkled with fresh seed, offended by a failure in the family's plans. The lavender bushes, one on either side of the steps which led down to the lawn, were big and flour-ishing, but cats were apt to get into them at night. There had been some montbretia when the Pascoes moved in; Dad split the clumps and set it round the border at the foot of the privet, where it fought for life but at a disadvantage: some prospered, some died, some merely survived, so that it showed variously round the lawn. From the next garden a half-domesticated weed called Golden Rod had invaded the Pascoe garden, thrusting up its common yellow head in some improper place—the rose bed or the lawn; and always peering meaningly through the privet, mocking the Pascoe exclusiveness: the Pascoes acknowledged its significance by calling it the Yellow Peril. It wasn't the only thing that came in from Next Door, either. There was a hole in the privet where a dog from next door came in, fought with Bonzo, and stole the dinner out of his plate: but Bonzo made up for that by going through the same hole and being sick in the plate of the dog next door. Then they would fight for who should eat it. The lawn always tended to grow dandelions and daisies, and the poplars had a way of flowering in April, and dropping long catkins on the lawn, which presently sprouted young poplars. These things all had to be watched. Gardening became largely repressive.

That was the garden where Elizabeth and I often had tea, seated in canvas chairs under the poplars.

> 'They move to a high new house
> He, she, all of them—yea,
> Clocks, and carpets, and chairs
> On the lawn all day.
> And brightest things that are theirs—
> Ah, no! The years oh!
> Down their chiselled names the raindrop ploughs.

Then the house. They found it decorated according to a dramatic and violent taste: bright reds and bright blues in distemper, and wallpapers with large rose-clusters, or Grecian urns. Outside was Nature, so to speak: inside was Art. The doors, and all timbering, were coated with sticky paint, with finger print texture round the knobs.

The Pascoes came to purify. Destruction was in their eyes, especially in Mam's, whichever way they looked. There was tearing down, stripping away, scouring and burning.

(So have I often wanted to purify my heart. Not to make it white like snow, but simply in honest and grave endeavour to find out what colours and shapes it really is.)

Doors came from their hinges to be scraped, glass-papered and scorched down to their grain. Then Dad reached for the permanganate of potash, but Mam and Elizabeth stopped him: pitch pine remained pitch pine, deal remained deal. The Imitation-Mahogany Period was over. Hinges were re-set, jambs trued, frames were lined with rubber to prevent draughts and slamming. They stripped the walls. They scrubbed and sluiced the red distemper away in thick rusty streams, and found purple distemper underneath, which in turn faded to a wicked, unexpected yellow; the past gave up its guilty secrets, till at last the plaster came through like the white soul of a child, before sin and shame had overlaid it. Then they attacked floors and ceilings. Elizabeth swabbed and scrubbed whenever she was at home: so did David before and after school. Mother never stopped overworking, 'her own thoughts drove her like a goad'.

They did not object to living in this protracted upheaval: they hardly saw it, their eyes were on the future.

The day came when the stripping and cleaning was finished. The walls in every room were white smooth plaster: so were the ceilings. The floors were scraped into the most secret corners, the skirting-boards repainted, the ornate electric fittings replaced by flush switches and indirect lights. The house was theirs to begin on. The painting began.

Elizabeth tinted very delicately, broken white with yellow for the drawing-room.

Dad: 'That's not a colour.'

Elizabeth: 'What is it then?'

Dad: 'White.'

Elizabeth: 'On large wall surfaces, strong tints must be avoided. It's primrose, actually. Keep stirring and I'll put some more in.'

Elizabeth produced a delicate oyster-grey for the living-room.

Dad: 'What do you call that?'

Elizabeth: 'Oyster.'

Dad (scratches head).

Elizabeth made up a delicate brown-tinged cream colour for the big bedroom.

Dad: 'For Christ's sake put some *colour* in. What's that supposed to be?'

Elizabeth: 'Biscuit.'

Dad (scratches head).

Elizabeth devised a flushed cream tinge for the hall.

Dad: 'What's that?'

Elizabeth: 'Apricot; what do you think?'

Dad: 'Dirty white.'

Elizabeth: 'Remember we've got to live with these colours.'

Dad (scratches head).

Artistic matters were settled by the balance of power. If Mam supported Elizabeth, Dad had to give way: on the few occasions when Mam supported Dad, Elizabeth was over-ruled. David's influence was approximately thirty per cent. Elizabeth was defeated in the choice of an electric radiator, thus:

The Pascoes, except Dad, were a remarkable family for baths: Elizabeth had almost a complex about cleanliness (she strongly resented a suggestion of mine that it might be due to an unconscious sense of guilt). In their previous cottage they used to bathe in a washtub in the scullery, locking the back-door and the kitchen-door, for they were, as a family, quite shy of seeing each other, or being seen undressed. Dislocation of domestic affairs, and exasperation, occurred whenever anybody took a bath, so they all looked forward to a better state of things in the new house, with its bathroom and hot water. But the hot water was a failure: there was something wrong with the boiler. The best bath they could get was only lukewarm, and you had to stoke the fire unendurably even for that. So they carried out a sweeping policy such as Mam liked. The coal fire was torn out, the chimney bricked up except for a narrow passage for ventilation, and electric heaters were used throughout the house. The old hot water system was converted into an electric one by means of heaters inserted in the storage-tank. Then came the choosing of electric radiators.

Mother: 'I've seen just what I've always wanted. It's in the window of the showrooms at Falmouth: it has two elements, burns three units an hour when full on, and it's made in the form of a *log fire*. I've never seen anything so nice before, it looks exactly like real logs burning, there's glow-

73

ing ash in the bottom of the grate, and a bit of smouldering wood—just perfect.'

Elizabeth: 'For God's sake, Mother, let's have things that look like what they are.'

Dad: 'A log fire will look real pretty in that little nook—old-world.'

Elizabeth: 'This craze for imitations: petrol pumps disguised as Burnham Beeches, etc. It's a neurosis. If electricity is better than wood, why be ashamed of using it? Put a simple panel heater in, to do the work it's meant to do, and leave it at that. After a couple of years with one of these imitation affairs you'll be as sick as hell of seeing the same flame flicker in the same place five thousand times every evening. Anyway, why are we having electricity? Just because it's cleaner and better than coal: and if so, why disguise the better as the worse? You might as well disguise a motor-car as a stage-coach, or put bottle-glass in the windows because the Elizabethans couldn't make plate.'

Mother (dubiously): 'That's all very well and good, but. . . . .'

And since Mother had set her heart on the log fire, Elizabeth was wasting her breath.

The Pascoes being now embarked on a programme of electrification, they carried it through logically, and bought, by various plans of deferred payment, an electric cooker, a vacuum-cleaner, and a radiogramophone. The coalhouse became a larder, the gas supply was cut off at the main, and all the services of the Pascoe house were operated by switches.

Which all brings me back to my point of departure: my first visit to the Pascoes. The electric fire was flickering rosily on the hearth, spreading synthetic cheer, which was reflected from a beaten copper ashtray nearby, which Dad polished when it seemed to need it since Mam still refused to polish metal. We had finished tea; I was in an armchair, lighting my pipe. Mam was clearing the table, clattering a little more than need, so that I suspected an unconscious grievance —as if unaware of it herself, she wanted Elizabeth, David and me to notice that she was working while we were not. But she was not actually doing all the work herself. Dad was

74

putting away the jam and the cheese, and emptying the tea-pot. He had taken off his glasses, which he lately had to wear for reading, and seemed handicapped without them, for he nearly dropped the tea-pot lid. Then he made towards the kitchen just as Mother was coming out of it, and obstructed her in the doorway. Finally it appeared he had put the cheese in the wrong cupboard. From all this I deduced that it wasn't usual for him to help clear the table: but I was quite wrong in this conclusion. As I found later, he always sprang to help Mother in whatever she was doing, and he always did it wrong. Or if he didn't, Mother said he did.

She stopped on finding the cheese in the wrong place, and looked at him with amusement and some irritation. He hadn't the knack of noticing how she did things, and she could never quite get used to this lack. He was now sweeping crumbs from the tablecloth onto a plate; some were falling on the floor. 'For Christ's sake sit down and leave it to me, John', she said with a humorous sort of forthrightness, 'you do me one job and make me twenty.' Quite unfair.

Dad grinned at her and me, and went on with what he was doing. 'Poor old devil, he can't do a damn thing right,' he said.

Meanwhile Elizabeth went into the scullery, and from the clattering which began I judged she was washing the dishes. So I went in to dry them for her. Mother, of course, came up and tried to send us away, as she had tried with Dad. 'You two go away and sit down, I'll do the pots.' Elizabeth firmly ordered her to go into the living-room, find a comfortable chair, and read: or to go into the garden and look at the flowers, before the blooms closed with the set of the sun. Dad was already out rolling the lawn. Bonzo followed him patiently up and down the garden once or twice, mutely suggesting a walk, till losing hope, he padded back into the house, and curled up on the carpet with his nose tucked under his flank.

Mother fussed round us for a minute or so, then went: a neat, nice little woman to look at, with Elizabeth's brown eyes, but darker hair, and with a tinge of rouge on her cheeks which, correcting an invalid pallor, was becoming; and wearing, over a simple black dress, a pinafore embroidered in intricate vivid colours which had an Oriental or Russian quality, and made you realize that she liked to dress nicely. As we washed and dried the dishes, we heard her in the living-room, first talking to David—who answered with grunts—and then playing with Bonzo.

Mother could never be quite unnoticed: she was like a sparrow, which, though it may have nothing to do but stand still, yet draws your attention by the tiny jerky cocking of its head first to one side and then to another. She had to be reminding you, however gently, that she was there—whether by fluttering round to do the work herself, when you were doing it, or by banging and rattling cutlery louder than necessary, or by talking to David or the dog (one wanting to read, the other to sleep) or by beating time with her foot to Mozart, a most unnerving thing to do. But there wasn't a grain of harm in her.

(Of course, you can regard the individuality expressed in her dress, her house and her furniture as part of the same birdlike quality that needed to be noticed.)

She was back with us before we had finished washing the crockery, and was putting plates away in the kitchen cabinet: then she took a floorcloth and dried the floor round the sink. Elizabeth flashed a brilliant smile of resigned humour at me, and I saw her father's share in her. 'Mother *must* fuss.'

There are so many ways of sitting in an armchair: some people are ravishingly animal in the way they behave to furniture, half-lying negligently in a chair as if they *will* not conform to its shape, but it must follow theirs. It is my fate to worship such people, on whom civilization has failed to impose more than a minor compromise. They are still animal, and warm with life; they are tender because intense, and they are beautiful because their soul lives freely in their body.

Elizabeth and David were of that race. No ostentatious negligence, which is revolting, but a preoccupied unconsciousness of their own grace. David, when he returned to the living-room, lay half-curled in an armchair, as relaxed, unself-

76

conscious as Bonzo on the carpet: his whole being was absorbed in the paper he was reading, an Aircraft Recognition weekly called 'The Spotter'. As we came in, both Bonzo and David cocked a questioning eye at us, then returned to their silent absorption: neither moved more than an eyelid: Bonzo's nose remained buried under his flank, David's relaxed limbs lay passive and unconstrained in the yielding cushions.

'David', said Mother, from the kitchen, 'Dad wants you to help him set the lawn mower.' David nodded without having comprehended, an involuntary reaction to the sound of his own name: his eyes beneath their lowered lashes went on with Boeings, Stukas and 109's. Then, perhaps half a minute after, came the response. 'O.K.' he said, and rose: folded his 'Spotter' and put it on the bottom bookshelf where all the journals were kept, and went out into the garden. 'Got the spanner, Dad?' we heard him shout; 'I'm bringing the oil.'

The family relationships were subtle: the four of them were quite different from, and in a sense, critical of each other, but all identified themselves very closely with the house and with each other. Elizabeth told me once that one of the most difficult thoughts, for her, was the realization that it was possible for distance to separate her from the others, and that David, Mother or Dad could undergo great or terrible experiences and she not even know. She could not reconcile herself to the limitation, the confining of her individuality in her own body. She felt she partly lived in the others, too. And there was that significant little act of David's, his putting the 'Spotter' on the shelf before he went out, an act which contradicted his natural abstracted carelessness. He was exigent in this respect, and disapproved if Elizabeth left papers or drawing materials about the house. It was an infringement of the Pascoe Constitution.

You can find out a lot about a family by looking at their bookshelves.

Among the Pascoes' books I saw two or three of Lawrence's novels, some Virginia Woolf, 'Mr. Weston's Good Wine', Auden's 'Look Stranger', and Warner's 'Wild Goose Chase': I thought I could see Dad's taste, in a couple of books by

J. B. S. Haldane, Haxey's 'Tory M.P.', Cronin's 'Stars Look Down', Huxley's Essays and the 'Brave New World' of his grandson: much H. G. Wells, Jack London's 'Iron Heel', and Upton Sinclair's 'Oil'. On a shelf for big books were some works on Architecture, Anatomy and so on, and 'Representative reproductions of Cézanne': ditto, Van Gogh. Then there were David's books, 'Dr. Fu-Manchu', 'Treasure Island', 'The Food of the Gods', 'The Time Machine', and some technical booklets about aircraft. Mother, I supposed, had no particular literary predilection. With tolerant catholicity she ranged over the reading of the rest of the family, and might one day have Cecil Day Lewis in her hand, and the next Chaucer—or a Cookery Book—or Ibsen—or E. M. Forster. Mothers are usually so, they try pathetically to keep up with their children, and the children, as they go ahead and exclude their mothers from their developing lives, do not realize their great cruelty till long after.

Mother came in and drew the black-out curtains across the window, standing on a chair to do it. One side was blacked out, and she got down to the other. Through the remaining half of the window I could see Dad's head as he pushed the roller up and down the garden. As he came towards me his face was in shadow, but the sunset glinted through his crisp hair. David was busy with the lawn-mower, immediately outside the window and below the sill, for he was stooping to adjust it. From time to time his head came up, dark in the sunny glory of his hair, as he rose from a crouching position.

Beyond these two intermittent figures were the hedge, the hollyhocks and the six poplars, all motionless in the calm summer twilight. There was no breath of wind, though soon that sigh, that tremor which stirs the land at sunset, would set the poplar leaves twirling a little, and gently would rock the hollyhocks. Beyond the hedge and the trees was a little hump of grassland which almost hid Tregonning Hill: and beyond that dark, shadowy hump was the sinking sun. The sky was a molten glow, transparent, liquid. The sun went down suffused, swimming in its own light.

Bonzo stirred, stretched, pushing his forepaws forward

and pressing his jaw down between his forelegs: then he went out, and I glimpsed him earnestly trotting about the lawn. Beyond and above the peaceful garden thus framed in a rectangle of window brooded the vast clear sky, paling from liquid fire at the horizon to pale night-blue tinged with amber at the top of the window. Three little horizontal clouds, floating above the sun like thin slivers of wood laid to dry over a fire, caught all the golden light, and shone out from the shining sky a hundred times brighter: as if the sky were a smooth backcloth with a dazzling lamp behind, and the canvas had frayed along the folds in three places, letting the light through. The long beams of the sunset fell redly on the dust which flecked the window outside, and drew in shadows a tangle of sweet-pea tendrils on the glass. Then Mother drew the other half of the black-out curtains, and war had shut out the evening.

Chapter Eight

Yes: there I sat, with Elizabeth on the arm of my chair, her fingers buried in my hair, which she liked because it was thick and gold-coppery: and the red light of Mother's precious log-fire flickered systematically over us, Mother being slow to switch on the light because she so loved the dancing, intense glow of her artificial fire, and would not in this world grow tired of seeing the same flame-light leap up the same patch of wall. What dreams the ruddy logs realized for her, from as far back as the story-books of her childhood: old-fashioned Christmas parties, roasting fowls, Tudor fireplaces, winter nights, warm lights, ingle-nooks.

But that was long ago.

Bonzo's ears were large and floppy. When he was interested or excited he would look straight up at you, and spread his ears out like wings: hence Elizabeth called him Batsy. When he was a puppy his tail was long and thin, like a whip, and he was known as The Rat, but later the tail developed a down-swept fringe like a modest fox-brush, and instead of waving out behind him as his rat-tail had done, it then circled up and curled over on his back like a tea-pot handle: and 'Bat', 'Fox', 'Squirrel' and 'Teapot' were amongst Elizabeth's terms of reference.

Dad was always uneasy with newcomers. He came in and talked to me for about half an hour, during which he plunged through countless topics of conversation, apparently afraid lest talk should flag: I could fairly see him ransacking his mind for subject after subject, so that as fast as one thing was exhausted he put another in. It almost made me feel nervous, too. After a brittle silence of at least two seconds, he took down from the cupboard his one-string fiddle and showed me it with a mixture of pride and deprecation, even timidity. He never played it now, he said: had not done so for years. We made barren chat of it for almost a full minute,

80

then he put it away without playing a note, and resumed his standing position with his back to the fire. I think he had wanted me to ask him to play, but in those days I wasn't alive to the undercurrents in the family, and I've always lacked initiative. Elizabeth told me that once a young violinist had visited them and played some Beethoven. Dad had produced his fiddle, half-apologetic and half-proud, and had played a tune, thinking to be commended by young Joachim: who raised his eyebrows in amused contempt and said 'it would be simpler to play the real thing than fool about with that object'—Dad laughed and agreed, but there's no hiding a flush or a hurt look in the eyes. That was about the last time the fiddle was played. Its voice, with that throb and quaver that Dad used to love, the voice with which he had told himself stories of life when he was off watch in African waters, or lying off Suez: and the rhythmic thump of the piano, the deep voices of the neighbours spending the evening with them, the chairs pulled up to the table, the whistle of the kettle, the smell of fish and chips that wafted up the stairs to Elizabeth years ago—all were gone now, and belonged exclusively to childhood and the past. And though in her turn Elizabeth now sat at the piano, and delighted to play Purcell, Mozart and Bach, it was a thing totally different from the remembered pleasure, the remembered vibrations, of childhood. Mother rarely played now, she said she hadn't the time: her fingers now seemed thin, white, and wrinkled. And when she did play, the old pieces had no longer the old conviction, she played tentatively, expecting to make mistakes and apologizing in advance. 'Le Poète Mourant' she played nervously, like a practice piece: and altogether the joys of Today were Today's, and fine enough, but the sensations of the past were become only griefs for what was lost for ever, and lived and trembled only in the dark, rich garden of memory.

'So *now* it is vain for the singer to burst into clamour
With the great black piano appassionata. The glamour
Of childish days is upon me. My manhood is cast
Down in the flood of remembrance, I weep like a child
for the past.

Elizabeth and I left the family, and went into the drawing-room to play the gramophone. We had a recorded version of the Beggar's Opera, which we had bought when we were together in Bristol, and some other records; but once I had closed the door behind us, and Elizabeth and I were alone in the room, I couldn't with any certainty have told you whether the gramophone was playing Palestrina or Bela Bartok. We had to play the records, for the reassurance of those in the living-room. But Elizabeth and I were sitting in the same armchair, and our lips were together, and we were not listening or moving much. We were *being*: that was sufficient.

We had not drawn the black-out curtains, because while they were undrawn we had a sufficient reason for not switching on the light.

What Polly had to say, as the music hung gently round our stillness, might have been said for us:

> 'Can love be controlled by advice,
> Will Cupid a Mother obey?
>
> Though my heart were as frozen as ice
> At his touch it had melted away
> When he kissed me so closely he pres't
> That I languished and sigh'd till I granted the rest.'

We heard a tapping on the window, and from infinite distance our souls returned, confused, as their separate bodies, and we sat up. It was David taking Bonzo to his favourite lamp-post.

We sank down again, ruffled but returning to peace. The record was to be changed. Elizabeth did that. Then once more I could rest my lips on hers.

Then came the slam of the living-room door. We hastily disposed ourselves. Mother made a lightning incursion.

She came in briskly but apologetically. 'Hello you two; I thought I'd just come in and do the black-out.'

'We'll do it, Mam', said Elizabeth, 'we're not going to put the light on just yet.'

'But you can't see,' said Mother.

We said nothing to that, for there was nothing to say.

'Don't you think you'd better have the light on, if you're playing the gramophone?'

'Later', said Elizabeth.

Mother stood undecided for a second or two, then found her way out with a dubious murmur.

Once more Elizabeth and I set out together for the country which is more real than reality, where two incomplete souls fuse into one, and that one perfect. To be aware of the buttons and barathea of my uniform, even of the feel of my shoes on my feet, and of Elizabeth's knitted jumper: to be aware of all these things precisely and yet from a distance, knowing them all to be mere bindings and accidents of circumstances, while within them, and yet independent of them the true natural life of us grew together and drowned our accidental selves in deep after deep of fulfilment and longing: to be passive, and sense the pressure of each other's flesh through those clothes. And the war, and the house, and the night, and the music, and the hours that led to this and the hours that would follow, were dwindled to their distant perspective and put in their places.

The living-room door slammed again, but this time it was David and Bonzo, returned from their walk. David came in, with obtuseness which verged on malice, and Bonzo flew round the room, panting, licking, and leaping about us. David was looking for a note-book. ('Where's 'ee to'? he asked himself as he searched.) 'Wanna play battleships'? he asked me when he had found the book.

'No,' I said.

As he and Bonzo were going, the living-room door slammed again, and Mother came in, fuming because Bonzo had been allowed to romp about the drawing-room. 'Dog-hairs all over', she lamented as she tried to pick them off the furniture in the almost complete darkness, 'you can't see these chairs for dog-hairs, and I cleaned them only this morning'. Elizabeth and I sat silent. In the hall Bonzo could be heard scrabbling, slipping and puffing: on the gramophone, Polly, Lucy and MacHeath stuck to their guns: David was saying something about barrage-balloons: the door flew open again, Bonzo shot in with Dad after him, and David after Dad. It was, after our peace, as if a hurricane had struck the room. Lucy again had some pertinent lines:—

'No Bow'r on Earth can e'er divide
The knots that faithful Love hath tied:
When Parents work against our Mind
The True Love Knot they faster bind.'

Then, outside the house, came a distant, terrifying wail: it rose and fell, and rose again, and suddenly was blotted out as the Polpryn air raid sirens came into action: and for forty seconds the air quivered under the most God-awful, dolorous sound ever heard.

The sirens sounded like the voice of Moloch, or the hungry roar of the Beast in 'Revelation'. We never heard it in our childhood, but now there is a generation which has been born to it, for which the Air Raid Siren is one of the Earth's natural voices. The mystery is, how many generations shall pass before the Beast howls for blood no more? Perhaps the buffalo-voice will be silent after a few years, and never be heard again. Or perhaps there are grimmer things still, standing behind the curtain of the future.

Mother's hand flew to her throat. 'There's the sirens, John.'

We went through the house, collecting oddments, switching off the fire and the lights, and out of the back door. All sorts of things were put into one's arms on the way out: I had a blanket, two overcoats, a pan of hot milk which had been prepared for coffee, and a copy of 'Gulliver's Travels'. Elizabeth carried Bonzo in her arms, in case he tried to make a break for it. Mother had a first-aid outfit, half a bottle of brandy, and five breakfast cups.

The Pascoe shelter was provided by the City Council: it was of brick, and more or less cubical. The City Fathers, in erecting air raid refuges, appeared to have the peculiar conviction that their occupants were vulnerable on three sides only. Material for a blast wall was hard to obtain, and what the builders might have done with ten per cent more bricks and time, Dad could not do in months. Therefore the shelter was highly effective and splinter-proof on three sides and on top. The entrance on the fourth side, was screened only by a flimsy wooden door. However, if they would, the Pascoes might comfort themselves with the fact that, as they were, so were ninety per cent of the shelterers in Polpryn.

As the sun had set behind the house, so the moon was rising before it. The shadow of the house lay half across the lawn. The leaves of the hollyhocks caught the moonlight and lifted it, as on silver plates, above the leafy darkness of the border and the hedge: whereas the poplars dappled the moonlight, played with it and crumbled it to nervous shimmering flakes of grey and silver. The stakes of the fence behind were so whitened by the moon that they were invisible against the moon-blanched knoll behind them. The sky was flooded with moonlight, the stars pale; even the Great Bear was hard to descry.

Dad was fire-watching. Elizabeth and I went round to the front with him, and looked down at Polpryn. It was not, by daylight, an attractive town; but now the moon, ruthlessly eliminating detail, and presenting the whole scene in simple masses of shadows and light, made a composition of immobile dignity. A bank or a warehouse, at that distance and in that light, was neither more nor less imposing than the Parthenon. The light fell on the eastward faces of the three rounded hills between which lay the town, and left behind them an irregular lake of shadow from which rose roofs and walls. The square tower of St. Jude's, catching the moonlight on its white pinnacles, seemed disembodied, rising from the still shadow of the furthest hill. This tower, and the smooth fields (blotted occasionally by copses and their shadows, and the black winding ribbons where walls divided field from field): and below, the many-armed sea of shadow: these, and the moon, were the simple elements of the picture. Occasionally a sound came up to us, the slam of a door, boots clattering on cobbles, a distant voice, 'take care of yourself, now'. The Pascoes' next-door neighbour, an Air Raid Warden, hurried out of his gate, wearing a steel helmet and overalls: 'Action stations, John' he grinned as he passed. In the town itself no movement could be discerned, but in a nearby street a motor-cycle suddenly roared.

'It's a bomber's moon tonight, Michael' said Elizabeth.

David joined us, carrying pieces of cherry-cake, which he distributed. We stood in silence, eating, till a faint sound reached our ears, and all jaws stopped munching. Very soft, very far, from some point incredibly high in the moon-flooded sky came the sound. Very softly the sky was singing. 'Vroom-vroom-vroom-vroom-vroom-'; the sky throbbed. 'Visitors from the Fatherland' said Dad.

The sound of the bombers throbbed over our heads, and then diminished till it was almost inaudible. Then came two great, instantaneous flares, over towards Falmouth, followed seconds later by the heavy crump of bombs. The windows rattled slightly. Over Falmouth stood a great cone of searchlights, whose apex shifted gradually from left to right. With each drumroll of the bombs, the distant drone of the bombers momentarily increased in loudness, as if the engines were roaring to pull the aircraft clear of the blast. Fountains of fiery stars played upwards from the land, slow dotted lines of wavering tracer, and shells. The anti-aircraft shells were vivid small blotches, splashes of white fire, which appeared and vanished like lightning in the sky—like twinkling splashes of lightning, no sooner seen than gone. The roar of the anti-aircraft batteries was a continuous drumming, drowned at intervals by the heavy, murmurous thunder of salvoes of bombs. When the bombs fell, a lurid redness glared up from ground to sky, and was gone: the door of Hell had opened and closed. The sky and the earth were quarrelling. From its infinite vault the sky was throwing death down on the earth: the earth was blasting fire and metal back into the sky. Again and again the bomb-light glared.

What hurt was the knowledge that human beings, with soft flesh like ours, were in the centre of the holocaust. You could see no injury and hear no cries: only the spectacular play of lights and the roll of guns and bombs. The guns were angry, the bombs were angry. They were arrogant, they shouted each other down. It was a mere side issue in their debate, that men and women and children were being briefly shouldered out of life. When in the old days a man was shut

86

in the Iron Maiden, you saw and heard nothing: only the blood that oozed from the joints of the machine indicated what was within the silent iron door. And we only knew, though we heard no cries, that every one of those bright flashes was costing life. The sky was painted with blood.

At that time my unit was under canvas, on Predannock Moor. It had been arranged that I should ride back to Helston on David's bicycle, and be picked up there by our M.O., who usually went over to Helston in his car each evening. I said goodbye to Elizabeth, and, having promised to ring her up the following day, cycled out of Polpryn along a lane drenched in moonlight. The lane was strange to me—in fact I had never before been in Cornwall, and there was a queer mixture of emotions in my heart. I felt that I was in a far corner of the land, far from the England I knew, a warmer, gentler, more pastoral land: the superficial connections of life were broken, but instead I was where Elizabeth lived. The sloping fields, the trees, the earthen walls by the lane's sides, the farm I passed on the left, all still and moon-soaked, were strange to me but they were not unfriendly. I myself was now alone, now completely an individual, chained by the army but living only in love, and all authority, all the scheme of the world into which I had expected to fit my life, had melted from round me. I was that same bundle of emotions and impulses which I had known and questioned for twenty years, but the world was not the same, the sky was flickering over Falmouth. The night was an old friend of my unquiet heart, and Elizabeth promised me rest, but nothing else remained. Nothing. Nothing was certain, except the fantasy I was living in, that I, uptorn so easily from the soil of twenty years and more, was cycling along a Cornish lane, to sleep that night in a tent on the moor's face. But the cool scented night breeze laid its fingers on my forehead and lifted my hair, as it did when I was a boy, and told me the mystery. And the calm moonlight seemed to say, hast thou then still the old unquiet heart? Not a retrospective mood, but one of unendurable sensitivity. The factors of my life's equation lay on me with the weight of years. War, war had flicked the toys out of my hands, the straws and the prayer-books. Let them go, I never had clung to them. But what was left then? Myself alone, and the infinite shadows of love and death.

The sky was still at last. There was now no sound, except the quiet singing of the telegraph wires overhead, the quiet crisping of my tyres on the road, and the infinitely gentle whisper of the long, dry grass stalks by the wayside. And no person. All still and alone, I stopped, dropped the bicycle in the long grass, and stood in utter stillness and silence. Not even Elizabeth was in my mind, though certainly her love had produced in me tonight this unbearable sensitivity. My mind was as it had once been, years ago, when I was a boy.

I was thirteen then, and out in the country, alone, looking for blackberries, and there was no human being within sight or sound. This was in Yorkshire. There was only the hot sun, and the whine of the flies and wasps in the bushes, and a cow's steady munching beyond the hedge: those, and the incessant singing of skylarks. I stood deep among grasses, convolvuli and tall nettles, close into a bramble hedge, the basket in my hand: the leaves were still, spider-webs glinted among them. My alone-ness in the teeming warm richness of Nature went to my very heart. There I stood, waist deep in the grass, not in any ecstasy, for there was awe rather than rapture in me—only trembling with the realization of my own individual life: and I prayed aloud. I spoke, not loudly, but clearly, truthfully to God, in my individual tones, my own voice: I said my own thoughts, unchecked by any thought of a human listener, and I was certain that my words were heard. He heard me. The air itself seemed to be listening, to be taking my words as they left my lips. The leaves heard me; above everything else, the hot blue sky heard me, and all replied silently, 'it is so'.

Chapter Nine

The great trouble, dear reader, is that all the genres have been tried. If one wants to write a war novel— Hemingway: if it's Nature, the result sounds like Powys, or Hudson, or certainly like Thoreau. If it's love, there's D. H. Lawrence, if it's the social problem there's Mass-Observation. It seems to make it hard for a simple soul like me, who isn't too certain what his own voice sounds like anyway, simply to model his simple personal story in the material of words. I'm continually looking back on the last page but one and saying 'now is *that* what I meant, or have I slipped again'? Even a digression like this, I know it, probably owes more to Sterne or Thackeray than to my own determination. And Heaven witnesseth it isn't for want of material: one thing I do *not* need is to pad this book; if I put in all the stuff which I suppose is relevant I won't finish it this side of Christmas '43. And don't (for Pete's sake) clap your hand down on the pages at this point and say 'how I hate novels where the author says "dear reader"!' Aren't you my dear reader—God knows you've cost me dear in headaches, cigarettes, qualms of conscience and night thoughts; and haven't I the right and the privilege of speaking to you directly, if I want to, as directly as if I were writing you a letter? Certainly I've written things for you here which I'd hesitate to put in most, even intimate letters.

Our tents at that time were in a wooded ravine on the south-west face of Predannock Moor, east of Ruan Major. The tents of each company were pitched in rows under the edges of strips of woodland, and separated by grazing, across which we scored our tracks. My unit left the area some time ago. I don't know whether anyone else moved in, but by now I should imagine the valley is left in quiet again, and the owls and wood pigeons have it to themselves. There was an enormous bull in a paddock near the mess tent. We often stood and admired his testicles, I wonder if he misses his public. I've often thought how the fields will look, years after we've gone, scarred by our inexplicable tracks: Nature, they say, has a long memory. The track of A Coy. office, which cut like a plough-furrow clean across a turfy knoll, will still catch the eye long after the men of A Coy. are dead over the sea, or demobilized. The short way from the Officers' Compound to the Mess, made by sheer idleness and chance, will outlast all the feet that trod it; and for years and years the rabbits will use the muddy path from Orderly Room to the guard-tent, and there will be no rattle of magazines or voice 'who goes there'? For years and years the grass will grow sparsely on the tracks which, from all corners, converge where the cookhouse used to stand. Lanes that lead nowhere, unexplained and unconsidered scars on the land, which will remain there, a kind of War Memorial, long after the men who made them have forgotten Predannock. Nature has a long memory. They say that tracks three thousand years old are visible, from the air, leading to Stonehenge.

I shared a tent with another subaltern, Dick Larwood: it was beneath the interweaving branches of some elms, a little thicket fringed with bushes, through which there were certain gaps which one had to know by touch and memory, because at night the shadow beneath the trees was impenetrable. Concealment from the air was, I suppose, complete, but there were disadvantages. The brightest sun never penetrated to our tent, the damp never evaporated from our blankets, and after a rainstorm our trees continued to drip on us for days after Heaven was appeased.

It was cautious going till I got into the tent. Dick was out, I could tell by the empty smell of the tent when I put my head through the flap. I let myself into the utter blackness and groped for the lamp, but before lighting it I dutifully closed the tent-flap. The oil-lamp threw out its tiny sphere of yellow light, showing me the positions rather than the characteristics of the nearest objects: beyond my bed and camp-stool, which intercepted the light, lay gulfs of shadow, hiding the canvas walls. My mind, after its abnormal sensitivity of an hour ago, was dead and normal. I began to undress, hung my Sam Browne on a nail in the tent-pole, and my tunic over the back of the camp-stool. I was tired, sweating a little from my ride; my shirt, as I removed it, was damp under the armpits. My bed looked formal, cheerless and narrow, and as I unfastened my trousers I wished with all my soul that I was undressing for Elizabeth. Though I usually had the habit of leaving my shirt till last, not removing it till I had put on my pyjama trousers (an idiosyncrasy rooted in some childhood modesty, so that I was not *entirely* naked), this time I took off all my clothes, socks and shoes too, and put them ready for the morning: and standing naked on the sacking of my bed, I considered my body, all that I could see of it by the yellow lamplight. This was how I wanted to be with Elizabeth: full nakedness, both of us. It was nice to feel the mild cool air *all over*, entirely. When the skin felt as free as this, the soul felt free, too. And after all, this creature so rarely seen was the real me, much more real than the uniform which went out with me inside it. Under the barathea, one must remember, always *these* limbs and these muscles were moving. This was the reality. Then with clothes, I must throw down shame, modesty, reserve. Those pubic hairs about which civilization had taught me to feel uneasy and slightly ashamed, were a far more integral part of me than the collar and tie I put on each morning, and had just removed. Nothing here to blush for: this was the real man Elizabeth loved, in his true shape.

I put him into his pyjamas and into his bed.

I was very tired. There was a time when my bed was a lot softer, at home, and yet I didn't drop asleep for hours. This was better, it was one of the best things, this sudden pounce which sleep made on my relaxed limbs as my head dropped into the pillow, this instant smoothing of forehead and easing of toes, ankles, knees: the smell of the extinct lamp, the blackness, and that was all, my life was wound in dark sleep.

Thwack! Thwack!

Like a diver I came up from the deep sea of sleep: consciousness returning to me was like the green daylight of the surface. Three o'clock in the morning, surely: pitch black in the tent.

It was Dick Larwood outside, whacking the tent with his stick. Drunk, I daresay.

There was a further whack, then silence except for the sound of hard breathing just outside the canvas. Then a movement, a sharp jerk on the tent, and a fall. He had caught his foot in a guy-rope.

Silence for a few seconds: I imagined him lying in the mud and bushes, trying to clear his muddled thoughts.

'Mike!'

I did not reply.

'Mike! Which is the way in?'

I was silent.

'Mike! Don't be a rotten bugger.'

He found the tent with his stick, and began whacking it again: then he stumbled round the tent, and at last I heard him pushing into the tent-flap. A smell of whisky entered.

He poked his stick through into the darkness, towards my bed, and caught me in the teeth. I jerked away, grabbed the stick and yanked it out of his hand—

'What the hell do you think you're playing at?' I said.

'I *knew* you were awake all the time', he said, with one foot inside the tent. 'You're not very helpful, are you? You might light the lamp.'

I lit the lamp. He had struggled through the tent-opening, and now stood holding on to the tent-pole, swaying a little. I wriggled quickly down again into my blankets.

'Don't go to sleep, Mike old boy, please. I want to talk to you while I undress. Then you can put the lamp out when I've got to bed.'

I didn't answer, but dug my nose deeper into my blankets. He had picked up his stick again, and prodded me with it, in that part of the blankets where he supposed my genitals would be: 'Now little Michael, don't 'ee go for to be surly with me, I means no manner of 'arm.'

Silence.

'Oh come on, Mike, play the white man. I've got to talk to somebody.'

'Oh you *are* a bloody pest, Dick. Get yourself to bed. It's three o'clock in the morning, you're drunk, and you'll probably be up in front of the Adjutant tomorrow.'

'Ssh, don't be intolerant, love. I'm not drunk, and it isn't three in the morning, and the Adjutant's as drunk as I am, and if you don't talk to me I shall stay here annoying you all night.'

I grunted. He prodded me again, and said, in a tone fatuous with self-consciousness:

'Michael, I want to talk to you about Sybil.'

Silence. Prod.

'I said I want to talk to you about Sybil.'

Prod. 'All right, talk to me about Sybil.'

'Michael, do you think you can understand how it feels, at this moment, to look round on this dark, cheerless tent, half-lit by a smoky lamp'—(Thwack! Thwack! he illustrated with his stick) 'and to realize that the light of my life, my Sybil, with her laughing, dear grey eyes, is four hundred miles away? Can you realize what it means to be here in Cornwall, talking to you about Sybil, instead of folding her in my hungry arms?'

No answer. I had just slipped off to sleep as he finished.

Prod. *Prod!*

'Yes. Yes, Dick, I can imagine.'

'What can you imagine, *love?*'

'Sybil.'

'Yes, love, but I don't want you to imagine Sybil, I want you to imagine me without Sybil.'

Prod.

'I said I wanted you to imagine me without Sybil.'

Prod!

'Oh Christ yes, I can imagine you without Sybil.'

'Oh. 'Tain't nice, though, is it?'

'Bloody horrible.'

'Wouldn't it be Paradise beyond belief if I could be transported this very minute to where Sybil is, and find myself in her bed, our heads on the same pillow?'

PROD! 'I said wouldn't it be Paradise if I could be transported—'

'Jesus, would it!'

'—into Sybil's snow-white bed, and see her open her heavenly eyes from sleep, and feel me by her side, and hear her say "Dick, darling, *take* me"!'

Prod.

'Are you listening, Mike, you dirty old ram? Or are you playing with yourself?'

'*Oh, go to bed!*'

'I am doing—look, I've taken my Sam Browne off. But surely I can talk to the only man in the world who understands me and gives me any sympathy. That's what I need, Mike, sympathy and understanding. Sybil is the only woman who understands me. When I said goodbye she said she would follow me to the ends of the earth—'

Prod. 'I said she would—'

'Follow you. Yes.'

'She's got intelligence, Mike, as well as beauty. She's cultured, Mike. She can talk about things that the average girl knows nothing about.'

Prod.

'Cultured.'

'I'll tell you what I've been thinking, Mike.'

'Thinking.'

Prod. '—Oh you bastard!'

'Wake up, love, you're slipping off again: do you know what I've been thinking?'

'No.'

'Going absent without leave.

'Wish to God you'd desert.'

'Mike, I can't wait for my leave. July, August, September —the summer will be over. I'll have spent the best months of the best year of my life in this damn wigwam, thinking every minute of what I'm missing. I can't face it.'

Prod.

'Mike, I can't even sleep for her.

'Neither can I.'

'Since the day I first saw her eyes I've not been the same. She's the only reason I have to go on living. To think that I'm in Cornwall and she's in Cumberland. It's past bearing.

I have to wait five days even for an answer to my letters. Every sunny day down here is torture to me, thinking how it could have been spent with Sybil. Instead it passes from morning to night absolutely wasted, without a spark of happiness in it. Mike, this place is Hell itself for me. I hate it more than you could ever understand.'

Prod.

Prod.

'Oh, what is it now?'

'You *are* a rude bugger, Mike. You went to sleep just when I was telling you about my feelings here.'

'Heard 'em before.'

'Yes, I daresay. Yes. But do you understand them?'

'Yes.'

'Do you understand that I *hate* this bloody tent, and my bloody Company, and the whole bloody battalion and everything about it, and the routine and the mess and the drill and every bloody thing I have to do from reveille to tattoo? Do you understand how I *hate* each separate minute of each separate day, and hate each night because it leads to another day? Do you understand why I go out whenever I can and get a skinful of whisky? Do you understand—?'

Morris, my batman, next woke me. It was a dull morning, I could tell from the greyness of the light which filtered down through the trees and in at the tent-flap. A wind was blowing in from the Atlantic, bringing moisture and cold freshness with it. All the leaves above us were hissing and whispering; though there was no sunshine, the air since before dawn had been full of the sound of birds.

For about twenty minutes I lay in bed looking up at the triangle of leaves and branches visible through the tent opening, and listening uneasily to Morris's brushes working on my boots and buttons—uneasily, because I was ashamed to lie in bed and have my uniform cleaned for me, but not so much ashamed as to make me get up.

When Morris had finished rubbing saddle-soap into my boots, and put them by my bed, I pushed back my blankets and went out under the trees to wash and shave. The officers' compound was coming to life. Through the trees I could see figures, wearing pyjama trousers, emerging from tents and stooping over canvas buckets and bowls. The wind being in the right quarter, a very attractive smell of hot tea, porridge and bacon was blown to us from the Mess Tent.

A sensation of not unhappy madness came over me as I passed through the wet bushes and stepped out on the soaking grass. It was now raining steadily. What a life. Should I ever become used to four walls and a roof again, after this redskin existence? At any rate, walls would never seem so solid again: they were obviously not the limits of possibility. The wavering rain soaked down: it hid the moor, it veiled the trees across the field, it blotted out the church at Treeth. When I reached the Mess Tent, the elm-grove dripped the rain on me in large collected blobs which smacked on my cap and plopped down my neck. A route march had been fixed for today, but I hoped Hadcock, the colonel, would cancel it.

As I sat down to breakfast, I saw Dick Larwood hobbling up, leaning heavily on his stick, and walking very bow-legged. He suffered acutely from piles. Drinking didn't help. He sat down, very carefully, beside me, and looked out of his eye-corners.

' 'Morning Mike.'

' 'Morning Dick.'

'Is the march on?'

'Haven't heard yet.'

'If it is, I'm going sick, old boy.'

'I don't wonder.'

We ate and drank in silence till Hadcock came in, chatting to Cuttle, the Adjutant. 'Perfectly wretched, Cuttle,' he was saying, shaking the rain off his cap.

'It *is* wretched, sir.'

'Morning sir'—'good morning sir'—'morn'n' sir'—'morn', sir.'

'Good morning, Berry. Morning, Larwood. Morning, Luke'. The colonel found a chair opposite us: the waiter was at his elbow like a shadow. 'Porridge, sir?'

'Porridge, Gordon? Ah, no. Bring me a Shredded Wheat.' Then, turning to the M.O., 'What form this morning, doctor'?

'Never better, sir.'

'Good. Good. Sugar please: thank you. What are you giving us this morning, James?'

'Eggs and bacon, sir,' said James, our Messing Officer.

'*Eggs and bacon!* James, no Black Market? Or should I not ask?'

'No Black Market, sir. Fair dealing and rations.'

'Oh excellent young man. Eggs-a-bread, Cuttle, eggs-a-bread. Nothing like a good breakfast to begin a march on —'

It was out. A ripple of disappointed eyebrows spread concentrically from the colonel to the far corners of the mess tent. I concentrated on eating somewhat more than I really wanted. If I was to march twenty miles in a Cornish downpour, it would do no harm to start with a full stomach. I turned to James—

'Mess truck going out with a hot meal?'

'Haversack rations' he said briefly: 'stew when you get back.'

My enthusiasm reached its nadir. Had there been only a hot meal: a hot meal half-way through a route march—the Mess Truck backed into some farm or inn yard—hot bully stew, carrots, potatoes, an onion or two, rice pudding with raisins in it to follow—beer and cider on the truck, too—such a meal transformed the day, even though the rain came down in sheets. You marched with a good heart in the morning, because of the meal that was coming, and you marched with a good stomach in the afternoon because of the meal that was gone. But haversack rations—tasteless bread and cold bully—worse still, hard dry cheese: perhaps a scrape of jam: army margarine, tasting not unlike ointment—haversack rations! I put my mind on breakfast. It was worth it, too—our first egg for six weeks, deliciously fried and fatty. I cut up a soft piece of toast, pressed a square of it on my fork, then a piece of bacon, and coated the whole with the thick yolk of the egg.

Morris, accustomed to my habits, was waiting in my tent when I dashed back after breakfast with only three minutes before parade. He slung my respirator round my neck as I entered. I spun round, hitching the haversack up on my chest, and he pulled the sling down my back, threaded the cord through, and passed it under my left arm, where I looped it on the S-hook. The gas-cape was ready rolled: he had it on my shoulders in an instant, the tapes through the respirator-D's, as I always liked them. Then the belt and brace equipment, then the epaulettes buttoned over the straps and pistol-lanyard: the small pack (the side-valise was already attached): the water-bottle; map-case on left shoulder: binoculars round my neck; and Morris completed the ceremonial Preparation of Childe Michael by clapping my steel helmet on my head—'That's it, sir.'

'Compass?'

'Side valise, sir.'

'Haversack ration?'

'Side valise.'

'Good man. How are you today?'

'Better, sir. The sore on my left foot is healed.'

'Did you get the boots changed?'

'Yes, sir.'

'Think you can make it today?'

'I reckon so, sir. I'm not over keen, you know.'

'No. What do you think?'

'I'll do it, sir. I am all ready.'

'Got your haversack rations?'

'Yes sir.'

'Right. Let's go.'

As I made my way, at the double, to the Coy. area, I remembered my promise to ring Elizabeth. No use trying to do it now, with the battalion about to move off. Anyway, the Polpryn Art School, where she was working just now, wouldn't be open yet. It was a problem to be solved. If I didn't ring her, after my explicit promise—well, I'd better do it: damn. An ill-considered arrangement.

There was a hasty conference in the Coy. Commander's tent—soaked Platoon Commanders, a soaked Sergeant-Major, and the Coy. Commander the wettest and most irritated of all—and we joined our platoons, and stood for three-quarters of an hour in the pouring rain, waiting our turn to move. A section of carriers had to get away in front, then D. Coy., then A. Coy., then most of H.Q. Coy. We had to wait till all these people had their distance on the road.

Hadcock was keen on officers wearing the same dress and equipment as the men. This morning he himself wore battle-dress, like the rest of us, and like us he was soon soaked. He then conferred with the adjutant, and shortly afterwards a runner brought us permission to unroll gas capes. There followed a scene of fantastic confusion as the men pulled their release-cords and discovered (many of them) that the capes were wrongly rolled, and wouldn't release. They assisted each other, and one by one the great yellow capes spread out, flapped, and enveloped their wearers, so that my platoon looked, through the screening rain, like a bed of gigantic buttercups tossed by a tornado.

At last we moved.

Once on the main Lizard Road, we turned North. Hadcock wanted to exercise our troop-carrying vehicles, so this was not to be a circular march; we were to follow the coast roads as far as Penzance, where the R.A.S.C. lorries would meet us and bring us back.

I do not like the Cornish roads: the incredibly bleak road which connects Bodmin, through Indian Queens, with Truro: the forlorn, semi-industrial, derelict roads of Camborne and Redruth: the unenterprising undulations between Falmouth and Marazion, the modest mediocrity of Penzance—Mount Misery—Land's End. In any case, a route march, when the rain continues, is not the best imaginable way to appreciate the Face of Britain.

The first ten minutes' halt found us unsmiling. We had not yet marched long enough to get the morning stiffness out of our limbs, we merely felt sore and disinclined for more. Our equipment did not yet feel heavy, merely uncomfortable. The gas capes, however, were a curse. They kept in the sweat and steam of the body, and they compelled the men to sling their rifles reversed—where, every time they slid from the shoulder, the muzzle got between the man's knees, or bounced irritatingly on his leg: the gas capes also prevented adjustments of pack or respirator. We all had beetroot-faces because of the body heat which the capes trapped.

The men were lighting cigarettes, with matches that spluttered in their wet fingers. I followed their example, not having time to get my pipe going.

The whistle blew, the platoon commander in front waved me on, and we took the road again. My leading section of seven men was in file—i.e. in two's—on the right of the road, followed by platoon H.Q.—myself, Morris, a runner, my sergeant, and two mortar-men. No. 2 Section was fifty yards behind, on the left, and No. 3 on the right again. It struck me that the Light Machine Gun was not moving around much in No. 1 Section—'Corporal Norris', I shouted.

'Sir?'

'How long has Wiles been carrying the L.M.G?'

There was a moment of enquiry, and I saw the gun passed from Wiles' patient shoulders to those of the man behind.

The Wheel Inn, the Bonython Plantations, were left far behind; by a quarter to twelve we were passing Nausloe, and our boots were slipping on the metalled surface of Meneage Street, Helston. The rain fell as merrily as ever, and made its familiar noise in the kennels, each a square-cut, deep torrent.

The 'phone call was on my mind. Nearly ten to twelve. If Hadcock, away at the front of the column, gave the halt at the proper time, my Company would halt in Helston, and I should be able to 'phone Polpryn. On the other hand, I knew the Colonel's objection to halting in towns. But what could he do? He must be away at Porthleven by now. However he timed the halt, *somebody* would stop in Helston. I began to look out for telephones. We were passing the Post Office now. The road here was very steep and treacherous.

Crash!

The man with the L.M.G. was flat on his back. I clattered downhill at what speed I dared, and examined the gun: cocked the action, and squeezed the trigger. No damage. March on.

We were passing the Angel, in Coinagehall Street. Luke,

in front of me, held up his hand for the halt. Good. Ten minutes to 'phone.

The telephone booth was occupied. An R.A.F. officer was inside, leaning on his elbow, chatting into the 'phone, with no hint of hurry or importance: 'I say, no! —yes?—Did she, though!—I say, really!—rather a bitch, though!—I say, no, old man—well, really—poor view taken, though!—I say, no!—'

Minutes were passing. I returned to where No. 2 Section was sheltering under the arch of the Angel. No. 1 Section had halted, by good fortune and some management, near a tobacconist and confectioner, and by a miracle he was open.

The back entrance to the Angel was fortunately obscure. I found my way in without remark, and was soon busy with the 'phone.

Conditions were against me. The line was engaged. After nearly five minutes I was at last put through, and then had to wait till Elizabeth was brought to the 'phone.

I said a few hurried words to her, listened to a few, said goodbye and rang off. Then came the proprietor of the Angel, wanting twopence for the call. It took time to get the twopence out of my back pocket, because of the equipment and gas cape. When I got out of the Angel at last, my platoon was out of sight, and C. Coy. was already coming round the corner of Meneage Street.

I overtook my platoon on the upward slope of the Porthleven Road. It was a gruelling climb. One seemed to force one's body up the hill as if it were a detached mechanism, like holding a plough hard down into the ground. The men's faces were bright red, but unexpressive, wooden. Respirators clung to our chests like clammy poultices, packs swung on our shoulders. The steady nine-pound drag of the rifle set the men leaning to off-set it; the weight of the steel helmet strained the muscles at the back of the neck, the gas cape retained heat and moisture, the tight belt rode up on the battle dress tunic. Underneath the serge, shirts worked up above the belts, vests rolled up under armpits. We set down one foot in front of the other, vindictively, breathing hard, jamming our heels savagely, rhythmically into the road. Our steps were short: packs jolted and bounced on our shoulders. The slope increased as we came out above the Penrose road, and the step was lost, we kept no time but our own, fixing our eyes on the road six feet in front. How many telegraph posts before we reached the farm on the first crest?

The sharp climbs over, we wound down into Porthleven, where women, children and old fishermen stood in shop-doorways and at corners, watching us go by; some of them making the ambiguous V-sign which was the delight of soldiers and schoolboys. Ahead of us, No. 1 Section was rounding the end of the harbour, and beyond them I could see the rear section of No. 10 platoon about to disappear around the bend of the road.

The road was climbing again. We were level with the sea-gulls which sailed above the harbour. One or two men in No. 2 section were beginning to straggle. I fell back and whipped up the step.

'Left, right, left—come on, now, hold it. What's your trouble, Shaw?'

'Blisters, sir.'

'I'll see you at the next halt. Got a change of socks?'

'No, sir.'

'Why not?'

'Two pairs being washed, sir.'

'God. I must look very young. Anyhow, keep that distance till we halt. Understand?'

'Yes, sir.'

We halted on the open road between Rinsey and Breage. The rain still came down steadily, but up here on the higher land the wind blew it at us from disconcerting angles, and clapped our wet capes to our bodies. This was the long halt, the bread-and-cheese halt. We had done some twelve miles. From my three sections, sentries were already taking up their positions in the hedge or over on the far side. The remaining men helped each other to take off their packs, or dropped into the long, soaked grass just as they were, reclining and using the pack to support their shoulders. I jerked open my haversack and took out a sandwich, which I ate more from habit than hunger. I never felt very hungry in the middle of a march: only towards the end, and on returning to camp.

I perched on the top bar of a gate to eat my sandwich. Shaw limped up, and I told him to take off his boot. His heels had a couple of small blisters at the back, and one had bled slightly into his boot. Both his socks had large holes in them, which he said were not there when he set out. I looked at him. He was very young, but old enough to know better.

'Shaw, if you persist in telling lies you'll get into trouble.'

Under my instructions he washed his feet in water from a brook: I applied Elastoplast to his sores, and lent him a pair of clean socks which Morris had packed for me.

From along the road came the sound of a whistle. The thirty minutes' halt was over.

The sentries scrambled back to their sections, the men, who had long ago finished their sandwiches, now snatched a long last swig at their water-bottles, or three final pulls at a cigarette before they pinched it out and put it in their pockets for the next halt. They got to their feet a little awkwardly and moved into formation with the stiffness which is unavoidable in the first minute after a halt. Tender areas of the feet, which would soon be easy again, were sensitive after the rest: joints were stiff, shoulders felt obscurely bruised.

In five minutes we were in our stride again, the easy, tired swing which depends on a half-weary relaxation of muscles and on an abstracted mind—the swing which makes one mile just like another, the swing which goes on steadily even though the man is falling asleep. The swing which never develops in much less than ten miles' marching. I looked back at No. 2 section. Shaw was falling behind again. I waited for him to draw level. He intensified a limp.

'Well, Shaw?'

'I can't keep up, sir.'

'You can. You will. No one drops out of a march unless he faints or dies. You're doing neither.'

No reply. 'Give me your rifle,' I said.

He passed it without a word. I slung it on my shoulder.

'Now get into step with me: left, right, left, right—hold

it, now. Never mind your feet, keep marching. What are you, a soldier? Be a soldier then. Left, right.'

I brought him up to the section and put him at the head of it.

'Don't let him drop to the rear, corporal. He stays where I put him.'

'Very good sir.'

As I went on ahead, I heard Shaw comment to his neighbour: 'What, break my f——g heart for half-a-crown a day—not f——g likely.'

The march went on. Slowly our five-mile column crawled, a sinister yellow worm, from Ashton, from under the shoulder of Tresowes Hill, towards the west: a column made up of numerous sections, like venomous little maggots, each one keeping its fifty yards distance, each one bearing its deadly sting, its Light Machine Gun.

The queer thing was that each of these impersonal sections, 'soldiers' to those who saw us on the road, was made up of men, and men comically disguised with their steel helmets and capes: in years to come they would roar with laughter at old photographs—'That was when your father was in the Army, son'. And I was more conscious of their diversity than of their uniformity. Here there were, trudging through the rain, bricklayers, dustmen, teachers, 'bus-conductors, plumbers, ploughboys, engineers, riveters, painters, bank-clerks, journalists, butchers—fathers, sons and brothers: middle-aged men down to boys like Shaw: their personal lives abandoned in scattered corners of the country, they trudged together unprofitably through the Cornish rain, everyone now lost in his own thoughts, not talking, but swinging mechanically forward, the mind almost released from the body, the mind far away, in other scenes. Belonging, all of them, still far more to their own lives and occupations than to the platoon, the company, the battalion which had usurped their bodies.

But for all that there were some for whom this temporary disguise was the one they would die in. There were some who, though they were only 'in for the duration', had no further future. There were some amongst these men who would not lay their uniforms by in this world. In quietened homes all over England civilian suits were hanging—pressed and cleaned for *his return*—whose owners would not take them down again.

And, for that matter, there were tears that would fall like this Cornish rain for some of these very lads marching now.

The rain eased, and stopped at last. My watch showed half-past four. We rolled our gas-capes, and felt the pleasant coolness of the wind blowing through our damp clothes. We were now coming into Marazion, and on our left, from time to time, we had glimpses, through hedge gaps, of St. Michael's Mount. Elizabeth and I had twice been to Marazion, and therefore the place was attractive to me. And St. Michael's Mount has an enchanted appearance. It fascinated the men, too. Despite their twenty-mile march, and their minor discomforts, they peered over the hedges to get sight of the island and the castle, and drew each other's attention —'see the castle, Jack? That's Goebbels' country house when they've conquered England, so he says. Some hope!' I looked back out of curiosity to see if Shaw found it worth a glance. Evidently not. He was marching sullenly at the head of No. 2 section, limping a little. Engrossed as he was in the road, he yet saw me looking at him, and imperceptibly exaggerated the limp. I looked away again. Self-pity is a juvenile trait. He had not grown up. No crime, but a pity, for himself and for those to whom he could have been valuable. He must learn to be responsible for himself. As it was, he sulked along, blaming me, blaming the army, blaming the world— it was an easy way to dispose of blame. I understood him: oh yes. Too neglectful and apathetic to report ill-fitting boots, too uninterested to darn his own socks, too lazy to wash his feet—oh God yes, I understood him, because I was all those things myself. But he must understand all that, he must learn to take blame himself, he must understand that he himself had inflicted sores and blisters on himself (on his soul as well as on his heel) and then he would be grown up. Instead he walked in at least tolerable comfort in my clean socks, wearing my Elastoplast—and cursed me, the colonel, the army, the war, the weather and the world.

Poor little devil, I suddenly thought, thinking of his sullen, hostile face when I ordered him to the front of the section, and remembering the lack of expression, the suspicion with which he accepted my socks and bandages. No more than a child, and with nobody he trusted. Somebody had failed him, surely: only a lack of love or sympathy makes such people armour themselves with hate, bravado and suspicion. He said he was twenty when he enlisted. I guessed he was seventeen: and emotionally, barely fourteen. Retarded development. A kid, hurrying into a man's world, and trying to carry through a man's part with nothing better than bluster and suspicion: a juvenile bluffer, giving himself a very raw deal.

Wiles's turn with the L.M.G. again: and here came the Company Runner on his cycle. Embussing one mile out of Marazion, sir. Captain Cross says form platoon into lorry-loads when the column halts. Embussing in twos, sixteen to a lorry, and moving off as a Company. Platoon Commanders ride in their first lorry.

The end of the march, and the sun at last breaking through the clouds. Mine were always good marching feet, but after twenty miles I usually found my legs growing heavy: it was the body as a whole which hadn't much stamina. Luke's hand went up for the halt. I closed the platoon in file and split them for embussing. Their faces were cheerful, with a satisfied tiredness: another five hundred yards and they'd be riding. Even Shaw had forgotten to look resentful, and with that lapse of memory the strained creases had vanished from his forehead. Wiles smiled at me. Morris, my batman, was showing off by dashing about on unnecessary errands. But he was a damned good, willing man, and would serve me till he dropped.

Corporal Adams had an astonishing face for collecting dust. Even on this day of rain, he was the same colour as the road, except for the black-margined furrows traced down his face by sweat.

We came smartly up to the lorries, and my lads doubled in like greased lightning. It pleased me. The colonel was watching, and liked it. Up they shot, helped by the man in front, helping the man behind. Young Shaw, however, clambered up slowly: what, break his f——g heart?—Not he. Hadcock's mouth tightened a little. But I could not feel furious with the little devil, though I said 'for Christ's sake *jump*, Shaw.' He looked tired, and startlingly young in contrast to the other men: and how thin he was. And that slum-schoolboy sullenness.

The driver clapped up the tail-board of my lorry. My platoon-sergeant, Sitwell, was climbing up beside the driver of the lorry behind. I went round to the front and got into my seat, and we pulled away to form up in company convoy. I sighed, relaxed all my muscles, and allowed my feet to lie idly on the floor of the cab. Back towards Marazion we moved. Twenty miles of road, every inch of it trodden out by our feet, would run smoothly under the tyres now before we made camp. Twenty miles of rest and ease while the throbbing engine did the work.

And a hot stew waiting.

Chapter Ten

When we got to camp, I found Orry, the M.O., washing and shaving ready to go to Helston. Despite my tiredness, I took the opportunity of seeing Elizabeth again. I just had time to wash my face and feet, change my socks, and eat my plate of stew, then dropped into the seat beside Doc., who was anxious to be off, and we roared away on the Lizard road again.

Pedalling David's cycle up Station Road, Helston, was a hell of an effort, I never thought my legs could have been so unwilling. It was a strain to keep my eyes open, too.

As I rode into Polpryn, the Helston 'bus passed me, going the other way, and I caught a glimpse of David, Mother and Dad, presumably going into Helston for the evening. A sick wave of nervousness swept through me at the possibility that Elizabeth might be out, and my ride be all for nothing. It was not so, however. When I leaned David's cycle against the wall and walked round to the back of the house, I found the door open, and went in without knocking.

Elizabeth was sitting on the edge of the table, biting her lower lip, her slowly swinging legs marking her thoughtful attitude. She turned quickly as I came in, and smiled: I could see the quick flush of delight and surprise in her cheeks. 'Michael, my sweet.'

One is so rarely *sure* of a welcome. I couldn't take my eyes off her, I was bathing in her gladness because I had come. I backed against the door, closing it with my shoulders, regarding her all the time, drinking the sweetness of her brown eyes and giving her the love in mine. The sun was always near setting when I was at Polpryn, and now its red light lay on her gold hair. I stood gazing and smiling at her. She had on a knitted jersey, on which the sun lay in the pattern of the window, across her shoulders, like a bright band of copper in the dimness of the room: the curve of her throat where it went beneath the neck of the jersey was inconceivably beautiful.

She loved me completely.

I walked up to her and took her hands in mine, and gently drew her down to me. She slid from the table unresistingly, her body against mine. I kissed her, gently, slowly, unpassionately, consciously taking all the sweetness from her obedient lips, as if the deliciousness of all her body lay on her lips, to be gathered from there by mine. I was not trembling or tense, but to the last corners of my being I was relaxed and passive, resting in her love. I had not spoken since I came in, and I felt that I did not want to move, ever. One only moves and hurries, in life, in order to put things by: to have done with them. But here life was so sweet that its principle must be slowness.

At last, still keeping one hand in mine, I led her to the armchair by the fire, and I sat down in it, whilst she sat on the arm of the chair, on my right, leaning over me, her arms round my neck, her hand still in mine.

'You're tired, darling,' she said, and laid her free hand on my forehead: then slid her fingers caressingly through my hair.

'Not now,' I said.

We had been so quiet that Bonzo, curled on the mat, had not wakened when I came in: but now our voices, soft as they were, stirred him. He unrolled, stretched, yawned, looked up at me, and licked my hand in undemonstrative friendship: then plodded aimlessly round the room.

'Has it been a hard day, dear?'

'Route march. We went to Marazion.'

'And in all the rain. You poor thing. No wonder you look worn out.'

I looked up and smiled into her eyes. 'I'm happy now, darling. I'm happy.'

She bent her head and kissed me. 'Oh my own heart's darling, I love you.'

'I love you.'

'Let me take your collar off. It looks uncomfortable.' Her cool fingers unfastened the knot of my tie, and slipped the collar off its studs: and unfastened the buttons at the neck of my vest. 'There, that's better.'

'My Elizabeth.'

I reached up for her hand again, and gently pulled her down beside me in the armchair, taking her weight in my arms. She laughed and put back her arms round my neck contentedly. And so we lay for a long time, completely passive, submissive to the intimate contact of our bodies from knee to shoulder.

Her lips were parted in absorbed bliss. At last I leaned very gently forwards so that my lips rested on hers, not pressing: remained so with closed eyes, thinking of nothing, absolutely nothing, letting my whole being soak in the fragrance of adoration for her. Very slowly her arms tightened round my neck, but hardly perceptibly: I responded immediately, turning my body towards her, so that my weight was partly on her, and we lay in close contact, all the front of my body touching hers. Because of this movement, my lips pressed hers. She wriggled slightly against me as she nestled down in the chair, and the need for her, the aching longing for her mounted like a flame through me, seeming to choke me. My thighs and my heart and my lips craved for her. Oh God how I wanted her. I drew back my head and looked at her beautiful face, and stroked her hair, I was filled with the pain of my love for her. 'Kiss' she said. I kissed her.

I caressed her hair, lifted it in my hands and uncovered her ear, and leaning across her, my cheek on hers, my lips touching the lobe of her ear, I whispered love to her, softly, half-formed words that meant everything on earth.

But I had come to that limit within which my inhibitions had hitherto constrained my life, and now I knew what long-built barriers must crack and crumble before I could be at ease and passive again: for now I was no longer resting in her love, but longing for a different equilibrium, a deeper —an ultimate equilibrium. And what would that mean to her? How *could* I do what all the blood in my body was *compelling* me to do? She would be shocked, wounded, she would lose her love for me—mad, crazy fears, the shadow of my own repressions, and yet they scared me. Oh Hell (I argued with myself), she loves me, doesn't she? If we were married——?

The regular flicker of Mother's electric fire played over the leather of the armchair. Puzzled by our immobility, Bonzo put his forepaws on the armchair, and very delicately licked my eyebrow; with an intense detached awareness I saw all the detail of the room within my field of vision, felt Bonzo's light breath as he sniffed gently, and heard the tick of the clock: my mind beyond that observation was agony, desire and fear.

Bonzo gave up the problem and returned to his carpet. No, she'd lose all her trust in me—

I drew back my head again and looked long and deeply into her eyes, and all my soul looked through my eyes: and her eyes gazed back into mine without any shame, affectionately, gladly. I crushed my lips on hers, wound both my arms round her and pressed her closer to me. So we lay for a long time, kissing with parted lips, so that the tips of our tongues touched, and I understood then what heaven was possible for me, I knew that I must take her, and that only Elizabeth herself should stop me.

I felt the warmth of her body through the serge of my battle-dress. The contact of her adorable flesh: God above, how very lovely she was.

I slipped my hand quickly under her tight grey jersey, felt the cool sheen of her silk slip and cupped her breast in my hand. She relaxed more in the chair, and we slid closer together. She disengaged her left arm from round my neck (for a panicky moment I thought she was going to push my arm away) and put it round my back, under my armpit, holding me closely.

Gently I squeezed her breast, caressingly, and kissed her closed eyes, her nose, her mouth: I could be very gentle and tender now, and patient in all my actions. Still kissing her softly and tenderly, I turned so that my knee came between her thighs, pushing her wide blue skirt back to the top of her stockings. She had been lying on her side, half facing me, but now she turned a little away, resting more comfortably in the crook of the chair: and moving her hand down

111

from my armpit to my hip, she drew me down towards her. Still I kissed her with a deep, tender passion, and she seemed to be all the sweetness of the world in a human form: and I moved my hand from her breast to the silk of the top of her stocking, though it was hard to leave the one sweetness even for the other; and I caressed the soft flesh of the inside of her thigh tenderly, always kissing her. As I kissed, she moved her lips against mine, and all her body: my whole being one ache of longing for her, I slipped my hand inside the wide leg of her knickers, softly and gently, till at last I felt the soft hair beneath my fingers. And all was as inevitable as death, and I knew and accepted all. I laid my cheek on hers again, whispering breathlessly broken words, 'my darling, my heart's darling, you are so sweet, so sweet'. 'Oh Michael', she murmured, in a trembling childlike voice, 'I know it's wrong, but it must be, now.'

Our lips met again, each seeking the honey of the other, and slowly I began to work her knickers down from under her. She lifted her body slightly, and they dropped to the rug. Her hand was quickly unfastening the stiff buttons of my battledress. Longing and impatience swept me, till the last button was done, the clothing released, and then the sense of freedom, the relaxation, the cool air at my loins, the infinite satisfaction as under her guidance I tiredly laid all my body down upon her: I felt my flesh touch hers, and enter there, and felt the warm throbbing of her: her arms went round my waist, drawing me to her, and my hips and loins moved as I pressed gently but insistently into the depths, inexorably overcoming the slight dragging resistance of her body, forcing the deepest communion, while the throbbing of her body beat always warmer in mine, and mine in her: and when at last I had fully subdued all the sweet resistance of her flesh, and had completely taken possession of her, the ecstasy reached its immense climax, and we strained, strained ever closer together, souls (if ever human souls were) in bliss, in Paradise.

And at last the wave receded, relaxation and ease flooded our bodies. I lay quietly in her arms kissing her gently, gratefully.

112

Chapter Eleven

I woke from a profound sleep, next morning, and was very happy. At breakfast I saw the Doc., and arranged to go down to Helston with him in the evening as usual.

There was a strong rumour going round, said Orry, that the battalion was to move shortly. Of course, it was all very 'security' just now, to be kept very dark. So far the impersonal powers upward of Brigade and downward from Whitehall had kept it so dark that the officers and men who would be affected by it knew nothing about it; but this ignorance was confined to them, and among the laity all the barmaids in Cornwall passed on the information that the ——Shires were moving. Occasionally, as time went on, the more charitable civilians took pity on the man in khaki, and let him into the secret—hence the Doc's knowledge.

From usually well-informed barmaids we understood we were going to North Wales. Another suggestion was Durham. In either case, said the man who supplied the Mess with coke, one thing was certain, we were going soon.

My happiness was gone. Gone in a flash. I tried to discount the rumour, but I felt it was pretty certain.

I was silent over breakfast, weighing the proposition that our days together were numbered. Probably I could count on the fingers of one hand the nights I had left with Elizabeth, before we went.

'What time do you think of going into Helston, Doc?'

'Oh—between tea and dinner.'

I should be in Helston by half-past six, Polpryn at a quarter-past seven. And I always had to leave Polpryn not later than ten.

Time seemed to be narrowing down on us already.

I was inspecting the rifles of my platoon when a runner came over from Company Office to tell me the Adjutant wanted to see me. There was the rear rank still to be inspected, so I acknowledged the message and carried on. Shaw's rifle, of course, was one of the dirtiest in the platoon: shiny enough in the barrel (anyone can pull a bit of flannelette through a barrel) but dirty behind the safety-catch, under the leaf of the backsight, and in the trigger mechanism. I looked up from the rifle into his defensive eyes, and slowly shook my head.

When I reached Orderly Room, Cuttle kept me waiting half an hour before he would see me. This was not uncommon with him, and I always assumed, charitably, that he had a lot of work. At last I went in and saluted.

'Good morning, sir. You wanted to see me.'

'Yes, Carr. I suppose you know why?'

'No, sir.'

'The fact is, Carr, I'm not satisfied with you.'

I was puzzled, but said nothing.

'Yesterday, during a route march, you left your platoon. You were seen, several minutes after your platoon had marched out of Helston, leaving a public-house. Why?'

'I wished to make an urgent 'phone call, sir, and I used the 'phone in the "Angel".'

'What do you mean by "urgent"? Somebody dead?'

'Not as urgent as that.'

'Hmm. You understand that this is a clear neglect of duty?'

'I don't think my duty suffered from my very brief absence, sir.'

'That's not for you to say. Did you inform your Company Commander, and ask his permission to leave the column?'

'No sir. I didn't intend to leave the column. I intended to have made my call and have rejoined my platoon before the march was resumed.'

'If you had to 'phone, couldn't you have used the public call box?'

'It was occupied, sir.'

'Why did your call take so long?'

'The line was engaged.'

He looked at the blotting-pad in front of him, pursing his lips.

'It isn't good enough, Carr. I won't have subalterns slipping up in this way. You are, whether you realize it or not, an example to the men, and if you are slack, you are a bad example. It will not do, and I will not have it. Such incidents lower the discipline of the entire unit'.

'It was not my intention to leave the line of march, sir, and I did not feel that to make a 'phone call during a ten-minute halt was a breach of discipline. I do not think that my conduct in general is such as to lead to bad discipline.'

'That's beside the point. Junior officers must understand that I will not tolerate slackness.'

I was silent.

'Very good', said Cuttle: 'you will do the duties of Battalion Orderly Officer for the next three days.' He turned to the Assistant Adjutant: 'Mr. Wilkie, you will see that an entry to that effect is made in B.R.O.'s., and that the Duty Roster is set back three days.'

I saluted and came out. There was a corporal standing outside, waiting his turn, who came to attention: I returned his salute but avoided his eyes, I felt so humiliated.

Resentment, indignation, but above all humiliation filled my mind as I went back to my platoon. I felt so wounded, so reduced in pride and status that it was an effort to command my men—I felt a mere sham, not trusted by my superiors. But mingled with this disagreeable shaking of my self-trust was fury and contempt for the pettiness of the army system, for the third-form sneakishness of the officer who had reported me, and for the silly, pettifogging, exasperating punishment. God damn it, were we in khaki to fight a war, or to scratch each others' eyes out? Was it an army, or had I strayed by mistake into a third-rate girls'-school? No wonder the men were bitter, no wonder the army was full of men like Shaw. This was how we squabbled, *'peached'* on each other, backbit, while the Nazis roared through Europe like a flame. We were much too busy to fight: busy seeing that Private Smith didn't overstay his leave, punishing Private Jones for being out of barracks at Retreat, or packdrilling Private Brown for failing to polish his capbadge for inspection. While the Nazis marched on Moscow and Cairo! Thank God the Bolsheviks were not polishing *their* badges.

An army! Not an idea in it, not an ideal, not a fighting spark, not a flash of imagination, not a capful of the fresh air of inspiration in it: just a dead, frozen, congealed mass of routine, restriction and prejudice, mud, leaves and dead twigs that any January might freeze together: paltry, petty, incapable, craven, dead-brained: betraying the faith and courage of the soldier: holding together, not by a common aim and a common resolution, but by the sheer weight of inertia and blanco. Blanco, symbol of the corruption of the army, blanco, as stiff as starch, and crumbling to dust under the first pressure.

Of course, the main purpose of my fulminations against the army was to ease my conscience; when you are about to injure anybody, you generally alleviate your sense of guilt by finding good reason why the victim deserves it. And I intended, if it could be done, to go to Polpryn on at least one of those three nights when, as Orderly Officer, I should be in camp.

There was this in favour of such a plan, I never spent much time in the Mess Tent, apart from meals. A general aversion to officers in mass, an antipathy to the ruling officer-types, kept me to my tent or walking in the lanes of Treeth, when I couldn't reach Helston or Polpryn. When I did spend an hour or so in Mess, it was to play chess with the Doc., or to attempt the Times Crossword Puzzle. No-one would miss me if I did not appear in Mess, even though I was Orderly Officer.

In the circumstances the crime would be pretty serious, so it was as well the risk of detection was no greater. As it was, I did not feel inclined to risk it unless it seemed fairly certain that the Battalion was leaving Cornwall. If the rumour of the move seemed likely to be fake, I would be a good boy.

The soldier who deserts his duty cannot be defended, of course: one would not attempt a defence. There have been times before today when my conduct has been indefensible, and I don't doubt there'll be such times in future. I'm not unique in that regard.

There were technical details to settle. If I was to break

bounds, it would be well to have somebody to answer the 'phone in Orderly Room in my absence. Dick Larwood might do that. In fact it was not uncommon, in the ordinary way, for the Orderly Officer to ask a friend to act for him: such arrangements were usually reciprocal, and a matter of convenience. But in this case that would be a direct contravention of Cuttle's orders, since the duties had been awarded as a punishment.

And therefore Dick Larwood couldn't mount the guard for me, as Cuttle might attend guard-mounting parade.

And I must appear at dinner. Hell. Therefore I must ask Orry if he would start off later for Helston; and if he wouldn't, I was sunk. And even if he would, that meant I could not reach Polpryn till after eight, and must return at ten. And something might crop up in my absence, there might be a stand-to of sorts and my defection be discovered.

And further, Dick Larwood might refuse to stand in for me.

Chapter Twelve

My illegal visit to Polpryn was very unsatisfactory.

I had no difficulty in persuading Orry to go into Helston after dinner instead of before, and so I was able to mount the guard and appear in Mess for dinner. Dick agreed to stay in camp from dinner onward, provided I bought him a bottle of whisky. His pockets were always empty. He also agreed to stay in Orderly Room when the Adjutant had gone, and should Cuttle return he would say I had just gone to the latrine.

Unfortunately I had had no opportunity, since my interview with Cuttle, to get into Preeth and 'phone Elizabeth. Hence I had to risk Elizabeth's being out when I went.

It was after eight, and my shadow stretched well ahead of me on the red-lit road, when I pedalled David's cycle up the slope to Pascoe cottage. I felt irritable and over-wrought, nervous lest things should have gone wrong back at camp, aggrieved that I had less than two hours with Elizabeth. I had hated every mile of the road between Helston and Polpryn, a road of which generally I loved every bend and bush.

I saw Dad in the garden, clipping the privet hedge. The snip of his shears was a peaceful noise in the quiet air.

David was weeding leeks in the front garden when I opened the gate. He put down the hoe to walk by my side.

"'Lo, Michael. You're a surprise tonight.'

'You wouldn't be expecting me?'

'No. I'm afraid there's a disappointment for you.'

'Elizabeth's out?'

He nodded. 'Um. She's over at Falmouth.'

I felt like twisting the cycle I held into a figure eight.

'Hell,' I said, and put the cycle against the wall.

'Never mind,' said David, 'perhaps she'll be home before you go.' He looked up at me. 'I hear the ---Shires are moving, then?'

'Do you?' I said naïvely.

David smiled with secrecy, screwing up his eyes. 'O.K. Michael, keep it dark.'

'Where did you get the rumour?'

'Ah. You'd like to know that, wouldn't you?'

Bonzo suddenly burst into the garden and hurtled up the lawn, a brown ball of dog, to fling himself on me, barking with joy, leaping, licking, seizing my wrist and mumbling it with mimic ferocity but never letting his strong teeth grip—prancing on his hind legs, fore legs stiff out in front of him, ears laid back, eyes alight with joy—he ducked under David's arms and came at me again and again, his jaws laughing with delight—'Oh you Bonzo, oh you little wristbiter' crooned David. At the noise and commotion Dad turned from his clipping and saw me for the first time. 'Why hello Michael', he said, 'I didn't see you come.'

'You were too intent on your clipping' I told him. 'I hope you're making a good job of it.'

'She'll do, I think—she'll do,' said Dad, stepping back to have a look at his work. 'How does she look to you?'

'Pretty trim,' I acknowledged.

'All done since teatime, and I think that's about enough for one night—what say you, David?'

David looked critically along the hedge. 'I wish you'd got down to the first tree. It would have looked neater.'

'Ah well' laughed Dad, 'I'll let 'ee do it, if you feel in the mood. I'm going in for a chapter of Aldous Huxley.'

I strolled towards the house with Dad, and observed that David did not follow.

'Coming in, David?'

He shook his head. 'I've leeks to weed.'

'Mrs. Pascoe', Dad confided to me as we drew near the door, 'hasn't been very well today, and David has been rather trying to her.'

I gathered there was ill-feeling between mother and son.

The cause I saw as I entered—a large fruit cake, very badly burned.

Mother was sitting bolt upright by her log fire, pretending to read a book. The house smelt not unpleasantly of burnt cake.

'Hello Michael,' said Mother when I went in. 'I thought I heard you.'

In time the story of the cake came out. Mother said she hadn't been well for days. She had been saving her rations of fruit, butter, sugar and eggs for some time, to make a fruit cake. David was very fond of fruit cake. Unfortunately Mother had put the cake in the electric oven, and forgotten to turn the switch to 'low': it had been at 'high' to heat the oven. 'I'd a splitting headache', said Mother in explanation. David had come in and taken no interest in the catastrophe: that had caused the trouble. The cake, after all, had been mainly prepared for him, the saving-up and the care had been to delight him—and then he gave no word of sympathy or regret, not even a show of interest, when it was destroyed. That he could take it so lightly was a snub, an unintended putting Mother in her place.

The fact was David simply *didn't* attach as much importance to his mother's cookery as she did, and as she pretended to herself he did.

As the children grew up and as she herself grew old, more and more Mother lived in an unreal world of wish, and desperately exaggerated to herself the part she played in the children's lives. She pretended to herself that the things they studied also interested her: she tried to share their interests because she was terrified of the bleakness of life if she were pushed out in the cold: and she kept up also the pretence that they were interested in her work, that every domestic thing she did mattered vitally to them. The precarious happiness of her life depended largely on the maintenance of this illusion: nothing was so calculated to shatter it as an uninterested attitude in the children.

David in his way understood this, and usually played up to his mother. It wasn't difficult because he still relied very much on her. But this time, thinking of other things, he had failed.

'I'm sorry, David—I've burnt your lovely cake.' And Mother was about to go on with the long story of how it happened, with information as to the saving of rations, etc., and amount wasted.

David, who had not clearly realized even that a cake was contemplated, said carelessly 'Never mind—make another. What's for tea?' But Mother couldn't let it go at that. She wanted to make her moan, and she wanted sympathy. The cake must be keened to its grave: was not a King of England involved in domestic difficulties over a matter of burnt cakes? Make another, indeed! Where would she get the stuff to do it? David didn't seem to realize . . . . . and so on, till David said 'Why go on at me about it, Mum? I didn't burn the damn thing.'

'I'm not going on at you, David, but you don't have much sympathy when people do their best for you. There's not much kindness in you . . . . . .' 'Well, Mum, after all, it's burned, and that's the finish of it. All the talking on earth won't put it right again.' 'It's all very well saying that—if you'd got the headache I've got . . . . .' 'Good Lord, Mum, if you can't cook the cake without burning it, why cook it at all? If you've got a headache, don't bake.' 'That's a nice way to talk to people who do their best for you, isn't it? A lot you care whether I've got a headache or not. I shall think twice before I bake you another cake.' David couldn't resist the opening—'I reckon you'd burn it, anyway, so it doesn't make much difference.' And so on, and so on, patience shrinking all the time, till David said something unforgivable, and Mother struck him as hard and as often as she could. David, seated at the table, couldn't escape: he hit back. Dad came in on this scene, and managed to put an end to it. Mother ran upstairs weeping and hysterical, saying she wished she was dead. David went out into the garden, where I found him: he being out, Mother came down again.

Mother, who seemed apt to burst into tears at any moment, did not stay downstairs for very long after I had come in. She took some aspirins and said goodnight.

'They're all loopy except me,' said Dad when she had gone.

Mother being in bed, David could leave his leeks without embarrassment. He came in. Dad settled to his book. David mooned about for a time: Bonzo, sensing a gloomy disquiet, padded disconsolately about the room, sometimes stopping to stare up into our faces. I tried to re-read D. H. Lawrence's essay on Keats, but my mind would not be compelled. I was on edge for Elizabeth's return.

David produced some square paper, and suggested a game of Battleships. I agreed. For twenty minutes nothing was heard but our 'A7: G10: F3:' and the responses 'No hits,' or 'Hit one destroyer.' Under the stress of the game David became happy and excited, but my ears were stretched always for the sound of the gate. Even David's enthusiasm could not carry the weight of my tense abstraction: the first game finished, he did not suggest another. 'Let's go out along the road and see if we meet Spud. She might have come in on the nine o'clock 'bus.'

Bonzo was round our feet at the first hint of our going out, prancing, barking, crying with eagerness. He preceded us to the front gate, and opened it himself by standing up on his hind legs and depressing the latch with one paw, bracing his other paw on the gate-post: at the same time (for the gate opened inwards) he inserted his nose between gate and gate-post, and pushed it open. This skill, David assured me, was spontaneous. They had never trained Bonzo to open the gate.

We were abstracted as we went down the hill, each sunk in his own troubles. Elizabeth was not to be seen so far. The sun had set, and I must soon go.

'I reckon we both feel miserable,' said David, with a rueful half-smile.

I nodded. 'Things seem to go wrong.'

'Reelly' said David (a true Cornish 'reelly'). 'I always feel sorry when Mum's been rowing me. She's not a bad ol' stick, reelly.'

'No', I said, 'it's a pity. Couldn't you have kept quiet, or got out of the way?'

'Well—I s'pose I could.' He half-turned to me, spreading his hands and looking up into my face: 'but you see, Michael, it was *on top* of me before I knew. An' then I got mad at her as well.' He sighed. 'I can't help it, reelly.'

I said nothing. After a time he continued.

'I know I did wrong, Michael. You don't need to keep

silent to tell me that.' He sighed again and shook his head. 'I dunno: grown-ups are sometimes as bad as children reelly. But she's not a bad ol' stick. She does a lot for me.'

Pause.

'So does Sis.'

Pause.

'And Dad as well.'

A long pause. We approached the 'bus stop in the centre of the town. No sign of Elizabeth.

'But why does Mum have to go mad at me?' asked David, looking up at me again. 'I'm only ord'nary. Other boys in Polpryn do worse things 'n I do, but their mothers don't go mad at 'em.'

'You'd like to swop mothers?' I suggested.

'*I would not!*' said David. 'Ah, you don't know Mum, Michael. She's better than all the world to me. It'd break my heart. She can't help being like that. It's her nerves. Ah, she's terrible touchy. Then when she gets mad she doesn't know what she's doing. You can't reelly blame her for what she does when she's mad at me.'

Another pause. Again he sighed, and shook his head. We had reached the 'bus stop, but though the 'bus was in, Elizabeth was not on it. I watched the passengers dismount, hoped her face would appear amongst them, hated each one that came in my view for not being Elizabeth.

'Ah, she'll be some disappointed when she knows you've been here, Michael,' consoled David. We set off heavily back. Bonzo, tired of unapproved rompings, walked at our side.

David continued his train of thought.

'You know, she isn't responsible for what she does when she gets *past herself*. It's her nerves, an' all the operations. I think she ought to have the doctor coming always, reelly. Once she did an awful thing.'

He was silent for a time, ruminating.

'Ah, I shall always remember that, Michael. I don't *want* to forget it. She just didn't understand what she was doing. Women are different. She never could understand, never.'

Pause.

'Once I had a jam jar with a lot of sticklebacks in it. Mam

got mad at me about something, I dunno what—maybe I answered back or something. Terrible mad she was, Michael. I didn't reelly know she was as mad as that. I was going upstairs, an' she took my jar of sticklebacks—it was in the garden—and threw them out in the field. I saw her out of the window, coming back up the garden with the jar in her hand—*Empty!*

'Ah: broke my heart, that did. I ran down to the end of the garden, and I could see some of the sticklebacks, through the railings, flipping about on the grass. Some of 'em were dead already, lying on their backs, an' most of 'em had slipped down among the grass-roots an' got lost for good. Just a few were flipping about an' dying. I c'd see their gills trying to breathe. Broke my heart.'

His voice was soft with grief. Certainly he could never forget it. This had become the prototype, the pattern for irreparable wrong; when he met in other situations a harm that could never be made right, it would take a colour from the episode of the sticklebacks. David was of those who heed the sparrow's fall. The agony of his sticklebacks was planted in his heart, and the inarticulate anguish that his mother had done this to him. 'I couldn't stop screaming, Michael.'

'What happened?'

'People—Spud came running down the garden, and after a bit Mum as well, and they tried to pick the sticklebacks up, but most were dead then. They put 'em in the jar with fresh water, an' I helped to find some of them, an' Mum said they were all picked up, but I knew there wasn't half of them. But I couldn't talk about it. Those that we *did* pick up mostly died. Sometimes I think about it at night, and sometimes when Mum gets me raving mad, I say she hates me an' that's why she threw my sticklebacks out. Then she goes *past herself* and says I'm a bad devil to remember things like that. As if I c'd forget it!'

We were back at the gate. Below us, the road to the centre of the town glimmered palely through the dusk. We stood there some time. At last we heard footsteps.

Bonzo was tense, pointing down into the town, his tail giving tremulous involuntary wags.

'Spud,' said David.

Bonzo shot down the road to welcome Elizabeth, and shuttled back and forth between us as we met. David faded into the house.

'Michael! Why have you come?'

I could see by her eyes that she guessed why I had come.

'Is it certain?' she asked.

'I think so. In about three days.'

'Oh God. Everything to finish like that. No warning. God.'

'Everything isn't finished at all, Elizabeth. I shall still be in England, and I'll spend my leave here.'

'Yes. Of course. I'm silly.—Oh Hell, Michael, it's awful. After having you here, and seeing you in Helston—almost every day we've been together—then to see you only once every three months.'

'Elizabeth, darling, don't let it hurt you so much.'

'Ah, Michael.'

'My darling, I'll come back to you. Elizabeth, I don't think I could even lie quiet in a grave. That's silly. But so long as there's life in me I must come back to you. It's in me, I can't change. I'm lost without you. Don't be afraid.'

'I'm not afraid.'

David brought the cycle round to the front of the house ready for my instant departure, but it was ten minutes after my usual time before I could bring myself to go. I couldn't even spare the time to open the front door and say goodbye to Dad. I rode away down the hill as fast as I could pedal, but turned my head at the bottom for a quick glance back. Elizabeth and David stood at the gate watching me into the dusk.

I dared not run any risk of missing the Doc. tonight. I took each bend and twist of the road at top speed, pedalling so hard that sweat burst out on my forehead and my lungs felt raw and sore from my hard breathing. The uphill stretches were very trying. I endeavoured to keep up my speed all the time.

About two miles from Helston, at a double right-angle bend, I ran along the edge of the grass verge with my front wheel. Two seconds' wild wobbling, my feet off the pedals and waving desperately, and I came off on my face with a solid jar.

I was grazed and scratched, and fragments of gravel seemed embedded in the skin of my palms and the end of my nose. Otherwise I had not suffered. The cycle was unridable (the front wheel had lost several spokes and was an ellipse). I found my cap a few feet away, and, wheeling the cycle on the rear wheel—I set off towards Helston.

I had been tramping perhaps a quarter of an hour, my mood completely black, when a car approached from the direction of Helston. To my great relief and gratitude it was Orry's; knowing the gravity of my position if I failed to return to camp, he had come to find me. We fastened the cycle on the top of the car, and went straight back.

We got into camp without trouble. Dick Larwood was asleep in Orderly Room, with a pressure-lamp waning at his side and a powerful smell of whisky about him. I woke, thanked and dismissed him, flapped the tent-door to get rid of the alcohol, and pumped up the lamp. Apparently I had got away with it. I arranged a mirror by the light and cleaned up my grazed nose. My hands were raw, and smarted severely when I washed them.

I turned out the guard at midnight. They had a prisoner, said the guard Commander: Mr. Larwood had put him in for drunkenness. I was not at all pleased to hear this, first because it might mean inquiries in the future as to why Mr. Larwood had acted instead of the Orderly Officer, secondly because I never put a drunk in the guard-room if I could help it—one could nearly always get him off to his tent, where his mates would look after him. But anyway, it appeared Dick had laid no charge against him—merely run him in for convenience, the sort of stupid thing Dick *would* do. I could send him out again and nothing said. His name had not been entered in the Guard Report.

'What's he like now, Corporal Wynne?'

'Quiet, sir. Asleep. He was disorderly when brought in.'

'I'll see him.'

'Very good, sir. I'll get a candle.'

He lit a candle from that on the table, and led the way

through the next tent, where the sentries off duty were already falling asleep again after my inspection, into the far tent. There, flat on his side, his head nestled in the muddy grass, his limbs totally relaxed on the earth (as if they were half-fluid), as still as a stone Crusader, lay Shaw. He had been sick without waking. The dark, beery vomit had seeped into the grass-tufts near his mouth, and trailed from his parted lips. His white face in sleep, completely abandoned by his soul, had a childlike content and innocence.

Corporal Wynne smiled, fatherly. 'I can let him go, sir, if you like.—Like a lamb, sir, isn't he?'

'How much do you think he's had?'

'A tidy whack, sir. And there's nothing on him to stand it, you see. He was very abusive when brought in.'

'But Mr. Larwood overlooked it?'

'He left it up to you, sir.'

'Was he violent?'

'Yes, he was violent, sir—such as he could be, considering there's no bone and muscle on him.'

'What time was this?'

'Quarter past ten, sir.'

'Where did he get his beer? NAAFI?'

'I should think he got it in Treeth, sir. I reckon he went down with a crowd of his mates, and none of 'em was mate enough to bring him back.'

'He's only been asleep a couple of hours, then. Better not wake him now, he might be noisy again. Give him till three o'clock or so, then wake him and send him to his tent. If you think he can't find his way, send a man with him.'

'Very good, sir.'

Shaw now joined the conversation. 'Lights out' he said, suddenly covering his eyes with his hand, 'Get that f——g light out.' Then, with a strange movement, he swung both his arms down and raised himself, head and shoulders, from the ground: 'I can see you grinning behind them f——g bars. White-livered bastards'. Then he dropped like a sack and was asleep, but groaning slightly. ' 'E thinks he's back in clink,' said Corporal Wynne as we came out.

Chapter Thirteen

The day before I left Cornwall, Elizabeth and I went to Land's End. We couldn't have chosen worse. The day was grey and cool, with a west wind. From the unenterprising bare road through Sennen, past the little windswept houses we went, down the rocks to where the water swang and slapped the sides of granite: we stood on the soggy shingle, rings of cold water round our boots, and looked into wind and spray and the sleepless splashing of the Atlantic. Bottles, and a half-eaten sardine sandwich in a soaked paper, lay at our feet. And there was no sentimentalizing the fact that the Atlantic didn't care a damn for us, didn't know we were there, and wouldn't care when we were gone. 'We never would be missed.'

The cold wet wind twisted Elizabeth's hair into lank rat-tails and dimmed its shine. And when all was said and done, we didn't want to hear the message of the waves. It was not comforting.

The sea's sound was a steady, vast, repeated roar: low, hollow, desolate. Every wave that rolled in said the same thing: desolation, desolation, desolation. But it went deeper than any words. It was so hollow, so uncompromising, so cold. It was death speaking. It was beyond history. It was beyond grief. It faded into a sighing murmur far along the beach, and then again began its roar. It came from endless spaces where there was no dawn. No comfort or recognition in it. Desolation, desolation, desolation. The sea merely talked to itself, groaned, could not sleep. Eavesdropping, all we learned was that we could die, and that it could be that we should never meet again, in this world or any other. I was afraid.

'Elizabeth, let me see into your eyes. The world and society and war are all nonsense and irrelevant. Our own names don't matter. The only real thing is that we two beings need each other. Let's always come back, whatever happens. There's no life for us away from each other.'

We never got the sound of the sea out of our ears. Back at Polpryn, for that last night we tried to listen to the music we liked most, but the sea drowned it. The 'Beggars' Opera' was meaningless. 'Jesu Joy of Man's desiring' seemed unbearably slow, as if it would take up the whole evening. 'It's no use, Michael, they don't seem to connect' said Elizabeth, looking at me almost tearfully. Our very souls were sore and uncomfortable. Till at last we found a record of Mendelssohn's 'Hebrides' overture, and the sea did its worst with us. The unearthly descending phrase of the main subject twisted my heart. I saw again the lonely salient of Land's End standing far out into the sea, absolutely motionless and grey, while the waves came in from infinite heaving remoteness onto the hard stone, sending high into the air their spires of hissing spray. There was no place now for the old music: it was too soaked in the sunshine of our happiness, and we felt too well that we had come to the end of that land. Land's End was in our hearts. We had not lost the sound of the sea, the melancholy long withdrawing roar. You could not drown that voice with madrigals. Whenever I have recalled that day, the heart-piercing descending phrase of Mendelssohn's has come to my mind—I can hear it now, it says too much to me—and the hollow, remote, inhuman trumpets which seem to sound far, far out over a never-resting brown sea.

'Ah, Michael' said David as we stood at the gate waiting, and Elizabeth went upstairs for her coat. ' 'Tis a bad thing for Sis.'

'I know, David. Be kind to her when I've gone, and remind her I'll come back soon.'

He sighed, fondling Bonzo's ear. 'She thinks a terrible lot about you. It's been good for her, you being here.'

END OF FIRST PART

PART TWO

Chapter Fourteen

Dearest Elizabeth,

Here we are, after preposterous trouble, bustle and contradictory orders. I have a room all to myself: imagine how I feel after all those months under canvas. I have the unpleasant sense that all the old life has been folded up and packed away: everything is new, times, places, duties, scenes, sounds. The strange thing is that though it has only lasted three days so far, it already seems right and natural. I'm already quite accustomed to my iron bed and four walls, and I get no pleasure out of them. Doors and windows and stairs—you see, at the back of my mind is the bald-conscious recognition that, in moving from Cornwall to North Wales, the significant change is that I've lost you, and gained domestic amenities: my unconscious regards it as a lousy bargain Yes, I miss you very much and I won't try to pretend otherwise. I'm no mental-lifer, I can't and won't be satisfied with recollections, fancies and hopes—it amounts to masturbation. They're all I've got, of course, but satisfied I am not. The want of you is in my mind always. Every fresh or beautiful thing I see brings the thought of you back, because I want you to see it too. There's no pleasure in the world for me unless I share it with you.

Pwllheli is a little seaside town, with plain grey houses, ugly pubs, and hideous chapels: that finishes the plain, the ugly and the hideous here. Cardigan Bay is due South, directly in front of my window. The coast is quite different from Cornwall, the whole sweep of the bay is bigger and smoother: no rugged cliffs. But thirty or more miles to the South-East, across the water, you can see the Cader Idris group of mountains, and Snowdon is to the North-West. Pwllheli itself is dominated by a couple of mountains due North, about ten miles away, called the Rivals. We are in a saucer of flat, fertile land, bounded by the sea along the South, and by hills, North, East and West.

From the little I've already seen of this part of Wales, I get a strong impression of grey, green and purple—stone walls, bushy tufty fields, and purple mountains. It's all lanes and hills, and I have to admit that the Welsh lanes are very much more beautiful than those of Cornwall. They are quite enchanted. They climb, they wind, they dip, they become so narrow—and the earth or stone walls that edge them become so thick and massy with briars, hawthorns and every kind of entangling plant—that any one such lane seems as if it must be the direct route to Heaven. Unhappily, that impression is quite correct—turn the bend in the lane, and sure as fate you're face to face with some great yellow chapel, the last convulsion of a diseased imagination, standing four-square amid the greenery, scowling at the sky and putting the mountains in their places—all pipeclay and yellow paint and stucco, with EBENEZER, BETHEL, or some other sinister cabalistic impossibility writ large upon its forehead (why not, oh why not MENE MENE TEKEL UPHARSIN!). An atheist, I stand stunned. Could any devout man look about him in such country and not know that the mountains have raised steeples and *the heavens are telling the glory of the Lord?*

(I do solemnly hate these beastly, ugly, hard, cheap, sub-human, bigoted, God-*fearing* chapels. God-*fearing:* that's the word. You see the natives trooping into them, Sundays, dragging their reluctant children, all humanity and nakedness pinioned in decent black, faces like fiddles, sore with soap and salvation—hurrying guiltily out of the sunshine, in from the hills, crowding into their yellow boxes to hide their shameful selves from God's creation, afraid the butterflies will laugh at them or the swallows turn them to ridicule—black crawling blots on the generous face of nature—in they go, out of the light, like beetles—God-*fearing*. They fear the sky, the hills, the trees, the sun—these ghastly chapels are psychological Air Raid Shelters.)

Cardigan Bay is deep blue, the beach at Pwllheli is smooth, regular and golden, proceeding miles to the West—to a place called Abersoch—but closed at the East by a great rock called the Gimlet, which stands out into the sea. The pilots from the neighbouring aerodrome make a practice of roaring along the beach occasionally, no more than fifteen feet or so from the sand (or even immediately above the promenade) in their Spitfires. When they reach the West End Hotel, they lift one wing over it (so to speak) and spin up sideways into the sky in a way which always reminds me of how we boys used to flip cigarette-cards.

That is the place, in general. My platoon seems to be happy to be out of canvas and under roofs again. We are no longer all together, as a battalion, but split up into Companies. This I like better. We don't have the old Mess Etiquette, for instance—one can have dinner in battledress, instead of the daily annoyance of changing into barathea. Also I see more of the men (my own men) and less of the battalion officers, God forgive me, darling, I do not love my brother-officers.

I haven't time to re-read this letter before sending it, my sweet, so I hope I've said all I should. Give my love to your mother and dad, and to David.

Your Lover Michael

Elizabeth wrote back:

My Darling,

'How like a winter hath thy absence been.' But that's no way to begin writing to you. It's so strange being without you, I haven't got used to it yet. Sometimes I fall into my old habit of gladness, then suddenly ask 'why am I glad'? and realize that you have gone, and my happiness is just a mistake, an old habit. There's no hurrying back from classes on certain nights now: I know you'll not be waiting for me at home.

Bonzo doesn't understand it either. All evening he lies with one ear cocked for the click of the gate. And David misses you. Now that you are gone, of course, Mum has no praise too high: but it makes it a bit too obvious to me that in her eyes your principal virtue is absence. She never trusted me with you. Which is understandable, my own darling. She often talks about you, apparently for my sake, but I wish she wouldn't, it makes me most uneasy. Her misunderstandings of you, too, seem so queer to me, who know you to the deepest corners. No, I'm not to be gratified by endless indiscriminate flattery of you: let Mum like you in her way, and I'll love you in mine. But the poor dear means nothing but well, and her natural appreciation of you as a man and an officer is able now to develop unchecked by the fear that you may be seducing me in the drawing-room. Though she will never take any earthly rank or honour seriously except that of a doctor. If you were but a doctor, sweet, I think you could do as you liked. I reckon Mum has had so much hell in her life, operations and God knows what, and doctors have played so big a part, that to her they have become an order of superior creative beings, gods. (And then, you see, they are rich, powerful, professional gentlemen, with cars and a brass plate on the door: far above the Working Class. Oh Mike my own, you should have been a doctor.)

Dad fell downstairs yesterday morning. He went from top to bottom with a terrible clatter. We were all asleep in bed —it was Sunday, and you know what we are on Sunday mornings. We all shot up in bed thinking it was the Invasion or the Millennium, and Mum shouted 'John! John!! John!!!' and Dad replied from the bottom of the stairs, 'For Christ's sake shut up, woman. Can't a man fall downstairs now?' whereon Mother, nettled, said, 'Oh, if you *like it*, bloody well do it again.' I couldn't help giggling, though I was sure Dad had hurt himself, and when I got downstairs —Mum ahead of me, flapping rather—he was bleeding from nose and elbow, and had an egg-bruise on his head. We grabbed the Doctor's Book and found out what to do with him—keys down the back is merely a superstition—and we ran cold water on the bruises. But I *did* feel sorry for poor old Dad. He's still limping stiffly about, I think he's bruised all over, and he sits down tenderly.

There's no other news, darling, except that David has gone back to school, and the objectionable Mr. Forbes has given him some fifty lines on account of his French homework: you know why that is. David is lost without you to help him. He was puzzling over Latin last night, and he looked up and said 'Ah Spud, I'm in a bad way without that Michael'. He has no one but Dad to play Battleships with.

We had an Air Raid Warning the night before last, and went into the shelter, but no bombs and no aircraft. Do you have warnings in Wales?

I am writing this now when the house is quiet. Mum and Dad have been in bed half-an-hour, and David has just closed his book with a doubtful noise and gone upstairs. So long as I am here. Bonzo refuses to leave the other armchair. There is no sound except the old clock: in the silence its tick is positively jarring. Well, I must creep upstairs soon, very carefully so as not to wake anybody—but I know the switch on the landing will go off like a cracker when I turn out the light, it always does. So goodbye my pet. Let's keep ourselves for each other.

Elizabeth

Elizabeth,

We've been out on exercises for the last eight days, that's why I haven't been able to write. Exercises are very curious things: every one I take part in helps a little to increase my profound ignorance of the art of war, and my immense distrust of all things which depend on people doing as they're told.

We hoped to be the enemy in the Exercise. It's a good thing to be enemy, because you wear soft hats instead of steel helmets, and you don't have equipment. But we were disappointed.

From the first day, the exercise became like all other exercises. One doesn't ever get to know what's happening: that information is usually given weeks after in a lecture by the Divisional Commander. God knows how he finds out. For a long time we were attacking the 9th Popshires, but as a matter of fact the 9th Popshires were not in the exercise, and the people we were attacking were the Home Guard, who conduct guerrilla warfare against both sides impartially, and never give any information. In default of information from higher up, one draws on imagination for inspiring bulletins to send down to the men. This is called Putting them in the Picture. Throughout the exercise one lives out in the open. It rains, naturally. Aeroplanes are used, and add greatly to the excitement. They dive and machine-gun friend and foe alike, giving a convincing air of reality to the show. From time to time an umpire sets off a Tear Gas capsule in the platoon area, which is funny if you've got your respirator handy.

Great sport is had when the enemy attacks. We lie down in the trenches we've been digging all night, and aim our rifles. Having no blanks, we can but snap our bolts at him, whereas he, having blanks, is far more minatory. Exasperated, we shout 'Bang, Bang'! The total effect is highly remarkable. Finally he charges with fixed bayonets. Our cries of 'bang'! make nature's buildings shake. The umpires, who have been darting like pale ghosts from tree to tree, run up and tell us who is dead, who wounded, and who missing. Argument ensues. Corporal Adams bellows in my ear that he shot the enemy platoon commander. The enemy platoon commander says Corporal Adams missed him. Corporal Adams wishes to God he'd had a round of ball up the spout: the enemy sergeant says he shot Corporal Adams. The umpire shouts, the sergeant shouts, Corporal Adams shouts, the enemy officer shouts, I shout. What's the use of playing if Johnny won't be dead? Then we return to our trenches and continue our interrupted Three-card Brag.

How I chatter: you can guess why. I will not turn my letters into everlasting moans.

I hope Dad's recovered now. Poor David. Honestly, I don't flatter myself I was *so* essential to his homework, I only helped him to be interested in it. Homework is a barbaric ritual: see Veblen, 'Theory of the Leisure Class', chapter on The Higher Learning. Chain of ostensible reasons: —if the children don't do homework, they won't pass the examinations: if they don't pass the exams., they won't be able to make a living. If it's untrue, what an imposition. If true, *what* an imposition! A fine world we've made of it, on such an assurance—so bloody complicated that we aren't clever enough to live in it. What will it be like a century hence, at that rate—let's hope the children of that period will have resolution enough to cut their throats rather than enter on the hothouse cramming, from two to forty-two, which will be necessary before they can wring a bare living from the earth which (we're told) provided at least *sufficient* before our intellectual race began.

What a race we are making of ourselves: all heads and no tails, and like all other double headed coins, without value except as a means of deception. All mental-lifers. Paul was misquoted, surely it's clear that 'it is better to marry than to learn'? All this merely to get Society's approval: the best years of life spent by the young, under compulsion, trimming their minds to the fashionable shape. How innocuous by comparison are the physical distortions practised by 'savages': how infinitely kinder to castrate a boy with a sharp stone than with a Latin Dictionary. How incredibly crueller is our idol, Society, than their Moloch or Juggernaut. Society, society: as we were sacrificed, so let us sacrifice our children to Society. Society which should have been a reasonable framework of law to help men live together, has become a colossal idol sitting on our shoulders and eating our souls. To hell with Society. Elizabeth, let's give it no more, life's too precious. We believe none of its mumbo-jumbo, we are not patriots, Christians or any other stock articles: the tribal customs don't impress us. Let's neither conform nor contradict, but concentrate on living as two creatures who love—only compromising where we must. To hell with Society. Our children shall not be sacrificed. They can learn enough of the tribal formulae to perform the *unavoidable* rituals, without sitting up till midnight over it. They can learn to stand for the National Anthem, use a knife and fork, speak Standard English, and keep silent in Church when they have to go: and the nature in them, if we let it live, will teach them something rather more important, to love their neighbours and to love themselves. For the last time, to hell with Society and rituals: one reason it's such a burden is, it's pullulating with fat parasites.

Do you remember Dick Larwood—you met him at a dance in Helston. (The one who has piles. They're improving now, he says.) He's married—yes, the famous Sybil: he has just come back from leave and honeymoon. I've seen Sybil, too. I won't give my comments, I'm prejudiced, but I feel she will turn out bad-tempered. Dick is in bliss just now, and just as he used to wake me in the small hours to tell me how lonely he was without her, now he wakes to tell me of his happiness with her. From my viewpoint there's nothing gained, in fact it's a dead loss, because whereas before I had you and he had not Sybil, now he has Sybil and I have not you, so I don't at all like to be wakened at three in the morning. But he has brought her to Wales, and means to apply for permission to sleep out, which I'll be glad when he gets. Did I tell you he has moved into my room, his own having been taken over by the Q.M.S.?

Goodbye for now, dear: Michael.

A letter from David:

Dear Michael,

I'm sorry I haven't written before, but I'll make this extra long, to make up.

Spud is terrible lonely without you.

We had a match with High Crag School a week ago. The referee was one-sided (on their side) so we lost 3—2, the pitch was covered in slime and we kept slipping.

I had some fun with Mum and Spud last Thursday. Went to bed earlier than usual, tied china elephant I have in my bedroom to a reel of cotton then I gently let the china elephant from my bedroom window until it knocked the door with its trunk. I heard Mum answer the door and heard her say 'There's no one there.' Then Spud went next time to the door. The same story. I thought that was enough for the night. On Friday night I tried the same but the cotton broke, elephant got smashed so the joke's over.

We have been recently to get some blackberries, but they were not ripe. As we were near a pool, Peter Trevithick and I got a stick, a pin which we bent, some cotton, with these we made a crude but efficient rod and had goes in turn till we caught a fish. All went well till Bonzo, who had been hesitating on the brink, jumped into the water and got entangled on the line. This was strange because he does not like water much. We did not catch any more fish. Do you remember the plant in the front garden which we thought was an American Blackberry? Well in reality it was a Chinese Strawberry.

This winter my homework will be taking up a lot of my time without your help. I get headache trying to think *how* to do things and no-one to ask. I do miss you Michael. When will your leave be?

Cheerio, David.

From Elizabeth:

My Dear Michael,

I feel very tender tonight. The house is at peace. David is outside mending a puncture, and Dad is cutting the lawn. There's a nice smell of mown grass coming in through the window. The first leaves began to fall from the poplars today. Mum is in the chair by the fire: it's quite cool tonight. She is reading Ezra Pound's 'Guide to Kulchur' and wrinkling her forehead over it. Poor dear. I think she hates to feel out of her children's world. She wants to share experiences with me. She doesn't realize how superficial my own understanding is, and that I haven't the remotest idea what Ezra Pound is driving at. She's seen me reading it, and concludes it's a significant part of my world. She thinks I know all about Kulchur! And that if she studies, she'll know too, and we'll have everything in common. It makes me feel horribly sad for her, taking so seriously what I merely skim. She reads Ezra Pound as if she were learning a lesson, as if she hoped to educate herself back into youth. It makes me feel guilty. I'm not earnest, I don't think hard, I merely take the obvious line in life, but Mum thinks I understand all sorts of things which she doesn't. It's as if we were bluffing the old folks. At their age they shouldn't be teased with lessons, puzzles and problems. They deserve peace and respect.

Do you understand what I've just written? I know you would if I said it to you, but written, it seems so hard and impersonal. Life is mainly sad (though when *that's* written, it looks like a comic phrase from a Russian novel).

I went to St. Ives for the week-end, to Margaret Lowrie's bungalow. She has the place all to herself, just for the winter, and cooks and does everything. You remember her sketches. She's selling a lot of drawings now, to magazines, and improving her technique a lot. She's most business-like, not a bit arty: says it's all a matter of bread and butter. She cooks

141

marvellously: she says she puts her talent into her work, her genius into her cooking. She has a black market arrangement with a local farmer for eggs and cream: she made a delicious raspberry omelet-soufflé with whipped cream—served hot, imagine it!

Yesterday in a fit of enthusiasm I bought a tin of some stuff called liquid lino (a pleasant brick-red colour—an enormous tin) and painted it all over the scullery floor, which is concrete. Today I'm very pleased with the effect. It is quite smooth and sanitary-looking. I shall give it another coat tomorrow, and so on till the floor is smooth and rubbery. Or is there a limit to the amount you can put on?

Dick Larwood did well to marry. He needed someone to keep him in order.

Goodbye Darling: Elizabeth.

Dear Elizabeth,

Excitement and worry: the Adjutant suddenly produced, over a week ago, an order that a draft of men and officers were to be sent from this unit for overseas service. There is a War Office letter instructing commanders not to 'offload' into drafts—that is not to get rid of their troublesome men by sending them abroad. But how strictly would you expect an adjutant to observe such an order? He's only concerned with his own unit. So long as *that's* fine and dandy, the war can go hang. 'Up with the gangway, I'm aboard'.

Don't be alarmed, darling. This body dropped not down. Though Cuttle loves me like a sick headache, he did not ink me in. But Dick Larwood's going, just when he had brought his wife to Pwllheli and got permission to sleep out. Poor lad. He came out of the Orderly Room—having been told he was for the tropics—looking deathly. He is said to have caused a sensation by telling the Adjutant 'but my wife won't hear of it'! Anyhow, he cheered up quite soon, considering, and just before he vanished on Embarkation Leave he was working out the chances of taking Sybil to India or wherever with him—not, I understand, as batman, despite Polly Oliver.

142

Now for my own private worry. The Adjutant, seeking what men he can get rid of, decides there are a couple in my platoon who 'never would be missed', and accordingly inks them in. They are warned for overseas service, their kit is made up (a multitude of sins shelter behind that phrase) and they are sent on belated embarkation leave, to have only three days before leaving for the tropics. I'm not going to insult you by telling you my opinion of *that*.

This 'warning for overseas service'. It means in effect that the men are clearly informed, before they go off on leave, that if they fail to return by the appointed time they are liable to be charged with desertion. The men sign a statement that they have had this read out to them and that they understand it.

Well, of course, one of my men *didn't* return. He came back a day late, when the draft had gone. He is now in the guard-room awaiting court-martial. I don't like court-martials anyway, and I certainly don't like them on any of my lads. I don't think I'm sentimentalizing: I simply don't accept the current notions of justice. Only an idiot could. 'See'st thou yond Justice railing upon yond simple thief? A word in thine ear: change garments, and handy-dandy, which is the justice, which is the thief?'

What worries me particularly is that the offender is no more than a lad. His name is Shaw, his age, I suppose, eighteen. He gave a false age when he enlisted. A child in arms. He never has been a good soldier, but whether it is more economic to knock hell out of him to make him so, or to get him out of the army altogether, is an open question. Every punishment he's had, so far, has led to greater faults and a still heavier punishment, which isn't much of a recommendation for the army methods. I hate to think of crushing a foolish boy under the solemn stupidity of a court-martial. But Fate doesn't spare my eyes and ears—Shaw has (not unnaturally) named me, his platoon commander, as his defending officer. God knows I can't save him. So I'm to watch him wriggle and squirm under the Iron Heel and pretend to protect him. Gloomy.

Ah well, I'll do what I can. He's got a pretty bad crime-sheet. This will give him a powerful push downwards. Society again. There's no mercy for those who can't conform.

In the long run, you know, one feels sorry for both judge and criminal: the criminal not questioning the rightness of the laws in general: and the judge, so solemn, so sure, so confident of the moral perfection of Society, which he represents. And yet the only real difference between them, as creatures on the earth, is that the judge has all the help he needs and the prisoner has none. I daresay Pilate took his job very seriously.

I can't quite put my feelings into words: I'd like to have a logical mind like T. H. Huxley's. But I feel that in our civilization which is based on a conflict between masters and slaves, crime is a projection of the world's guilt. The criminal is a reflection of the judge. Do you remember in 'William Wilson' where Wilson finally stabs his double to death, and seems to see a mirror, in which *his own image* lies bleeding, dying—'Thou hast conquered and I yield. But see, in slaying me, how utterly thou hast slain thyself?'

I had a letter from David which I haven't answered. Please thank him for it.

This retreat into letter-writing, returning into the same world where you still live, contrasts violently with the real, present, objective world. The ideas we share are so impossibly different that if either world is sane, the other is hopelessly mad. You and I seem to believe in nothing. We've thrown away so many traditional attitudes, particularly about morals and ethics and religion—about patriotism, politics—in fact all the things which seem to make up the external world, we reject. And yet I often feel that as a matter of fact we have far more faith, earnestness and belief —I'd rather have a positive belief in nothing than a negative belief in everything—it sounds priggish and complacent, but why not? With my equals, in Mess, I talk smut: with my superiors, shop. The only other permissible subject appears to be dancing—criticisms of the last dance, anticipations of the next. Bridge is played endlessly by two or three religious-solemn groups (beer and whisky to their hands, outrage to interrupt them). The radio is a curse, since the general taste of officers, as of troops, is contemptible: they will hear nothing but the most infantile 'light music', Boogley Woogley Piggies etc.—they are connoisseurs on the stuff and take it very earnestly. There's a unanimous howl of hate should the radio, remaining tuned after such bleatings, broadcast Handel, Mozart, or Beethoven— 'SWITCH IT OFF'! It's far more than mere ignorance, it's a burning poisonous hatred of beauty and grace. These are the men who are fighting, inter alia, for Culture. And their eyes continually on each other for slips which might be brought, indirectly, to the Colonel's notice, thus crippling a competitor for promotion.

What a nasty spiteful toad I am! God, the last paragraph says far more about me than about my fellow-officers. It shall stand, as an Awful Warning.

I won't be due for leave until the second week in October. Apparently something has gone wrong with the leave roster. I've been asking for the possibility of a long week-end, but the C.O. won't sanction so long a journey in a week-end. It isn't any worse than we expected.

Goodbye, Michael.

Dear Michael,

This will have to be a short letter. We're in the midst of jam-making. David is writing your name on a large pot of gooseberry jam which we are putting aside for you. I'm longing to see you eat it. I love the greedy sparkle in your eyes when you see gooseberry jam and cream. I hope you can read this writing—a wasp, amongst the greengages, stung my hand this morning, making me clumsy with the pen.

You sounded to be in a bad temper when you last wrote, or probably it was worry about this court-martial of yours. I hope it doesn't go too badly. But you shouldn't feel so responsible. It may sound bitch-like, but to be quite truthful I'm much more concerned that you should be happy than that justice should be done to this man Shaw. Just because the times are out of joint, you don't have to shoulder the burden of putting them right. It's a form of conceit. If you can't help the victims, it's no use feeling sorry for them. It's better to think of your good luck than other people's bad.

You said yourself, 'to hell with Society'! If you want something to sigh for, just think how *we* would have felt if you'd been on the overseas Draft instead of Larwood. And I'm not sorry if this philosophy seems callous. I *am* callous where it's a question of your happiness. Nothing else really matters to me. I take your advice much more completely than you do yourself, probably because I'm a woman. The only thing I'm interested in is you.

The Larwood business horrifies me. A newly-married couple to be separated like that. Fancy us having to say good-bye on the station here, and neither of us knowing where you would be in a month's time, except that you wouldn't be in England.

I'll have to stop now. Mum is tying covers on the jampots, and if I don't help her they won't be done before midnight.

Love, Elizabeth.

Dear Elizabeth,

Peace at last. I'm on the golf course, my back against a bunker, and facing out to sea. There's only one human being in sight, an elderly man who is the Colonel of the local Home Guard. He hasn't seen me, he is playing golf. I have to keep an eye on him in case he brains me with the ball. This is a perilous golf-course. Returning by it yesterday after a cross-country run, I was chased (a) by a horse, (b) by a goat. A picnic party watched the second chase, and seemed to like it. I am watching the Home Guard Colonel partly in the hope that he will be involved with the goat.

You are right, the last letter I wrote was unworthy of me. I was in a sour, savage mood.

The colonel is teeing his ball very close to where the goat chased me yesterday.

Thank you all for setting aside a pot of gooseberry jam. I long for the day when I shall eat it and have you opposite me at the little table in the garden.

My court-martial has been and gone. I did *not* help much. I think I let my man down. (But even if I'd gone to work differently, I think the result would have been the same.) The legal point was this: Shaw was charged with Desertion, a serious charge, punishable in the field by death. Normally, desertion implies an absence of not less than 21 days: *but an absence of an hour, or even less, can constitute desertion,* if it can be shown that the prisoner was absent in order to avoid some particular military duty (i.e. (here's the rub). If a soldier was absent from a draft of soldiers ordered for overseas service, and if his absence was due to a deliberate intention to dodge the draft, then he is a deserter.) *But* if he can show that his absence was *not* due to any intention to dodge the draft, but to some other cause, then he may be Not Guilty of Desertion, though (possibly) guilty of Absence Without Leave, a much less serious offence.

(The Home Guard Colonel, by the way, has just driven his ball slap into the sea. He knows I saw it, and is trying to look nonchalant.)

To return—Shaw had a story of the unexpected illness of his mother. He claimed to have gone on leave with every intention of returning for the draft, but during his leave his mother had become seriously ill, and he could not leave her. There was much more to it. And in evidence that he had intended to return for the draft, he said that he had volunteered for it in the first place (and had not simply been inked in by the Adjutant as I had supposed. This statement proved to be true). I verified his story about the trouble at home by 'phoning the garrison of his home town, and by obtaining doctors' certificates, etc.: and drew up a paper defence which was based, more or less, on the *letter* of the law. Undoubtedly his mother's illness had occurred: whether or no that *was* the prime cause of his missing the draft was more a question for the prosecution than for me.

At the court-martial itself I thought I had a reasonable chance, and decided not to allow Shaw to present his own case. However, I made a mistake in procedure. I know *now* what I ought to have done: I should have forbidden Shaw to open his mouth unless I told him to. But what happened was this: the President of the Court asked Shaw if he wanted to go into the witness-box. Neither Shaw nor I realized that this was another way of saying 'will you put your own case?' (Oh my bloody stupidity.) Shaw said 'yes', and immediately found himself defending his own case against the Adjutant, without my having opened my mouth.

Well, Shaw did very badly indeed, as you would expect, since the only possible defence was a legalistic one based on King's Regs., which he didn't understand. It became a personal struggle between himself and the Adjutant, with the odds overwhelmingly in the Adjutant's favour. My careful case was not even heard (except after the verdict had been reached, as a plea in mitigation of the offence). Shaw was a hopeless witness in his own defence. The Adjutant got at him again and again, and in my opinion, gave oblique evidence as to bad character before the verdict had been reached, which is illegal—but when I brought this up I was ruled out of order. Shaw was like a cornered rat. He could feel the opinion of the court against him, and grew truculent.

His sentence has not yet been promulgated. I fear a stiff one. So he will soon be in a military prison, which is as close an approach to the Dark Ages as anything surviving nowadays. A pity he hadn't the savoir-faire to be born into the Upper Middle Class instead of the Lower Working Class. He'd still have been at school! My darling Elizabeth, I can't and won't avert my eyes from this sort of thing to live in the Ivory Tower of my love for you. That love itself would be poisoned and worthless if I used it only as an escape. I know I'm born to fight, to use my voice and my strength and my wits for those who are suffering. I shall never be able to ignore it. 'So long as there is on earth a man crushed by oppression, I am in torment: so long as any man is in prison, I am not free.'

Michael.

Dear Michael,

Suppose I come to Wales for a week?

I suggest it because I've sold two designs to McMasters, and have a five pound note in my purse. Either I come to Wales, or I spend it on gramophone records for when you have leave. I'd much rather come to Wales, even if we only saw each other in the evenings or such odd times. Could you find somewhere in Pwllheli for me to stay? You mentioned a West End Hotel. I could come any week from next Friday to the middle of September, so perhaps you could arrange it for a time when you haven't a great deal of training to do.

I was sorry about your court-martial. I hope the sentence is not as severe as you expect.

I can't think of anything else now I've got this idea of coming to you: I'm too excited. I'll send this note off now, and go down to the station to look up train times. David came second in Maths., fourth in French, *ninth* in Latin. Top in English, though.

Elizabeth.

*   *   *   *

TELEGRAM.

LIEUT MICHAEL CARR THE —SHIRES PWLLHELI NORTH WALES BOMBED OUT MOTHER AND DAD IN HOSPITAL DAVID DEAD COME QUICKLY ELIZABETH

*   *   *   *

Chapter Fifteen

When the sirens blew, Dad took up the coats, books, cups and comforts which they were accustomed to take on such occasions and the family went into the air-raid shelter, Elizabeth carrying Bonzo. Mother made herself comfortable at the back of the shelter, with Ezra Pound's Guide to Kulchur. Bonzo, after sniffing at a suspected rat-smell, threw himself down at her feet and went to sleep. Dad buttoned his overcoat up, since the night was cold, and strolled round to the front of the house on fire-watching duty.

David was not with the family. He had been spending the evening with the boy next door, and went into their air-raid shelter, where the two boys continued a game of Battleships.

Elizabeth came out to the front with Dad. The first faint throb of aircraft was audible.

Dad, at the gate, was about to set off on a tour of the neighbourhood, which was fairly dark: it was an unusual night for raiders, since the moon was a week short of full. 'Wait a second, Dad,' said Elizabeth, 'I'll get my torch.'

She returned to the shelter. High above, the sky throbbed softly. The man next door (at the other side, not where David was) could be heard asking his wife if he should bring her coat out to her. Elizabeth went into the shelter and looked for the torch.

'Going with Dad?' asked Mother.

'Yes, when I've found my torch———Hello, what's that?'

'What's what?'

'Listen!'

There was a faint, long whistle, accompanied later by an equally faint metallic tinkle. 'Incendiaries' said Elizabeth, hurrying out of the shelter.

She had gone three steps from the shelter, and stood at the corner of the house. She could hear Dad walking round the house, apparently towards her. The faint whistling had stopped with a gentle thud. But the tinkling continued.

'What is it?' shouted Elizabeth, 'incendiaries?'

'No' came a voice over the hedge, 'it's a land mine in your garden.'

A full second seemed to intervene, and then the earth screamed and reared up. The concrete shrugged sharply from under Elizabeth's feet. She went flat on her face: there the explosion clapped down on her like a lead sheet, squeezing her into the ground. An instant of utter silence and emptiness. A colossal pressure. No slightest movement.

A sense of the splitting of something immense and very hard, a sense that a final word, a decision of unimaginable malignity had been spoken.

Like the flick of a whip, the first part of the explosion finished and the second began. Great weights fell down onto the earth, slabs of masonry and bricks and shards of wrinkled iron. The debris fell thicker and faster and heavier, now like a curtain hurrying down, the sky emptying itself furiously of the unwanted weight. Elizabeth was battered by the falling stuff. Blow on blow, striking almost simultaneously, numbed her. Her legs were buried in broken stone, it was over her shoulders. Now the lighter stuff came down, fine soil that poured into the interstices between the stones, levelling everything like snow, hiding the broken bones of buildings. It covered Elizabeth entirely. She was buried and could not breathe. She scrabbled, scrambled wildly up, and debris still fell as she did so: as fast as she struggled she was buried again. Her mouth was full of grit and blood. She fought madly upwards for air.

There were noises. Very abruptly the rubble fell no more, except for distant rattlings of stones on roofs. She was standing. Rubble was up to her knees still. The house was gone, except for two broken walls only eight feet or so high, and one corner where a part of a bedroom stood up in the blackness. A light had been left on there. It still shone, and now there was no roof to cover it. It shone brightly up into the sky. The sky was still droning. Only ten seconds ago all had been normal.

Dad was calling somewhere in the blackness, his voice sounded thick and mumbling, not at all loud: 'Marion! Marion! Are you all right. . . . .Where are you?'

Elizabeth tried to run forward, and fell. Her hands sank into light slippery soil and ragged splinters of wood. She got up again, went forward, and at last found Dad, at the side of the house, groping with both hands along a bulging wall.

Voices were dull, distant and metallic. Somewhere there was a continued soft screaming, not loud, but breathy, demented. Elizabeth stumbled through the dark to the air-raid shelter. It was different: low down in the ground, only three feet of the entrance showing. It appalled Elizabeth: she could not understand. From within came the terrible screaming. Somehow Elizabeth got inside.

'Elizabeth, I'm dying. Oh is that you, my bairn?' said Mother. 'Fetch a doctor, Elizabeth, I'm dying. Oh my God, my God, what have they done to me?'

'Darling, darling don't cry, you'll be all right,' said Elizabeth, feeling her way forward. She touched Mother's face in the dark. Above the eyes her fingers found warm wet blood, no hair that came to the touch, only slippery blood. Blood was all over the face and the little woollen sports-coat, and blood spouted in a shower over Elizabeth's legs. 'Oh Christ, Mother's dying now in here.' 'Get me a doctor, love. They've killed me. Where's Dad, is he all right. . . . ?'

'Keep still, Mother darling, I'll get a doctor.' Elizabeth climbed out again. The air was strong with cordite. The electric light still blazed. No-one———

Elizabeth screamed.

'Won't *anybody help me*———'

Noises. People were there. A motor-car somewhere. Mr. Taylor had broken through the hedge, he was running to Elizabeth. 'We're here my poor lass, we're coming.'

Elizabeth was back at the shelter. Somehow she herself lifted Mother out. Mr. Taylor helped. There were men with a stretcher, Elizabeth saw them carry Mother away, and put the stretcher into the ambulance. Dad was not there now. The ambulance went away. There were many men, a lot in uniform. Elizabeth asked them where David was. 'A boy? Ah well, he will be at the First Aid Post by now. In with his Mother, wasn't he?'

'No, he was in the other shelter—there.'

'There—ah well, I don't know about that. Better ask Bill Burrows.'

Bill Burrows could not be found. Ambulances were arriving and departing on a plan unknown to Elizabeth. The people standing about seemed mainly spectators who didn't know anything. Elizabeth found her way over the debris to the back of what had been the next-door house, where the air-raid shelter was. A ring of uniformed men stopped her.

'But David's there. In that shelter.'

Voices. 'It's Pascoe's lass. It's 'is sister, get her away.'

'But David—David———'

'He's dead, my lass. He never felt any pain. They're all dead in there———the sides collapsed———aye it's a bad job———'

She could discern the shape of the shelter. It had been one of the early 'Anderson's', an arch of corrugated steel with a foot thickness of cement all round. The explosion had lifted it and folded its two walls on each other. Everything inside must have been mashed at a blow between two jaws of concrete. The smell of blood was in the air.

Mother and Dad were gone. She was in the street. She had lost the sequence of events. The street was covered with rubble. Policemen were about. Nothing else alive. Bonzo was in her arms. She did not remember picking him up. Her arms were locked round him.

She was in a first-aid post; they gave her something hot to drink and asked her to put her Bonzo down. She apologized and did so, but then took him up again. She asked them to take her to Mother. Mrs. Pascoe, where was she taken?

Dad they had taken first, to the same post. His face was bloody and had pieces of gravel driven into it, and he was bleeding continuously from mouth and nose. He told them he was all right, but would they bring him news of his wife? A warden said yes, and went out to find Mother; he did not come back. So Dad asked another man, and he too went out and did not return. They were kind to Dad, but he wanted to know about Mother. He tried to get up from the stretcher, but found he could not. He thought perhaps they could not find her, or had forgotten, or she was dead and they could not bear to tell him. At last the ambulance came again and took him to the hospital. He still did not know what had happened to Mother.

In the ambulance which took him away was the woman from the next house but one. She had been in the shelter, her husband in the house, sitting by the fire. The explosion had blown in the end wall and crumpled the floor. Her husband had been trapped between the twisted floor-joists: at the same time the fire had shot out from the grate. He had roasted slowly: the wood round him took fire. His wife had heard his shrieks and seen the charred creature jerking and writhing. The rescuers had thrown water over the flames, but could not put them out. The woman was demented. She screamed continually in the ambulance.

At last they took Elizabeth to Polpryn County Hospital, which stands a mile out on the far side of the town. She found Mother there. Her head, above her eyes, was covered with yellow gauze bandage soaked in blood. Bandages were about her chest. Her eyes were closed, her face very small, shrunk and blue. She did not seem to be breathing. Elizabeth spoke to the nurse. All sounds were strange, her voice was not like her own, did not seem to come from her own mouth. A small metallic voice.

'Is she dead?'

'No,' said the nurse. 'She's had sutures to head and chest and two blood transfusions. Now we've given a morphia injection, to rest her. She is very poorly indeed.'

'She won't die, will she?'

'Oh no, we hope not,' said the nurse kindly, 'we are looking after her very carefully. Dr. Alexander has been in to see her almost every ten minutes since she was brought in.'

'How long ago was that?' asked Elizabeth.

'Almost four hours ago. It's three o'clock now.'

For almost four hours Elizabeth had been wandering mutely from place to place. She was not yet accustomed to the new life which was now four hours old. At eleven o'clock on a calm night, in one second, twenty years had been cancelled.

Bonzo, sleeping and silent, was still in her arms.

They led her to Dad, in a different ward of the same hospital. His face, including the eyes, was entirely covered with bandages, but she could see by the slight movements of his head that he was awake.

'Dad.'

'Elizabeth. Is that you, Elizabeth?'

'Yes. Are you all right, Dad?'

His voice was very thick and slow. 'Ah, I'm all right,' he said. 'My dial's had some terrible bash. They've given me an injection. How's your mother, Elizabeth?'

'She's very poorly, Dad, but she'll get better.'

'Where is she?'

'Haven't they told you? She's in this same hospital as you, only a few steps away.'

'Is she, Elizabeth? My God, that's good news. What a bloody good job David wasn't in the shelter as well. Is he there with you, or have they got him in bed somewhere?'

Elizabeth could not answer. She struggled but found no words. Instead she broke into tears. She could not control her sobs, which reached Dad's ears. The blind bandaged head stirred grotesquely, in an agony of bewilderment. His hands beat feebly the starched sheet. The thick, slow caricature of his voice said, 'What's the matter, what is it? Is anything wrong with David?'

'Oh Dad,' she sobbed, 'he's dead, he's dead.'

Margaret Lowrie, who had been looking everywhere, found Elizabeth at the hospital, and brought her and Bonzo to her parents' house in Polpryn. Once in the house—where all was safe, warm, light, untouched by explosion—Elizabeth broke down. Her right leg was almost useless, being black and yellow with bruises from hip to ankle, and very swollen.

There were great bruises and inflammations on her shoulders. Her head was gashed. Her clothing was shredded into mere grey ribbons which trailed from under a coat which had been put on her at the First Aid Post. Her hair and clothes were full of powdered plaster and brick-dust. She was very deaf, and her ears began to ache intensely. They gave her a hot bath, aspirins and hot drinks, and she went to bed, but could not rest, for as soon as her eyes closed and her breathing steadied, she would wake up again screaming 'I can't breathe—I'm buried alive!'

Chapter Sixteen

I had been with Luke for a drink, and had returned to my billet on some minor errand. It was then that I found Elizabeth's telegram waiting for me.

I went straight down to H.Q. Mess, and found the Colonel with a book and a glass of whisky. He gave me permission to go immediately, and Orry drove me, though it was near midnight, to Bangor. I caught the morning train out.

Trains were bad. It was early on the following morning when I reached Polpryn: and the telegram had not reached me till nearly twenty-four hours after the bombing, so that altogether it was nearly two and a half days after the disaster when I got to Polpryn.

Curtains were drawn at the Lowries' house and all was in darkness, for it was barely dawn when I arrived. Margaret let me in. I took a hot bath to recover from my journey. Then Margaret and I had breakfast together, as we thought it better not to wake Elizabeth.

'It's the first good sleep she's had,' said Margaret. 'She's worn out, but too overwrought to sleep. But last night Father made her have four aspirins and a big glass of Horlicks, and she has slept soundly all night.'

'Is she hurt?'

'Terribly bruised. It's a miracle she's alive. She has some cuts and gashes on the back of her neck and her shoulders, but they're healing now. She's very deaf and has terrible headaches. Yesterday she wouldn't rest, but kept going up to the hospital. She fainted three times. Fortunately I was with her.'

I asked about her Mother and Dad.

'Mrs. Pascoe's very seriously injured. She was in the air-raid shelter when it happened. There was no baffle-wall to the shelter. We think the door must have been shattered by the explosion, and some fragments blown in. Elizabeth's father is not so seriously hurt so far as we know, though his face is badly mauled. And there is some fear that his heart may be affected.'

'What about David?'

'He was in the shelter next door. The two sides of it came together. There were four people in it, including David. All were killed.'

So far, I learned, nothing had been saved from the wrecked house. Elizabeth had been unable to go and watch the demolition. Mother had now had three blood transfusions, and was 'in a critical condition'. David was to be buried today, in the afternoon.

Elizabeth wakened at half-past nine without being called, and came downstairs. She was very changed. Her face was chalk-white and pasty, her eyes yellowish, her hair untidy and dull: she came downstairs slowly. I could see her hand gripping the banister. On her forehead was the frown of headache and deafness.

'. . . . . . .It was getting beyond me, Michael. Waking up to it each morning, only me left to bear it all. I thought you'd never come.'

'The worst's over now, dear. The weight's on my shoulders now, you can rest. I'll see to everything.'

'It was just about driving me mad. There's such a lot to be done: I didn't seem as though I could *start:* my memory doesn't seem to work, and then I can't hear what people say. There was the house, and David's funeral, and Mother and Dad, and all sorts of things. . . . .'

She only had one pair of shoes, her oldest: the dress she was wearing belonged to Margaret Lowrie. At first I couldn't always remember to speak loudly to her, and it broke my heart to see her leaning forward and smiling apologetically, 'What did you say, Michael?' The explosion seemed to have frightened the soul out of her, she was timid and self-effacing and nervous. And yet she forced herself to go about all sorts of business arising from the disaster.

We went first to the hospital. I was still wearing the battle-dress I had on when I got her telegram. I tip-toed into the quiet ward on the iron toe-caps of my boots.

Mother was asleep when we first saw her. She lay rigid on her back under the white coverlet. She was shrunken, withered to a leaf-like thinness. Her face seemed mere skin folded over a tiny skull. Above the eyes a mass of bandages rested on the pillow. Her mouth hung slightly open. Her artificial teeth had been removed. Her left shoulder and the left side of her chest were thickly bandaged.

Her face was a maze of wrinkles. The pale skin had sagged as if there were no flesh under it.

Her breathing was very light and quick, and so shallow as not to stir the body at all. You could have thought her dead. Her wounds gave off a faint smell of festering flesh and of medicaments.

On the chart at the head of the bed I read 'severe wound to scalp, and deep penetrative wound to left shoulder. Severe shock. Radiant heat'.

Elizabeth was weeping. I got her a chair and supported her. She sat where Mother could not see her. 'Michael, when I think how she was so proud of the house, and everything was so clean and nice, and we'd just made the jam. Poor Mum lying like that now. It'll never be the same again. You can't get it back. Everything's gone now.'

She was drying her eyes, but fresh tears swam up. 'Her head was terrible Michael. All the skin from just above her eyes was sliced off and peeled back, hair and everything, right to the top of her head. I touched it in the dark. Oh poor Mum. All blood.'

Mother had awakened. I saw her eyes moving in painful questioning about the ward. She still didn't quite understand the place. She was still numb from the blow of sixty hours ago.

'Ah my love.' Mother's lips shaped the words, 'my lass.' Then great tears came up into her eyes and ran down her thin face. 'Oh they have hurt me, Elizabeth. They can't help it, it's for my own good. But I can't stand it. I think I'm dying, love.'

'Oh you foolish Mother,' said Elizabeth leaning tenderly over her, kissing her and trying to smile, 'you won't die, Mum, you aren't anywhere near dying. I've been talking to the doctor. He says all the danger is over now. You're in great pain, but you've just got to bear it for two more days, then all the pain will be over. The worst is finished now.'

'Did he say that?' whispered Mother. 'Did he say I was out of danger?' Mother actually smiled, a tremulous smile as she slowly formed the words. 'Oh it does cheer me up. I've been lying here thinking I should die, Elizabeth. How long have I been here? My old head's so stupid. I don't really know where I am.' There was a pause. 'I couldn't breathe, with my chest.'

'There, Mum, don't talk too much my sweet. You know you're in the hospital, and you're going to rest for a long time now. I've brought somebody to see you.'

I stooped by Mother's bed and kissed her. I never felt such pity in my life. I remembered how neat and pleasant she had been, her dainty black-and-red pinafore, her busy, fussy little ways, and her hair which had been like Elizabeth's.

'Michael!' she whispered, 'fancy you coming to see me. Have you come all the way from Wales?'

I nodded and said 'Don't talk a lot now, Mother, don't strain your eyes looking up at me. Close them, rest them.'

She did so, then opened them again with a heart-breaking reminiscence of her old half-humorous smile. 'Aren't I a terrible fright, Michael? Did you expect I should look like this?' Then tears of weakness rose again. 'Oh Michael they have hurt me.'

Elizabeth was stroking her hand with infinite gentleness. 'Poor Mum.'

'They've taken the stitches out of my head,' whispered Mother. 'There were seventeen. . . . . Just fancy. But they don't want the wound in my chest to heal, because there might be something in it. They've given me three transfusions, two of blood and one of plasma. They put a needle in my leg, near my foot, and put something in. It hurt me. I thought I should go mad. I must have been mad, Elizabeth, because I swore at them and said 'why won't you leave me alone?' I thought they wanted to hurt me, like Germans. Isn't it funny?'

She relaxed, panting after this long speech. There was a

pause, during which we gazed at her but kept very silent. Her eyes were closed. Suddenly she said, 'When are you bringing David to see me?'

'Soon, Mum, soon.'

'He isn't hurt, is he? Not badly hurt like me?'

'No, Mum, he isn't badly hurt, but he can't get up yet.'

'Poor kid,' murmured Mother. 'It's better for him not to see me like this. I look such a fright, I know. Is Dad all right now?'

'His poor face has been knocked about', said Elizabeth, imitating Dad's own jocular tone, 'but he is improving wonderfully. They say he'll be walking about long before you are.'

Mother lay still, with a faint wistful smile on her face. Then she said, 'I hope you are getting plenty to eat, Elizabeth.' Her mind was wandering a little. 'I know I'm a neglectful woman, not looking after you, but you understand, don't you, love? There was some stew in the pantry, and all the tinned stuff. You know where it is. What a good job I got it in. I must have known this was coming. Now do look after yourself and get plenty to eat, my bairn. I ought to be up now and get it for you, but. . . . .' her voice died off. She was not sleeping, but her mind had given up the attempt to follow a thread of thought. Often, months after, I saw the same puzzled, half-frightened frown as she suddenly realized that her thoughts had slipped away, she had forgotten what she was saying.

We left Mother when we saw her sleeping at last. We felt treacherous to forsake her in her pain.

Dad was more visible than when Elizabeth had first seen him. Bandages covered his nose and the central part of his face only, leaving eyes and mouth free. 'Hello, Mike lad' he said thickly when he saw me, 'you've come to see the old crock, have you? I reckon I had most of the surface shale of Cornwall in my face when they brought me here, but they've picked some of it out now.'

Dad's cheerfulness was almost frightening. Fate seemed unnaturally wicked to overload such willing shoulders. Life seemed, with cynical cruelty, to have taken him at his word.

His brave kind heart still supported all the disaster, but David's death had driven him to the extreme edge. Yet he kept smiling, for one reason only, to help Elizabeth.

Apparently all the air-raid victims, as they were brought in, had been inoculated with anti-tetanus serum. Dad was now in the worst stages of stiffness from it, and although he tried to joke, the pain and his general, hopeless, anguished condition got the better of him from time to time. 'My leg's giving me hell' he said. 'It's as swollen as a football. And blood keeps dropping into the back of my nose and mouth . . . .my heart flutters pretty badly, too,' he added.

My boots clinked on the tiled corridor as we went out. The air outside had the autumn warmth, a faint ubiquitous scent which one would hardly notice except by contrast with the antiseptic odours of the hospital. Our next visit was to where the house had stood.

The area for a radius of fifty yards from where the mine had fallen was devastated. Houses as much as half-a-mile away bore traces of the explosion—here and there slates whipped from a roof, or windows shattered, and in one case a door split down the edge. But the houses nearer the crater were ravaged. There was an entire block of houses, eight in all, standing longways to the mine, which had been half-capsized by a terrific push on the end wall. The top of the block, roof, lintels and all, moved two feet or so along. The end wall and the house of which it was part, were burst in like a broken box. Every window and door along the whole block was pushed into a new shape, a diamond-shaped parallelogram, bursting panes, panels and all. From one side of the roof, the blast had stripped every slate: on the other side, not a tile was disturbed. As we approached where Elizabeth's home had stood, the mad dance of houses, road and earth grew wilder. A cottage yawned at us, all its face blown away, revealing the joist-ends and laths of its sagging floors and ceilings. Plaster still trickled here and there, a little powdery movement amid ruined stillness. Odd ends of carpet, pattern blotted out by plaster and mud, hung out from under banks of plaster and rubble. There was a young tree beheaded by the explosion. Its long white shards and splinters of wood, raw and jagged, stuck up from their sheath of bark, above the bole of the tree still firm in the earth, as if a giant had twisted off a tree-top. All the hedges and trees were stripped as bare as winter. The blast had not left a single leaf.

There used to be a lamp-post near the Pascoes'. All that remained now was the truncated stem.

The gate which Bonzo used to open was still there, and could be used as readily as ever: but it was no longer the quickest way into the garden. The explosion had opened fifty quicker gates. Planks, roofing, masonry, rubble, plaster and earth had levelled the privet hedge. The private Pascoe world stood open, broken open to all the world.

One end wall still stood, but dangerously. A strong wind might bring it down. This wall reared up as high as the eaves had been, and within it—the front wall entirely gone —was a corner of David's bedroom. The floor had been wax-polished. Pieces of polished floor stood out from the rubble. The front-door frame of the house still stood, held by the half-open door which was jammed with debris. From the wreckage of the bathroom, above the doorway, the broken washbowl hung down on the end of three feet of waste-pipe. The asphalt path we stood on, which went round the house, was lifted in wave-shapes and rolled back on itself along the edges of a long central gash.

It was not safe to go under the fallen ceilings and fabrics which hung, caught up on each other, at varying distances from the ground. We looked in through the empty front window, which the ceiling slashed with a great diagonal, and saw the piano, burst open at the corners, its hammers and action spilled over the keyboard. A little porcelain statue of Garibaldi with his horse still stood on the window-sill, but his head, which had always been loose, had now vanished altogether. In the woodwork of the window were embedded thousands of tiny slivers of glass, driven deep into the wood. Though it was unsafe to explore under the wreckage, it was easy enough to move about on top. We climbed over where the stairs had stood, and found ourselves on a great bank of rubble which covered the living-room. We found the remains of a part of the bookshelves. A few pages fluttered when the breeze caught them, as they protruded from brick-dust and splintered wood; a copy of the 'Spotter'. There was also a piece of metal, with a switch attached, which we recognized as part of the log-fire. The furniture of the living-room was somewhere under our feet. Bits of the wall were recognizable by their oyster-coloured enamel. There was also the collapsed fabric of the bedroom above. We found eiderdowns and mattresses tangled into this great rubbish-heap, riven by glass and full of plaster and splinters. Elizabeth pointed out a tiny visible patch of the scullery floor, coated with 'liquid lino'.

We were able to get a few undamaged tins of food from the ruin of the pantry. The cupboard's situation was denoted by a chaos of broken china. We discovered a pile of twenty large-sized willow-pattern plates which seemed intact, but on touching, we saw them fall to pieces—great cracks ran down through the entire pile.

The asbestos-lagged electric water storage tank still stood on its struts, caved in on one side, but assertively high and solid when all that had concealed it had fallen away.

We saw why Elizabeth had had the grotesque impression, at the time, that the air-raid shelter had sunk into the ground. Tons of earth, brick and rubble had fallen, and the level of the ground round the shelter had been raised almost two feet. There was left an opening only just large enough to get in and out of the shelter.

I went inside, and passed to Elizabeth a few things we might be able to use. Blood was splashed all over the interior. The 'Guide to Kulchur' was soaked in blood. Blood was spattered all over coats, blankets, sheets, and a cut-down mattress on a bunk: in one corner these things were stiff with blood. This was the practical issue of the conferences of statesmen, of 'failures to reach unanimity on certain points', of high principles and councils of war: this was what the talk of Empire and Sovereignty and Fatherland and Motherland *really* meant. This was how they solved their problems. Just this.

Two of the trees beneath which Elizabeth and I had often

sat, had been ripped furiously out of the ground. The filthy blasphemy of force.

The crater which marked the course of this devastation was between ten and fifteen feet deep at the centre, and about thirty feet in diameter. I saw a piece of the exterior casing of the mine still in the crater. It was a jagged, heavy piece of metal and its curvature suggested it had formed part of a cylinder about the size of a large milk-churn. In exploding, it had caused damage in a wide area perhaps a mile in diameter, and completely demolished eleven houses, and rendered twelve others fit only for immediate demolition. It had killed seven people, three of whom were children, two women, and two men. It had injured twenty-three.

We buried David in the afternoon. It came into my mind as I sat in the coach that we had not seen his bicycle among the ruins—somewhere twisted up under the wreckage, no doubt. He had finished with homework, too. All trifles to the God of War, who deals with large incomes and with Principles so Vital to the Integrity of Nations that they must always be printed with capital letters—whereas 'a dead boy' may be printed just so.

We had neither singing nor ceremony at the funeral. We could hardly be happy to tell ourselves that he now slept well, having escaped a bad world. A bad world it was: by God it was: but it was the only one he was offered. He was bloodily cheated out of his life, before he could touch or taste the treasure of it. *We* needed no comfortable thoughts: *he* was the victim, it was not up to us to say if he was well off or ill, or to dispose of his approval. All I know is he loved his life, he was a happy boy: he didn't ask to die. A human boy, and all civilization could do for him was to smash him between two blocks of concrete. In the thirteenth year of his life, we were putting him into a hole in the ground so that he shouldn't rot on the surface—that and no more. Let those who helped to commit the crime expiate it.

Over the bodies of children and old people the wolves are scrambling. Diplomatic wolves, wolves who knew all about oil concessions, international credits, trade routes, and a steady five per cent. The diplomatic wolves show their grinning, polite, pointed teeth. Over the bodies of children and old people.

Once, in England, wolves' heads were worth a silver shilling.

And his mother did not know that he was dead. She thought he would visit her soon. Perhaps she was thinking of him now, muddled in her thoughts, while we watched the sextons lower the coffin (swinging, clumsy) hand over hand on the rope, till it stopped suddenly on the bottom of the long, narrow, deep hole. There it lay, a long wooden box, deep down between the narrow walls of clay, and David lay under that lid. No goodbye. The sexton threw onto the coffin lid a spadeful of earth, crude lumps of clay, and the last signs of him went under, beyond all those who loved him. He was under the ground. His mother did not even know that he was dead. The clay soon covered him and lay solidly upon him: David.

John and Marion Pascoe, it was this that your long lives and your struggles led him to. But such incidents may be unavoidable in the maintenance of a steady five per cent.

Chapter Seventeen

The bitter thing was that in this period Elizabeth was given no rest. Surely there could be few emergencies in a human life calling for more remission of duties, more assumption by others of the burdens habitually carried by the victim. There could be few occasions when an entire neglect of the outside world were more justified. Elizabeth was deafened, bruised, exhausted, ill, overwrought, and driven to the limits of her emotional endurance. Yet it was just this period which the world exasperated by its claims on every side. There was money to be found: I could support Elizabeth out of my pay, but my money wasn't enough to rent and furnish a house and have it ready for Mother and Dad when they left hospital. Clothing must be obtained somehow for the three survivors. Claims must be made to cover the total loss of all that was in the house, so Elizabeth had to draw up from memory a list of all furniture etc. which the house contained, and to figure out what it cost. And coupons for rationed food—all had been destroyed in the house; and countless offices of one sort or another, as far afield as Bodmin, to be visited.

One such place we went to immediately after the funeral. Like all these war-time offices, it was in 'temporary premises'. In an ante-room attached to a chapel a bald man sat behind a table, at which a small and shabby queue of air-raid victims waited their turn. There was a young married woman who had lived in the cottage I had seen riven open by the blast. She had a young baby in her arms. Her white face had a sharp, malevolent bitterness; her lips were tight. She had been waiting long, and was propping herself against the radiator. 'Oh I'm all right', she told Elizabeth in answer to a question, 'you've got to be all right to stand this bloody game. I've been here three-quarters of an hour, waiting for a form to claim for my bits of furniture. They don't give you much rest. This morning I was waiting at the Food Office from nine till half-past eleven. God help them that's injured. It's bad enough for us that can stand on our feet.'

I never saw so many forms before. It was the technique of the Circumlocution Office. Some of the forms were remarkably complex, and seemed to demand principally the very information which was most likely to be lost in the destruction of a house by bombing. What, for instance, was Dad's income during a representative working year, what was the rent of the house, what were the amounts of any weekly or monthly payments for furniture and equipment, what Insurance Policies, Income Tax, any scholarships or earned income of children or other contributors to this, that and the other, and many more: this was for a claim 'in respect of' Dad's injuries, and when completed was to be attached to a certificate signed by the 'competent medical authority' of the hospital, showing the 'nature and extent' of injuries received etc. etc. Since the doctor was very busy, it might be necessary to wait over an hour for such a certificate to be signed. Then there were similar forms regarding Mother: details about David: forms without end. To each of these fantastic forms were appended numerous provisoes, codicils and emendations, statements of amounts which might or might not be available forthwith if the applicant could show that he or she intended immediately to re-furnish some particular house. Meanwhile we had to have medical aid for Elizabeth herself. And each form we obtained seemed to involve fresh journeys for further forms, and fresh investigations for information which Elizabeth had never possessed, and Mother and Dad had forgotten. Dad had to be worried with questions which he could only answer from memory. But we were not the most unfortunate. We saw wretched people (mainly women with young children), who at a blow had lost most of all they prized in the world, tormented and harassed by a niggling, suspicious, hostile, inadequate and incompetent system of Inquisitorial Assistance such as left in their hearts only bitterness, grief and contempt. There was a scene in one of these Relief Offices when we were there, when an old woman shouted 'It's to be hoped the Government is fighting Hitler as hard as it's fighting us.' There were murmurs. 'Aye' said somebody, 'I reckon *we* must be the bloody enemy, not Germany.'

The details of those days are now blurred in my memory to a distasteful, profitless going about—usually on foot: a succession of dreary makeshift offices in warehouse-corners, converted shops, committee-rooms, municipal halls and chapels: tables piled, piled with forms, shiny forms, dull forms, smooth forms, long forms, mere slips and chits of paper, typed forms, hectographed forms, cyclostyled forms, forms with appendices and forms without: of windows whose lower half was painted in with green, through whose upper half we looked out on pointed iron railings and rubbish-choked 'areas'—windows with names of solicitors, corporations, departments, all written backwards: of bald little men who 'were extremely sorry for you, but', who 'thought it was a very sad case, but', who 'promised to do everything in their power, but'. So we trudged on, tired to the bone, our hearts like stones, seeking comfort and warmth and succour from the country whose enemies had so stricken us.

Hell has a special devil on the shores of the burning lake, in the uniform of a life-saver. He watches for those who flounder desperately in the fiercest eddies, and he extends to them, on the end of a long pole, an application form for assistance, to be completed in block capitals and returned to this office not later than thirty days after the date of issue.

When disaster has cracked the armour of the heart, a feather of a breeze will agonize it. A straw will be a spear. There are times when motes and midges are unendurable. The doctor who examined Elizabeth's ears was not sympathetic or gentle. She was in tears when she came out of the consulting-room, hurt beyond all rational explanation. He wouldn't understand that.

Vain efforts, strangeness: dislocated life moving with stiffness and pain. Journeys with unimagined sad purposes, to hospitals and cemeteries, and about the neighbouring villages in search of a house we couldn't pay for. Tired returns with the object unaccomplished. Nights of pondering, in the unaccustomed furniture and rooms of the Lowries' house. Meals at a strange table, dependence on kindness and pity for all those things which had been the natural treasures of home. Climbing the stairs in a different house, sleeping in an unfamiliar bed, waking to the sounds of a family with a life of its own to carry on. Anxiety, worry, and the deepest uncertainty for every day of the future.

Petrol was rationed: there were narrow limits to the extent we could use the Lowries' car. I spent a lot of money on 'bus fares. We searched every village in the district for a little, inexpensive house, far enough from Falmouth or Polpryn to be safe from further bombing. We took 'buses out into the country and then went from door to door. In vain. Every cottage was crowded. The district was a reception area. Every house had its evacuees and refugees, some from Falmouth, but most from the bigger industrial centres of England. Not a house was to be had; the villagers shook their heads without any hesitation. But where, in two or three cases, we did find a house shortly to be empty, the rent was fantastic, a wartime rent, a blackmail rent: refugees could be made to pay a good price for safety. It was no use. We would have paid, if we had the money. But Elizabeth simply couldn't buy safety at the market price. She lacked the golden key of the fields.

We found a partial answer to the money problem by marrying by special licence, before I returned to my unit. Margaret's brother, a Flight-Lieutenant, came home on leave in time to act as witness. The Polpryn registrar seemed to combine many other municipal functions, and moved briskly in and out of a warren of cubby-holes, being a different official in every one. His quality depended on which door you entered. In a different room of the same building he issued to us coupons for bacon, margarine, and sugar: and when we came in from a different direction, he appeared behind a different counter and made us man and wife. But it was as Registrar of Deaths we first saw him.

We went every day to see Mother and Dad. After six days Mother began to recuperate, and looked very different, though racked by headache. A swab was kept in the chest wound to prevent it from closing till all fragments had worked out. She said she felt as if the left side of her chest had been crushed flat and would not expand again. For a fortnight she could not take any food other than broth.

During the first week of their being in hospital, beginning five days after my arrival, Polpryn was heavily raided four times. I was there for the first two of these blitzes.

It did not begin till nearly midnight. It was the night after we were married. We were sharing a room at the Lowries'. Elizabeth and I were asleep, though I was on the edge of waking, when an unrecognized irritation began to fret me. I woke sufficiently to realize that the irritation, the insistence, was the drone of a bomber: it was a loud drone, the sound of many planes, not one. Suddenly there came a sharp, loud, roaring whistle, rather as if a distant train were to approach a station at such a colossal speed as to arrive in a second or so: this ended in a splitting metallic *crack!* the windows flew open, and the blast hit the room like a flapped sheet. The sirens screamed, wise after the event.

Elizabeth crouched silently beside me, shaking with fear. I could hear her teeth chattering. I was appalled by my powerlessness to help her.

The anti-aircraft had opened up. We could tell from the steely quality of their reports whether the barrels were leaning towards us or away. The noise of the guns was formidable, but they were only the rattle of a kettle-drum compared with the solid, bitter thunder of the bombs. The sudden instantaneous glare of the bursting projectiles lit and re-lit the room. As the raid developed we seemed to learn its plan, and to expect the repetition of its phases. First the distant bombers: these rapidly grew louder, till they dinned and throbbed overhead: then the shriek of the bombs, the furious onslaught of the Anti-Aircraft guns, then the smashing finality of the bombs' reply. Obscene violence rocked the little town under the startled sky. The peaceful houses were shaken as if all the unsuspected brutality of man had sprung up out of the core of civilization, to blast them and destroy them. The dainty bedroom we were in, with its mirrors and dim-seen pictures, was never meant to shake under such hellish blows. It quivered, it danced as the bombs burst among the houses. The walls now flickered with rosy lights as houses in another part of the town lit up in flames: flames where men and women were burning threw a rose-petal glow on walls and windows. And those flames with cores of agony were used by ingenious airmen to guide them in for further slaughter. The next wave of bombers droned faintly, far away, approached, roared over the barrage, and released their bombs. The walls shuddered at the monstrous, implacable attack. The nearer bombs, screaming like express trains, came down to their battering eruption, then, seconds later, the avalanche of bricks and rubble came thundering on the ground, dwindling rapidly and finishing with the light patter and crack of small stones on slates.

Elizabeth, before the disaster, had been controlled and steady in most emergencies. Now she was sick with dread: her ears were strained for every sound of the blitz. 'It's so *final*, so remorseless' she said when a bomb exploded fairly close. For fear of flying glass we had got out of bed, and lay wrapped in sheets on the floor, having the bed between us and the window. The floor at every great explosion bounced under us like the vellum of a drum. We lay listening to the waves of bombers, waiting for each salvo of bombs: we heard them come down and burst, and heard the lightened bombers drone away. It was a quarter to three when the last wave of bombers faded into silence and was not replaced by a new drone from the south.

The raid being over, Elizabeth was anxious about Mother and Dad, so I made her go back to bed, and set out myself for the hospital.

It was not dark in the town, since many of the streets were lit by burning buildings. A cinema was blazing in Turkey Street. On the outskirts of the town I had to pass a cattle-shed which had been struck by a bomb. Blood, entrails and riven flesh were scattered about the road and hedge.

A building immediately behind the hospital was in flames, and many windows were broken in the hospital itself, but it had not been directly hit. I had some difficulty in persuading various people to let me into the wards, but I was determined not to return to Elizabeth without having seen Mother and Dad.

Mother was awake when at last I got to her. She was composed, and very glad to see me. She even smiled when she told me about the raid, and said that her one fear had been that the building would be struck and something fall on her wounded head. Many of the patients, bomb victims, had got under their beds, she said; but she dared not, for fear of fainting or dying if she got out of bed. (As a fact, she could not have got out: I knew that, but she didn't.) And, she said, even if she had contrived to get under the bed, she might have caught her head on the mattress above her.

Dad looked very tired. He could barely keep his eyes open, so I did not stay more than a few seconds. He said little. He would have thought it preposterous to have talked seriously about his feelings during the raid. A whole lifetime of concealing his own anxieties, doubts and fears had indisposed him for admitting he was alarmed. I believe that what had strained him most was that Elizabeth and Mother were undergoing the blitz in separate places and without him to help them.

Chapter Eighteen

I returned to Wales.

I never was so at ease in the army as to live its life with either confidence or calm. My own happiness has never been sufficiently portable. Right from childhood, as I remember, I've always given too much of my heart away, not to places, but to people. Joining the army, in war time, meant leaving people. That was hard.

When I first entered the army, as a ranker, I experienced a blank misery such as far grimmer situations which came up later failed to provoke. It was misery not due to any rational, proportionate cause. I was in no danger. Though the food they gave me was strange, ill-smelling, eaten off chipped enamel, yet it was food and plenty. The battle-dress I had to put on (with difficulty, due to unexpected buttons and stiff button-holes) was stout and good: and though I slept on the floor, I was at least under a roof and in England. What then?

The truth was, I was deadly afraid of being deprived of my own soul.

My roots were dug out. Even my old civilian clothes had something intrinsic of me—flannels, or my serge suit, with the choice of wearing one or the other. But now I was not *allowed* to take off khaki. I hadn't comprehended such a loss of independence before: I *couldn't*, wasn't *allowed*, to put on my own clothes even when the day's work was over. My shoes must be returned home. I must wear army boots always, except for nights, when I could wear army P.T. shoes —no familiar, worn slippers. Each morning I opened my eyes, not to my own quiet bedroom, but to a dusty dilapidated provincial dance-hall converted into a billet for a hundred men. And I could not go away. Not even at week-ends. It was beyond anything I had imagined. Not the lightest decision seemed left to me. The little town I had been sent to was my prison. I was not allowed outside its boundaries. The prospect of leave in three months' time meant not a thing, even if it were more than a rumour: three months was eternity. And I was not even myself. Not only imprisoned in my billet area, but imprisoned in my own dumbed body, in its khaki that could only be removed for sleeping. Nothing, nothing of me was left. Sometimes I saw my soldier-reflection in a mirror in the window of a confectioner nearby: I looked, sad and puzzled, at this strange lost creature in new khaki, with his hair short and empty eyes.

But there was a way to make things go. After the first week, I took the army noisily. I told dirty stories, better dirty stories, funnier dirty stories than the ones I got in return, I chanted dirty songs when I shaved at reveille. I worked at P.T. as though it mattered. I was merry at all times. I was hearty. Meanwhile my soul crouched behind the barrage and hoped to get by.

It was the Pascoes' disaster which ended that phase. After that I said to hell with pretending.

It's easy (or I had found it easy) to be a Boy Scout in the army. Perhaps it's the best way to take it. Successful officers often seem to live on the level of Baden-Powell's boys. Loyalties are straightforward and unsubtle, training is a thing demanding all one's heart (and that's the fun of it!): one goes slap through the hedges and ditches, rain or shine, one consensus of concentration on duty. And other things in life, however interesting, are holiday stuff unrelated to the great game of Work. Enthusiasm, a measured heartiness, a complete absorption in the task of the moment—these make the good Scout and the good Soldier. Never ask the ultimate question, 'to what good?'

I admire those qualities, but I know they aren't mine.

I have not a scout mind. I have this sort of mind—sometimes coming back to billets, say, in driving rain, long after midnight, after night training during which we had in imagination thrown grenades, bayoneted enemy and taken positions, as I led my platoon along the dark lane, squelching underfoot, I would seem to see, white against the unfriendly black, Mother's tortured face as I had seen her that first day—the bloody bandage, the sunk cheeks, the mouth half-open, the afflicted face, the body so wrecked by foul, foul wickedness. Then my heart would grow sick at this Scouting of ours, this hearty play that sent me scrambling through hedges at night and left her in agony, the crying example and shame and victim of the rule of those wise men, the Boy Scouts of the world. And at times, when we played with explosives or trained in the field, at odd moments my mind would sketch David as I last saw him, standing by the gate fondling Bonzo's ear before he went back into the house which was so secure and permanent. This Boy Scouting is a fine and pleasant game for some, with its victories and defeats, but there are those for whom the fun was expensive. There were those who paid and never understood the game. Oh yes, *our* Boy Scouts stand up in voluble indignation and blame Hitler, and Hitler blames them, and both sides take good care not to look at the bodies. But they may, for they can be confident that, on whatever side the blame finally stays, those bodies won't get up and walk again. Score up, by all means, as many points against each other as you can in this military, political game: the last word has been said about humanity if our first and only reaction to the massacre of millions of innocents is, how evade responsibility and fix it on our enemies. Is that all it means? Is guilt so easily discarded? Why worry for all the perfumes of Arabia? No Good Scout can seriously feel implicated, thank God.

I went back to three months' training in Wales. I was now less inclined than ever to support between myself and other officers the nexus of superficial flippancies and accidental agreements of taste. There were irreconcilable divergencies. Perhaps I grew morose: I don't accuse myself of Pharisaism. I had sufficient honesty to my own character to recognize when and where I was not at ease, and to know what relationships I should avoid. One interest alone I really had, the happiness and security of my wife and her parents. Beside the magnitude of that care, Mess small talk was inane, and I ceased to dabble in it.

There was a financial aspect also. I could not afford now to run a Mess bill.

There are sufficient people who approve of the army, the Officers' Mess, and All That, to do it more than justice, so my conscience is clear. I didn't approve. If I tried to be jolly about it, I think the ink would turn sour on my pen. A failing no doubt. I like children better than brigadiers, in general. There are no apologies coming.

The Pascoe business precipitated a change in my character. I dropped some diffidence and became more positive.

I wrote to Elizabeth every day, but she didn't reply as often. At first she had a bad time. I had had to return to Wales without having found her a house, and leaving her with many problems. Then her health broke down, and she was in bed for a week. When she got out to the hospital again, neither Mother nor Dad was there. They had been transferred to a larger hospital at Plymouth. Elizabeth set to work alone on all her problems, the greatest of which was still to find a house. Lack of money crippled everything. Various voluntary relief organizations helped her greatly in the first weeks, and they also provided clothing. The Lowries gave her a home for as long as she wished. Her marriage allowance came through after a time from the army, and this made an immense difference, and I sent her all my pay after meeting my obligations. After a month, she found herself able to save money against the time when Mother and Dad should be discharged. But the amount she could save seemed quite inadequate to obtain a house: we had tried, in ignorance and desperation, a Building Society when I was in Cornwall, and found we hadn't the shadow of a chance of getting a house that way. A human being without a home is a strange thing in Society: one feels unsure almost about one's own reality.

Every fortnight Elizabeth went to Plymouth to see Mother and Dad. She couldn't go more often because of the expense.

Six weeks after my return to Wales she wrote:

My Dear Michael,

I've been offered a house, not a big one—two living rooms, kitchen, three bedrooms, bath, electric light: furnished (not too well). The owner wants 35/- a week, and can let it at that price to others if I don't take it. It's three miles from

Polpryn, in a fairly safe situation. Wire back immediately yes or no, because if I don't let the owner know by the day after tomorrow I shall probably lose it. I'm rather in favour, but 35/- is a hell of a hole in our money. God knows what we'll live on. I may be able to sublet a room.

I'm trying to get a job in an aircraft works, doing some kind of draughtsmanship. It's no use thinking of going on with my art studies now, because even if I got my exams., the chance of a teaching job can't be very high just now, and the position if I failed the exams., would be too grim altogether.

I went to Plymouth the day before yesterday. Mother is worlds better. She doesn't get so absent-minded nowadays, and she's past the stage of weeping at the least thought. She takes an interest in things. Asks me have I got a house yet, am I looking after myself, was anything saved from the old house, and so on. The bandage has been completely removed from her head now. The wound is very bad, there is a puckered slash right across her forehead, going back into the hair on either side. Her hair has all been cut off at the front by the doctors, and now that it's beginning to grow again she looks very strange, with short frizzy hair from forehead to crown, and the livid gash, from end to end, must be over nine inches long. It runs forward from over one ear, down in front of the temple, across the forehead almost to the right eyebrow, then back into the hair on the other side and along the scalp almost to the crown. Of course she can't get out of bed yet, but she is now on a normal diet, and recovering much quicker than I thought possible. Dad is more of a worry to me, though. His face wounds are quite healed, except for a little eruption at the side of his nose where a fragment of bone is working out: and he was due to be discharged a week ago, but the doctors changed their minds and won't let him go. I think, and he thinks, that it's because his heart condition has deteriorated. He has been walking about the hospital some time now, and finds he can't climb the stairs, and even on flat ground he has to stop every few minutes because one of his legs seems to go paralysed ('seized up' he says) and he has to wait for it to come to life again. The doctors are giving him digitalis.

I'm much better, except for my *bloody* headaches and deafness. My ear still discharges, but Dr. Craven has given me some ear drops which are fully as good as those from the hospital, and don't hurt at all.

Elizabeth.

Chapter Nineteen

I was away from my unit for four weeks, on a Gas course, and I judged that on my return to Wales my leave would be due. However, when I got back I found that another overseas draft had been called for, and this time I was on the list. This was quite a severe shock to me. I did not want to leave Elizabeth alone.

Tropical kit would be required. I was to pack my things and take the next train home for my embarkation leave.

I went into Orderly Room and read my draft order. Officers selected must have full training, as they were likely within a short time of arriving overseas to be in contact with the enemy. There were financial details and regulations about advances, and instructions to report to a specified Draft Centre on a specified date (ten days in the future). There were some documents to sign, and finally an interview with the Commanding Officer, who gave me his good wishes. Then I returned to my billet and began packing.

Morris, my batman, volunteered to go abroad when he heard I was going, and several men in my platoon did the same, expecting to go out with me.

I believe the Unit hardly noticed my departure. My men were sorry I was going, and so was Doc. Orry. The last service the Doc. did me was not the most pleasant—he inoculated me against typhoid and tetanus—a parting shot, so to speak. He had an ingenious technique for giving two injections. He charged the hypodermic needle with T.T. serum, thrust the needle (skilfully, with hardly any pain) into my arm, and made the injection. Then, without withdrawing the needle from my flesh, where it lay sheathed to a depth of an inch and a half, he unscrewed the barrel of the syringe and took it away, leaving nozzle and needle sticking in my arm. He then re-charged the barrel with T.A.B. and screwed it back into the needle, or, if you like, screwed it onto me, and made his second injection into the same hole as the first. 'Two injections, one jab.'

At the Quartermaster's Store I got various articles, including two khaki shirts which he said (justly) could readily be altered by a tailor to a tropical pattern. With these, my railway warrant, sundry documents, two suitcases, my pistol, my valise, my respirator and my steel helmet I left Pwllheli.

Elizabeth's house, when I found it, was cheap, flashy and new, quite without personality, with a lot of fanciful glass about the door, and bright green paint on the gate. At the click of the gate, to leave me in no doubt that I was right, Bonzo came skidding round from the back, leapt for my face, barked, laid back his ears, cried and howled with joy, pranced on his hind legs seeking to rest his forelegs on me, licked wherever he could, opened his mouth to the widest in a joyful dog-laugh, wagged his tail beyond belief, scampered, darted away and then back, crouched (his upturned eyes always on me) swung his hindpart round and about as if his whole body must wag, let his long pink tongue hang absentmindedly from the side of his stretched jaws, curled, uncurled, turned and returned, made noise enough with yelping, barking and almost talking to rouse the district, ran boldly up my chest (supported by my hand behind his head) to lick my face, and thus escorted me in.

Dad and Elizabeth were in the house. With one glance direct into her eyes I knew she was not the girl I had left. She was less my wife than before we were married. She had gone further from me than ever she had been before. There were two things wrong; she was very ill, and she was hysterical. I thought her nerves were about at their utmost stretch. Even her voice was different when she welcomed me in; it was a tight, brittle voice.

She was trying to conceal her despair that I was going away. She didn't want me to be unhappy during my last days in England. But her effort defeated itself. It's easier, and kinder to oneself, to admit such truths. Besides, ever since the bombing she had been concealing fears, and pretending to be confident. Repressions of that kind take a vicious revenge. She had used up all her reserves of nervous energy, and all she had left was the brittle shell of her assumed cheerfulness and confidence. Once these were shattered she might break down completely. She had carried too big a load for too long. She must have love and re-assurance. I must win her back to me, melt down her intense defences: she needed me to face the world for her, to settle out of hand the countless tiny problems that lay on her mind night and day, and to bring her scared soul back into its body. And yet it was just now, of all times, that they were sending me abroad, away from her. The shadow of my going, the knowledge, absolutely certain, that I could not possibly be with her to shoulder her burdens, the knowledge that I should be far away, beyond the possibility of helping her, lay upon her like a pitch black shadow covering all the future.

Dad had been out of hospital a fortnight. He was much changed. As I remembered him, he was a fairly broad, healthy, cheerful middle-aged man, with the shadow of a stoop, the suspicion only of increasing years, lightly on him. Now he was an old man with the last gleams of middle-age leaving him. The night had advanced with a bound. His face was not scarred. But he walked slowly, he hesitated, he repeated himself when he spoke: his deafness was pronounced, and he had a trick of walking with his hands held loosely slightly in front of him, as if he had just put something down or was about to take something up. He was washing some pots when I came in.

The days before I left England were very unhomelike.

Not even the plates and the pots from which we ate recalled the dear old house. It was all gone, we ate from cheap, elaborate china instead of the fine solid stuff of old, the table had one leg too short and rocked, jarring the pots. The chairs were worn in places where the Pascoe chairs had not been, and (worse) were not worn where the old chairs had been. The carpets were different and not nice, the stove was gas and not electricity, the bathroom was narrow—the house was all right, and complete enough, it wasn't its fault that it wasn't home. But the differences were always there: another individuality, not a Pascoe one, had assembled the house and furniture. It was as if a stranger were always amongst us. Our roots were not there, it was just a temporary shelter, not a home. There were no household gods in it at all.

The days were bleak: bleaker because we had waited so long for them, and because they were to end with complete separation. The old ease would not return to us. Endless trivial things to be done in the house, fires to be made, laid, cleared and what not, hearths to be washed, continual dusting, all reminding us that we were not now in the old house with its clean electric heating. There were dozens of makeshift arrangements of one kind or another. The old recreations were gone, too. If Dad sat down to a book (in an unfamiliar and uncomfortable armchair) he had no longer the laden bookshelves at his side, but must be content with something from the lending library or the daily paper. The gramophone was gone, and all our records, so there was no Beethoven or Handel or the Beggars' Opera. There was a radio, but its distortion was abominable when we remembered the one which had been destroyed. In the front room was a piano, quite out of tune, with stiff keys and two broken hammers. Then, 35/- a week. The thought hung over us always. We dared not switch on a light till dusk was well advanced, because of the electricity bill, and for the same reason, we did not burn two lights at once.

Under the shadow of my going, we seemed chained down to onerous trivialities; laying or clearing the table, washing pots, making beds, breaking coal, laundry, chopping wood, and countless little repairs, to window-fasteners, door-knobs, ill-fitting doors—things which contrasted sharply with the previous home. Then there was shopping and other errands, journeys to various offices, claims of one sort or another, and Elizabeth's search for employment. Mother was expected home any day, so the house must be clean and respectable for her. We never had any time to ourselves. Elizabeth and I never settled down to be happy with each other. There were too many and too urgent things to do. Frustration and emptiness grew in me as the days of my leave went by. My last days in England, perhaps the last days I should ever spend with Elizabeth, did not unite us. We were harassed.

There was a dumb, strangled desperation in me, and I sensed it in Elizabeth too. The broad stream of communication between us was strangled. The very desperation which this knowledge brought inhibited still further our endeavours to unite. We almost became artificial and tried to force the relationship. Our life was endlessly interrupted by small things. I could have wept with disappointment and forlornness.

Dad had fits of blank absent-mindedness during which his eyes became empty and he looked about him without any comprehension of where he was or what was happening. I cannot describe the sadness of seeing him once, with an expression of benign, pleased anticipation, reach up to the top shelf of the cupboard and fumble about there for some time: then the gentle light died off his face, a puzzled look replaced it, and he turned to me, with a face that became quite a blank. He had been looking for something, but not finding what his fingers expected to feel, had questioned what it was, and found he didn't know: didn't know the source of the pleasant anticipation. But I knew what the enjoyed routine of long ago had been leading him to, that he had been feeling for his one-string fiddle: unplayed for years, and now smashed to splinters in a smashed home.

The house was full of ghosts. Behind what *was,* we always saw the shadow of what had been. Three to a meal was a strangely small party to sit down at the rickety table.

Mother came home half-way through my leave. The scar across her head was frightful. At one point a small area of skin had adhered to the bone of the skull, so that the patch of skin was below the level of the surrounding flesh, and purple-red in colour. She wore a coloured silk handkerchief lightly wound round her head to conceal the short hair and as much as possible of the scar. She was thin and shrunken, but sun-tanned from her convalescence, and seemed to be in fair health.

After her return, the atmosphere of restlessness and strain grew worse. She could not hide her hatred of the house. She would look round the place and sigh bitterly. This hurt Elizabeth, who had had such labour to find a house at all.

The house was not clean—certainly not clean according to the standards of the old house. Nor was it possible to clean it; such a re-building as the old house had had was quite beyond the powers of the family now. They had put their best into the old house, and now——it was all gone.

Mother's hysterical moods now were sometimes blackened to tragedy. She was very unbalanced: she alternated between a heartbreaking timidity and quietness, and outbursts of utter despair. Then she would try earnestly to look on the bright side and be thankful for those who were spared. Her old impatience with Dad sometimes broke out with neurotic vehemence, intensified by her discordant nerves and Dad's much increased slowness, dullness and absence of mind. The least thing could make her weep.

So my last days in England went by, with the uprooted family which never could regain the security it had lost. Wretched unhappy bickerings, passionate reconciliations, misunderstandings and tears, thwarted love and tormented hearts.

The day after her return, Mother asked us to take her to David's grave. Having once seen it, she said, she would be satisfied and go no more, for no good could come of it for the living or the dead.

At the grave she broke down and knelt on the worn path beside, touching the headstone and kissing the carved letters of his name. The soil on the grave was now smooth and regular. It had not been disturbed except for weeding. The stone had a light film of dust, and dust lodged in the letters: already the stone had the settled, permanent appearance of the older stones about it. David was no longer a novice in the community. There were newer stones in the cemetery.

While Mother was on her knees, weeping over the grave, Dad was supporting her. Tears were running down his face. 'Don't upset yourself Marion, we can't do him any good,' he was saying.

I left Cornwall on a day grey with the coming winter. I had sent my heavy luggage in advance, and so had only one suitcase and the inevitable respirator. The situation seemed grotesquely like a play, or an old silent film about the last war. I the young officer, tall, straight, British and determined: clean-shaven, and wearing beautiful barathea and gleaming buttons: with peaked cap, gloves and cane. Elizabeth, the girl-wife, a Mary Pickford rôle. Bonzo on his lead, puzzled and not happy. It was acting an old, dated melodrama, it was the Soldier's Farewell as on the cheap prints: it was not the real, beating life in us that brought us to the station-platform to act these parts. Our very grief was not our own. The situation was so stale that we were only repeating other people's passions. Yet our hearts were leaden heavy. Compulsion was on us. We had to play it through. But when would the curtain come down on it? What if it were so arranged that I should die in the motley, and never come back to real life, off the old-fashioned, time-washed stage.

I hated the long shining rails which were my road away from Elizabeth, as I stood on the platform with her. Porters were jostling past, at that of all moments, barrows were trundling, there were shouts to stand clear of this, that and the other, the children hopefully thumping the empty chocolate-machine, the smell of stale breath from the waiting-rooms, the bookstall where I bought 'Picture Post' and 'Kindness in a Corner' to keep my mind off the new, never-healing wound. Then the train ran in, there was a dry sickness at my heart as I hurried to find a seat in a first-class compartment, put my impedimenta on the rack, and turned to say all that, having failed to be said during our last days together, could not be said now. Elizabeth was holding Bonzo in her arms so that he could not get under the train. The last dry, hard, wretched minutes when we looked miserably at each other's eyes: unutterable longing. The knowledge that these minutes were the last. Time was closing like a door between us.

Elizabeth standing there on the platform, ungovernable pain on her face, tears forcing themselves out of her eyes: the train moving out. She waved her right arm, woodenly, holding Bonzo with her left: Bonzo's eyes followed me, amazed, he was whining absentmindedly: he yelped suddenly and tried to break free to follow, I saw his hind legs shoot out, I leaning from the window, till Elizabeth's form became small, small, tiny, dim, and the platform and the station itself became a far grey blur, still just in sight as the train curved round to that side: and at last gone completely. Gone completely.

Sitting down in the corner of the compartment, my whole soul one raw wound: aware of the rhythmic throbbing of the train, and my heart thumping painfully: the man in the opposite corner opens his 'Times' with a smooth rustle.

END OF PART TWO

PART THREE

PART THREE

Chapter Twenty

At the Assembly Centre I was given a draft of rather less than a hundred men to take abroad with me. These did not include any of the men from my own unit who had volunteered in order to go with me. I never saw any of those men again. But among my draft I was surprised to find young Shaw, whom I had last seen at his court-martial four months earlier, since when he had disappeared to a North of England military prison—'gone into the Glass-house'. The prison pallor was on his face. He was silent, pinched, sullen. I supposed he had been drafted abroad as a commutation of the remainder of his six months' sentence. Whether he were pleased or not to find I was his commanding officer on the draft I could not say. I never saw his expression soften once while we were awaiting the embarkation. There were few smiles among the men, for that matter. But one in ten had volunteered—nearly all 'inked in'. When their documents were handed to me, I found, as I had expected, that the majority had bad army records. They felt that their inclusion in the draft had the force of a punishment—or rather, that their units had thrown them out.

There was a waiting-period of about a fortnight before we left. During that time the men were inspected and their kit made up (while the Quartermaster rightly denounced the Q's. of their previous units, who had sent them—merely into battle—with all the rubbish and junk of their stores, and little attempt to replace worn and useless clothing and equipment). Tropical kit was issued to them. In that period I also visited the local military tailors and filled the gaps in my own outfit. I was not told my destination: nobody at the Assembly Centre knew it, which was as it should be.

Once I had left Cornwall, the bitterness of my regrets was finished. I even felt excitement and anticipation for the future, for I had not been out of Britain before, and now I was to go far, into incredible tropical waters, to see things which I knew only as phrases in geography books, and to take part in real war, not the hedge-scrambling, blank-cartridge-firing shadow-boxing of our 'exercises'. If there is anything more soul-killing than real war, it is imitation war.

The day of our departure came. The men were handed over to me, paraded in threes on the square. The weather had suddenly turned bitterly cold. We were leaving an English winter. I inspected my men, preceded by a good-natured major who was handing them over to me. Their equipment, respirator-haversacks, small packs, etc., were in poor shape. The major cursed unit quartermasters again, gave the men 'close order', and I said a few words, on orthodox lines. I introduced myself, said I was their draft commander till I handed them over at the other side. We all, I said, had mixed feelings about going abroad. If we nursed any regrets, the only result would be that we ourselves would be less happy than we might be: but we should go just the same, therefore the thing to do was to forget our regrets so far as possible. I said that after months and years of monotonous training which had no direct effect on the war, we were now going out to fight: henceforth our actions mattered, and we must behave like men. I said also that we were going into parts of the world which were new to most of us, we were going to see things which otherwise we should never have seen: therefore we should try to get the most out of it. No grudging, but make this all an adventure, as it was. The chance of a lifetime. I remember also referring to their equipment, and saying I hoped to be able to look after them better than their previous staff had done.

During this little speech they looked at me without resentment, without expression, without interest. I might have been talking to a wall. The good-natured major told me they were a tough, bad crowd, and I should have to post sentries all along the train, till we reached the port of embarkation, to prevent any of them making a break for it. In this, as it proved, he was wrong. I posted sentries, but am convinced that the idea of trying to desert never occurred to any of the men.

They *were* tough, and many of them were twisted. But so is oak. I don't regard myself as one of the Little Flowers of Saint Francis, anyway.

A day later, after travelling all night by train, we embarked. The troopship lay at X-docks. She was a big ship, the 'Huntley', some thirty thousand tons. My men and I were checked on board by the Military Police, and once on, were not allowed off. This prohibition had quite a damping effect on my spirits, and on the men's too. The door was closed. Even though the ship still lay in dock, our life was cut off from our country. I was worried about the men's kit, too, which we had left stacked on the quay. Would it all—and my valise with my typewriter inside—find its proper way into its proper hold? It did.

I dumped my suitcase in my cabin—cabin luggage was limited to one suitcase, other things I might need being labelled 'Wanted on Voyage' and stowed forward—and went to find my men. Their accommodation was: three hundred men living, eating and sleeping on one mess deck, with just room to sit down at their long narrow tables, and a space six feet wide for promenading. It was as if the passengers in a nicely-full tramcar or 'bus were to be informed that, instead of dismounting at the next stop, they were to live on the vehicle for the next two months. Each of the men held a rolled hammock, and didn't know where to put it. The crowd was dense, the through traffic was ruthless, the atmosphere unharmonious. When, that night, I saw my men hanging in their hammocks like hams in a pantry, side by side in rows, and each row interpenetrating the next, so as not to waste space, I wondered. The air down there was hot, dank and breathy. Naturally they were crowded. It wasn't intended for a pleasure cruise: the 'Huntley' was a ship loaded to the line with fighting men. It would have been criminal if the ship had not been crowded. But why then were the officers allowed so much room? Why did we officers travel so much better than we should? Remembering our lounges, our dining-room and our cabins, I believe four men at the very least could have been accommodated in the space allotted to each officer. Not that I disliked the luxury.

193

I selfishly and thoroughly enjoyed it. I like good food, drink, and comfort, and I had all those on the voyage out. But they should not have been given. The officers should have travelled on the same terms as the men, and the ship should have carried five thousand instead of four. Even if equity didn't demand this, the necessities of war did.

Four days after we had embarked, the ship having now taken on all the men she was to carry, we were pulled by tugs from the quay into the middle of the dock to take the tide: but either we missed it, or the captain did not like the look of a fog which had come down, and after an hour in mid-dock we returned to our berth. Once again we were gazing from our formidable height onto the long, wide, sloping grey-roofs of the docksheds, themselves thirty feet from the ground, and the ground twenty feet above water: and we, on the promenade deck at high tide, thirty feet above all. The umbilical cord, not readily snapped, still held us all to England like the mooring-rope from the bows. We humorously speculated on the chances of dodging the draft even now, by jumping down onto the roofs and thence by easy stages to earth. We concluded that anyone who tried it would either go clean through the roof, or become an ugly splash on the slates.

The electric gong rang for Boat Stations. We dived below, put on our life-jackets, and paraded in the appointed places. I had my men up on the Sports Deck. The Boat Drill took a long time: there was chaos in companion-ways. When we did get on deck, the authorities seemed to forget us, and left us at our stations an hour and a half, in the cold fog.

The following day, more pulling out by tugs, and this time we sailed. Wharves and sheds, bridges and dock-gates slid away on either side as the fuming tugs drew us backwards through a chain of docks. Where the dock-gates stood open for us, pedestrians and cyclists waited without impatience for the ship to pass and their road be open again. They were looking up at the vast ship. To them our heads, peering over the rails, could seem no more than a row of peas. They, to us, were dolls on a miniature quay. The ship's tall moving side was between us as we moved out, out and far away.

At the mouth of the dock the ship was born—its heart began to beat. We felt a new, faint tremor along the decks, and saw the smoke thicken from the only one of the four funnels that was not as false as a Prime Minister. We were moving under our own steam. And then, nose first this time, we went like an arrow down the river.

I was still child enough to be thrilled by the sheer speed and power of a big ship. I watched the great V, the arrow-head of her wash, rolled up by the prow-blade, open out in a wide, dappled, rocking, deep-green, bubble-suffused, foam-patched carpet right back to the dropping land on either side. The wind of our movement sang steadily over the deck, and would have taken off my cap had I not removed it myself first and let the wind blow through my hair. But the approaching evening was cold, so I did not stay on deck to see the last of England. I went down to my cabin, feeling the new life already vibrant in the ship, and the almost imperceptible stirring of floors and walls.

My cabin-mate was a young infantry subaltern, a lad of twenty, who had spent most of his life, since leaving an Elementary School, in the army. He was a natural soldier, very good with his men, and extremely conscientious and able, though he pretended to take his duties lightly. His name was Ted Carrick. His batman was already laying out his service dress for dinner when I got down.

I had just selected my own batman out of my draft: a man called Wells, who said he had been batman to a Brigadier. In fact I found him very good. He was married and had a two-year-old baby. When he was working in the cabin he used to talk to me about 'the best little woman in the world', and show me photographs.

Successive mornings brought us into the open Atlantic. At first the weather remained grey and cold. Wind and waves taking us on the port side, we developed and maintained a list to starboard, and the long pitch of the ship had a roll superimposed on it, and became an oblique, wallowing movement, at one time fairly pronounced.

Each morning I took a stinging hot sea-water bath, with the so-called Sea-Water soap which never really lathered.

The water always stood sideways in the bath, low on my right and high on my left, seeming to contradict Archimedes. After my bath I would go back to my cabin just as the steward set two cups of tea on the dressing-table. Wells would be in the companion-way polishing my shoes.

The companion-way was a corridor, cream-enamelled, perhaps sixty or seventy feet long, with cabins all along the port side and the engine-room casing on the starboard. I travelled the length of this corridor countless times a day, between my cabin and the bar, the lounge, the dining-room and the mess deck where my men lived. Also whenever the gong rang for boat-stations I had to force my way along.

There were many women officers of the auxiliary services aboard. Like some of the male officers, they had no responsibilities on the ship, and were (reasonably) anxious to make the best of the trip out. They formed coteries of half a dozen or so men and women who used each others' Christian names, and were further subdivided into couples. They played deck-tennis, quoits, bridge, etc., and walked briskly or idly (according to the temperature) arm-in-arm about the upper decks. The existence of this butterfly class formed a distasteful contrast to the life of the men, cramped down below and living most primitively and monotonously. The men, of course, had their own very congested decks for promenading and fresh air.

There seemed little to talk or think about communally, though I suppose we all had plenty of personal matter for reflection. We talked of the convoy, which we were to overtake somewhere out in the Atlantic—for we were alone but for two destroyers. We had weighed anchor late, two days after the convoy had sailed. It was rumoured that if we failed to pick up the convoy we should return to England rather than sail dangerous waters alone.

The Huntley was a big experience for me. I was a very ignorant landsman, not in the least blasé about big steamers. To me it was wonderful that a structure so ponderous and gigantic, far larger than any hotel, could race forward with the speed of a train. Holding the rail of the Sports Deck, I braced myself against the gale and watched in front of me the great, wide, long nose of the ship, the wide deck and its buildings, the immense mast, the forecastle deck, the entire frontal part of the ship, steadily, gigantically lift itself up from the sea (with a lull in the roar) and then lay itself mightily down, plunge down onto the dark swirling green, while the gale suddenly screamed from every rope in the rigging and the spray came up and over and down the deck like a whip: and along the twin wrinkles that stretched out and back from our bows surged a sudden thick tumbling froth like curdled cream. All the time the ocean ran past our sides as the fields fly past a train. The thought and the sound of that water racing past was at the back of my consciousness always. Along my companion-way, as the ship got into her long stride, I could always sense the tremor of the plates as the engine thrilled through them, and every ten seconds or so, with a long, regular rhythm, came the vast (but not loud) creaking, like the sound when you sit in a basket-chair— only this creaking was the long stridulation of the entire fabric of the ship, giving, yielding very slightly through all her length to the shifting support of the sea. Again and again, that regular, slow, respiratory crepitation, a multitude of tiny grunts and squeaks, beginning in a whisper, rising to a voice, and then dying again through a whisper to silence.

This was the Atlantic, which Elizabeth and I had watched and feared one day in another life. This was the heart of the mystery: this grey-brown tumbling, this restless water, with white crests blowing like smoke: with a misty edge where the sky came down, and where the distant waves were tiny specks of white that appeared, stayed a few seconds, and were gone. Far away in the grey distance our destroyers manoeuvred and tacked about: they came across our way, far in front of our bows, or crossed and recrossed behind us, like two grey dogs frisking round a gamekeeper. Except for them, the sea about us was empty; its unceasing movement was its own, had nothing to do with us on our sharp-edged world. To look down from the ship's high moving side into the water, the heavy, swinging depths of wrinkled green-brown, was a kind of apprehensive recognition. This was, indeed, the sea, that swung and burst on our iron walls, the sea whose green volumes we had watched at Land's End slapping heavily on the rock: but then we had seen it from a point beyond its power, as one sees a tiger in a cage. We had seen it confined and limited, we had seen its edges. Here the sea was master. There were no rocks, nothing solid for it to break on except our floating walls. Down into the depths, and away to the horizon, it rolled and splashed, and launched upwards its white feathers. There was a loneliness that became almost an entity. And beyond the horizon lay another tract like ours of tossing waves, but—unlike ours—without a ship, without anything floating, without an object, without anything to interrupt the unmeaning play of the waves: a brown-green desert which heaved endlessly and was not seen: which made the noises of meeting waves, and was not heard: which stirred endlessly and purposelessly under the empty sky. Mendelssohn caught, with a faint, long, hollow trumpet call, the voice of the sea where there is no land.

Chapter Twenty-One

I did not spend much time at deck-games. For one thing, I found I loved my brother-officers no better afloat than ashore: I don't play bridge: and preferred to interest myself in the men. They soon were instructed to write their first letters home, for dispatch at our first port of call, and I had to censor these letters. I was getting to know the men by now. Wells, my batman, had an inseparable friend called Fitzjohn, a tall intelligent man whom I made up to temporary lance-corporal. Then there was Marlowe, who had soldiered in India: an older man, the humorist, grumbler, Bolshy, and barrack-room lawyer of the draft. When I had first brought them aboard, he had had a grumble about not having had any food since the previous night:——'Sir, can you expect to have contented men when we're not even given *food?* I'll tell you straight, sir, I can't go on much longer. They put you on a draft, stick you under the decks *packed like sardines,* and keep you without *food* from six o'clock at night till two o'clock the following day. Man cannot *live* without *food,* sir. Sir, my belly is under the impression my *throat's* cut. If, sir, you issued me at this moment a scabby donkey, I should *consume* the beast, sir'.

'What's your name?'

'Marlowe, sir.'

'Marlowe. Well, Marlowe, first, don't speak to me like that. If you have a complaint, make it. I shall listen to complaints, but not to grumbling. Second, nobody on this draft, including myself, has eaten since last night, so you can assume that I'm doing what I can.'

'Yes sir.'

Another man I soon got to know was Craddock, a soapy person. He ingratiated himself with authority wherever he could, joined groups of men to whom I was talking, and usurped the conversation. Craddock was young, twenty-one or so. He attached himself to Shaw.

The average age of my men was twenty-seven. One or two were as old as thirty-five, many were steady married men of thirty, and there were a few boys of twenty or even less—Collinson, a quiet, dark lad perhaps nineteen, Shaw and Craddock. The worst crime-sheet was that of Shaw, who was also the youngest of the draft.

On the third night out from England I came down to the mess-deck and found young Collinson dead drunk, flat out on the floor, unconscious. Marlowe had been drinking with him, and was himself quite drunk. They had drunk enormous quantities of tinned American beer. In the morning I said a few words to the draft—I don't remember what sort of argument I developed, but the theme was that the older men were responsible for the lads. I mention it because, long after, Marlowe referred to this talk of mine, and said it had made him blush for himself.

Day by day the attendance at meals decreased. I began to feel, if not precisely sick, at least uneasy myself. Our meals were always ambitious—the officers', I mean. The men fed plainly enough.

The officers' dining-room was elaborate, in an ornate, sugar-icing style. Its solid and massy appearance accentuated the psychological disturbance aroused when it tilted. It was as if Covent Garden Opera House were to rock. A long velvet-and-brocade curtain hung at a window near my table, and as the ship rolled, it shifted in relation to the wall. Ted Carrick took one agonised look at this curtain at breakfast on the third day out, and left the room. I never looked at it myself. On the fourth day the sea became choppy. Most of the men were sick: even the waiter at my table looked pale. I ate modestly, but I ate. About the wide dining-saloon sat the few officers who had survived. They ate little, carrying the food to their mouths with quick movements, between which they rested, sometimes with closed eyes. They did not look at the curtains. From time to time a deep roll would shoot crockery off the table with a gratifying crash.

I instituted a compulsory P.T. parade for my men, up on the Sports Deck every morning. Shaw and Craddock failed to parade. I gave them a warning: next morning Craddock appeared, but not Shaw. I scratched my head, and rather thought it was up to me to succeed where, evidently (judging by his crime-sheet) many had failed. So I sent for him to my cabin. A remark of Marlowe's occurred to me—'you've got one of the most stubborn men in the army on this draft, sir —Shaw.'

He came in, saluted, stood to attention. It was a good position of attention. Training evidently counted for something, if not much. He reminded me of one of Hitler's Boys in uniform. I looked at him.

He was pleasant-featured in a juvenile way: his face suggested thirteen years rather than eighteen. He hadn't yet had to shave. His hair was brown and wavy. His eyes were blue, his brows strained, and I guessed he was short-sighted. His teeth were good, but never clean. His frame was thin, his legs long in proportion to his body. He was underdeveloped, undernourished. His face was noticeably white by contrast with the other men.

'Stand at ease, Shaw.'

He did so.

'What's your Christian name?'

'Frank, sir.' Though standing at ease, he did not look at me when he answered, but stared straight in front of him.

'How long were you in my platoon, Frank?'

An apprehensive shade crossed his face. 'About a week, sir. Just when we left Cornwall.'

'And in Wales?'

'My court-martial was after we'd been in Wales about three weeks, sir.'

'Altogether you've only soldiered under me for a month?'

'Yes sir.' He never once looked at me, but straight over my head.

'Tell me, Frank, why you failed to parade this morning.'

The unfair use of his Christian name took him off his balance.

'I've nothing to say, sir.'

'You prefer to take your punishment?'

'I can take my punishment, sir.'

I looked at his crime sheet. 'I can see that. But it doesn't seem to have helped very much, does it? Have a cigarette.'

His eyes suddenly met mine, and immediately looked away again. He was flushed and confused, and fumbled the cigarette. It did not put him at ease.

'See now, Frank, this is only the beginning. You and I are going to be together as soldier and officer for some months. I'm in complete charge. I have a very free hand with this draft. I may have to sling you into the cells in the end: but maybe we can do better. At any rate, let's start clear. Let's have a man-to-man understanding to begin with. Here's my viewpoint: I want this draft to be disciplined and efficient, and I don't want to do it by punishment. Because of your bad record and your youth, I'm particularly anxious not to punish you. That's my side of the case. What about you?'

'I'm not frightened of punishment, me. I can do my duty, sir.'

'But you don't.'

No answer. Then after a long pause—

'I got no embarkation leave for this draft, sir. Straight out of clink and on board, that's what they did with me.'

'You know why: because you deserted the last time you were given embarkation leave. But I'll tell you the truth, Frank: I think you should have had leave, even so, and I'm damned sorry for you.'

'I've never had a square deal in the army, sir.'

'Tell me about it.'

But silence fell on him again. After struggling for words for a few seconds, his expression suddenly became indifferent. 'I've nothing to say, sir.'

'All right. Don't miss any more parades, Frank. And when you have any complaints, or you think you've had a raw deal, come to me and say so and we'll see what's to be done. Don't just keep your trouble to yourself and act stupid. Do you understand?'

'Yes sir.'

'Good. Off you go.'

A day or two later we came into clear skies and blue water. The North Atlantic seemed to be characteristically green, tending even to brown, but this was a true deep blue, ultramarine in the troughs of the waves, cobalt on the crests, where it frothed into bubbling white foam. The temperature had risen sharply, and the sun arched much higher overhead. At the same time a very brisk wind increased on our port, and the ship began to roll very markedly to starboard. Passengers who had just determined to leave their cabins and attempt the meals changed their minds. I was about normal by now. I seemed to have overcome seasickness and become immune. It was not easy to sleep at night because of the constant rolling of the bunk. However firmly I lay down on my right side, as soon as I began to relax in sleep I found myself wallowing from side to side in my sheets. This was very heating. Ted and I found it necessary at last to throw off all clothing and lie naked under the ventilator. The crepitation of the ship now was very loud, and I wondered what sort of noises the old wooden ships used to make, in the time of Drake, or even Nelson. I imagine the squeaks, creaks and groans from those hearts of oak must have been deafening in heavy weather.

I wrote to Elizabeth:

My Dear,

This is a voice from the middle of the Atlantic, where I'm floating about in a cabin. I have your photograph here. As I write I glance up at you from time to time, to see if you are interested. You always are. This encourages me.

All is blue here. Deep blue as it is, the sky is paler than the sea, which is more like blue paint than water. One expects blue stains on the ship's sides. It's very hot. This morning all the ship's staff appeared like Angels Ever Bright and Fair, Clad in ducks of Virgin White. They looked very leisure-class and immaculate. Tomorrow we are to wear our tropical shorts and shirts, and our Gorgeous, Ostentatious, Ridiculous and Useless Topees (or *tepees* as Ted Carrick says: he also declares 'papoose' is a verb—by analogy with 'vamoose' I suppose).

I got your lost letter, your telegram, and the parcel with my silk underpants and the tobacco. Thank you.

There are many things I'm not allowed to say in this letter, so don't be surprised that I don't tell you the name of the ship, etc. As for where I'm going, I couldn't tell you even if the censor would allow, because I still don't know. Nobody in the ship seems to know where he's going. Very odd, if you think of it, and reminds you of 'Outward Bound'. Lugubrious parallel.

I'm absolute monarch (apart from the O.C. troops) of ninety-seven men. I like it. By the way, you remember young Shaw of the court-martial—he's in my draft. He comes from prison worse than he went in, both in health and temper. I suspect he has tuberculosis. They played him a *bloody* trick, sent him abroad without leave. He's always scrounging below decks, and thinks I'm persecuting him when I send him up into the fresh air. The other night he got wild drunk —not sleepy—drunk, but blustering, hysterical. I thought the ship's police would have him in the cells—however, my batman and I kept him out of trouble. He pitched his cap and some other things overboard, demanded to see the captain, and finally collapsed. My interview with him went something like this:

Me: 'Shaw, you had an expensive night last night. You
         lost your temper, your senses, your money, your
         cap and your boots.'
Shaw: (mumbles) 'Yes sir.'
Me: 'You've not written home yet, have you?'
Shaw: 'No sir.'
Me: 'Do you mean to write home?'
Shaw: (long silence: then) 'Yes sir.'
Me: 'I think you ought to tell your mother you were
         very drunk last night. What do you think?'
Shaw: (*l'œil farouche*) 'All right sir.'
Me: 'Good. Now look here, Shaw. I'm going to give
         you all the rope I can. Then it's up to you whether
         you hang yourself with it, or do something useful.
         Here's a pound-note. You can spend it on more
         beer, if you like, or you can go to the Ship's Quar-

termaster with it and replace your cap and boots, or you can save it, or you can sling it over the side. It's up to you. That's all, off you go.'

Shaw: (mumbly) 'Thank you sir.'

We, the officers, live so well that we don't like to think of any of our menus getting by chance into the hands of the troops. We have a very good lobster salad, the asparagus mayonnaise is delicious, and there are excellent ices. Champagne (I'm told good, but I would not know) is 12/- a bottle: in fact all drinks are about half their English price. It's all duty free. Some officers are sopping up oceans of whisky.

Troopship rules include no smoking below decks and no gambling. It's fantastic, because nearly all the men both smoke and gamble, and so do the officers. I may be old-fashioned, but I don't approve. Either enforce your law or repeal it, I think.

Now I'd better tell you what it's like being out in the Atlantic.

There's a continual wind blowing across the exposed decks. This is partly due to the speed of the ship, which is moving through the water at rather more than the speed of the Falmouth 'bus. One has to hold tight at exposed corners. I often feel I shall be blown off my feet, but it doesn't happen. The vivid blue water is blown up against the bows and side of the ship, so that there is a perpetual sloshing and roaring of spray beneath us. The ship rolls and pitches. The roll makes you stagger, the pitch makes you sick. Every so often the ship changes course (we sail in zig-zags) and when it changes there is a terrific pitch and a terrific roll, and the passengers make muted squeaks signifying inward uneasiness. The sun rises steeper every day. I see it from my port-hole as I'm shaving, for I'm an early riser these days. It goes up like a balloon from the water's edge, into a clear blue sky, and by half-past eight the boards on the deck have dried white and hot, and all the metal is hot. This dislocation of the sun makes me feel out of place. I remember the 'winter arches' the sun will be making in England.

There are flying fish, but my eyes are not as good as the

men's. I've only seen one solitary flying fish. It did not look very wonderful to me, a sort of celluloid flash in the air just above the waves. (But maybe what I saw was not a flying fish, but an optical illusion.) At night there are little gleaming patches of phosphorescence in the water, and the moon comes right over the mast, looking very outlandish because it's a three-quarter moon and the quarter seems to have been taken off the wrong place. The old constellations are dropping behind us now. Orion stands on his head on the horizon astern, the Great Bear crawls on all fours on the edge of the sea. I couldn't find Pegasus at all last night, but I daresay I wasn't looking in the right place. I haven't yet seen the Southern Cross. It's rather an experience to be on deck at night, hearing the roar of wind and water as we drive forward, and to realise that the whole fabric of steel, timber and plastics is racing along, with thousands of people on her (like a small town) into utter blackness, without so much as a glimmer to show what's ahead. On she goes at more than twenty miles an hour, stone blind, neither showing the faintest spark nor seeing one.

One hopes the Captain knows what he's doing!

She must have been a lovely ship in peace time. One of the ship's officers was telling me the other day how she used to look—bright paint, white, red and brown, broad bands round the funnel, 'snowy decks' (vide 'In Memoriam'), brilliant gleaming brass. Now of course she is sober grey, but still very comfortable in the somewhat vulgar style that the average first-class passenger of a decade ago might be supposed to appreciate. Moorish cafés full of minarets, Oriental windows, palms, etc.—Olde Englysshe lounge, oak-panelling and tapestry—rococo dining-saloon. Everything suggesting the Super-Pub. circa 1925 rather than a sea-going craft. But all extremely jolly and ingenious. Of course there's a swimming-bath, not very large, but a Godsend these days. I can imagine the leisured cruises of pre-war days, with lights beaming on the water at night (no black-out then), dancing, orchestras, rather more champagne than now, cocktails and ices galore, deck chairs. . . . .

M.

Chapter Twenty-Two

Next day we overtook the convoy. There was excitement, and crowding forward to look, and one by one appeared on the horizon the tiny lumps of which we were soon to be one. In a couple of hours we had reached the great procession of freighters and fighters; they came obliquely, first across our bows and then all about us: we slackened speed and adopted their course. Big ships of war drew past us, aircraft carriers, cruisers, and an enormous battleship. The separable armour of the convoy, they swam out on our flanks, we could see them every time we came on deck, steadily maintaining their position. Many destroyers chased about on the periphery of the convoy, rearing or plunging in the heavy waves: but the big fighting ships lay majestically on their courses, riding the waves evenly, only lifting and sinking with the immense horizon as our own ship rolled. David should have been here to see them. There were aeroplanes, too, which he would have liked. They came up from the aircraft-carriers and roared over the convoy, dipping over each ship.

As the trip went on, I spent more time with the men, organising whist drives, concerts, spelling-bees, debates and so on. Lotto ('Housey-Housey') was played a lot by the men. One way or another, too, I had to give a fair amount of attention to Frank Shaw, who was the problem child of the draft. I had him examined by the ship's M.O., who reported that he was not tubercular, though undernourished. Shaw was one of a group of men who spent a lot of time below decks, playing illicit games of four-card brag.

My pound-note he brought back to me, having signed for the new kit: its cost would be deducted from his pay. I refused to have the money back. It was a gift, not a loan, and he must have it.

'I've made up my mind never to drink again, sir,' he said.

I looked at him sadly. I would much have preferred a more modest resolution which might conceivably have been fulfilled.

'Don't promise more than you can perform, Frank.'

He didn't spend the pound. I learned by roundabout channels that he gave it to Fitzjohn to keep for him. This, I gathered, caused great annoyance to Craddock, who had hoped to have the drinking of most of it. Craddock was apt to drink steadily at somebody else's expense, and still be sober when his host was drunk.

Marlowe usually despised four-card brag, and played solo. Shaw was usually in a brag school: so was Craddock, and Collinson joined in sometimes. When I was about, they kept up the pretence that they were playing 'for love', but we all understood the position One day Ted Carrick's batman dropped a hint, and I verified by observation that Shaw often cleared a profit at brag with Craddock's assistance, when Craddock wasn't actually in the game. Craddock would stand at the other side of the table, opposite Shaw, looking at the cards of Shaw's opponents. Shaw got all the information he needed from Craddock's expression.

In talk about 'clink', all gave way to young Shaw. That was one respect in which he had the better of them. With expressionless face, but evident enjoyment of his pre-eminence, he would tell his prison experiences—Army prisons all the time—the tough birds he had met, the fatigues he had done, the brutality, the pack-drill, the way his gaolers learned to expect him back after each discharge. I picked up a lot of information.

'. . . . . .I'll go into clink any day, me. I'd sooner go in than standing messing about. No excuses for Shaw. I never say a word when I'm in front of the C.O. It's no use. Why, I did fourteen days only for volunteering for the guard room, you can see it on my papers. Do you know, I've only been out of clink six months in the last two years, me'? While he talked his face was expressionless, but in the pauses he grinned (one felt he did so in case any other expression should find its way out). 'Then I was up for drunk, and using obscene language to an N.C.O., and failing to comply with an order, and urinating in my barrack-room—I was drunk then. Then desertion. . . . .Pack Drill? Every morning for a steady hour, round and round the prison yard, with old Nick calling out the time—left right left right left right— full pack! That's clink! Two years of it, nearly.'

Young Collinson was quite different. He was a strong, though slender, keen-eyed, dark, tough young animal. His soldiering was far more than a superficial smartness, it was deep in him. He wore his Glengarry always at the old soldier's angle—so did Shaw, but on Shaw it was noticeable, even out of place. On Collinson it looked right. And when Collinson got drunk, he came out of the rabble and 'got his head down'. Collinson didn't talk much, or gamble much. He could see a joke, but only smile at it. Not easily shaken, and able to look after himself. Shaw seemed always to have to convince himself and others that he was a tough egg.

One morning I opened my port-hole and saw Africa in front of me. A row of slate-blue mountains crowded up over the horizon. The convoy was moving into harbour.

'Ted—Africa!'

Ted was not excited. He grunted without opening his eyes. After breakfast we came slowly into a wide estuary, perhaps two miles across. I retain now only an impression of vivid green palms on the shore, and at the mouth of a lagoon: and a long green promontory of flat land, with white houses amid the green, stretching far out into the sea. As we came further into the estuary we came opposite the town itself, backed by shaggy hills. We anchored about a mile from the shore. All the ships of the convoy lay at anchor about us. We passed a cruiser, brilliantly spick-and-span. Aircraft, their wings folded down their backs, like mosquitoes, were on her decks. Astern, in the shadow of an awning, the ship's band was playing.

Then came another troopship, with row on row of tiny heads, watching us as we watched them.

We anchored far enough from shore to be immune from mosquitoes, though even so we were ordered to wear slacks after sundown, or turn down our shorts (they were the un- gainly type with turn-ups). But we were not out of range of the bumboats. We had been warned about them long in advance, and trade with them was strictly prohibited, since it was said that every kind of tropical parasite and pest and disease was transmitted by their fruit. Like so many things which were prohibited on the ship, bumboat trade prospered.

They skimmed towards us over the smooth, oily, sparkling water, like water-skaters on a pond, and seeming no larger. The canoes were large enough to hold one, or two, persons only, and were all shaped more or less like a banana. They were paddled by ebony negroes, none of whom wore more than a loin-cloth, though they put on immediately any cast-off articles thrown down to them from the ship. Their tiny boats bore just the same proportion to the Huntley as a peanut shell bears to a row-boat. They had odd phrases of English—they asked us if we came from Glasgow, and used the expression 'Glasgod tanner', which was too recondite an allusion for me—but I did not hear enough English to discover whether it was their adopted language or not. The only use they seemed to make of the language was Caliban's—

'You taught me language and my profit on't
Is, I know how to swear.'

Their obscenities caused a not unpleasant sensation on the ship, and enabled men and women officers to peep briefly at each other through the holes knocked, momentarily, in the chivalric convention. This catharsis without guilt, this exhilarating encounter with concepts which our own tribal taboos bury in silent obscurity, was not the only benefit the primitives conferred on us. They brought fruit out from the shore, principally bananas and oranges, and exchanged them for money or articles of clothing. It was significant that here we had our first serious outbreak of theft. Things had been stolen earlier in the voyage, among the men, but here the matter suddenly became serious. Men were stealing each other's kit and exchanging it over the side for fruit. Money also was stolen, and not only among the men. Ted Carrick lost £3-10-0 which he had left in a drawer in our cabin.

It was here, too, that I first saw natives diving for money.

I observed that there was a technique of deception. The divers did not in fact retrieve half of the money thrown overboard, but they made a point of pretending to get it all. The infallibility legend was, I suppose, essential in order to persuade the passengers on the big ship to part with their money. The negroes would not dive for copper, ostensibly because they couldn't see it in the water. Silver reflected the sun. (Or so they said. I found Frank Shaw below, wrapping a penny in silver paper.) Once the coin was thrown, the diver never admitted a miss. Confidence had to be maintained; if we aloft didn't think the divers would get our coins, we wouldn't throw them. To a man conditioned in western civilisation, to take half-a-crown out of his pocket and throw it into a river, straight down to the bottom without the possibility of its being saved, is like tearing out his own heart. 'The soul and body rive not more in parting'. I verified my suspicion of the infallibility legend when the wind caught my sixpence and carried it a good twenty yards from the boat of the native who was watching me. He dived, struck vaguely downwards, but certainly did not go within fifteen yards of the coin—then broke surface, went through the motions of taking a coin out of his mouth, thanked me with a gesture, and clambered back to his boat.

We lay in this estuary for a week, till all the convoy had taken on water and fuel, and then put to sea again. Soon after we crossed the line. We were now right under the sun, which stood above the mast at noon. Most nights the men had a concert on the deck forward. I shall always remember these concerts, the full moon directly overhead, the shadowy rushing water (yellow on the crests and gleaming backs of the waves), the ship riding on, the warm air, the men crowded silently on the decks, the cigarette-smoke, and a figure standing on the hatches, a voice singing 'The Rose of Tralee' —romantically incongruous, the English voice, the khaki drill clothing, and the full African moon.

My crowd of tough guys, whom the Major had expected to be troublesome, were quite good. I remember most of them with respect and liking.

On the second stage of the journey, I took a decision to

stop all gambling in my draft. I did so because I was sure, from observation, that there were very few habitual gamblers in the draft, and therefore I had a reasonable chance of making the prohibition effective. Gambling was responsible for the persistence of stealing on the ship: and it produced a characteristic and bad attitude to life, a gambler's attitude, which could easily be recognised.

I paraded my men and told them of my resolution, explaining why. Nearly all the men were clearly of the same mind as I was.

Two days later I found Shaw playing brag with some men from another draft. There was no money to be seen, but I was suspicious, and asked the party, in general, if they were gambling. They shook their heads.

'Playing for love, sir.'

Somehow I was not convinced. I asked again,

'Once more I ask all of you. Are you gambling?'

Again they quietly shook their heads. There was a pause, rather strained, then Shaw said, 'Yes, we were gambling, sir.'

The faces of the others were expressionless. Their eyes flickered over Shaw, who sat still. I left it at that. The game broke up as I went away.

A couple of days later I found him gambling yet again, and told him to report to my cabin. He did not do so, and I went below, very irritated, buttonholed him, and said 'Shaw, I gave you an order, which you haven't carried out. You will be at my cabin at four o'clock precisely'. I then detailed two men to bring him at that time.

When I got back to my cabin, the steward had placed on my desk a bottle of whisky which I had ordered. I poured out a couple of fingers and censored a few letters. Then I looked at my watch. Five to four. I considered the Shaw problem again. Clearly, to make a man of him was going to be a task of some magnitude. I still had the alternative of letting him run his own way. He would be in the cells before the trip was over, and I should have a bit of peace.

However, the fact was that I was not made that way, and that was the end of it. For better or worse, I had to do my best for him, according to my own lights. I had to see it through.

He came in with a very sober face, even paler than usual. This tough guy, I commented mentally, is *always* scared. That's why he bluffs. And his bluff is anti-authority, and is partly due to his fear of authority. It's a kind of penance, a self-torture, a neurotic compulsion. He won't let things go easy. He *forces* this conflict (which he dreads) with authority.

He stood rigidly to attention, his face tense. Masochism. Inflicting very real nervous strain on himself. Having found me kind, he had forced me to be an executioner. Now we were in the rôles he understood.

However, I knocked the bottom out of all that.

'Hello, Frank' I said, 'sit down a minute, will you? I'm busy with one or two letters.'

A straight left would have disconcerted him less. I had a glimpse of a sudden tumultuous flood of emotions in his face as I turned back to my letters. But I didn't leave it at that. I was drinking whiskey, so I poured him a glass. 'Have a drink while you're waiting.'

He tried to refuse, and say thank you. Finally he took the glass. I settled down to censoring for two minutes, to give him time to think. When I put my pen down at last, and turned to face him, the whiskey was untouched.

I filled my pipe in a leisurely way, pressed down the tobacco, and lit it carefully.

'Now, Frank, what is the trouble?'

He took the cigarette I offered him, but did not light it. Shaking his head unhappily, he said 'I don't know, sir.'

'Why have I sent for you, do you think?'

'I expected to be put in the cells, sir.'

'I won't put you in the cells. You can be sure of that. Honestly, haven't you had enough of that? Honestly?'

'Yes sir.'

'Pack drill. A kid of your size. Is it the sort of thing you want to do?'

'No sir.'

'You know, Frank, I reckon no human being can ever really understand anybody else. But I understand a great

213

deal about you, I think. You're only eighteen years old, and you've spent two of those years in prison. But you've got the right to go to Hell your own way, and I can't stop you even if I wanted to. All I want to do is to make sure you understand which way you are going. I'll tell you why, in my opinion, you break rules, and drink, and gamble. You do it because you are younger than the other men, and you want to bluff them into thinking you are grown-up. That's why you act tough, that's why you like to be thought the best gambler in the draft, that's why you boast of your prison life. But that prison life wasn't *really* a good thing, was it? Behind all the bluff, you know that it hurt you. And the whole bluff is a hell of a strain, really, isn't it?'

He sat silent for a time, then nodded slowly. 'Yes, sir.'

'You think I'm right, more or less?'

'Yes sir. I think you're right.'

'Frank—look here, kid, see if we can get all this straightened out. There are better things in life than you are getting out of it. What did your mother say about the detention you were always doing?'

'She didn't know, sir. I told her I was going on a course.'

A course. Pack drill.

'But she guessed, I daresay?'

'I think she guessed sometimes.'

'You didn't see her at all before coming on this draft?'

'No sir. I haven't seen her since I deserted.'

Pause. Then he went on. 'I wouldn't have minded if they'd let me see her. But I might never go back. Every man's got a right to embarkation leave.'

'I've just seen the letter you've written home, you don't tell your mother about the night when you were drunk.'

He looked profoundly worried. 'I *couldn't* tell her that, sir, it's no use. I couldn't. She doesn't know I ever drink. I never did before I joined the army, sir.'

'She probably guesses, Frank. She would understand you better than you think.'

'I couldn't tell her, sir. I've thought about it.'

'O.K. Now, this disobeying of orders. You were gambling. Since I'm not going to punish you, I'm failing in my duty.

I can't help that, I'm prepared to fail if it's going to put you right. But watch the effect on the other men. I find them gambling—what then? If I punish, they want to know why you were not punished. If I don't punish, what becomes of my order?'

He flushed deeply. 'I'm not frightened of punishment, sir. Take action against me.'

'No', I flicked the pages of his crime-sheet. 'That's what happens if I punish you. I've promised myself to save you from that, Frank; from that black record, and from the cells and the pack drill. And I'm not going to fail. So that means no more gambling: no more at all so long as I'm your officer. No more at all. You understand?'

'But what is there to do all day, sir, if we don't gamble? It's the only way of passing time, and besides——' he broke off suddenly.

'Go ahead, say it: "And besides, the officers do it". True enough. But my order is an order. And look at it this way. If *you* gamble, there are two dangers: one, that you may lose, and two, that you may win. The second danger is the more serious, because even if you win fairly, your gain is another man's loss, and it makes you selfish and callous to other people, which in the long run is worse for you than for them: partly because you get to the point of winning by any means, fair or foul: such as having Craddock tip you off from behind your opponent's back. And that's not a man's game——Don't get excited, son, I'm not blaming or praising, and I'm speaking of what I've seen.'

Sullen rage and shame was in his face. His colour was high enough now. 'I'm not the only one who ever did anything wrong, sir.'

I looked at him. 'That's true. But you feel ashamed at this moment, and that's why you are furious with me. Well, listen: you do not have to feel ashamed in front of me, I've done worse things than that in my life, and shall do worse again. Only since you are not going to play cards for money any more, this particular question won't trouble you again. When you're out of this draft, or out of the army, you can gamble then, if you like, and you can cheat if you like. It's entirely up to you. I am not the judge.'

There was quite a long silence. At last he looked up into my eyes.

'I'm sorry sir,' he said. 'I won't gamble any more.'

'Frank, I don't believe you, and you only half-believe yourself. If you are thrown amongst gamblers a lot in the future, you will gamble, and we both know it. I shouldn't worry about that if I were you. At this moment neither of us knows which way your life is going to take you. The only big thing for you to care about is not to waste the goodness and the strength and the honesty in you. Live your life right out, wherever it goes, don't let it trickle away in empty bluff and bluster. Be real. Be a man. And on this ship, obey me. When I tell you to come to my cabin, do so.'

'I will, sir.'

'One other thing. Just get this down into the deepest parts of your mind: you can trust me to the limit. You can put *all* your weight on me, and I won't fail—not for a second. Lean on me as hard as ever you like. Do we understand each other, Frank?'

'I understand you, sir. I will try, honestly. I won't give you any more trouble.'

Chapter Twenty-Three

So far we had not set foot on land since we left England. We next put into Y——, and here we knew we should be allowed ashore. In fact I was signing shore passes as we entered the dock.

When I try to analyse my delight in seeing foreign towns, I find that it isn't so much the differences from home which strike me, as the similarities. When I go to Heaven, I shall be interested for once in a way, to see the cherubim and seraphim singing praises round the throne, but I shall only be enraptured when I see them sitting down to a cup of tea and a biscuit. It's the parallels which storm the imagination: to see the old relationships in a new plane; the old principle but a new circumstance. To see the same trading company or travel agency which one knew in a grey street in the North of England, open its chrome-plate doors and windows under the hot blue dome of Africa, is to be teased out of thought by the singular invisible root from which both grew. It's in this ubiquity of civilisation that the magic lies: not to be surrounded always by a dead, portable sphere of England even in China or in the jungle, but rather to realise with a shock of delight that in these alien circumstances some of our own tribal gods have got themselves established, and here, out of their element, they lose the dullness of custom, and are seen comical, romantic and impermanent. One sees the pleasant hollowness of our solidity, one is reminded by the very stretch of our banks and businesses that the Sun Life Assurance Company, for all its plate glass, has not lived as long as a tortoise, and is nowhere near as permanent as an oak.

It was very good to see from the ship a shining metalled road between and beyond the dock buildings, with trolley-buses rolling along it, and with white-fronted buildings, shops, hotels. My feet hungered to be on that road. When I did at last put my foot down on the solid quayside and, walking out at the dock-gates, showed my pass to the native policeman there, I re-experienced forgotten childish sensations of joy, as when my parents long ago had taken me to the seaside. Not, as I say, the differences particularly—the rickshaws caught my attention and made me marvel, but they were less mysterious and unfathomable than the trolley-buses. For after all, the rickshaws *grew* there. They belonged to the romantic picture, but the trolley-buses with their fascinating African destinations placarded on the front did not. The good smooth tarmac road, in magical contrast to the bright green palms that fringed it and the hot blue and gold of the sky, gave me joy to feel it under my feet. Slick American cars hummed along towards the city centre. I came across some of my own men, eating fruit and drinking lemonade, on a grass patch in front of a church canteen. They told me of fabulous meals for sixpence, and oranges free. They were like lads at a picnic, grinning all over their faces. Ted Carrick's batman had been invited out to tea. Marlowe, Hutchinson and Fitzjohn had just gone into the city in rickshaws. Would I like a bunch of grapes from the canteen? Bloody fine spot, this.

The continual chirping of crickets increased to a remarkable loudness when you came near grass or a garden.

In the city centre, the sunny white buildings were so much like the current impression of Hollywood that I never quite escaped the suspicion they were stage sets. Neon and chromium and snow-white plaster. Opulent. Opulent cars rolled up to the opulent swing-doors of opulent blocks of flats, and opulent business-men sprang out, slammed the opulent door behind them, and ascended the opulent steps. Grand. I found my way to the beach. Shops, cafés and milk-bars (neon and chromium) had fruit which we in England had not seen since the beginning of the war. I went into an octagonal café overlooking the beach, and ate a mixture of fruit, cream and ice-cream: and visited the aquarium.

There was no black-out when night fell. Blue-purple lights shone above the smooth roads, there were lights in the shop-windows, and tinted light streamed from the uncurtained hotel-windows. Above this fairyland of light and colour was the shining African sky, greenish towards where the sun had set, and the waning moon. Africa. As I walked back to the docks, I repeated the word to myself, like an incantation, looking all round me to take in everything. Far back, beyond the edge of the city, I could see low hills shining under the moon.

The hottest weather of the journey came when we left Y—. We had trans-shipped to the Ilyssus, a big ship built for the Atlantic. She had not as much deck space as the African waters and the Red Sea demand; she was a huge iron box which, under the vertical sun, became an oven. The men were much more crowded even than on the Huntley. Conditions were bad. There were bugs, fleas, cockroaches and rats, particularly in the men's quarters. The Ilyssus had been in constant wartime commission for two years, and needed disinfestation; as the heat increased, some of the men went down with stomach disorders, and most of them had heat rash.

For one thing I was very thankful, she was a 'dry' ship, or nearly so. There was not enough beer aboard to sell it regularly in the canteens and bars. We officers drank cocktails and whisky in the cocktail bar, through the ornate windows of which we could see the men's crowded hammocks. And they could see us. The O.C. troops said, in a talk to the officers: 'Gentlemen, you will please remember that as you drink, in the luxury of the lounge or the bar, there are men quartered all round you in conditions of extreme discomfort, and they can see you. You will therefore not aggravate the position by drinking to excess, or by any conduct unworthy of your rank.'

One day was appointed as beer day. There was none for the officers, who could get other drinks, but it was on sale without restrictions in the troops' canteens. That night, as I went down the aft stairway towards the canteen, I came upon a small riot. At the centre of the disturbance were Craddock and Shaw. Craddock was shouting apparently in defiance of the Military Police. Shaw, his back pressed to a rail, was struggling with Mulgrave, my senior N.C.O. A dense and curious crowd pressed round, hostile to Mulgrave and the M.P.s, who were forcing their way through. Both Shaw and Craddock were drunk.

The excitement of the two drunks was fanned by the shouts and surge of the crowd. It was the sort of incident which could be serious. All the men had more or less beer in them, and the noise and confusion were considerable. I was the only officer there: fortunately my voice was strong. I secured silence and ordered the men to clear the landing. As this order was not immediately obeyed, I found it necessary to post a policeman at the four exits. The crowd now thinned rapidly. I turned to the centre, and found that Craddock had vanished. Shaw still strained to break away from Mulgrave. I told Mulgrave to release him.

The landing was half-cleared, and quiet. I crossed to where Shaw hung panting on the rail. He missed Craddock, spun round, saw two Redcaps approaching, and went berserk.

'Where's my mate? Where's Craddock? You've put him in clink, you bastards. Come on then, all of you' (squaring up drunkenly). 'Put me wi' my mate. I'll fight every f----g Redcap on the f----g ship. Come on, put me in clink, same as usual.'

'Get him below,' said Mulgrave.

'Yes, that's right' echoed Shaw bitterly, 'Get him below, get him out of the f----g daylight'. He went for the Redcaps, fists flying. Without a word they caught him by the wrists. At the new uproar the crowd was looking back, edging back. I stepped forward to the struggling group.

'I should stand back sir,' said one of the M.P.s. 'It will make it worse for him if he happens to strike you.'

'He won't'. Shaw was throwing himself about in complete frenzy, screaming and swearing. 'Leave go my f----g wrists —leave go my f----g wrists—leave go! let me go, you bastards, let me go, will you, let me go—you cowardly rotten f----g bastards—all on to one f----g kid—let go, will you— where's my mate—Craddock! Craddock! Help me—oh you *bastards, bastards, bastards.*'

His face was violet. Sweat was running from him, and a

white, creamy froth oozed from his lips. I clapped both my hands on his shoulders and looked full into his eyes.

'*Frank Shaw.*'

He stopped dead. His utterly confused, bewildered eyes looked back into mine. His lips shaped words which he did not speak.

'Let him go' I said to the Redcaps, without taking my eyes from his.

One of them did. The other, being bloody stupid, didn't get the order because I hadn't looked at him when I gave it. Instead of releasing Shaw's wrist, he twisted it into an arm-lock. Perhaps he thought that was what I wanted.

That broke my control. He began tugging, writhing and screaming again. Mulgrave unfortunately stepped forward and said 'Stand *still* when an officer is talking to you.' That finished it. Shaw got one hand free, and lashed out at Mul-grave. (Very reasonably, too.) Both M.P.s sprang on him, and one of them got him by the throat. He became com-pletely hysterical, and was taken off to the cells.

I stayed behind to see the landing cleared, and to see where Craddock had got to. He was already in his hammock, making no movement. I would have loved to put him in the cells, but he took care to give no opportunity.

I went below to the cells, far down in the entrails of the ship—or so it seemed to me, though I daresay there was as much ship below me as above, even there. Four or five cells —with barred, small windows in their heavy doors—opened off a small central space, where the policeman on duty sat and read 'lech' books, or drank cocoa. The atmosphere was hot and stuffy, since the black-out made it impossible to open the ports, and there were not sufficient air-scoops. The Redcap who guided me down said they had put Shaw in the padded cell as a precaution.

From the cell came threats of the bloodiest nature and obscenities. The cell walls and door quivered as Shaw bat-tered them with his fists. Yet the most characteristic thing of all was that the cell door was neither locked nor even completely closed. He made no attempt at all to come out and wreak the destruction he threatened. It was completely typical of him.

I went to the cell door. The Redcap assured me he would be violent and advised me not to go in. I couldn't see it.

The cell was six feet square, and fairly dark. Shaw stood back in a corner, swaying, moving his fists as if he were shadow-boxing. He went for me erratically, but though his fists whirled all over the place, he didn't hit me. He didn't mean to: he dared not. It reminded me of Bonzo's wrist-biting. He didn't know who I was—probably couldn't see.

'Now Frank, you wouldn't fight me?' I said, putting out my hands to him.

He immediately collapsed in my arms. I had to hold him up—but he was no weight. 'No sir—I wouldn't, sir—it's them buggers sir—I wouldn't—give—you—any trouble sir —they pinched—my mate sir—I—didn't—know it—was you —sir—I wouldn't—give—you—any—trouble—sir—I would-n't—sir.'

'Don't talk, son. Steady now. Get your breath.'

He was sucking breath convulsively, his lips and chin covered with foam, his heart thumping so that I could feel it shaking all his frame, and he was sweating so much that not only his own khaki drill was soaked, but mine too, where I held him. 'They—wouldn't—wouldn't—let go—sir. They would—wouldn't.'

'Easy, lad, easy,' I said, feeling like an ostler with a nervous horse, 'sit down on the floor, now—I'll help you—there.'

He slid submissively down on the padded floor. I eased his shoulders to one side, and got him stretched out, his head on my arm. The Redcap at the door watched in amazement: 'Lord, he's like a lamb with you, sir.'

Shaw was almost in a fit. His throat was working in violent spasms, a sort of intensified sobbing which obstructed his breath: his face was blue. I sent a Redcap for the M.O. But after seeming to lose consciousness, the lad slowly recovered. I put my hand on his forehead.

'I know—who—that—is—without opening—my eyes,' he said between his sobs, 'it's—Mr. Carr—he's the—only—one who—ever—ever does—anything for—Shaw'. Pause. Then his eyes opened a little. 'Sir—I can't—see—for tears. I can't see—anything—sir.'

'Sir—don't be hard—on Craddock—sir.—I—know you—don't—like him, sir. Sir—he's my mate—sir.'

'Sir—is Craddock—there? Is he—in—clink—with me—sir?'

I said yes, to quieten him.

'I—know I'm—in—clink—sir.'

'Sir—you leave—me—now—sir, I—shall be all—right.'

'Sir—I'm sorry—for causing—you—this trouble. I'm bad—sir. Shaw's no—good. You'd—better leave—me sir.'

'It's—no—use sir. You can't—keep—me out—of clink.'

'Shaw's—no good—sir. You—leave 'm. No mate—for—you sir. Shaw's—too fond—of—beer—sir. Sir—leave me—here. I can—take my—my pun'shment.'

'Back to—the cells—with—Shaw.'

'Sir—where am—I?'

'Sir—don't you—think—too hard—of—Craddock.'

'I'm—sorry—I've given—you trouble—sir.'

'Don't you trouble—any—more—about—Shaw, sir. Let 'm—take his pun'shment.'

'I—can't stop—crying, sir.'

Pause. Then, very quietly. 'Sir—I can—see now.' His hand came up and pointed erratically at the barred opening in the door. Very softly, 'One—two—three—four—five—six—seven—eight—nine. Nine bars.—You count—sir. Are there—nine?'

'Yes,' I said.

'Nine bars. I'm—in detention—again. Am I—sir? Bars. Seems funny.'

'It's them bars—sir. I can't help—looking. One, two, three ———Sir—I'm behind bars again.'

'Makes—my—head ache—sir.'

I told him I would take him out soon.

'Will you—sir?'

'Bars. Shaw's—in jug—again.'

When the M.O. came, he was asleep, so we did not disturb him. 'Good Heavens' said the M.O., 'he should be at school still.'

I was not sure how or when he would wake, so I spent most of the night down in the cells, drinking cocoa or playing cribbage with the M.P's. About half-past two, Shaw suddenly flapped on the door with his hand. 'Sentry! Come'n take me for a piss.'

On his return from this expedition he became very difficult. Evidently he confused his present surroundings with his earlier months in prison, and the discrepancy of the padded walls of his cell made him furious. He raged, stamped, and shouted for the Adjutant. He could see the shadow of a sentry near the still-open door of his cell, and threatened to maim him if the Adjutant were not brought to see that he, Shaw, had been put in a padded cell. 'You white-livered bastards. I'll cut your eye out with this' he yelled, and 'this', flew out of the door—a cheap cigarette-case (he threw it feebly and with no sort of aim). Then he fell into a weird muttering to himself—'It's no use Frank, there's six of 'em out there. You might as well give in. You're beat.'

Then he found his AB 64 in his pocket—'All right, you whispering buggers, if you don't bring the Adjutant to me, I'll tear up my AB 64, that's all. Just wait till the Adjutant knows you put me in a padded cell. I've warned you. Bring the Adjutant or this paybook goes west. Are you bringing him?'

Silence.

'Answer me, you snigg'ring sods.'

Silence.

'Right. Here goes.'

He ripped the pay-book in two, and having started, went on as if by compulsion, talking to himself all the time. His voice as he shredded the book dropped steadily to a sad, preoccupied mutter, as a child cries itself from frenzy to sleep. Now that his fingers had something to do he was slowly forgetting his grievance: self-pity crept into his voice. 'I'm tearing it up' he announced lugubriously, then paused (though without any real hope) for us to make some move. Then, talking to himself, 'Put me in a padded cell. Ah, it's no use. They won't take me out. They'll never put this lot together again, anyway. Tear it up—small—tear it up. . . . . .'

He continued till the book, and the papers it had contained, were a heap of tiny scraps on the floor: he ran them through his fingers, tore them smaller, and examined them by the light from the window. 'That's the finish of that' he said, 'and the Adjutant will want to know all about it tomorrow. Huh! I wouldn't be you when the Adjutant wants to know. . . .' Then a familiar scrap of yellow paper caught his eye. He stopped dead, looking at it.

For some time he sat silent and still, with this piece of paper in his hand. Then he said to himself, 'Now I've torn the old woman's letter up'. Apparently he had carried his mother's last letter to him in the flap of his AB 64. It was torn into tiny scraps. With the slow uncertainty of drunkenness he tried to sort out from the heap on the floor, the other pieces of the letter. I watched him trying incapably to fit two pieces together, two pieces which obviously didn't fit. He turned them slowly about, trying different positions. Looking at them with gloomy earnestness. 'No use,' he whispered to himself, 'no use.'

At half-past three he fell asleep again: I told the M.P's. to wake him at six and send him to his own quarters, and I went to my cabin.

His pre-occupation with the bars of his prison haunted me. The prison bars of the last two years had left scars on his soul. Caging a child. The cruelty of it was medieval. He was a fool: but the answer to folly is not wickedness. We must not torture children when they are slow to grow up.

Chapter Twenty-Four

That day we passed Aden and sailed between two deserts, Egypt on our left and Arabia on our right; and the sea was that which had parted to let the Israelites cross. So far as I could see from the Sun Deck, there was nothing to choose between the land they lost and the land they gained.

Did they ever reach the Promised Land? Their wanderings were so weary and so protracted that *I* never did: and the recollection of their barren pilgrimage sets me positively against finding out. Arabia looked no barer or more desolate than the book of Exodus, and I don't much care to see either again.

Next day we anchored in a smooth sheet of water off Suez, and debarked into motor-transports: flat pontoons, each holding two hundred men. The sea journey was over. I had brought my ninety-seven from England to Egypt.

The transport chugged out from under the shadow of the Ilyssus and set off over the smooth water. It was evening. We felt a new coolness, in fact a not very welcome chill in the air. We had become accustomed to hot days and hot nights. I buttoned up my shirt to the collar. Behind us dwindled the great, immobile Ilyssus. Now we had left her, she lay still, dead and empty on the shining Egyptian water. End of the voyage out. 'God, she's a big bugger' said the men, seeing her for the first time from water level. She lay as calm as a cathedral, slate-black, immense against the orange sky. I watched her till she became only a tiny black point in the distance, and our own chugging little pontoon was nosing into the quayside. As the sun dropped, the cold increased. We shivered. Greatcoats appeared from packs. Soon we would be familiar with the cold nights of North Africa.

We were on the quayside two or three hours before a train came to take us to the Base Camp. We found a canteen, where a good mug of tea cost a piastre (we had changed our money into Egyptian Currency before landing) and all were in good spirits, though I was worried about my valise, which contained my typewriter, and which I had not seen since leaving the Ilyssus. There was a good deal of congestion and confusion on the station, but fortunately the moon was bright.

The train, when it came, reminded me of the one which climbs Snowdon by the track railway. The coaches were not subdivided into compartments, but were like an old-fashioned English tram. Seats were wooden, and windows without glass. If you wanted to keep out of the raw night air, you pulled up a slatted wooden shutter. There were no lights whatever. We were tired, cold and subdued as we crowded in. The men were docile. A strange, unfriendly, hopeless sort of rail journey, in a primitive train, at night, and in a foreign land. No voices calling 'goodbye', no hands waving from the platform. One's heart was bruised, empty and numb. The moonlight showed us glimpses of Suez as we moved out: white Eastern buildings with tall, thin, knobbly spires to them, all drenched in the white moonshine, all still and silent, but a chink of light appearing occasionally from an Arab eating-house.

I sat shivering in the darkness. My greatcoat was in my valise, and my valise was God knows where: and we might be all night in the train. The men were falling asleep. Marlowe, in a voice decently low, was telling stories indecently low. At the other end of the coach Craddock was giving a sotto-voce impersonation of his last R.S.M. taking Battalion Drill. The rest were snoring.

Much sooner than we expected came the order to detrain. I got down first, and found the train halted in a moonlit desert. There were no buildings, no shacks, no station, no platforms, no huts or tents—nothing but barren sand and the rails, and on the left, the black bulks of a range of hills. Some British N.C.O's. had come to meet the train; a sergeant joined me as guide.

Meanwhile the men were throwing their bundles of kit —the sea-kit bags and their own black kit bags lashed together—out of the windows, and assembling. In the moonlight Mulgrave drew up the draft in three ranks, and our guide took us a couple of hundred yards, to where, just beyond visibility in the deceptive light, stood a row of vehicles. The kit was soon loaded, and then, relieved of our burdens, we set off in column across the desert, and soon came to a road, which we followed. The men were cheerful, marching well in step, swinging along the hard road—their first march since England. Now on our right, the black bony hills caught on some of their ridges a tinge of yellow from the moon. The land was alarmingly desolate. But for the hills, unbroken desert lay all around us, and the glossy road, yellow-gleaming, divided it like a sword. The guide said we had a mile to go to camp.

A building started up on our left, and proved to be a cinema-hall, built in reinforced-concrete. Then, tiny and hardly seen, scattered on either hand, came tents: not belltents, but flimsy rectangular bivouacs, though larger than they looked.

Soon after, we right-wheeled into a side road. There were a few widely-dispersed tents just discernible on the desert's face. 'Here we are', said the guide, 'this is your area'. He sent the men off in groups of eight, each to a tent. It was as if he had taken us to the middle of Dartmoor on a cold night and said 'here are your quarters.'

'Off, off, you lendings.' Furniture, timber, carpets, and strong stone houses are not life. You can drop the lot and hardly notice. I peeped dubiously into a tent—it was quite empty. Not even a ground sheet. The men slept on the sand, in a house of calico ten feet long. How now, Thoreau? But not for a worthy reason.

'I'll take them to the stores now, sir' said the guide, 'and issue blankets.' This relieved my immediate anxiety.

'What about something hot, sergeant?'

'I think the cook's got some stew ready, sir. I'll slip over now and make sure.'

This was welcome news at two o'clock in the morning.

I got the truck driver who had brought the men's kit to run me over to the Mess, where I found many new officers from the Ilyssus, drinking beer—the bar had been re-opened. I had a beer, and returned to the men. They were in the dining-tent, each man with a bowl of hot stew and a hunk of bread. I had a bowl of stew with them, and then went back to the Mess, where I spent the rest of the night in remarkable discomfort, trying to sleep in two armchairs.

In the morning I had a better view of Infantry Base Depot, as I shaved in the brilliant cold sunshine, behind the Mess Tent: but I didn't like it even so. They told me this was the best place in the Middle East outside the Delta. To me, after the luxury of the trip out, and with English thoughts in my head, it was simply the wilderness. There was a bright black road, straight as a spear, through the area: military trucks and vehicles roared along it, keeping always to the right. On one side, parallel to the road and a mile from it, ran the wall of brown bare hills: on the other side, the Bitter Lake. Our vast, dispersed camp straddled the road, between the hills and the water; tiny tents lost on the empty face of the sand. You could walk many miles along the road without leaving the camp. In the camp were canteens run by the Egyptian NAAFI, every one just like every other one: there were two cinemas, two miles apart: there were tiny stalls (watchmakers, confectioners, whatnot) with Egyptians behind the counter. There was a wooden shack which was the Church of England, and a wooden shack which was the Ottoman Bank. Down towards the Bitter Lake there was a tiny, filthy, biblical Egyptian village which did not appear to have been emancipated from the Plague of Flies. Apart from these things, there was nothing nothing nothing nothing except khaki khaki khaki khaki, sand sand sand sand and flies flies flies flies.

No women, no children in our lives now, only men, and men only in khaki. On the ship one had not noticed it, because the ship was only a transitory stage, it even moved all the time, it was an interlude. But this was the destination: final till the war ended: the blank yellow desert, the empty blue sky, the plank canteens, the Mess tent, and men in khaki, till weeks became months and months, years. No sight of women, no sound of children. The sand and the shacks and the sky. Life meant either being inside your tent, or being outside: in both cases there was sand. There was never even a skylark or a singing bird in the sky.

I still had *de facto* control of my men, for though they were now included in the Base Company, I was an officer of the same company, and as I alone was familiar with the draft, I naturally dealt with their affairs, paid them, went with them on training, and so on.

The training was a desert hardening course: P.T. for an hour after breakfast, then a run across the sand and straight up the hills. The hills were only a couple of hundred feet high, I suppose, but rough going, sheer in parts, and very dusty. The run-and-scramble generally covered six or seven miles of this bad country, and took rather more than three hours. All the time the sun roasted us, and the desert gave us no shade, not even for the half-way rest. It was sweaty, dusty, parching work, but it satisfied. I felt harder with every run. Unfortunately some authority had promulgated an order that men on training should wear shorts and boots only. The Egyptian sun smote our shoulders. Some of the men, and I, were soon seriously inflamed, particularly on the back of the neck, and upper part of the shoulders, and the arm down to the elbow. Blisters developed, we lost a lot of sleep, and the M.O. had to treat some cases.

At Base there were two sorts of people—the Base wallahs and the fighting wallahs. You could not distinguish them by behaviour or speech—both types were 'sick as hell of this bloody place', despised its smug safety and disliked its bull-shit. The difference was that, whereas sooner or later the fighting wallah was sent up to the front, the base wallah never shifted. He remained at Base, always indignant, always browned off, always hoping to be sent up the line—but 'the C.O. seems to think I'm indispensable', etc. Each base wallah pulled secret strings of his own: and in conversation, avoided the word 'cushy'. I knew one whose line was Courses. He had been on seven army courses in England before the inevitable draft order caught him: he said that, when his children asked 'what did you do in the war, daddy'? he would say 'I trained successively for every emergency, possible, improbable, and unthinkable, and my training was almost complete when the Armistice was signed'. When I last saw this amiable cynic, he was off to Cairo on an Intelligence Course. Coals to Newcastle.

Once or twice I was able to take my men down to the Bitter Lake for a swim, though I wouldn't go in myself because of sunburn. Once we went through the native village. It could not have altered much since the days of the Israelites. There were bearded elders in dirty robes, walking by twos along the stinking canal, and gaudy, filthy younger men, and one or two children, filthiest of all. The air sang with flies. There was a characteristic smell of putrid human dung. The 'houses' were of wattle, tin, wood, mud, and anything else that came to hand—tiny lean-to sheds like fortune-tellers' booths, built up against the sun-dried wall of the village caravanserai, or the trunk of a tree. We saw one woman there, veiled. In an open hut by the roadside sat a native barber under his board 'Hairs cut very good'. The butcher's shop was three stout beams by the canal. A cow was led up and killed with an axe. A rope was looped round its hind legs, and fastened to the heads of the three beams, which formed a tripod. The villagers all lent a hand to push the feet of the tripod closer together, so that the intersection of the beam-heads was progressively raised, and at last the cow swung clear of the ground, hanging head down between the beams. The head was hacked off. The beast was slit open down belly and chest, evisceration and skinning proceeded simultaneously. An old man caught the blood in a basin. The flies were indescribable.

There was a letter-rack in the Mess-Tent, in which I had been allotted a pigeon-hole. The supervision of that pigeon-hole was the most serious thing in Egypt to me. When I went in to breakfast I went round by the letter-rack to see if the vacant space had been filled. I would find reasons to drop into the Mess every time I passed. I scrutinized the letter-rack before and after every meal, and gave it my last disconsolate glance before I went to bed. I looked at the addresses on the letters in the holes to right and left of mine, and above and below, in case the orderly had carelessly put mail of mine in the wrong hole. But there was never a letter for me. Though one or two of my men had Air Mail from home, my pigeon-hole was still empty on the day I saw it last.

Young Collinson had a letter from his sister telling him that his mother was dead: he had left her in perfect health. He fainted on reading the letter. The shock must have been very great, after the excitement and pleasure of having a letter before anyone else. The world must have become very black for him. I found him in his tent, sitting still, silent and white-faced, and said what little I could to comfort him. He took the letter from his pocket and gave it to me, but could not speak. It was a very gentle and kind letter—'Dearest, this will be a great shock to you, but you will have to be told. Mum passed away suddenly yesterday. She had been poorly for two days. . . . . .Poor Dad has been very upset, but I think he is getting over the worst now. Mum was getting a parcel ready for you, but we have not got it finished because of this. I will send it as soon as I can after the funeral. . . . . .Do not worry about us, dear. Dad will go and live with Emily for the time being, and we shall look after him well. . . . .'

Tears were streaming down the boy's face. He showed me the last photograph that was taken before he left England, himself in uniform, standing with his hands on his mother's shoulders: and asked me if I could get him a bit of crape to put on his sleeve.

Chapter Twenty-Five

Some of my men were warned to be in readiness to reinforce units 'out in the blue', and I was to go with them.

'Jerry' said an officer opposite me at breakfast, 'is sitting down right on our door-step at A——G. I should travel light, if I were you. Leave your camp-bed, suit-case, all non-essentials. You may have to cover long distances in short times.'

I followed this advice.

Next morning, at half-past seven, I inspected the Mess letter-rack for the last time. There was nothing for me. Any letters that came now would have to be forwarded to my new unit, out in the desert. Despite regulations, I had written to Elizabeth every day since reaching Base. Something must get through.

An hour later we were climbing onto the train. All my kit, including even steel helmet and respirator, was in my valise—I carried only revolver and food-haversack. A crowd of Egyptians swarmed round us at the station. My valise, more than I could well carry myself, was hoisted up with great effort by a slender little Egyptian lad of twelve or thirteen: he got it on his head and tottered towards the train. Such was the power of custom that the child did the work, the man walked unburdened, and no anomaly was observed. I gave him five piastres for my conscience's sake. Conscience should be the White Man's Burden: but he finds ways and means to make the black man carry even that.

Ted Carrick had been posted to the same unit as I. It was good to have his experience and competence on the journey. He kept an alert eye on rations, an old soldier's eye. We were taking fifty men, all from my draft, the 9th ——Shires. It was a convenient number, easy to handle. At Ismailia we gave them tea, biscuits and bully, and I drew £10 from Lloyd's branch there, and had coffee and sandwiches at the French Club. Then the train came in which was to take us to Ben Har. In our compartment was a stout, youngish man, a civilian, whom I set down as something between an American, a Greek, and a commercial traveller. He was very amiable, and pressed sweets and chocolate on us. He told us he had spent the previous night with a nice prostitute, who had given him a good time, but about dawn he had wearied and left her sleeping. Apparently he had not been able to get a good meal anywhere, so had filled all his pockets with chocolate etc.

While Ted chatted with this kindly gentleman, I looked out of the window. We had now left the sand, and were entering the cultivated region of the Delta. Still there were never any fine, or even decent, houses, only the shocking one-room hovels, the filthy, flimsy sheds of the village by the Bitter Lake. The Egyptian natives lived in conditions literally as bad as those of pigs in England. Ted suggested that the natives were merely cattle for working the land. The civilian, with the most amiable smile, told us that the produce would go to swell the state of the landowner, who probably kept up a big Neo-European establishment in Cairo or Alexandria. But one didn't need telling. The contrast between the rich land and the starving peasants told its own story. An invisible parasite, worse than any liver-fluke, was eating them. Out of the misery and inhuman degradation of these creatures certain ingenious spirits were digging gold: many noble sentiments and noble fortunes, much light and laughter and luxury and power, was being squeezed out of them daily, for others to accumulate and enjoy. These withered wretches were the hosts from which the native vampire and the foreign one sucked their fill: this was the reverse of the Bankers' façade. And those who destroyed them, mocked them. They that wasted them, demanded of them a song. To their foul injury they added foul insult—trod them into the dung, then called them 'dirty Wogs': starved them till their ribs showed white, and their children's shins were no thicker than a stick of celery

—so that they *prayed* for even a crust—then 'all Wogs are beggars': kicked them till they flinched at a shadow—'shifty Wogs': robbed them till there was nothing but their breath to steal, then 'every Wog is a thief': and remember always —it is the glory of our civilisation—that it's all free contract and legitimate trading. There's no hint of slavery about it. A man doesn't *have* to work on the land for a piastre a day. He can always starve.

For the Delta is rich land; that's the blasphemy of it. The land which, four thousand years ago, cradled the civilisation of the western world, now supports on its face only a race of beings so fantastically impoverished that their life is but a hectic, unequal and losing struggle against poverty and disease. But oh, the subtle mechanism of exchange, which fosters, in that rich land, great towering weeds whose roots are invisible, but whose blossom is a fine house in Cairo, a couple of yachts on the Mediterranean, fifty or a hundred servants, half-a-dozen Rolls Royce cars, a five-figure bank balance, a racing stable, and credit all over the world.

The level fields of mud were covered with vivid green, like an English market garden in Spring, but brighter. All the plots were strictly rectangular. They were irrigated by shallow ditches, all running as square as the lines on a chessboard, so that the Egyptian countryside was like Looking-Glass Land. These ditches were constantly replenished with water drawn from a well by a chain of buckets, and the wheel over which the chain passed was driven by a horizontal wheel, pulled round by an ox yoked to a radiating pole. There was such a well at every furlong or so, with its ox moving steadily on its circular path, treading out its track, the wheels turning, and the buckets continually tipping muddy water into the irrigation system. A native or two might be encouraging the ox, or stooping at some field-work nearby. Every now and then one saw a camel, tall and ungainly but not out of place in this bright landscape, with the occasional shapes of palms above the fields.

At Ben Har we changed trains, and bought some eggs from a native. Soon after this the train rattled away with us, soon to take us far beyond the cries of 'Eggs-an'-bread', 'Ice-kald limonade' and the rest. As night fell we rattled towards Alexandria.

We were now on a troop train. Our compartment held six officers and a great deal of luggage. The men no longer had separate compartments, but were in the old, wooden-seated, full length coaches. I went through at one of the halts and joined them. They were hungry, but rations were not accessible, except for a case of biscuits and a large tin of marmalade. I forbade the opening of these: to have issued marmalade in the darkness would have been too horrid.

About midnight the train stopped, and from the total darkness around came a strong, hot, sweet smell of tea. We tumbled out, cramped and cold: a hot meal was ready for us. In a little shack set apart for officers there was a rich bully stew and a dixie of tea, together with all necessary plates, mugs and utensils. It was one of the most welcome meals I ever ate. The tea was very sweet. Half an hour sufficed to feed the train, and we moved on again.

For democratic reasons I decided to travel with the men, and had a very bad night: trying to sleep in the aisle between the seats, on kit bags, rifles, a case of biscuits, and my respirator for a pillow. There was no room anywhere: you could not stir a leg without kicking someone's face. The blackness was complete. There were men asleep under the seats, men asleep on the seats, and men asleep on each other. It grew cold: some of the men took out blankets from their bundles, others put on greatcoats. Too sullen to beg half a blanket, I steadily froze. Grey morning found me sitting high on the back of a seat, hands in pockets, too dispirited to light my pipe. The coach looked nightmarish in that first light, chockful of immobile, contorted figures. Young Shaw, curled like a kitten in someone else's blanket, alone seemed comfortable. Craddock was not in sight, having found a cubby-hole at the end of the coach, intended for the guard: there he lurked, secreting rations about his person.

The lads woke one by one, yelping with pain as they stretched their stiffened limbs, and coughing. They all lit cigarettes and coughed more. Somebody, in a voice of inexpressible mournfulness, began to sing

'When this bleeding war is over,
Oh how happy I shall be.
When I get my civvy clothes on
No more soldiering for me.
No more Church Parade on Sunday,
No more asking for a pass.
We will tell the Sergeant-Major
To stick his passes up his arse.'

'What about biscuits and marmalade, sir?' asked Shaw.
'Lash them out, then—you, Fitzjohn and Marshall'.

We were all completely sticky, and holding service biscuits running with viscous marmalade, when the train checked its speed and presently halted at the seaside resort on the desert's edge—Mersah Matruh.

Mersah at that time was a city without life. To walk through it, as I did in the afternoon, was an experience positively eerie. Tall white stucco buildings, villas, shops, offices, all were empty and blind—mere square holes instead of windows, never a voice from the hotels where holiday-makers had laughed and planned their days, never a step on the sidewalk. The transit camp, where we fed, and awaited the next train, was tented, and outside the town itself. I came into the town to visit one of the few inhabited buildings, the Officers' Shop. There I bought for 60 piastres a quilted sleeping-bag, and returned with it under my arm. One car passed me as I went back to the camp: otherwise, I had the sun-soaked town to myself. Its silence was terrible. Not a voice. Not a footfall. Behind all the white walls was mere emptiness. No sleepers ever lay in the bedrooms. No table was ever laid behind the windows. No summer-dressed shoppers ever crossed the wide white streets to buy swim-suits or cool drinks.

The smart shops had lost their windows: bombs had shattered them, and sand had silted into the corners and crevices. Many of the villas were riven and broken by bombs. White walls ended harshly in great jagged edges, showing the raw red brick under the plaster. Smashed plaster crumbled from walls of lath. But I had seen London, Coventry,

Plymouth and Hull. Mersah was battered, but I had seen as big an area, in the living heart of an English town, *laid flat*. It was not the bomb-scars; it was the dead silence of Mersah which filled me with quiet horror. Whenever in the future I think of what the war has done, one thing I shall remember is how it left Mersah standing dead, empty, and utterly silent —all gay voices, bright dresses and holiday laughter cancelled—on the desert's edge, by the sea.

We left Mersah in a long train of cattle-trucks. There were twenty officers on the train, and we travelled ten to a truck. The men were more crowded. We had been warned that these trains were very jerky, and took precautions. I spread my new sleeping-bag and made myself comfortable. The jerking was fantastic, but nobody was injured or flung out of the open space mid-way along the truck's sides. I had brought in a tin of jam from the rations, and both Ted and I had haversack rations from Mersah. These proved to be sardine sandwiches. We ate the sardines, and spread jam on the bread. The taste was horrible. All night we headed west. Despite the inconceivable jolting of the truck, I slept well in my sleeping-bag, and woke refreshed to a grey, dewy, cold desert dawn. In this dawn the train stopped. Around us was as blank a waste of sand as you could wish to see, with a couple of tiny tents and a derelict lorry, swallowed up in miles of desert. This was the transit camp at Fort Capuzzo.

A dreary place: we stayed two nights there. There was not enough tentage, and a sandstorm blew up and raged fiercely all the hours of daylight. Ted and I were reasonably snug, though the sand blew right in on us, and when we woke in the morning our eyes, ears and nostrils were full of sand. But the men were under odd flysheets and scraps of canvas, which the screaming wind sometimes plucked off the desert's face like an old dry piece of sticking-plaster. The yellow fog of dust was everywhere. We could not see more than a couple of yards ahead at the best, and had to tie handkerchiefs over our faces in order to breathe. We had little idea of direction, could only orient ourselves by the railway, and the tents were widely dispersed to avoid the attention of enemy planes. Even old inhabitants of the camp often lost their way. We made certain of the line between our tent and the Mess: that was the important communication. Then, when we had washed down sandy porridge with salty tea, we set out to find the men.

They were queuing, in the thick of the yellow dust-storm, for bully-stew, at an open-air cookhouse. We did not know whom to pity most, the cooks who made the stuff or the men who had it to eat. Later we visited all their improvised tents, and found them—ten men to a tent—lying side by side, sucking tinned beer and reading pornographic novelettes. All were grey with sand. They took it light-heartedly. Marlowe groused less the more reason he had. When we left the men, the wind was a hurricane, the sand was impenetrable, we could not find our way back to the Mess, and spent a couple of hours prowling in circles round the cookhouse.

The tea at Capuzzo was salty because the water was. Henceforth, from Capuzzo on into the desert, we had only salty water. The reason was that it was well water, and in the fighting between British and Axis forces in the whole of the desert forward of Mersah, the wells had continually changed hands. Each party, being driven back, had salted the wells in its area to inconvenience the enemy: and on readvancing, had found them double-salted by the enemy: so now it was a matter of drinking from the wells till all the salt water should be used up, probably a matter of years. This, at least, was the explanation I was given. The water now was rationed, too, though not so strictly as in the front line.

The sandstorm ceased completely when night fell, so Ted and I went for a starlight walk round the camp, and fell into an argument about the position of British agriculture after the war. During this discussion we lost our way again, and by using the stars as a guide, succeeded in returning five times to the cookhouse. It was after ten before we broke free of the cookhouse and got back to the Mess. There a captain joined us at the counter, and we stood each other gin-and-limes for some time. On the counter was a copy of Roger Martin du Gard's 'Les Thibaults' in an English translation. I wanted to take it away with me, but the P.M.C. objected, and the Mess corporal, who apparently was reading the book, became impertinent. It was a library book, and I proposed to take it away to the front line with me: no doubt the corporal concluded from this that I was drunk. He said the book was the property of the Y.M.C.A. library, and must be returned. I said that as I was going up the line, I stood the usual chances of not coming back, the library rules might be broken on this occasion, particularly as I was prepared to pay double the market price for the book, so that the Y.M.C.A. could buy two copies in Cairo to replace the one I wished to take. Further, I said pointedly, I could not help supposing that the intention of the Y.M.C.A. was at least *as much* to provide recreation for soldiers in the line as to benefit those in base and transit camps on the Egyptian side of the wire. This pronouncement of mine seemed to have a chilling effect on the Capuzzo Mess. Ted remarked with unnecessary clearness that he was going off to bed now, and looked at me. He said it again, and went. A major told me stiffly that the Y.M.C.A. library did in fact exist mainly for front line troops, as I had conjectured: and therefore, when I got into the line, I should find plenty of books there, which would be changed regularly: many more books than here at Capuzzo. Probably (he went on) that very book I was so eager to have was up with my unit at this moment. Capuzzo only had Y.M.C.A. books because the camp was well up towards the front. (Unnecessary to say that I never saw a Y.M.C.A. book, or any library book, from that day forward anywhere between Capuzzo and Tripoli.)

The discussion continued some time. I left at last, and found Ted outside the door, waiting to take me across to our tent. Undoubtedly he thought I was drunk. Perhaps I was.

With morning the sandstorm rose again. The blast was so sharp and rough, so heavy on the eyes, that I had to walk backwards to the latrine (which was to windward, and black with flies and greenbottles). In the yellow hell of the storm we crowded at midday all onto three-tonner lorries, and set off by road to Tobruk.

Between Capuzzo and Sollum we passed the graves of many soldiers, British and Italian. They were marked by neat wooden crosses. Out on the sand, whenever the wind dropped or opened a rift in the curtain of dust, we saw occasional burnt-out tanks, or derelict trucks: here and there a wrecked gun, probably Italian.

Immediately after Capuzzo we passed through the frontier wire, and were in Libya.

Chapter Twenty-Six

The day on the road was not unpleasant. By now we were all accustomed to travelling on top of piles of kit and warlike impedimenta: we passed the time with bawdy songs and similar matters. We sang 'The Hole in the Elephant's Bottom', 'Sweet Fanny Adams', 'Coming Home from the Wake', 'The Man that Did it the Last Time', 'Blaydon Races', etc. Just before dusk our driver told us he could not make Tobruk before nightfall. What should he do? The question concerned our stomachs. Tobruk was too near the front line to light up cookhouse fires at night. If we went on, therefore, we should not have a hot meal to finish the day. We needed a hot meal. I ordered the convoy off the road, and we 'laagered' in an area on the right. In the remaining hour of daylight we set to work cooking bully stew, tea, and biscuit porridge. We cooked in four-gallon petrol tins, over a petrol fire: each truck-load of men cooked for itself, and Ted and I went round to see everybody got something. Our own stew, containing three tins of potatoes and six of bully, was excellent between ten of us and the driver. The biscuit porridge contained condensed milk, and we had apricot jam with it. After the hot, sweet, luscious meal we all felt happy. I looked round almost with affection at the barren desert and the sinking sun. This had been a battlefield, as we could tell by the fragments of Italian grenades scattered around.

I put down my sleeping-bag, set up stakes and fastened my ground-sheet to them to keep out the sandy wind, removed my boots for the first time in three days, took everything off but my shirt, and wriggled down into the sleeping-bag, adjusting my body to correspond with the unevenness of the ground. Tired as I was, however, I could not sleep for a long time, but lay watching the Libyan stars, which after all were pretty much the same family as those of Cornwall. The Pole-star, of course, was nearer the northern horizon, but the Great Bear sprawled straight above me, brighter than ever. Since it was ten o'clock in Libya, I guessed it must be something like eight o'clock in England. So distant were the stars that in comparison I could not feel very far from Elizabeth. The Great Bear was over both of us. The subtended angle was too small for measurement. The light of those seven stars was falling simultaneously on me, and on the gleaming surface of the Loe Pool: on Tregonning and Tresowes, the hump of Castle Wary, the plateau of Sithney Common. At Porthleven the surge would be running along the harbour wall: the open sea would be splashing round Tye Rock: the long waves dying on the Loe Bar. Polpryn dark in its threefold valley. And there, in England, in Cornwall, was the one thing precious to me, and belonging to me, one human life that was as much mine as the life even now in my limbs. Dear, divine, beautiful flesh, lit by the divine mystery of life: sacred lamp of flesh, lit my life. Dear human hair and lips and eyes: heart-subduing loveliness of flesh, created flesh for me, for the incarnate hunger that was me.

The night was very cold. When I came out of my sleeping-bag at seven the next morning, my clothes, boots, socks, bedding and all were soaked in icy dew. We had a good breakfast, shaved miserably in a drop of dirty water saved from the bottom of some vessel, and packed our kit. Under my sleeping-bag I found a snake, which apparently had spent the night with me. Collinson wished to kill it, but I forbade. Collinson was now my batman, Wells having been left behind at Base.

Though we passed close to Tobruk, we did not enter the town. I was disappointed to pass so epic a spot without seeing it. About midday we reached a tiny transit camp which had no name that I can recall, but a number; which I forget. The Commanding Officer of this camp appeared to be a lance-corporal. It was all very strange. Our transport left us here, and we, who had long since given up all attempts to comprehend the organisation which was bearing us west, watched the departure of our three-tonners with indifference, and cooked a bully stew. Our water ration was getting low, and the little camp did not seem to have any. There were rumours of a bulk NAAFI just round the corner, but as there was nothing but undulating desert, and no corners at all, for many miles in every direction, we did not try to find the place. We were all very tired and very dirty, and the noon sun was very hot. We took off shirts and boots and lay in the sun, thinking of quart flagons of cider.

Half way through the afternoon came a couple of R.A.S.C. trucks to take us to our unit—the final stage in our journey to the war in the desert. We gathered we should go up to B echelon, which was five or six miles behind the front line, and would remain there till transport was available to take us into the line itself. We moved off, and henceforth travelled, not by road, but by desert tracks. These tracks run straight across the desert, since there never were any obstacles to make them wind. A track is usually a wide ribbon of tyre marks, sometimes a quarter of a mile in breadth. Originally most of these tracks were trodden out by Arab caravans with camels, and where they intersected, a roundabout was marked out with cairns. The general times of the regular caravans being known to each other, I suppose it would be common for parties to meet at these cross-roads, or Rotundas, and exchange merchandise and news.

My imagination suggests (perhaps inaccurately) scenes of drinking, bargaining, chatter, greetings, interchange of correspondence, and goodbyes, before we came along. Now there were no more camels at the rotundas, only dusty military vehicles that bounced and jarred along the tracks, and took their individual directions where the ways met. The tracks were not smooth. The passage of many vehicles over sand scores it and ridges it, till progress is a continual slithering and jarring in and out of other people's tracks. In addition, the desert is stony country, hard on the springs of vehicles. Since the centre of the track soon wears down to stone, and becomes intolerable for driving, vehicles tend to be always making new tracks for themselves along the outer edges of the existing tracks. Hence the prodigious width of the main desert tracks. In appearance such a track is like a hundred sandy, deep-rutted cart-tracks laid side by side—all the ruts criss-crossing. It runs straight across the desert, linking the two horizons. It has no single building on it, nor on the whole expanse of the desert is there ever to be seen so much as a house, a hut, a post, a pillar, a tree or a bush: but scattered here and there in the remote spaces are primitive forts made of rocks, like those in Foreign Legion romances: and 'Birs', wells made years, centuries ago by the nomadic Arabs, and usually to be seen from a good distance because of the great pyramid of spoil, dug out of the well-shaft, which marks each one.

We were a long time scudding across the desert. We had left the Lance-Corporal's Command at three o'clock in the afternoon, after a bully-stew which was quite inadequate, and we were still bouncing and chasing each other's tails along the tracks when the sun began to drop in the clear west. Ah, bitter chill it was. The keen desert wind, added to the speed of our trucks, got its teeth into us: we were jolted, jarred, and thrown wickedly about amid countless hard objects with sharp corners. I was on a side-board of the open truck, my legs buried in kit bags, rifles and respirators. Without serious risk I could not release my grip on an iron canopy-strut, which I could only reach with my left hand.

Marlowe was among the men on my truck: he kept up all our spirits with his humorous grumbling and agonised expression when the truck bounced. At last, however, we lost our resilience, became too tired, cold and uncomfortable to laugh any more. We hung inertly on our perches, occasionally soaring, to fall again with a helpless thump. We were very hungry.

My peaked cap flew off when we went over one of the bumps: this caused Marlowe great amusement, which spread to the rest of the truck. I joined in the laughter with as much heartiness as I could, but it was hard to find unmixed pleasure in the sight of a two-guinea Bond Street felt going under the wheels of the truck behind. I was annoyed at my own lack of resolution in not stopping the truck. Secretly I found I had enjoyed wearing that cap. I liked the spurious dignity it gave me. It had helped to elevate me above criticism. I was fond of the Regimental Badge, of the shiny but not assertive chin-strap, of the soft thick felt. As Marlowe said in a remorseful moment between laughs, 'it's a pity, it suited you sir'. I took my glengarry out of my pocket and sadly stuck it on the side of my head. Really it was more comfortable, and no doubt I looked as well in it: but a certain military distinction, importance,—even romance— was left battered in the desert. Peace to the camel-driving nomad who finds it.

Night closed down on the desert. The dusk deepened, second by second, and still there was nothing around us but blank, stony waste. The drivers kept confidently on; the sun at last dropped below the edge of the wilderness, and the shadow from the east advanced with a great stride. Within half an hour it became impossible for me to see that we were following a track. No lights were shown. I had distressing anticipations of a night in open trucks, cruising desperately about the desert in search of our destination.

Just as the night grew really black, our trucks halted, and we climbed down, cramped and hungry, outside a solitary tiny tent. This was the officers' mess at B echelon.

A captain-quartermaster took Ted and me into the tent, while the men were marched off to a cookhouse which was said to be somewhere in the surrounding blackness.

It was not the end of the journey, but it was the end of the day's travelling. We still had a mile or so to cover before we reached the front. But here we were back in our own regiment again, the accent of the captain in the tiny mess was our own county brogue, the badge on his cap was ours. It was a kind of home coming. It was not the indifferent promiscuity of Base.

The only thing I recall of our journey, next day, to the front line, is a halt at an immense track-junction in the desert, and reading on a signboard the startling name KNIGHTSBRIDGE. Later I found that the Libyan desert had its Piccadilly, its Oxford Circus, its Leicester Square and its Hyde Park Corner—most of them lonely, cairn-marked cross-roads where no traffic ever roared except the occasional dusty desert truck. Their silence and their immense loneliness gave tragedy to the dear homely names they bore:

'So the lights, the London lights grow near and plain
—So I rowel 'em afresh towards the Devil and the flesh
Till I bring my broken rankers home again.'

Imagine:—A single wooden signboard with crude lettering, PICCADILLY CIRCUS: and nothing else at all—
round the grooved wheel-ruts, round the up-ended barrel
or the dozen cairns of brown stones that mark the place, the
lone and level sands stretch far away. You stand by your
truck, in the shadow of the sign-board, and you are wrapped
entirely in the everlasting silence of the sands. Piccadilly
Circus. Not a movement anywhere under the blue bowl of
the sky. The bare brown desert is still and empty, to the
horizon.

Chapter Twenty-Seven

We were front line troops. Two misconceptions may arise from this statement. The first concerns the word 'front': the second, the word 'line'.

My Company, which was B Coy., occupied the rear of the Battalion position, and faced back towards Egypt. Thus, though the battalion was in the front line, I was in the rear of the battalion.

The line was not a line in the Maginot-Siegfried sense. It was not a system of fortifications. It was simply a long strip of desert running sixty miles south from the coast at A——G, a strip of varying width, from a hundred yards to a couple of miles. This strip was surrounded by a trip-wire, nine inches from the ground. The ground inside the wire was sown with mines. That sixty-mile minefield was the only thing that could be called a front line.

Down the 'home' side of the minefield were the front line units, looking out across the mines to the West, the enemy's country. On the enemy side of the minefield was about fifteen miles of empty desert—corresponding to 'No Man's Land'—and beyond that, the German and Italian divisions.

Apart from the minefield, the only things between us and the enemy were patrols, out in 'No Man's Land': armoured car patrols, and one or two standing patrols of infantry. Our job was, if attacked, to defend the minefield with fire, prevent Jerry's engineers from lifting the mines and making gaps for his tanks: and to hold our positions till our mobile-armoured forces in the rear could see where they were most needed in support.

The lay-out of the battalion was roughly triangular: two companies forward—west—protected the minefield, one company, my own, being in the rear—east—to contain any attack from behind, should Jerry break through the minefield elsewhere and attack us from the East.

This was simple; but the Engineers soon made it more complicated by laying minefields to the East as well as to the West: so that before I had been there a week, a brand-new minefield encircled our company front, and when we talked about minefields, we had to distinguish carefully between the one in the front and the one in the rear. This process went on all along the line, till the front line brigades were all enclosed in minefields to the right of them, minefields to the left of them, minefields behind them and minefields in front of them. The desert became explosive: driving one's truck was a nervous effort.

The desert in our area was very flat. The few hummocks there were never rose more than twenty feet from the surrounding sand. Occasionally a low escarpment ran across the desert, marking the edge between two levels which only differed by a few feet. My platoon was on such an escarpment, a slightly swelling fold of rock and sand, which allowed us to look across five or six miles of flat. There, since we were looking East, we could detect vehicles approaching from the back areas, signalled by the yellow-headed snake of sand their wheels flung into the air, and which followed their course like the pillar of cloud by day: in the desert, long before any vehicle was visible you saw the plume of sand snaking up, thick and dense at the head, thinning off through light smoke to nothing at the tail. When you saw a number of these smoke-clouds crawling across the distance, you knew that a column or convoy was on the move.

The three sections of my platoon occupied three corners of a square, which was completed by Platoon H.Q. The forward sections faced East, directly across the new minefield, which was only a few feet away. Each morning the sun came up beyond the minefield, beyond Egypt and Suez. By nine o'clock the day's heat was on us, but work did not become onerous till noon, when the sun scorched down from overhead. Then we stripped off shirts and dug, picked, and hammered at our rocky slit trenches, the sweat smarting on our foreheads. The battalion had only just moved to this position before I came, and all digging was still to be done.

After four o'clock in the afternoon the sun began to lose

its fierceness, dropping over to the West beyond Battalion H.Q. and finally we saw it go down beyond the main minefield, beyond the enemy's country, beyond the Jebel and Tripoli.

There were four of us in Platoon H.Q.: myself, Phillimore (my platoon sergeant), Collinson (batman) and Shaw (runner). Our life was very simple and very arduous, but not unpleasant or monotonous. Phillimore was far and away the best sergeant I ever had. I liked working with him, had great trust in him. We slogged away at the digging, and at last had a very respectable platoon position. Most of the men, however, had been out in the desert a year or more, and felt bitter. Some time or other, apparently, they had got hold of a copy of a newspaper from home in which was printed a letter from a soldier stationed in the North of England, complaining of his conditions, distance from home, infrequency of leave, etc. This letter formed the subject of a great deal of sardonic humour and imitation. The men would sit round their breakfast dixies, looking glumly at the empty sky and the empty land: then one would say 'Dear Mr. Editor, I am stationed five miles from the nearest town, and can only go to the cinema on Tuesdays and Fridays. I only get leave every three months, apart from week-end leave, which doesn't count. If I want a drink of beer in the evening, I have to walk a quarter of a mile to the nearest pub., which is very hard when a man has spent the day blancoing his anklets web. We sleep in a village hall with a wooden floor, with nothing under us but a mattress, and nothing over us but blankets, and nothing but a pillow to put our heads on. Dear Mr. Editor, is it not f——g 'ard?'

One did not hope to escape enemy observations in the desert. Every morning at about half-past ten the enemy sent over a Dornier recce plane with a couple of fighters escorting, to have a look at our positions and take a few photographs. Certainly the German G.H.Q. was taking as deep an interest in the development of our defences as we were ourselves. If the Dornier came impudently low, as he did sometimes, our Bofors guns would go into action, but I never saw him hit. Undoubtedly we were correctly pinpointed on the German maps. But that did not mean that concealment had lost its value. It was one thing for their H.Q. to have mapped us; another for their troops to see us when they attacked. As we dug in, we gradually disappeared: vanished completely from the desert's face. Henceforth he could find us on the map, but he would have to look very hard to find us on the ground. When I first joined the battalion, it had just moved in, and was all on the surface. We pitched our bivouacs at night like ordinary tents. The digging began. Every day there was less of us on the surface, more underneath. The first task was to dig pits from which the Bren guns could be fired, and a narrow slit trench for every two riflemen. When these fighting positions were complete, we went on to dig 'bivvy-holes', in which we lived and slept. These holes, usually six feet square, went as deep as the digger's patience; probably four feet: and the bivouac-sheets were stretched flat over the top and camouflaged with nets and sand.

By some luck and some management I sited my own bivvy-hole in good digging, and went down more than six feet. When finished, it was a neat dug-out. The walls were smooth, cut out of a kind of soft sandstone, as soft as cheese. There was a level floor, and a raised shelf of earth running the full length of the dug-out, which was my bed. I built into each wall a box, with the open side facing inwards, and thus obtained cupboard space, and also let into each wall the bottom of a four-gallon petrol tin, to act as reflectors for candles. Taut wires braced to two iron pickets formed the supporting network for the roof, which was made of ground-sheets laid flat and sanded over. But for the steps which led straight down into the earth, the dug-out was quite invisible: and though I burned six candles at once, to get a brilliant light for censoring letters at night, not a trace of light could be seen from the surface of the desert.

The dug-out was my luxurious retreat. I had no books there, and did not miss them. If I was not too busy to read, I was too tired. But most afternoons, when it was too hot to work, I was able to get underground for half an hour, and lie stretched in calm, weary bliss on my sleeping-bag in the cool half-darkness. A photograph of Elizabeth was clipped in a cheap frame in a little recess by my head. My food cupboard was stored with tins of pineapple and peaches, bars of chocolate, a tin of condensed milk, coffee, sugar, tea, a tin of Nadler's fruit drops, a bottle of grapefruit syrup, and a bottle of White Horse whisky. Such a store fostered contentment.

Each section position, and particularly the position of Platoon H.Q., was a warren of underground dens and holes for stores. Everything went below the surface. Returning from other parts of the Company area to my platoon, I had no visible sign to guide me, unless any of the men were working up on top.

Shaw and Collinson shared a bivvy-hole, Sergeant Phillimore and I had one apiece. Shaw altered for the better whilst he was in the desert, partly because there were no temptations. He remained always a grumbler and a scrounger, but there were good qualities as well. Towards me he showed gratitude mixed with scorn. He thought me simple.

He and Collinson did not like each other. Often after I had gone to bed I would hear them quarrelling and arguing in their bivvy before going to sleep. Shaw said Collinson was greedy and wouldn't muck in. Collinson said Shaw was just a schoolkid—'He'll never soldier.' George Collinson was a decent batman, but lazy: and he had a superior air, a trick of silently disapproving my suggestions, which irritated me.

Spring in the desert was a loathsome season. It was bone dry and windy. Sometimes we had a clear morning, but the afternoon generally brought heat, wind and dust—the Kham-sihn. Not sand: sand is clean stuff found on seashores. Deserts are not made of that, but of dust which cakes with moisture: it gets in your ears and eye-corners, and chokes up your nostrils with a permanent lining. A desert gale could be seen approaching from miles away—not the tall thin columns of sandspouts which the heat produced, which stalked waveringly about the desert, drawing up the dust in a graceful spiral that leaned and curved up to the sky and there dispersed, but a great sullen purple bank which first lay low on the horizon, and gradually rose till it covered half the sky and threatened the sun with its fringes, while its slaty sombre shadow tinged every tent and every eye. Then Collinson would dash quickly round platoon H.Q., making my bivvy-sheets fast and as sand proof as possible, and putting everything under cover, and Phillimore would wrap up his rifle and the Very Light pistol, watching the cloud warily: in the cookhouse the cooks would cover water and all open foods. The flies now would bite worse than usual: in the minute or two before the storm burst they would bite like hell, and return to the same bite with wolfish persistence.

Then the sound of the storm, coming over the desert, a thin, sustained, distant scream. It would rapidly increase in loudness: the cloud would mount up to the zenith, its metallic edge would cut off the sun, switch off the light. The desert now lead grey and dim, from edge to edge. 'She's here, boys'. Away to our front, a tent, not fully dug in, would flap sharply and fill like a sail: then the storm would be on us, and down we would plunge into our bivvies out of the dark, cold, stinging sand-blast (surprising how cold the sand-cloud was. After the scorching sun we would suddenly be shivering in a dark, chill gale).

Such a storm often did not last long. Much more exasperating were the merely windy days, the restless days when there was always a fog of yellow dust hiding every section-post, dust in our hair, our food, our blankets, our water, our weapons. There was no keeping it out. When, in Mess, we had a dish of marmalade on the table, even though we kept it covered except when we were using it, it was soon completely coated with dust. Dust blew into every bivvy-hole, all the time. Maps, letters and papers, lying on shelves, vanished under a smooth layer of dust. Although each day I turned my sleeping-bag inside out, I always slept in dust. It caked to the body, and as our personal issue of water was only a pint and a half per man per day (the remainder of our six pints per head went into the cookhouse), you could not have a bath. But occasionally we got some impure water from one of the local Birs, sometimes as much as a gallon per man. It was not fit to drink, and generally contained a lot of rabbit-dung, but after filtering it was good enough for a stand-up bath, and then for washing clothes. We made percolators of very tiny stones in a petrol-tin, and when we had any well-water in Platoon H.Q., the four of us pooled our ration and bathed in turn, filtering it through the perco-lator when necessary.

One learned to live on human terms, with human beings. Whether he likes it or not, a platoon commander, like a teacher, is *in loco parentis*. It is humanising. Even such inti-mate matters as excretion and urination were quite com-munal: there was only one latrine per platoon. It was a simple wooden box set over a deep hole in the ground, with a suitable hole in the seat, and a lid. If any man in the platoon developed crabs, it was obviously a matter of immed-iate significance to all his fellows who had to use the same latrine. We were living so much together that we had to be intimately aware of each other.

Remembering the latrine at Capuzzo and its flies, I did the essential work on our latrine myself, sealed the excavation with oiled sacking, stopping up all interstices in the wood-work, and fitted a fly-excluding lid. In the after breakfast period there was a steady procession (in which I took my turn) to and from it, and the man in occupation could be seen from half a mile away, seated on the square box, solitary on the desert's barren face, and holding in one hand a sheet of newspaper, or an old letter.

You love yourself and your fellow-man better when you are constantly reminded, by proximity, that you and he are subject to the same necessities. Bowels are as much our com-mon heritage as hearts.

It was the universality of this process that made us more human to each other. We lived so very much under each other's eyes; our lives were common property. Similarities and the dropping of protective reserve endeared man to man. So many of our old, complicated, sophisticated reactions were not needed, and fell away. We talked to each other with the understanding frankness of some children. And we did not talk much. There was no chattering. Our lives were steady and taciturn, like those of farm workers. The only man who talked a lot was Marlowe, who could generally be found, work over, standing or sitting with his pipe in his hand, a sardonic grin on his face, pulling the government to pieces, or criticising the administration of the battalion.

I liked Marlowe. He was his own enemy. There was no man grumbled more, and no man worked harder. He was absolutely dependable and faithful. In everything but his talk he was a saint.

God, when I recall my good intentions and my ineptitude! The foolish oversights, mistakes and miscalculations, which innate stupidity combined with inexperience led me into. The men, simple and generous, credited me with my intentions as well as my achievements. They trusted me: but whom else had they to trust? I did not always deserve their confidence. I made certain serious mistakes. I was not always even honest with the men.

One special task of all the front line units was to patrol the desert on the enemy side of the minefield. Each platoon spent about one day and night each week 'in front of the wire', contacting other patrols, and looking for signs of enemy activity. Even on patrol, one knew that there was still an armoured car screen between oneself and the enemy, so it was not very anxious work. There was just the odd chance that we *might* strike a German patrol, but we bristled with tommy-guns, Brens, rifles and grenades: and I never felt so nervous as to go without sleep. Patrols were popular with the men: there was just enough uncertainty and risk about them to make them attractive; scudding about the desert in a truck was a pleasant change from routine work in the company area: and there was an element of picnic about the tea, bully stew and sausages which we cooked for ourselves in the desert: and again, we were off on our own, not under the inspecting eyes of our superiors. We all felt the relief of being entirely responsible for our own movements, 'masters of our fate'. We slept on desert sand in our dug-outs, therefore it was no hardship to sleep out on desert sand elsewhere. Wrapped in blanket and greatcoat, under the cold desert stars, with three light machine-guns and six sentries guarding you round, you could sleep well. My only trouble was avoiding minefields—their arms reached out in unexpected directions, and the old minefields, out in the remote spaces, where nobody seemed to worry very much about maintaining the trip-wire, could be nerve-shattering.

Out in the desert, one relied entirely on compass bearings and Trig points for direction. The desert was a web of tracks, but they might be anybody's. They were highly treacherous. I never was lost in the desert, but once I thought I was, with all my platoon. It was a sickly sensation.

I liked to take the wheel myself when out on patrol, but the men on the truck did not like my driving, and in deference to them I only took over if the driver was tired, or not keeping on his bearing. My own sense of direction was very poor, but I could be mathematically correct with a compass, and was scrupulous in checking direction every few minutes: so I could generally get dead on to an objective when necessary. My principal trouble was that I was a little short-sighted, and when driving fast in the desert I would often fail to gauge correctly the heights of the ridges, bumps, depressions and boulders I had to pass over. Hence I often took rough country much too fast, and shook the men up. A much more alarming consequence of my myopia was that once or twice I almost took a truck over the trip-wire into a minefield.

The men's great weakness on night patrol was smoking. It was an idiocy which needed ruthless elimination. Curious that men who would have laughed if you had called them heroic—who wouldn't touch a scorpion, and were scared of desert lizards—should yet insist on lighting their 'Camel' brand cigarettes even under the enemy's nostrils.

I enjoyed patrols, and enjoyed commanding my men in the desert, knowing that we were doing a real job. We were the listening-line, the eyes and ears of the Middle East. We mattered. I was happier lying out in the desert, among men I trusted, than I ever had been on our schemes and exercises in England: even though I had no comfortable billet, no village, no pub, no Polpryn, to return to when the patrol was over. It was real; I was in the war, not watching from the side. I saw my life in perspective, a perspective that was due entirely to my journey, and the distance from home, and the German lines to the West. I knew that I should return to Elizabeth a better man, because of this. I should take back a heart that had grown up, was more at ease, kinder, and stronger. The clear unveiled light of the Libyan stars and the moon seemed then, and still seems, to have shone into my soul.

Chapter Twenty-Eight

'**B**ut what actually *are* they, sir?' asked Shaw, gazing up through his glasses (which I made him wear) at the brilliant sky, which was absolutely crowded with stars, shining much brighter and clearer than in England. I believe he had never really noticed them before.

'Mainly, suns', I said: 'very large globes, much bigger than the earth, and so hot that most of the metal in them is either permanently liquid, or a gas. But some of them are cool like the earth or the moon.'

This confused him. 'I don't understand that, sir.'

'Well—hm. Let's get the first things right. Sizes of things. If the moon were as big as a pea, the earth would be a marble, the sun a barrel.'

'What *is* the sun?'

'Er: well, a ball of fire. It's composed of the same things as the earth, but all blazing hot.'

'And bigger than the earth?'

'Oh yes, much. I dunno—say, a half-million times as big.'

'Phew!'

'And the earth—which is ninety million miles away from the sun—moves round it, in a great circle. It takes $365\frac{1}{4}$ days to get round, and we call that a year.'

He looked at me, fascinated: suddenly struck by the wonder of it, and without words to express himself.

'Does the moon go round the sun as well?'

'Well—yes, with the earth: because the moon is much smaller, and goes round the earth just as the earth goes round the sun. But it only takes a month.'

'I see. A month is a moon's year—sort of.'

'Yes. That's true. Well now: some of these stars we can see (but not many) are other earths, like our own, but perhaps bigger or smaller, and like us they are going round the sun. There's one, that bright one near the horizon:

that's Venus, and it is much nearer to the sun than we are. It goes round in quite a small circle. There are others, too, nine or ten of them, which we can't see now, and anyway I don't know them. They all have their own paths round the sun, and if they are much further away than we are, it takes them much longer to get round. One of their years may be a hundred or a thousand of ours.'

'It's—wonderful.'

'Um, I think so, too.'

'Does anyone live on the ones that go round the sun?'

'So far no telescope has been built with sufficient power to look closely at the surfaces of the planets, or even the moon, which is quite close by comparison. And the general opinion seems to be that life, as we know it, is only possible under very special conditions of climate and atmosphere and light and one thing or another, and there's no reason to suppose that those conditions exist anywhere except on earth. It's possible, so far as we know, that this tiny earth is the one spot in the whole universe where there is life. Outside us, for ever and ever in every possible direction, nothing alive at all. . . .We—the animals and fishes and insects and men—may well be the only living things: the only life there is, anywhere and everywhere. And we shall never carry life out to the stars, because we can only live on the earth.'

'By Christ, sir—I dunno, I can't hardly believe—can't hardly understand it—it's *too big.*'

'It's bigger than that, Frank. The stars you can see now—not the planets, the stars themselves—are some of them thousands of times bigger than the sun: bigger even maybe than the furthest circle which the sun's outermost planets make in travelling round him. Yet they are so far away that to us they are pin-points of light. Do you know how fast light travels?'

'No.'

'It goes a hundred and eighty-six thousand miles in a second. And yet some of those stars are so far away that their light takes, not minutes or hours or even days, but thousands of years to reach us. The light by which you see one of those stars, left that star before Julius Caesar was born, before

Christ was crucified, before the pyramids were built'.

Shaw was rapt. 'Nobody's ever told me such things. I could listen to things like that for ever.'

★

One thing about our life in the desert, we were always aware of the unhealed raw end of the life in England from which we had been torn. The immediate task took our attention, but behind it was the sense of something unfinished, unresolved, hung up and waiting to be carried on. It is such a raw end to a part of life, that parting on a noisy railway platform, the dwindling shapes in the distance, the agonised waving, the last hurried letter. Death probably comes just the same way, all hurry and broken threads and agonised stretching of hearts over the ineluctable gap. The last remaining thing of all must be the wish that it were not so, the bursting wish to continue relationships. So I longed for a letter from Elizabeth, and lived a life of solid immediate satisfaction in my desert work, with always a fluttering submerged uneasiness. Every time the mail was brought up to the platoon, my heart shook me with its thumping. Every time came bitter disappointment. Elizabeth's photo, when letters did not come, was a mute, hurtful, inscrutable thing. 'Oh Elizabeth, write to me.' And the photo looked back at me with the inward smile I loved so much.

I knew she had written, probably every day. I knew it well enough. That made it worse: the words she had written for my eyes, could not reach them. Some of the men had had their first letters from home. I could see how it made them more settled and content with our strange desert life, to be in touch with home, and to read words written back there, at the old table, in the old room. What it meant!

Collinson and Shaw began to write a book, but never got further than the following first two paragraphs—

THE DESERT RATS.

' "Stand to" roared the sergeant in a voice like a rusty foghorn, as he tumbled out of his bivvy at a quarter past five in the morning.

' The Desert Rats cringed at the sound, rolled themselves tighter in their blankets, and dug in their heads for the last few seconds of sleep. Down below the surface, they lay coiled in their dug-outs like rats in their holes. The sergeant coughed to clear the fog from his throat, and bawled out again. "Wakey wakey: Tumble out, now, sharp. Stand-to." The sun had not yet risen, and the dark, bleak, bare desert was soaked in dew and fog. The bivvy flaps were wringing wet.'

A fair enough description of the beginning of a day. Meanwhile, as Phillimore's voice retreated to the sections, I would be sitting up on my sleeping-bag, weary and creased with insufficient sleep, looking miserably at my feet by the candle-light, poking caked sand from between my toes, and sniffing at my fingers. The sweat of bed clung to me, but the clammy coldness of morning struck through it. I felt smelly, through sleeping in my shirt: wanted to wash my hands, and face, and neck, and knew that I had only half a cup of water; and I craved a good shave. The air was bitterly cold, raw, and damp. I pulled on damp socks, hard with sweat: underpants: my trousers, cold and too familiar, but not dewy. Then knocked out my boots upside down, in case there was a scorpion inside. Unclean clothes round an unwashed body. No freshness. My greatcoat hung on its peg with all my web equipment still attached: I put it on, jammed my steel helmet on my head, and plunged out of my dug-out, up the steep steps, out onto the uninviting desert.

The men clambering into their trenches: every weapon theoretically ready to go off at a touch: a full magazine on the anti-tank rifle: the mortar-bombs laid out ready. The platoon is standing to.

At seven o'clock in the morning, after some Physical Training, an inspection of arms, and a muddy wash and shave, we had breakfast. I always combined shaving and washing: lathered first, shaved, then covered all the area of my face, ears and neck with the shaving brush—a shaving brush wash. Breakfast was usually tinned sausage or tinned bacon, with service biscuits: porridge on lucky days: and always a delicious pint of tea.

'Tasting of Fauna and an onion stew,
Sand and Egyptian salt and sunburnt earth.'

The biscuits were very good fried in bacon fat.

After breakfast, work: digging or training. I preferred the digging because you could see results, and it might be useful. Training throughout the British Army, generally struck me as elaborate preparation for improbable contingencies. No more till midday, when the sun was overhead and frying us: too hot to eat. We had tiffin, probably a biscuit with margarine (liquid) and jam, and another pint of tea. We felt empty, not hungry. The tea was the great thing. One thought of strawberries and cream, and cider.

If the afternoon were very hot, we generally had a siesta from tiffin till four o'clock: we went below into our bivvies out of the sun. Too hot to sleep, but it was pleasant to lie naked and sweat in peace—if you could endure the flies. I was able to exclude the flies from my bivvy with the blackout curtain. Work began again at four, and continued till dinner at seven: a stew, followed often by rice pudding: no tea! Evening stand-to was from eight-thirty to nine-thirty in the summer: after which, said the men, the remainder of the day would be observed as a holiday: unless you were on guard, patrol, or whatnot.

The most interesting event of each week was the arrival of the Naafi goods. Of course, there was no other shop of any kind, except Y.M.C.A. travelling shop, which came round once. You could buy tinned fruit, chocolate, whisky, one tin of beer, and a few other things from the Naafi. Tinned pineapple was the favourite. In platoon H.Q. we had the following arrangement: I bought a dozen tins of pineapple each week, while Phillimore, Shaw and Collinson bought four tins each: thus we had two dozen tins between us, which we pooled, and ate three per day: pleasant feasts, the four of us sitting like schoolboys in my bivvy, eating out of tins. I usually drank a bottle of whisky each week.

In my bivvy also we used to make tea, whenever I could get tea, sugar and milk from the Naafi: water, of course, was a great difficulty: we used to contribute half a pint each from our water bottles: George would brew up over a petrol fire. Once he set the bivvy on fire, but we extinguished it before much damage was done. Another time, when he crouched over the brewcan, he felt a tickling on his knee, put his hand down, felt something biggish, looked—a spider about as big as a mouse, hairless and flabby, with thick, jointy legs.

There were a few disagreeable insects in the desert—scorpions, spiders, and ticks. The scorpions were either yellow or black, the yellow one rather like a small lobster: it had a long, jointed tail, perhaps two inches long and a quarter of an inch thick. The ticks were about as big as a bedbug, very hard, and very quick: sometimes one of them would get on to one of the men, and bore in under his skin. If the creature once got all its body under, sepsis and an unpleasant sore would follow: but if the tick had only got his head in, it was often possible to make him change his mind by means of a hot cigarette-end.

There was also an insect which none of us ever saw, but all heard every day. We called it the 'Man on the bicycle'. It free-wheeled round us with a measured, metallic tick, all through the hottest part of the day. Presumably it was some small winged insect, perhaps a beetle. Though it could be heard quite plainly, and seemed to pass only a foot or so away, we never were able to see it.

I never saw another snake in the desert, but there were many lizards, some over two feet long, and all quite harmless.

As the weeks went on, the concealment of our positions reached something near perfection. Where iron pickets had to be driven into the ground, we 'vanished' them by painting with oil, then sanding: or a sprig of scrub was wired onto them. Every bivouac was at last level with the surface. Corporal Willis, of No. 5 Section, so obliterated every sign of his tent that one evening, strolling round the section positions, I walked in on him, clean through the roof. He was drinking a tin of beer when I came down on him. 'What the bleedin' 'ell——?'

Still no letters for me. Not one. Collinson had two. Frank Shaw had one from his mother.

George Collinson hated washing clothes. He found so many good reasons for not washing out my shirts that I wore the same shirt for three weeks. At last I gave him a direct order: 'You will wash my shirts, shorts and socks before 1600 hours. You will report to me at that time with the laundry.'

At 1600 hours, he came to me, carrying a petrol-tin which contained all the garments, soaked in muddy water.

'What's this? They should be dry by now.'

'You can't get 'em clean in one washing, sir. They've got to steep first to loosen the dirt.'

'But I want to wear the bloody things.'

'Well, sir, if you don't want me to do the job right. . . .'

'How long are you going to steep 'em?'

'Take two days, sir.'

'Listen, George. Get the soap out of my bivvy, and start dhobying now. Let me see you start.'

I got my way.

Frank Shaw by now had altered quite perceptibly from the lad he was in England. He would still scrounge, and seek reasons for avoiding work: but by contrast there were times when he gave of his best, and dug or shovelled as long, as hard and as doggedly as anyone in the platoon. He developed an unexpected reliability as a runner, was nearly always at hand, and could take a message to the right place in the shortest time. He seemed to have a silent admiration and awe for Phillimore—a tough resolute character. Phillimore, though always a rigid disciplinarian, was gentle in his firmness, tolerant: particularly so with Frank Shaw. Shaw said to me one day:

'You swear a lot more these days than you used to do on the ship, sir?'

'Do I? I daresay I do. The desert alters all of us.'

'Um.'

'You think I swear too much?'

He nodded thoughtfully. 'Yes, sir.'

This was an unusual and welcome gravity.

In May we began battalion training, but no night operations, since there had been a couple of accidents lately on the minefields at night. The minefields were treacherous,

264

even if you knew the area well. One night, returning on foot from Company H.Q., I walked in the darkness right through my platoon area, crossed the trip-wire without touching it, and only realised by falling over a cairn that I was in the middle of a minefield across my platoon front. I was very badly shaken, and came off the field on my hands and knees, guided by my compass. All the fields in the battalion area were sown with Egyptian mines, which were said to explode under 120 lbs., but they were unreliable: men laying them had been killed merely by a hand's weight on an armed mine. In the field near my platoon there were seven rows of mines, each ten feet apart, so that the chances of detonating one were not really high for a man on foot.

Chapter Twenty-Nine

There came an order cancelling all training till further notice. Ten German tanks had been reported, moving from Segnali to cut the Trigh-el-Abd between Mteifel and Cherima. Burgess, our company commander, instructed platoon commanders to turn all available men on the completion of defences—'Battle—lats, section stores, guide-wires for riflemen—everything must be done now, down to the last detail.'

The Colonel came round two days later, inspecting defences, and was followed by the Brigadier. The Corps Commander's car was seen dashing in and out of D. Company's gap in the main minefield. In short 'there was a flap on.'

'There'll be more sandbags this afternoon' said Burgess, 'and new picks and shovels (if they come!) to replace the useless ones. The R.S.M. has some reserve ammo, including sticky-bombs and Ity grenades, which he's going to issue down to companies. I'll give you details as soon as I can, so that you can allocate in advance down to sections. . . . .'

I passed all the news on to Willis, Drake and King, my N.C.O.'s, who took in the main an academic interest: and to Phillimore, who was more realistic. Everybody was pleased that training had been cancelled, and nobody lost any sleep over ten Jerry tanks. At the end of a week, situation reports gave no further indication of enemy movement, and there were whispers that training would soon be resumed. The perennial rumour that the battalion was to be recalled to Alexandria for a rest also re-appeared.

Then a report came in, announcing movement forward of Cherima and Segnali of five hundred enemy vehicles and ninety tanks: and this was immediately followed by a warning order from Eighth Army H.Q. that a full scale German attack was expected in the near future, most probably on the 28th of May, which was full moon. Further, naval observation gave the impression that the attack would include an assault on Tobruk from the sea, and mass parachute landings in rear areas. It was not anticipated that a frontal attack would be made on the main minefield: there were three possibilities: (a) that the enemy would try to break through near the coast at Gazala. (b) That he would try to turn the south end of the field, by going right round Hacheim. (c) That he would try to break through the centre gap.

The centre gap was our position: D. Company gap.

We pushed on in the next few days with a lot of work which might be useful if we were directly attacked. The Engineers let us have a lot of barbed wire, and we laid an involved mesh of trip-wire most of the way round each platoon, to disorganise any possible infantry attack. Under the threat of immediate fighting, one became much more critical: defences which had seemed adequate now looked flimsy and unreliable. We knew that if the attack came through the D. Company gap, the first wave would be tanks. We were, according to plan, to maintain our positions and let the tanks go over our heads; then we were to pop up and destroy the enemy infantry which would be following. That was the way we talked, but in our unspoken thoughts was the recognition that tanks were perfect anti-personnel weapons, and that it was hardly likely that the German tanks would go peacefully past and leave us fighting fit to hold up their infantry. The tanks, I believed, if they once broke in on us, would not leave us till we were—'neutralised'. But such considerations were not part of our job. We had our orders.

The general plan was to allow the German force to come in, allow the tanks (if they must) to cross our positions and make their way East. Then we would spring up and detach from them their supporting infantry and their maintenance vehicles. We would thus engage in a man-to-man battle in the front line, whilst in our rear the vast tank forces which lay between us and Tobruk would engage and destroy the enemy tanks. That was the theory: yield slightly to the first blow, then strike like a thunderbolt.

Only it seemed rather to depend on the enemy's doing

those things which he was not likely to do, and not doing those things he *was* likely to do. But I daresay we only saw a fraction of the plan.

We never spoke our doubts. Burgess was an acute man: the mere fact that he passed this strategy on to us with matter-of-fact gravity, just as he received it from the colonel, gave us the cue. This was the plan, the only plan, and therefore the best possible plan. We passed it on to the men without comment. When they asked questions, we found answers. We declared ourselves satisfied.

I was talking to some Tank Corps men soon after this, when we were taken to look at some of the American 'Grants'. I asked questions about the famous 'blindness' of tanks—we foot-sloggers were encouraged to stand up to tanks at close quarters by the statement that no man in a tank could see the ground within a radius of twenty yards. It was below the field of vision, below the depression of his guns. Hence, if a tank came as near as that to our concealed positions, we could lob a sticky-bomb at him and watch him blow up. Was this true, I asked a tank sergeant.

'No' he said laconically.

'You *can* see, then?'

'Down to about five yards, in these things. Reckon Jerry's about the same'.

I suppose my eyes grew reflective. 'Hm. So if we're attacked by tanks, we can consider ourselves under observation till they're actually on top of us?'

'Yeh. And under fire.'

'Cramps our style rather.'

'Why? Doesn't affect you blokes. When the tanks come in, you'll be way back in the rear, to hell out of it.'

'No', I shook my head, 'that's not the idea. We stay up in front. We can't go back now, anyway, our transport's been sent away. We stay put.'

He took the cigarette from his mouth and looked at me with thoughtful interest. 'Uh-huh? Somebody made a balls-up?'

'No. It's according to programme. We sit tight and let the

tanks come through, for you fellows to deal with. Then we intercept his infantry.

'You're gonna squat down in y'r holes an' let his Mark Threes go over you? Huh. Sooner you th'n me.'

'We have good, solid slit trenches: we can get right down.'

'Uh-huh. An' you reckon he's gonna go past with his tanks an' leave you?'

'Yes. We have cover. That's our job, anyway.'

He looked at the end of his cigarette. ''Tain't much of a job, is it?'

★

How solid were our slit trenches? Seeking immediate information, Burgess arranged for H.Q. Company to send over a section of carriers, which carried out a mimic tank attack on our positions. Phillimore and I got down into two of the trenches, and the carriers drove over the top. Apart from sand down our necks, we were untouched. But of course there is a difference between a five-ton carrier and a twenty-five ton tank: and it was said that the tanks made a practice of swivelling on slit-trenches. When a tank swivels, it throws up in a second, from one track, as much spoil as a man can excavate in a day.

We drove on with re-inforcement of the poorer trenches, with wiring, blasting, picketing and sandbagging far into each night, sometimes working almost to midnight as the moon grew brighter, bringing the expected attack nearer. As the strain of expected battle, and the feverish work, began to fall on them, the men worked more heavily, mechanically and regularly, as if by inertia. They looked at me with hate when I came to them with more work, and when we went out in front on patrol they went doggedly, without smiles. Lack of sleep. With extra labour in the increasing heat of May, we all craved more water. Old Herring came to ask me if it would be safe to put a couple of sterilising tablets into some filthy well-water we had—for washing—and drink it: I said no. Characteristic of Herring to ask me. He was a steady, dependable old soldier, with touching faith in me. Who else can a soldier trust, but his officer? It makes the officer strongly conscious of his shortcomings. All the men turned to me for judgment, assistance, and advice: because they had nobody else. But often I was unworthy.

When I said 'don't piss on the ground about your section-post—always go to the proper place,' they obeyed. When I advised them how to conceal the shadow under the bivvy-entrance from aerial observation, they took my advice. They came for information about the enemy, for credit in their pay-books, to talk about their wives and children—for vaseline when the desert wind cracked their lips—for advice about letters home.

But no man is a hero to his valet. George Collinson drank filthy well-water on the sly, and never was any the worse. He would much rather drink it than wash my clothes in it.

'Sir' said Herring to me, loading spoil on the platoon truck —while the sweat dripped from his grey moustache, and he permitted himself one parsimonious mouth-rinse from his water-bottle, 'if ever I see my old woman leave a tap running when I get back to Blighty, I'll be the death of her.'

On the twenty-fifth of May I had to provide a small patrol outside the Western minefield—a 'wire' patrol, solely to ensure that no enemy had crept up to the wire to lift the mines. I made a mistake about this patrol.

New orders had been issued, increasing the patrol from one party of one N.C.O. and two men, to two such parties. I took out only one party, while it was still light, and put them down, according to orders, outside D. Company gap (which was closed, with wire and mines, at sundown, by D. Company—hence my taking them before sundown).

Burgess was up at Orderly Room that night, receiving operation orders, and had called a conference of platoon commanders in his bivvy for when he came back: which might presumably be any time after ten. I worked with my platoon till about ten: the men dug, filled sandbags, hammered pickets, wired, all in grim, resentful weariness, longing for their blankets. Shaw was in one of his old, sullen, cheeky moods, standing about instead of putting his back into the work: he made a comment, loud enough for my ears, about men not being bloody machines. My stoicism gave out: I brought him up sharply, and told him and the whole platoon that the next man who complained would go up to the guard room in close arrest. After this work went on rather better. At ten o'clock I left Phillimore in charge of the platoon and went over to Company H.Q. Burgess not yet back. Dewitt, Ted Carrick and the Sergeant-Major, looking worn out. I waited with them for an hour, then returned to the platoon, stopped the work, and sent the men to bed. Shaw, when I came up, had been leaning on a shovel. 'Watch it doesn't fall down', I said, and felt the rottenness of the remark even as I said it. He looked at me queerly, in the moonlight, turning back unenthusiastically to the work.

As I dismissed the men, there came a loud explosion from somewhere to our left, perhaps half a mile away. Everybody froze.

'Christ, he's coming,' said Hutchinson.

'What was that, sir?' asked Corporal Willis—as if I knew.

'Can't say. Didn't sound like a shell.' (I had never heard a shell in my life.)

'Mine, sir?'

'Yes—may have been a mine. Or a bomb.'

Nothing followed the explosion. The men went to their bivouacs, and I returned to Company H.Q. The others were still waiting. Burgess not back yet. Twenty minutes later we heard his truck outside, and he came in.

'Sorry to keep you all waiting. Major Marrick ran himself on the minefield. Got his leg blown off. His batman's dead, and the truck in bits. Shaken Corporal Figgins—he daren't drive me back, so I drove myself. Well, the news is: Jerry's expected to come in any moment now. Everything's to be tickety-boo. Don't let's have any balls-up now. The code word "Dorothy" is our signal for stand-to, and will not be used except for the real thing. Patrols—all patrols have gone, of course?'

Ted Carrick said 'yes' for his patrols, I for mine.

'Very Light pistols—have your two parties got a pistol apiece, Mike?'

'My *two* parties? I've got the wire patrol tonight.'

Burgess stared at me. 'I know: but it's a two-party patrol,

271

according to yesterday's orders. I underlined the passage for you.'

'Oh Christ yes. I remember now.' I went hot under the collar.

'Do you mean to say. . . . . .'

'Yes.'

'You've only sent one?'

'That's all.'

'O Jesus, Mike! That's a bad slip. Um. Um. They go out at twelve, don't they?'

'Yes. I've got one party sitting outside the gap. I could take——'

'Yes. Do. That's what I was thinking. Slip over now and rouse your N.C.O. and two, get them tee'd up, blankets, arms, Very Lights, pistol, etc.—can you get 'em through the gap before midnight?'

'Yes.'

'You can take the Chev., it's outside. You'll have to drive yourself, since I've sent Figgins to bed. You know the bearing to D. Company gap?'

'Yes.'

'Right. Watch out for that wire half a mile past B.H.Q. D. Company will have closed the gap, of course, so you'll have to pick your way through the mines. Lead the men through the gap yourself, to make sure there are no accidents. All clear?'

'Yes. Sorry.'

'O.K.'

I saluted, crawled out, and spun the Chev. over to my platoon.

Chapter Thirty

I had to rouse Phillimore, to get from him the names of the N.C.O. and men next for duty: then I ran over to No. 4 Section and woke Willis, who had only just got to sleep.

'I'm sorry, Willis, I've got to take you out on patrol immediately.'

He crawled out of his bivvy and looked at me, blinking, dazed with tiredness. 'Eh, sir?'

I repeated it. 'I'm certainly to blame. I made a mistake. You should have gone out before sunset, with the other party. I'm taking you over to the gap. How soon can you have yourself and two men ready?'

'Less than five minutes, sir.'

'Good man. Climb on the Chev. when you're ready.'

I went back and got the Very Light pistol and cartridges from Phillimore, who had them ready. 'Do you want me to come with you, sir?' he said.

'No, sergeant, get your head down while you can. This is my own bloody stupidity.'

I went over to the truck and took a bearing. There was a barrel some distance away, glimmering in the moonlight. I must drive on that. Then I slipped back into my bivvy for a mouthful of whisky.

When I came out, I found Frank Shaw waiting up at the top, his greatcoat on, and his tommy-gun in his hand.

'Hello, what are you doing out of your blankets?'

'I heard you waking Sergeant Phillimore, sir, and I heard you say you were taking a patrol out, so I got up to go with you.'

'With me? Why?'

'I'm your runner, sir'.

'Runner, hell. If I want you with me, I know how to give an order. Go to bed.'

'If I'm not to do my job, sir, I'd like somebody else to be runner and I'll go to a section.'

'Christ Almighty, man, don't worry me now with your scruples. George is my batman. If anybody should come with me, he should. But I'm taking nobody. Get back to your blankets.'

He hesitated a moment, then turned back to his bivvy. The movement and the droop of his head made me pause, and I changed my mind. 'All right' I said, 'you'd better come with me after all.'

He got up beside me on the Chev. Willis and his two men were already there, in their greatcoats and equipment. I handed over the Very Light pistol, and drove off on my bearing.

Half an hour later we heard the challenge of the Sentry at D. Company gap. I dismounted my patrol, and led them in single file over the wire and through the gap—behind me, Frank Shaw, and after him, Willis and his men. We stepped carefully to avoid the mines which had been laid in the gap, and which were not always very evident because of the deceptive character of moonlight.

Having seen the patrol out, Frank and I returned to the Chev., and I set off back to the Company area. After five minutes' driving I still failed to pick up a beacon by which I had turned to approach the gap. I drove slowly, and brought the Chev. round in a wide circle, straining my eyes through the dim moonshine, but no glimpse of the beacon. The minefield, so far as I could tell, should be at least a hundred yards away, but I did not like to run about too much, unsure of direction. It was much too easy not to see a tripwire in this light.

Again I turned about in a wide circle.

I had been too confident leaving the gap. And now, once off the track, I could learn nothing from my compass.

Every bit of the desert, in the still, pale light, looked just like every other bit.

I grew anxious. I guessed at the direction, using the moon as reference, and drove slowly on for nearly half a mile. Still nothing recognisable.

I stopped the truck and got down, pushing my cap back on my head to let the cold wind get at my forehead. I walked round the truck, searching for some familiar shape, a cook-house, a brazier, a dug-in two-pounder. Frank had got down also, and was wandering round.

No use. Nothing here. We got back into the Chev.

'Keep on to the wire, sir, and follow it round behind C. Company,' suggested Frank.

I nodded gloomily. These minefield wires rambled in all directions. I pressed the self-starter, and we went slowly on. Still nothing that we knew. Dimly humped about the desert were the gunners' quads, half dug-in. No movement. No sound. I stopped again for another fruitless reconnaissance.

The stillness and unfamiliarity of the desert were getting on my nerves. The desert was a big place.

There could be no real risk. I must be somewhere in the battalion area: couldn't well get out of it without encountering a minefield wire. Unless unawares I had gone through one of the gaps to the rear.

I drove on again. Frank sat by my side, hunched in anxious silence. The desert wind was cold, he had buttoned up his greatcoat to his ears. I was sweating.

Suddenly two dug-outs which I remembered, part of B. Company's stores, came into sight on our left. Then we were only a quarter of a mile from home. and not far off the track. I spun the wheel to the right and accelerated, changed gear, accelerated again.

Then Frank grabbed my elbow with a snatch like death— — — —'MINEFIELD, SIR!' and at the same moment I heard the tripwire swish under the wheels.

I threw all my weight on the handbrake. The Chev. was moving fast. She stopped, skidding, in about sixteen feet. For seconds I thought she was never going to stop. For seconds after she had stopped we sat, paralysed, waiting for the bang.

The two dug-outs were not the ones I had supposed. I had done just the same thing as Major Marrick.

I had stalled the engine, and was gripping the hand-brake with all my strength. Frank still gripped my elbow. He was arched out of his seat. The truck creaked, the metal of the engine ticked with heat.

I switched off the engine at last, re-assured myself that the brake was hard on, and put the truck into neutral. Frank sat back dumbly in his seat, never taking his wide eyes off me.

I took out my handkerchief and wiped the sweat off my face: got down onto the running-board, looked at the ground, and stepped down: then trod carefully round to the back of the truck. Here, where Shaw couldn't see me, I leaned on the truck and fanned myself with my cap. Then I called to him to stay in the cab, and proceeded to locate the mines immediately round the truck. There was one under the rear axle, between the wheels, and two between the tracks of the vehicle as I traced them back to the wire. It was difficult searching for them in the tricky light. One on the right I had missed by less than a foot. I wanted to take it up and carry it well clear of the tracks, but I wasn't equal to taking it up, in case there was some arrangement I didn't know about which might cause it to go off in my hands. I returned to the Chev.

'O.K., Frank,' I said, 'we'll get her out on her own tracks.'

He did not like the idea. 'Can't we leave the truck here till tomorrow, sir, and find our way back on foot?'

'She's coming out now. But if you feel nervous, I'll take you off the minefield first. Come on.'

He got down, ready to walk off the minefield, and then took his resolution. 'Christ no, sir, what am I here for? If you're going to get her off, I'm helping you.'

'Good. You can guide me off. Stand back here, where the first mine is, and as I reverse, you watch that I come back dead on my tracks. If I go off at all, put your hand up.'

I put the Chev. into reverse: and stalled the engine twice, because I forgot to release the brake. At last I got her moving, and followed Frank's signals. In ten minutes we were back to the wire. I spun her out onto safe ground, and Frank climbed up beside me. He was icy cold, I could hear his teeth chattering.

Once off the field, a certain nervous reaction overcame me, and for a minute or two it was useless to try to drive on. I was trembling too much. I got down from the truck and walked about, spying out the run of the trip-wire to right and left. I also crossed to where I had seen and mistaken the two dug-outs. From here I was able to orient myself to some extent. Half an hour later we were back at Platoon H.Q.

It was three o'clock in the morning when I got to bed, and we were all up at five, working again at defences by the half-light of the morning. We downed tools at seven, and were glad to hear that a consignment of Naafi goods, due today, was expected to come up despite the general tension. No further news had come in. Mail was still going backwards and forwards. I censored a couple of letters and handed them in at Coy. H.Q., bringing back my platoon mail—two letters for Corporal Drake, one for Phillimore. Still nothing for me.

At nine o'clock, when I was busy about platoon H.Q., Burgess walked across with a little, excited smile on his lips. 'Stand 'em to, Mike, it's coming. Fifty Jerry tanks are cruising up and down in front of the main minefield, looking for an opening, and a couple of hundred of 'em are going south by Hacheim.'

I got the men into their positions: then Phillimore and I went round and examined every weapon in the platoon, every rifle, Bren, and tommy-gun, the anti-tank rifle, the two-inch mortar, the three rifle-bombers, the stickybombs, and every grenade—the old 'pineapples', the new bakelites, and the Italian 'pillarboxes'. Also we made sure that every man knew how to use all his weapons.

I was chatting with No. 5 section about the coming battle when a Stuka flew over and dropped a bomb behind Company H.Q. It made a colossal noise and pillar of sand, and a lot of stone fell about us, but, so far as I knew, did no damage. No-one was disturbed, but all felt it was the starter's pistol.

When the platoon had been checked, I stood them down, leaving a sentry in each section, and told the men to sleep. Then I summoned George and gave him two shirts and a pair of shorts to wash. He was deeply offended at being given such a job at the outbreak of battle, particularly when the others were getting down to sleep. I told him it was one of the disadvantages of being a batman. The advantages he knew. I sent Frank—who was sleeping—over to Coy. H.Q. to report my platoon ready for instant action: and I wrote the following letter to Elizabeth:

*   *   *

My Darling Elizabeth,

We shall be doing some work shortly which may prevent my writing, so I am sending you this letter now, just to tell you how I love you.

Dear girl. Light of my heart. We have never talked or written about the worst things that could happen, because they always seemed far enough away to be neglected. But really they aren't. We can be separated for ever. Oh Christ, if only I could have you once more in my arms, before the future rolls over me. I want to tell you, my darling, that behind all the kindness and fun and fooling and ignoring lies the chance that we may not see each other again. In your heart you've considered this, as I have. But we mustn't close our hearts to each other, even on thoughts like that. This desert soldiering is simple enough stuff, routine and all, but for all of us here there is the odd chance that we may be killed. It's better for us to know this, and it will comfort me to know that you know it. Suppose it *did* happen, how horrible to die with a false grin on my face, without having said to you the deepest things in my heart—without even a tear. Let us not be regretting, at the moment when it's too late, that we had not said *all* to each other. Let's know each other's deepest hearts, let's have our eyes open.

And I want you to remember this, if it *should* be so—if you heard some time that I was dead, or missing: you *must not*, then, imagine me tricked or fooled or betrayed into death, or dying by accident, in any hole and corner, foolish way. If I die, I say now, Elizabeth, it will be because I so decided, with my eyes open, and having counted the cost and the gain. It will not be in error or misjudgment. Do not pity me or think of me as a trapped creature. If I should have to lose my life, it will be as a result of decision, confidently, consciously, deliberately, and for a worth-while reason such that you would not have me do otherwise.

278

Don't be depressed or surprised at this letter. I have had it in mind to write ever since I left England, and now that I have it written, I feel at ease, for whatever may happen now, I know that I have said to you the deepest things in me. My love for you is all my life.

Michael.

I learned, long after, that no mail posted that day, or sub-sequently, ever left Libya.

Chapter Thirty-One

The day was very hot and calm, and passed almost as peacefully as an English July day. There was a sense of relief as well as excitement in the air, seeming in the heat itself, which bathed and relaxed our nerves. I was much less the tyrant to the men. After tiffin the Naafi goods came up, and when I had got them out to the sections, I brought Phillimore, George and Frank into my bivvy, and we celebrated the twenty-sixth of May, the first day of battle, with a pineapple party and three or four bars of chocolate. We saved our tins of beer for the evening.

We talked about the prospects of fighting with a certain thrilled curiosity, anxious to see what it really would be like. No-one seemed depressed or doubtful, but simply interested to see what the next few days would show. 'Mrs Shaw' apostrophised Frank, 'your son's going into action.' Much laughter.

Marlowe said that after all the digging we'd done in that bit of desert, we were not likely to let Jerry shift us in a hurry.

'Grumbling apart—and I admit you have reason—' I said, 'still, after all this digging, won't you feel happy to start digging all over again, West of Benghazi instead of East?'

During the afternoon we heard some distant explosions and gunfire in the South, and about four o'clock a Stuka flew over, very low, and machine-gunned us. This caused some rapid diving for cover, but nobody was hurt.

At nearly six o'clock I had a note from Burgess, warning me to give my platoon an early dinner and be ready at seven to move, with all arms and digging tools, into a new position in the Western minefield, over on the battalion front. The enemy had attacked in force south of our position, and was expected to make an assault on our section of the minefield very soon. Apparently many of his tanks were already burning on the minefield to the south. Ted Carrick's platoon and mine were to be withdrawn from the Company area, where there was no threat, and put in at the front to protect the main minefield and prevent any attempt to rescue tanks or lift mines. No attack at present was anticipated from the rear, since the enemy had failed to break through to the south, between us and Hacheim—therefore we could be spared for the more important work on the main minefield.

We filled all water-bottles from reserve, loaded reserve biscuits, bully, and ammo on the platoon truck, and moved over on the signal, arriving on the threatened front as the daylight was fading. We moved silently to our new positions in the minefield, speaking quietly, each man heavily loaded. Ted Carrick led his platoon in half a mile south of me.

Still further south we could see seven Jerry tanks burning, in a long straggling row, perhaps a quarter of a mile apart. They burned with a beautiful rosy light, sometimes brightening to a clear flaring yellow. The more distant ones were specks of light. Beyond them still, from time to time a white Very Light blazed out in the sky, like a great white star.

Though our trench positions were spitlocked on the ground, they were not dug. We were in the middle of the minefield, which was almost two miles wide at this point, and we reached our position by a narrow path which I took to be clear of mines. Next morning I found this was not so, there were three or four mines in the path. Fortunately nobody walked on them. We began digging as soon as we got there. The Engineers had not been able to supply any extra picks or shovels: we had only two shovels per six men, and H.Q. had only one pick. Phillimore flung himself into the digging as soon as he had checked the platoon in. He was very strong and tireless, working steadily, like a machine. I posted a sentry well in advance of each section, to give us immediate protection, and then took Drake and three men, with Very Light pistol, tommy-guns and grenades, along the path straight ahead till we came out on the further side of the minefield, the enemy's side. We walked softly here and spoke in whispers. We saw no enemy: I posted Drake and his men about twenty feet from the edge of the minefield, with instructions to destroy any small body of the enemy who might approach, to signal with Very Lights any big movement, and if the enemy force was too strong, to fall back on the platoon. They lay flat behind some scrub, so well concealed that George could not see them from the edge of the minefield.

Drake's position was nearly a mile forward of the platoon. I walked the distance, there and back, three times during the night, keeping contact with him.

Back at the platoon, when I returned, a Signals man had laid a telephone between Ted Carrick's platoon and mine, and then back to Battalion. The wire he was using was thin enamelled stuff, not much thicker than thread. As the men moved about, they got their feet entangled in this completely invisible wire, and snapped it. The Signals man was yapping round them, warning and cursing. At last he got my end of the wire repaired. But it didn't work. He announced he would have to go along the wire, looking for breaks. I therefore took Frank Shaw off digging—he was working with Phillimore—and gave him the phone, and Signals went off into the night.

I went round the platoon, testing defences and impressing the need for silence. Everybody was disgusted with the digging. They had all struck rock about a foot below the surface. Progress was very slow and arduous. On my return to platoon H.Q., I found Burgess there.

'You're out in flat desert here' he said, 'and visible for seven miles. There's no question of concealment, Jerry will see you as soon as day breaks. All you can do is to dig your holes, so you'll stand a chance if he tries to shell you out. Spread your spoil behind the position. Men very tired?'

'So-so.'

'Good. I'm going down to see Ted Carrick now, I'll see if he can spare some picks and shovels.'

An hour after midnight Frank—who was rolled in his greatcoat, the night being cold—reported a sound on the telephone. I put on the extra phones, and got through to Ted Carrick, wished him a quiet night, exchanged a private joke or two, and rang off. Signals returned soon after, and spent the rest of the night trying to get through to Orderly Room. He got Ted's platoon every time.

It was after two in the morning—and I must have walked eight or nine miles in all during the night—when I got the opportunity of digging my own slit trench. I didn't want dawn to find me up on the deck under the enemy's eyes. Unfortunately I had failed to give George explicit instructions, when I last saw him, to start digging, and he had taken advantage of this neglect to curl up in his greatcoat and go to sleep. It was no use cursing him, I let him sleep on while I did the first part of the work, maliciously aware that when it was his turn, I should have got down to the rock.

When I began to swing the pick, I found I was pretty well exhausted. This was the third night of only two or three hours' sleep, and the days had been spent energetically in the main. But Phillimore, in addition to supervising the platoon, had got his own trench nearly three feet down, and he and Frank Shaw were working steadily away at it as if they would never stop. Frank was not even fully sleeping in the intervals, as the others were, since, being runner, he had to relieve Signals when he was not digging. Phillimore shouldered the main burden of the digging without a murmur. I was grateful for Phillimore. I never gave him the slightest hint of a wish without he executed it immediately, and better than I had expected. He never grumbled, and never allowed the men to grumble. Towards the end he was very tired. I saw him, after a spell of digging, stand with his eyes closed, practically asleep on his feet.

I worked hard for perhaps fifteen minutes on my trench, got down to rock, found a solid slab, and cleared round it with the point of my pick. Then, pretty suddenly, the pick became too heavy for my hands. I dropped it and sat hard down on the ground, head on knees. A couple of minutes gave me breath and determination. I began again, but not for long. Phillimore's spade went on like a machine, slow and easy, without a pause. As I rested, panting and dizzy, I could hear the steady clink, scrape and swish of the spade. Then Frank took the pick from my trench, where I had dropped it, and stepped into Phillimore's place, picking out the rock while the sergeant rested.

I did an hour, then roused George, who apparently had hoped to sleep till dawn. 'Dig' I said. I was trembling, sweating and footsore.

'Wha'—wha'—?' said George vaguely from his blankets.

'Dig—for an hour. Then wake me.'

I was in my sleeping-bag, fully dressed, boots and all, and asleep before George was out: but aware, as the black-out of sleep came down, that Phillimore had left his digging and gone down the minefield path to contact Drake's patrol, as I had arranged.

An hour later George shook me. It must have been four o'clock. The night was hateful, my brain sore with tiredness, I couldn't see the stars, only flashing blurs of light, and I didn't care if I got killed. I decided to turn over and go to sleep again. What the hell. George never knew, he had already dropped into his blankets, careless whether I got up or not—he had done his job.

I knew not a thing, I was not merely asleep, but stunned with tiredness, till Frank woke me. It was still dark. 'Breakfast, sir.'

Burgess had sent us up tea and bacon. The Q.M.S. was very anxious to be off before first light, since his cook's truck was at the rear edge of the minefield, half a mile away, in full view of the enemy. I was too tired to be hungry, but the men were not. I was in a mood of utter self-disgust because of my lapse during the night.

Spades and picks had been clinking all night, and did not stop for breakfast. I went back to my half-dug trench.

Dawn came. Drake brought back his patrol according to instructions. We waited for a sign of the enemy. But daylight showed the desert in front of us bare to the horizon. We heard later that Jerry had attacked again in the south.

We were nervous about aeroplanes, and continued to dig in. By nine o'clock in the morning, as the sun grew hot, we were mostly fairly well down: George and I had four feet, John Phillimore and Frank had five: all sections had reasonably good positions. The night's work had been heavy on water. By mid-day we should all be very thirsty.

I put down my pick and crossed to a patch of scrub to relieve my bowels. Odd thing, life.

During the morning I rested the men: one sentry per section, and two men to complete urgent digging. Frank and Signals were still taking turns on the phone, but since we had now resigned ourselves to being cut off from Battalion, they slept most of the time. I lay down to sleep myself, first ordering section commanders to test their guns. Two minutes after I had given this order, Corporal Willis shot himself.

He was clearing the Light Machine Gun, according to the order. The drill was to point the gun into the pit and fire a short burst. Willis's gun had a bad magazine (Bren guns were always a curse). The magazine was put on by Kenworthy, an extremely able and conscientious man: it did not snap correctly into position, though it seemed to have done so. Kenworthy then cocked the action, pushed forward the change-lever, pointed the gun into the pit, and squeezed the trigger. The action slid half-way forward, and stuck. Willis came up, cocked the gun again, and tried it himself. The same thing occurred. Leaving the action half-forward, Willis stood the gun on the ground, knelt in front of it, and struck the magazine with his hand—forgetting that the action was half-forward and therefore independent of the trigger. His blow on the magazine released the action, which snapped forward and discharged the round.

Willis half rose to his feet and rolled over, curled up like a caterpillar, making a noise between a scream and a moan. Phillimore and I ran like hell to him. Others seemed inclined to converge, too—Phillimore stopped them and sent every man back to his job. Two men were holding Corporal Willis, who was covered in blood. The bullet had entered his left thigh two inches above the knee, making an oblique tunnel wide enough to take a pencil. Striking the bone, it had flattened and come out again higher up his thigh, tearing out a large hole, and had gone into his arm (his elbow had been resting on his knee). It had entered the thick part of the biceps, making a hole as large as a boy's fist: from the edges of the hole, thick, heavy flaps of flesh stuck out. The wound was pouring out blood.

Willis was in great pain. Phillimore cut away the material of his shorts, to get to the wound higher in the thigh, and I looked after the arm. The cloth of his tunic was driven into the raw flesh of the wound. We talked to him soothingly while we worked. His leg at first seemed to pain him more than his arm. I was alarmed by the thick stream of bright red blood which rolled continuously from his arm: I felt for the artery under his armpit, located it, and pressed it to the bone with two fingers, while Kenworthy knotted a large handkerchief for a tourniquet. The pressure on the artery greatly decreased the flow of blood, but after a minute or so Willis complained of great pain in his arm. The hand and wrist turned wax-white. Phillimore by now had got a couple of field dressings on the leg wounds, and was chafing his hand to keep it warm, while Marlowe put a dressing on the arm wound. I released the artery for a time. The wound was so large that the dressing did not entirely cover it.

To my dismal fury I was overcome by nausea at this point, and had to sit for a short time with my head between my knees so as not to faint. This must have been due to tiredness. It was ridiculous, I felt very ashamed.

All this time Frank Shaw had been plugging the phone to see if he could contact battalion and get a stretcher sent up, but he could get no reply. I told him to keep at it, and sent Marlowe off to take the message verbally. I shall always remember Marlowe's conduct throughout the battle. At this time, though he had been slaving his guts out all the night, he ran the entire mile and a half to D. Company, the nearest company to us.

While he was gone we did our best to keep up Willis's spirits. Phillimore was very good, chatting easily with him all the time, assuring him that the wounds themselves were quite unimportant, though painful. Willis asked for a cigarette, which Phillimore lit and put into his mouth. I looked over the dressings. Much blood was still oozing from under the arm dressing, but I dared not tighten the tourniquet further. I told him he had a couple of unpleasant flesh wounds, which would not incapacitate him at all when they were healed, but would give him a great deal of pain for the next few hours. It was only soreness, I said, and nothing to be afraid of, but he would be damned uncomfortable. Could he set his teeth and stick it? He said he would do his best.

In a remarkably short time a truck came up to the edge of the minefield, and two stretcher bearers came along the path. We lifted Willis carefully, slid the stretcher under him, laid a couple of blankets on him, and sent him off. Then I appointed Herring section commander.

Chapter Thirty-Two

Early in the afternoon Burgess came and instructed me to withdraw the platoon, section by section. Transport was waiting behind a ridge which he indicated, a mile away. He had no general information to give me, but we had heard firing in the south for some time, and I formed the impression that the main attack was taking place there, beyond Ted Carrick's position. This was not quite the case, as I learned later. What had happened was that the German and Italian forces had swept right round the south, beyond Hacheim (the southern end of the minefield), had come up north again in the rear, and had occupied many of the Divisional H.Q. areas back between us and Tobruk: and were now extending back west again towards the rear of the front line positions. What it amounted to was that my platoon was now more likely to be needed in its original position to the rear of the battalion.

Immediately Burgess had gone, I organised and began the withdrawal of the platoon. It turned into a ragged business, untidy and unmilitary, straggling between the transport and the position we were evacuating. Burgess had said, send the men by sections, each under its section commander, each section four hundred yards from the one in front, and each section carrying all equipment, ammunition, weapons and kit. This we could not do. The mortar-men, for instance, had to make four journeys to get all their heavy gear and extra bombs away—four times there and back journeys is eight miles, four of them with a heavy load. All the sections had the same problem in a greater or less degree. We had far too much stuff to get away in one carry. So I told John Phillimore, who went ahead to the trucks, to send back men for more gear as soon as they reached him. The minefield path became dotted with straggling, laden figures, and Burgess, coming back again, gave me a terrific blowing-up for withdrawing in a disorderly manner. I felt this keenly.

As soon as we got back to our old position, I told Phillimore to post sentries and send every other man to his blankets. Then I dived into my bivvy. I had not been stretched out more than five minutes—hearing all the time, through the thrilling earth, the thudding of distant guns, and occasionally a faint whining scream—when a runner came in from Company H.Q.—'Captain Burgess's compliments, and will you take your bedding and batman over to Company H.Q., to Capt. Burgess's bivvy, and take charge of the company. Captain Burgess was going, with Mr. Dewitt and No. 12 Platoon. to re-inforce C. Company'.

From this I deduced the enemy had struck north along the rear of the minefield, and come up against C. Coy., the south-western angle of the battalion triangle. Ted Carrick's platoon had not been withdrawn when mine was. I imagined he must now be North-West of the battle which would be developing on C. Company's front. His job would now be to protect C. Company's right flank. My platoon was thus the only one left in B. Company's area.

The position, when I took over Company H.Q., was odd. Burgess gone, Ted Carrick and his platoon still in the Western minefield, Dewitt and his platoon gone with Burgess to C. Company. Hence I had a company front, and only one platoon to man it. I was uneasy in my heart, since one always feels that the enemy will find the weak spots. If he should attack me, I could foresee difficulty in defending the empty positions of ten and twelve platoons, which must be defended if only to keep the enemy from taking cover in them.

It was late afternoon when I took over. I drew up a guard roster, giving Company H.Q. staff (cooks, runners, clerk, etc.) the task of patrolling the empty platoon positions, reporting to me every half-hour throughout the night. I determined to keep my own platoon concentrated in their own position, which was familiar to them, for it seemed too risky now to try any experiments involving dispersal and difficulty of control. But my platoon was to provide a patrol which would also cover the whole Company area, would contact the H.Q. men, and, like them, would report to me. If an attack should be made on us, I allotted the men their alarm posts in Company H.Q. area, from which I would direct the Company H.Q. battle, leaving Phillimore to command my platoon in its own position.

The next thing was food for the two platoons which were out. The Q.M.S. had a hot meal ready in containers. I sent him off five minutes before sunset, so he could take his truck up close under cover of darkness. By now the night was full of noise from the direction of C. Company, the continuous battering of guns: the distance was too great to hear the lighter rattle of small-arms. I rang up C. Company and told Burgess I had sent his dinner off. 'Good man' he said. He seemed exhilarated, and said there was a sharp battle going on. What was happening on my front? 'All quiet' I said. 'Lucky bugger' he laughed.

I tried to get through to Ted Carrick also, but—as I had expected—the line was not working.

At about eight o'clock, Jerry's white Very lights began to go up, not only in C. Company's direction, but all round us, right over to the East. He must have worked right out on his right flank, and was now all along my front. None the less all was still quiet, and the flares to my front were at least half a mile away. Though my heart beat thickly, I was not apprehensive.

At half-past nine the Adjutant rang me, and told me to detail a patrol of two or three men, who were twice during the night to leave my platoon, go South-West from the corner of my minefield (across the Brigade gap) and contact C. Company, which was at present resisting attack. I sent for Phillimore and we arranged it. Hutchinson and Marlowe were chosen for the job, and were to carry tommy-guns and grenades. They would wear rubber desert-boots. I imagined the patrol would take them close to, or into, enemy positions.

The guns now were not so loud as before, but the attack on C. Company evidently went on. The Very light display continued along our front.

The Q.M.S. reported back after taking out the food to ten and twelve platoons. He said there was a battle still going on in C. Company's area. I told him to arrange to take out breakfasts before dawn.

Immediately after this the Adjutant rang again, and cancelled all orders for the night:

'The battalion is withdrawing.'

As they say in the North, I was fair dropped on!

'*Eh?*' I said.

'The battalion is withdrawing from this position. Have you got that?'

'Yes sir.'

'The route of withdrawal is due north of Battalion H.Q., through the North gap, and into the area at present occupied by the Glenskillings. This route will be indicated by two pin-point lanterns immediately north of this H.Q. You will evacuate the whole of B. Company area. Have you got that?'

'Yes.'

'You are responsible for clearing the area. All ammunition, water, rations, stores, tents and equipment will immediately be packed up and laid in dumps on the surface, ready to be loaded on trucks. Nothing will be left underground. That is your first task. The second task will be to load all that material on four three-tonners which I shall send you. The order of loading will be this: first, weapons, ammunition: *all ammunition will be loaded first*. Next, water. All water will be carried. Next, rations. Last, stores, tents, baggage. If anything must be left, leave some of the baggage and tents. Have you got that?'

'Yes.'

'O.K. You will send off these trucks, fully loaded, at 0330 hours in the morning, and will at the same time evacuate your men on foot. That's all. Repeat the order back to me, beginning with the first task, and finishing with the route.'

'I am first to bring everything in the Company area to the surface, and lay it in dumps convenient for loading. I am to clear the entire area. I am next to load everything onto four three-tonners which you are sending, and the order of priority in loading is weapons and ammunition, water, rations, stores, baggage and tents. At 0330 hours I am to evacuate the area by taking the trucks and the men out through the

North Gap into the Glenskillings' area. The route to the new area is due north of Battalion H.Q., and will be indicated by two pin-point lanterns.'

'Good. Begin on the first task now, and report to me when it is done.'

'Very good, sir.'

I sat down on Burgess's bed, and rubbed my aching forehead. I had been looking forward to half-an-hour's sleep. Rommel had murdered sleep. Pity. I shouted for a runner, and summoned Phillimore, the Q.M.S., and George Collinson, who were still over in my platoon position.

When they were all in the bivvy I told them what was on. They looked as blank as I felt.

'Sergeant Phillimore', I said, 'you are responsible to me for bringing everything up to the surface. Your platoon is the only one in the area, and it will first clear its own positions. Then you will take a squad of men to clear No. ten platoon, and you will detail a further working party, commanded by an N.C.O., to clear No. twelve. You will report to me as soon as the three positions are cleared.

'Quartermaster, you will be responsible for the cookhouse and for Company H.Q.'

Phillimore said nothing for a few seconds, but looked worried. At last he said 'What's the time now, sir?'

'Eleven o'clock.'

'What time are those trucks arriving?'

'I don't know. The Adjutant said he was sending them shortly.'

'The platoon has to clear all the Company area, load all the stuff onto four trucks, and get them away in four and a half hours?'

'Yes.'

He was silent again, lines of anxiety on his face. Then he said: 'The patrols, sir?'

'Cancelled.'

'One sentry per section?'

'Yes.'

The Q.M.S. spoke up. 'It can't be done, sir. It's impossible to get all H.Q. stuff on one truck. You won't even get it on three.'

'It's going on one. I don't care if the driver has to do the distance in bottom gear.'

'You'll be putting ten tons on a three ton lorry.'

'That's enough argument. It's going on.'

'I hope to God the trucks come soon' said Phillimore. 'I can get the stuff to the surface quicker than I can load it.'

'There'll be no sleeping tonight, watch that,' I said. 'The men are tired and want to get their heads down. Don't let them. See that every man works his guts out.'

'Very good, sir.'

'How many forty-four gallon water containers can you get on a three-tonner?' I asked the Q.M.S.

'Fourteen, sir.'

'And then it's fully loaded?'

'Overloaded, sir.'

'We've twenty containers to go, not counting anything else', I said. 'They'll be distributed over the four trucks, five to a truck, standing on their ends. You can put some of your water on the cook's truck, Quartermaster, as well as the cookhouse gear. You may have to carry some extra weapons and ammo. on the cook's truck, too. I shall hold you responsible for the loading of the cook's truck. Any questions, Quartermaster?'

'No, sir.'

'Sergeant Phillimore?'

'No, sir.'

'Get busy then.' I turned to George Collinson. 'Now George, go to my bivvy and pack *everything*. Put all you can into my bedroll. When I come over to the platoon, I want to see the bivvy-hole empty and all my stuff neatly packed. O.K?'

'Yes, sir.'

I sent him off, and told Burgess's runner to do the same with his tent and kit.

Half an hour later the work was well on the way. The cookhouse was dismantled and all stores, dixies, cookhouse water reserve and so on were stacked on the cook's truck. I went round the Company area watching the progress of the job, but dared not stay away from H.Q. in case the Adjutant should ring again.

He did. The Q.M.S. had just come over to tell me there were three water containers he could not get on the cook's truck—hence they would have to go on one of the four three-tonners in addition to the fifteen containers from platoons and H.Q.—when the Adjutant rang me to cancel one of the trucks; so I should only have three now.

I was pretty worried about this. Particularly as it was now nearly one o'clock, and the trucks had not yet come.

I was much more worried when the trucks had still not come by half-past two. Three and a half of four and a half hours had gone, and the loading, worst task of all, still to be done. And three extra water-barrels to carry, and one truck the less. By now Company H.Q. had vanished. All that was left was a compact group of huge bundles, bales, boxes and barrels, and nine or ten great gaping holes in the ground.

I hurried over to my platoon and found Phillimore and all the men asleep, lying sprawled among each other in empty bivvy holes. Phillimore said the work was done, everything packed and on the surface: why not sleep till the trucks arrived?

'Is every bit of ammo, kit, etc. throughout the whole area on top?'

He hesitated. 'It's all handy to load, sir.'

'Is it on the surface?'

'No, sir.'

This shook me profoundly. I had never known him fail before. I was too accustomed to leaning on him. I realised that he was so tired he could hardly stand.

The expression of deep worry intensified on his face. 'Sir, I've only got seventeen men to play with, and the stuff I've left below is as easy loaded from there as from the surface. Men can't do the impossible, sir.'

'Take a party over to ten platoon immediately and pack everything as you have done this.'

'Very good sir', he turned away, then back again: 'You see, sir, I'm sergeant of *this* platoon. I know where everything is, here. But when I get over in ten platoon's area, I've got to look for all the stuff. I've even got to search to find the section positions.'

'All the more reason for getting on with it.'

'You've got more stuff here, sir, in your own platoon, than two three-tonners can carry——'

'Rot. Don't bullshit, Phillimore. We can load the stuff, and you know it.'

'You can't carry a company's stuff on four trucks, sir.'

'It's going to be carried on three—they've docked one. I've nothing more to say.'

'Very good, sir'. He went off, a very worried man.

I crossed over to my bivvy, and found most of my stuff packed up on the surface, but the bivvy-tent itself still pegged down over the hole: and George asleep under it. I roused him, looked around, and found several articles he had failed to pack.

'You don't want odds and ends like that, sir'? he asked, when I showed him my plate and mug.

'Don't be so bloody wooden, George. When I tell you to pack everything, I don't mean leave out the things you can't be bothered with. For Christ's sake wake yourself up and do your job. Get this bivvy off and rolled up, quickly. You'll be buggering about with it when Jerry walks in.'

A thought struck me as I went away. I turned back and asked, 'What about those things I gave you to wash two days ago?'

'Oh Christ,' he said, dismayed, and began searching. I looked round and found the shirts and shorts in a tin of fusty water, smelling horribly. 'See George', I said, 'I'm wasting no more time over you now. Get on and do your job, and don't stop till it's done. That's the last word I've got for you.'

When I got back to Company H.Q., the three three-tonners were just coming in. The time was five minutes to three. At half-past three they had to be loaded and away.

The phone buzzed for me: the Adjutant. He told me to hang on for the Commanding Officer.

'Got your trucks yet, Carr?' asked the Colonel.

'Just come this minute, sir.'

'Good. You'll load everything in your Company area, beginning with ammunition: at three-thirty you will send them off to the new area, and evacuate your men on foot. Is that clear?'

'Yes sir.'

'Any problems?'

'Yes sir, two. First, I can't get all the stuff on three trucks. Second, I can't, with only one platoon, load three trucks in half an hour.'

'Carr, understand me. *All* the stuff will go on your trucks, and they will leave at three-thirty. I don't care if you smash every spring they've got. Forget about how much they are supposed to carry; they will carry everything. It will be done, and you will do it. Is that clear?'

'Yes sir.'

'Very good. Goodnight.'

I had sent the three-tonners off to platoon areas, under Phillimore: I ran over to my platoon, and found them loading. But it was apathetic, Phillimore was not controlling the work as he usually did, it was a scramble, and the stuff was not being properly stowed into the smallest space. Worse when I looked close: kit and baggage, in which the men were personally interested, had been thrown on before weapons and ammunition. I went wild, jumped up on the truck, grabbed stuff with both hands, and pitched it to hell out of it. 'Stop loading this bloody truck.'

They were muttering, half-awake, resentful. 'Listen', I said, 'you will load this truck right, and you will load it faster than you ever did in your lives. Bloody fools: do you understand that you're not practising now, you're withdrawing, and Jerry is just over the wire there? Let me catch one man slacking or grumbling now, just one, that's all. Sergeant Phillimore, get up on this truck, and bring Marlowe up with you. Load it, ammo first to the front, weapons, then water. Pack it so that the load will ride twelve feet high. Load flat up to the front, as high as ever you dare. When you've cleared this platoon, move over, taking everybody with you, to ten platoon and start there, filling up the same truck. Corporal Drake, get any six men and bring them with me, to twelve platoon.'

At half-past three the trucks were still not fully loaded. I ordered the driver of Company H.Q.'s truck to drive over to twelve platoon for more stuff.

'You've got it wrong, sir' he said, 'this is a three-tonner, not a thirty-tonner.'

Behind him, in the direction of C. Company, a tiny point of fire appeared, over a mile away, and grew to a red rose of flame. It waxed, then waned, then settled to a steady molten brightness.

'Driver', I said, 'you will obey my orders. If I tell you to put thirty tons on your truck, you'll do it. Otherwise I shall arrest you for court-martial after the battle. That's all.'

Even when I had put such a load on the trucks that the chassis was flat on the axles, I had not got more than two-thirds of the stuff on. It was now a quarter to four. I continued loading.

The same driver approached me again. 'Excuse me, sir, don't think I'm insubordinate, but I'm responsible for these trucks, and in my judgment, sir, the tyres are likely to burst under the load we've put on. It's better to save what we've got than to lose everything.'

I made up my mind. 'Very good. Sergeant Phillimore, take two men and get up on these trucks. Guide them out by the North Gap, and wait for me at the other end. I'll bring the men.'

The trucks moved away, the men formed up, carrying full equipment, all personal ammunition and grenades, rifles slung. The time was five to four. Twenty-five minutes behind schedule. And to make the North Gap I had to march first South-West for a mile, to Battalion Headquarters, before striking north.

I determined to take a risk. If instead of going first to H.Q., then north, I went ten degrees west of north from my present position, I could gamble with almost complete certainty on bringing my men straight into the gap. On both sides of the gap, I knew, the minefield wires converged, bringing you in like a great funnel. I could not go wrong.

All I had to do was to march so as to leave ten platoon on my right. Thus instead of the two sides of a triangle, I would travel by the hypotenuse.

The men formed up in file behind their section commanders. George came to my side, Peter dropped back between the first and second sections. I led off on a bearing of 350 degrees.

I guessed it was two miles to the gap. We had gone about four hundred yards when I tripped over a wire.

'Hell's bells' I said, disconcerted. So far as I knew, there should be no wire here. The minefield should be two hundred yards to our right by now.

The men were coming on, I did not want to halt them. Suddenly I realised what had happened. This was one of Ted Carrick's extra trip wires, with which he, like me, had surrounded his platoon position. I had never had the chance to see how he had disposed his wire, and had completely forgotten it. I now realised that he must have zig-zagged it back from the minefield itself, right back over the unmined land. Straining my eyes, I could see this crisscross web of wire, see its fringes just within sight.

I struck off to the left, keeping to the wire, passing the word back among the men, ''ware wire'. Had I gone to the right I must have hit the minefield: and had I gone straight on, stepping over the wire, I could not be certain that any of the wires I was crossing was not the true trip-wire of an outlying arm of the minefield. The only safe thing was to go round to the left, and hope to get completely round the wired area.

Ted Carrick must have had a lot of wire. It stretched ever further to the left, and at last began to turn back on us like the horn of a crescent, forcing us back in a circle. I wished now that I had gone right ahead over it and risked mines. All the time I was going further off my course. Ten degrees west could not possibly be right now. I couldn't tell whether we were east or west of the North Gap. Still the wire went on. Could it be all Ted Carrick's wire? Perhaps some more wiring had been done up here, that I knew nothing about. Perhaps there were even fresh mines laid.

When *would* it end?

'Sir, the men can't keep up with you,' said George.

'I know—can't be helped—they must do their best. You move half-way between me and the leading section.'

Then the wire turned, sharp right at last. We must have reached its furthest South-West point. But where the hell were we now with reference to the North Gap?

The wire was pretty straight now, leading about forty degrees west. I followed it for some two hundred yards, then again it turned sharp right, and right again, back on itself. I went straight forward North, into open desert, away from the wire.

Five minutes later, with not a landmark, I stood in blank black desert, looking round me desperately. I dared not guess the direction to the North Gap, for there might be any amount of extra wire to mislead me. There might be arms of the minefield of which I was ignorant. I might be messing about with my platoon in the deadly light of dawn, in an evacuated area, in front of the enemy's guns and tanks. Already it was twenty past four. Dawn was at half-past five.

I did not know where I was.

'Oh God, oh God' I was saying to myself, 'this is the worst thing I ever did.'

My men were shuffling up quickly behind me, in the moon-darkness, sweating under their loads, faint with tiredness. I was sweating more under dreadful anxiety. I alone had any knowledge at all that could bring them through the North Gap, and my knowledge was gone. I did not know where I was.

God. God.

George was level with me now. 'Which way, sir?'

I gulped: looked round like a trapped rat. The leading section of the men was almost up to me.

George saw something.

'Some transport ahead, sir.'

'There is'? (Oh Christ, the relief!) I shot forward, and soon made out a number of gunners' quads, drawn up and halted. I reached the first one, running. The driver was asleep. I grabbed him, woke him.

'Where are you going?'

He blinked. 'Dunno.'

'What?'

'Dunno, sir. We was told to wait here.'

'Wait for what?'

'Dunno, sir. For the order to move on, sir.'

'Move on where?'

'Dunno, sir.'

'Where are you now?'

'Dunno, sir.'

'Christ, man—is there an officer with these quads?'

'Dunno, sir.'

'Well God damn you for a bloody nit—who the hell is in charge?'

'Sergeant, sir.'

'Where is he?'

'Dunno, sir.'

'Well, get out of your bloody seat and take me, now, to somebody who knows where this transport is going.'

He led me to four different quads. The occupants knew as much as he.

I did the only thing I dared. Marched South.

Certainly the North Gap was somewhere north of east and north of west, but I dared not march at hazard to find it. I might lose the whole platoon on a minefield.

And this artillery transport was probably going up through the North Gap: but what if it wasn't?

I took them south, looking for Battalion H.Q. Full in front of us, now, shone the rose and molten brightness. I marched, almost ran. The sweat, in great drops on my forehead, rolled into my eyes. 'God help me' ran on my own voice inside me all the time. 'I've failed them. An officer. God help me now. This is the worst thing I ever did.'

I was lost. Quite lost, casting desperately round in unknown desert.

Marlowe had run forward from No. four section, and was at my side, using his keen eyes. He knew no more than I did where H.Q. was. He was free from my appalling fear that it was all evacuated and we wouldn't know it when we saw it. He had an instinct for the escarpments and declivities of the desert.

'What are we looking for, sir?'

'Two pin-point lanterns.'

'Near Battalion H.Q., sir?'

'Yes.'

Silence while we sweated on.

'Slightly right I think, sir.'

'Do you know where we are?'

'No, but I've a vague idea.'

Silence. We marched quickly on, straight towards the great rose of fire. We were nearer to it now, we could see its pulsing. 'What *is* that burning yonder, sir?'

'Don't know. Maybe a dump of some kind.'

'Maybe a tank, sir.'

'Maybe.'

Silence. Hard breathing.

We bore right again, again: and then my aching eyes, before his, saw a tiny point of light off to the right.

A tiny point of light.

It was as if a new soul had entered my body. I was born again.

Marlowe said, in a voice I hardly knew, 'Thank God.'

I marched due north from the light: four minutes later came the second light: and five minutes after that we were swinging at racing speed along the North Gap track itself. I steadied my pace a little because the men simply could not keep it up.

We marched so fast that it was not yet dawn when, on our right and left, the tripwire appeared, converging, and we came into the North Gap itself. I never before experienced such a sense of salvation as when I led my straggling men between the wires.

Several officers of the Glenskillings were at the mouth of the gap, checking in the retiring troops. One of them, I saw as I passed him, was the Brigadier. I contrived a salute.

301

He looked very tired. He asked me what I was, and I told him No. eleven platoon of B. Coy.

'Where's the rest of B. Company?'

'Don't know, sir. I imagine they've already come through.'

'You don't know where No. ten platoon is?'

'No sir.'

'Didn't the company move off together?'

'No sir. Mine was the only platoon remaining in the company area. The other two were detached to re-inforce other positions. No. ten platoon was in the minefield south of D. Company's gap. They would withdraw independently.'

He looked even more worried. 'Right you are, my lad,' he said, however, 'take your men in.'

Dawn was just breaking when we reached—half a mile beyond the gap—the bare slope which was to be our new platoon position. A Glenskilling captain showed me where trench positions had already been spitlocked on the ground, and said I should get the men digging immediately, since there would probably be shell-fire as soon as daylight gave the enemy sight of us.

I was so exhausted with the last hour's marching that I was trembling, sweating, and could only stand with difficulty. The men, waiting for the next order, had dropped to the ground and were enjoying the delicious luxury of not having to support their own weight. And now, when their eyelids were as if weighted over their eyes, they must be up on their feet again and dig, dig. I went over to them. Frank Shaw grinned up at me with a face as white as paper. 'We made it, sir.' Something strained about him made me look twice. Then I saw he was wearing, not boots, but light canvas shoes.

'Good God, Frank, you did that march in sandshoes?'

He nodded.

'But you'll be crippled.'

'Not too bad, sir. It was hard keeping up, that's all.'

I thought of the stony stuff we had come over, and the load we were all carrying. My own feet, in strong boots, were raw.

'What on earth did you do it for?'

'I put them on for patrol, sir—I was detailed for patrol last night. And when the orders were changed, I hadn't time to get my boots on again.'

'Surely you had. Orders were changed at eleven o'clock: we didn't march till nearly four.'

He looked guilty. 'I fell asleep, sir.'

'Do we eat yet, sir?' asked Corporal Drake.

'No. I'm going off now to look for Company H.Q., and to find out about breakfast. Meanwhile I want section commanders.'

I got them round me—Drake, King, and Herring—told them where to dig, and sent them to get their men working immediately. Phillimore now appeared from behind the flank of a little hill, and said he had unloaded the trucks there. The N.C.O.s were already sending men off for picks and shovels. Phillimore had contrived to get half an hour's sleep, and was his efficient self again. He took charge of the platoon while I went round the hill to find Burgess and Company H.Q.

The entire company was disposed in this area, about the little hill. Mine was now the left hand platoon. I met Burgess returning from twelve platoon, and he came back with me to see my position. On the way he told me that the North Gap no longer existed, having already been completely mined, very soon after I had come in. Our old battalion position, into which we had put so much work, was abandoned to the enemy. Half of Ted Carrick's platoon had straggled in individually; the rest, including Ted, were missing. (I understood then the Brigadier's questions at the gap.)

I heard long after that Ted had led one section in an attack on a machine-gun post, just after midnight. At short range the enemy had spotted them and turned the gun on them. Apparently all were killed.

Everything was going well in my position. The men were digging hard and steady. 'Christ, sir, I could do with a drink' grinned Herring through a mask of sweat, sand and stubble.

'I'll send tea up as soon as the cooks can produce it' promised Burgess. 'For the rest of the breakfast you'll have to issue bully and biscuits, Mr. Carr.' (He was always scrupulous with his 'Misters' before the men.)

Day had come, and artillery was already blasting away behind us and in front. I made no attempt to feed the platoon till the holes we were digging were deep enough to give some protection. It did me good to see that Frank Shaw was working himself to the limit, and looking cheerful too. As usual he was digging with Phillimore, and going all out to equal his partner. Phillimore was kindly towards him, evidently pleased with him, as I was. The child was learning to be a man.

George was also working like a beaver. I took a spade and got down into our joint slit-trench to help him: he immediately began criticising my efforts and my method of cutting out the earth. I bore this meekly, because I was not in fact doing very well, being too tired to overcome my natural unskilfulness. I am not a handy man, though sometimes weak enough to pretend to it. Anyway, George's derision was obviously intended to re-establish himself in his own eyes, after the reproof he had received during the night. I did not grudge him it.

Chapter Thirty-Three

As soon as the men had slit-trenches deep enough to lie in and be safe from splinters, I issued bully and biscuits, and—as no tea had yet come from H.Q.—I drew on the platoon reserve of water and brewed sufficient tea over a scrub fire for half-a-pint per man. We were certainly under enemy observation, for we could now see the German motor-transport, tanks and guns spread out on the desert plain, rather more than a mile away, and covering the desert in all directions to the horizon: it looked an immense force. But we were a negligible target. He was firing over our heads, at gun positions to our rear.

The platoon drew breath, rested, ate and drank. The sun climbed and became pleasantly warm. We were all very dirty and bearded. None had washed, shaved, or removed any article of clothing for three days. Nor had we now either time, water, or energy for ablutions. If there were a pause in the digging, sleep.

In this first respite, as we ate the bully for which our empty bellies craved and rumbled, and drank the hot tea (tasting of sand, salt and smoke), we had time to listen to the thin scream of the shells which passed invisibly over us.

Ceasing work was risky. Most of us fell asleep as soon as we had eaten and drunk. I did so myself, and was awakened by Burgess.

Burgess's orders were brief. No sleeping for any man till all pits were four feet deep. But I was to be considerate with the men, and rest them all I could.

I forced my leaden limbs round and round the platoon area, bullying here, coaxing there, keeping the men at it. My platoon stores, on the face of the desert, were a target, said Burgess. I must dig them in or hide them. More work. By now some of the men (including George and Frank) having dug their pits four feet down, came to the end of their enthusiasm, and I had to slave-drive them to get the extra work done. George and Frank forgot their differences and joined in muttering abuse of me when I did not seem to be looking. I watched all like a lynx, all the lead-swingers, chivvied them, made Phillimore stand over them, gave them no rest. Get it done, get it done. From time to time I went back to my own kit and took a quick mouthful of raw whisky.

There were some of the men—Herring was one, Marlowe another, and Kenrick, my mortarman, another—who worked like hell itself all the time because I told them to, who asked no questions even with their eyes, who grinned and were cheerful and plugged away at the digging and the carrying and never needed a word from me. These were among the older men, the twenty-fives to thirty-fives. I felt it an honour to command such men.

As the morning drew on, the sound of artillery to our left rear intensified, while before us on the desert the German vehicles scurried excitably, formed and re-formed. Burgess came and looked at the enemy through his glasses, and gave me the news. The enemy was all round the Brigade box, which was now the shorter by our withdrawal from our extreme position.

The main German fighting force, having turned the end of the minefield at Hacheim in the South, and occupied the areas between us and Tobruk, had now broken through between the northernmost battalion of the Brigade, and the brigade on our right. His forces had now united behind us. Thus the brigade was completely surrounded, and in no communication—other than wireless—with the remainder of the British forces. The enemy transport which we could see to the West—my new front—was mainly B echelon stuff, his supply lines in fact. Most of his fighting strength was now behind us, to the East, from which direction he was at present attacking. We hoped that before he could bring all his armour to bear on our little infantry position a British armoured force. probably the —— Armoured Division, would come to our rescue from the south-east and break him up. The ——Armoured Brigade was also fighting its

306

way to us from Knightsbridge in the East. We must hang on at all costs, since the area we held was to be the jumping-off point for the second stage of the British counter-offensive. This counter-offensive was already launched, and a colossal tank battle was in progress some five miles to our rear, near Knightsbridge. The enemy had lost ninety tanks already. Since we could not get supplies through, we must henceforth live on the food and water we had. The water ration would be cut to half a pint per man per day, and half a pint of tea at breakfast and tiffin. At that rate the Brigade had water for ten days, which would be ample, since we should be relieved long before then.

It was not easy to sleep even when we had completed digging and hidden our stores. The noise of battle, the battering of the artillery, the singing of the shells over us, and the high, sudden snarl of the ricochets was too stimulating, and so much was continually happening in the air. A formation of British planes, Kittyhawks, attacked the enemy out to our front, and were instantly surrounded by thousands of tiny white clouds, stationary puffs of cotton-wool through which the planes went like arrows. The din of the German anti-aircraft fire was much louder and more sustained than ours, though I don't know if it was any more effective. We saw one British plane shot down: it circled about very low over enemy territory as if looking for a place to land, and black smoke poured backwards out of it all the time. In contrast to the German fire, when three Messerschmitts came over our area, we put up only a very staccato barrage, mainly Bofors—but the firing was notably accurate, though at that time none of the planes was directly hit. Planes came over at such a speed that it was often impossible to know whether they were friend or foe, we had to rely on the anti-aircraft fire to tell us.

Nor were the gunners always a safe guide. Burgess came up with a message that we were shortly to have colossal air support, and sure enough, an hour later, fifteen Kittyhawks roared over our position and *machine-gunned our own medium artillery*, killing four gunners. Our own Bofors guns opened fire on them: they zoomed away over the German lines, where they were left absolutely alone, and finally flew back home, no doubt very happy. To offset this, two Italian planes came over a little later, sported above us unmolested, then bore off to the German side. The Germans opened fire with everything they had, whereupon, to our infinite satisfaction, the Italians dive-bombed them with great skill and daring for a couple of minutes.

In the early afternoon, while Kenrick the mortarman was sitting smoking on the side of his half-dug trench, and talking to me—I was six feet away, sitting on my own trench— a two-pounder shell suddenly alighted and exploded on the brink of his trench, not two feet from his hand. It was very rapid and startling—a terrific 'Whoosh-bang'!—blew a lot of his trench in, and left a crater about two feet deep. Also it ripped the tail fins off a rack of mortar-bombs. The reaction, when the smoke cleared and we found ourselves unhurt, was to roar with laughter, which we did. 'Christ sir, did you see the little bugger—came down like a f----g swallow— wumph! Thought I was a goner that time.' We peered into the warm crater and fished out bits of ragged metal. Impressions of so instantaneous an event are hard to recapture, but I rather think that for one split second I saw the shell— a little fellow, bright and steely, as big as a beer-bottle perhaps—resting on the trench side before it exploded. Kenrick had the same impression. We carried the damaged mortar bombs clear of the platoon area, in case the impact had rendered them unstable. I was surprised they had not exploded, in which case Kenrick and I and the whole of platoon H.Q. would have been—'neutralised.'

Somewhere over to the North-West, a British position, a kind of large scale outpost, remained intact and spent its time quietly lobbing fifteen-pounder shell at the Germans to our front. The range and the ground were tricky, and overs were frequent; so that the only indication we really had of the effectiveness of their fire was when an occasional shell droned into our area and went off with a skull-splitting *crack* that sent us to the bottom of our shelters, feeling ourselves all over to make sure we were all there. Bits of riven steel flew about, invisible, making loud, fluttering whistles through the air. One time, returning from defecation in a nearby hollow, I heard a most singular thrumming, nasal wail, and shouts of surprise and warning from the men. Looking in the appropriate direction, I saw a large silver wheel bounding with fearful speed towards me, across the platoon area. I dropped flat, unnecessarily, as the thing passed about ten feet to my right, and finished fifty yards away. It was simply a twenty-five pounder shell which had hit the ground nose-first and, failing to explode, had shot forward, spinning end-for-end, with enough speed to take it, I imagine, through a two-foot wall: spinning so fast that it screamed as it bowled over the ground, for all the world like a great disc of silver.

In the afternoon we felt the need of water and sleep. Some of the men were able to sleep profoundly despite the noise and the heat, but most only dozed, starting into wakefulness from time to time. Frank, George and Sergeant Phillimore however all went off into complete unconsciousness. Frank was stretched like a corpse in the bottom of his trench, and George similarly occupied his and mine. I hadn't the heart to disturb him, so I rigged up a canopy for myself with a groundsheet, on the surface, and crawled under it, determined to sleep. It was delicious to sit down on my bottom, stretch my legs, and wriggle my toes. Dare I take off my boots?

Why not?

I removed puttees, boots, hose-tops and socks, and bared my reeking feet to the fresh air. First time for seventy hours. Gently I poked between all my toes with my fingers. My toes joyfully wriggled of themselves. I stretched in the shadow of the canopy and reached for the almost empty whisky-bottle. No water? No matter.

In the immediate relaxed second before I fell asleep, I deliberately banished the desert, the sound of war, the heat, the flies from my mind, and thought of the sweet things in England. Into my mind came a certain picture, a scene, as bright as enamel: the stone steps which lead down from the bowling-green at Helston to the park. Standing at the top of the steps, I saw the little oval lake, sparkling blue below, flashing up yellow reflections of the sun. Children were playing on the swings across the road: their high, thin, excited voices came up to me. Four white-clad figures dodged about the tennis-courts far below. Castle Wary and Sithney Common were brown with corn. At my back was Coinage-hall street, the voices, the people, the water gurgling in the kennels, the Alpha Hotel. I was in Cornwall in August, not in the Libyan desert with roaring guns. Then sleep dissolved the picture.

No sooner was I asleep, than dreaming. I dreamt I was a little boy again, in the house where we used to live before my mother died. (This house often re-appears in my dreams, and the world then seems older, more stable and more diffi-cult to me, not I younger.) It seemed that my mother wanted me to go across the road to the grocer's to buy some house-hold articles (*what*, I do not know, but had no doubts about getting it). I went out of the house and crossed the road to the grocer's, and at the corner where his shop was a sombre uneasiness came over me. Walls and doors had changed positions and aspects, the street was foggy and unreal. But I forced the door open, despite the heavy spring, and came to the counter, which was level with my shoulders. It was dark inside the shop and there was very little for sale, only a large card on which were strung packets of soothing-powders for babies, and on an empty shelf stood a card-board clockface which I thought was to indicate closing-time. Surely it was closing time now, it was so dark in the shop. I was uneasy and tight-throated. At last the door at the back of the shop opened and the grocer came through wearing his white apron. He had been eating his supper, I supposed, and was resentful at being disturbed. Meanings passed between us, to get what I wanted. But as soon as he had gone I saw a bottle on the counter with a wonderful label, and I suddenly knew—with a deep conviction of cer-tainty in my heart—that if I stole and uncorked and drank the contents of that bottle, come what might of discovery, I should be beyond punishment and thirst—I should have had life, life itself, the secret of life, the potency and fulfil-ment we live for and die without. But I must take it now,

310

ravish it, steal it, without any deadly risk of refusal if I asked, or reasons why not: there it was, there, for this one brief flash of reality, before it melted or receded hopelessly from my hands: drop all acquired ambition and get it *now*. I grasped the bottle in both hands, felt the weight, hardness and rondure of it with gladness that almost burst my heart, and threw myself down on the filthy floor by the counter, amongst cigarette-ends and mud and scraps, hugging the bottle in my arms. I twisted out the stopper ravenously, with my teeth: the thirst for it was not in my mouth, but aching inside my whole body, inside my heart, down my spine, and between my thighs. The stopper came out. I spat it feverishly away and got my lips to the bottle. If only I could drink drink drink quickly before anything possible happened to prevent, if I could swallow and put inside me the Reality, I should have drunk life, the craving in my heart and in my thighs, the throbbing ache would have its utter complete satisfaction. But—the—liquid—would not—flow, just a tiny heavenly drop of the essence, oh it was nearly, nearly—if I could tilt the—bottle—higher and abandon myself, relax to it quite—quite fully, I knew it would come, and then I should know all—all—and be satisf—ied, sure, yes, sure it was—there, just—nearly—*Oh God curse, curse*, the grocer was back, leaning right over the counter, grasping my shoulder,—shaking——

'Captain Burgess's compliments and would you come over to a conference at Company H.Q., sir.'

With that sense of utter unsatisfaction, panting life-thirst for ever disappointed, I woke and looked up at Burgess's runner.

The sand had clogged my watch, it wasn't going. Kenrick said I'd only been asleep two minutes. Sullenly I put on socks, hosetops, boots, puttees, and stood up. Sweaty and sandy my shirt and shorts and socks. My shirt was rucked up under my belt, my nostrils clogged with sand, my mind heavy with whisky. My dream still on me, I felt as though Burgess's runner had cheated me of a colossal fulfilment, or an orgasm: I looked sourly at his returning form: he shambled over the sand. Oh God for a long, hot, clean bath, with gallons and gallons of sweet pure water. Oh God to see these stale limbs of mine stretched out in steaming water, to have insidious soap-bubbles stealing into every carnal cranny. Meanwhile the whisky bottle was empty. Must replace. I stuck my compass in my pocket, my map-case under my arm, hung my glasses round my neck, put on my steel helmet, looked glumly at my platoon. Most of them were down trying to sleep, all but the sentries and Kenrick still working at his mortar position. I looked down into Phillimore's trench: flat on the bottom lay Frank Shaw on his back, as if in a grave, his shoulders lightly gripped by the walls of the trench. Phillimore lay up on the surface, snoring. George, in my trench, had a filthy handkerchief over his face. The flies liked it.

Burgess, over at Company H.Q., was red-eyed with lack of sleep. 'Hello Mike', he said, 'I want you to give me a statement of your position as regards ammo, water and rations.'

'Now?'

'Yes, if you can.'

'I can't. I'll have to see Phillimore and check up. I'm complete as regards ammo., though, I can tell you that now.'

'Right. Check up on the other stuff and let me have a statement immediately. It's a question of consolidating all rations and water in the battalion, possibly in the brigade, since this position must be held till we are relieved. In future, also, there can be no further issue of water by platoon commanders. I am responsible for all water held by the company, and none will be issued except by my authority and in my presence. O.K?'

'O.K.'

'One other thing. Your platoon has had no real sleep for at least three nights. You must not slack up in the least in digging or defence work, but the colonel has promised us a night's sleep, so as soon as possible after dark you will mount one sentry per section and every other man will sleep. You've got to get the men fighting fit as soon as possible.'

'Very good.'

Just before nightfall Burgess came over and supervised the issue of half-a-pint of water per man, the first water ration that day. As the evening closed, the artillery at last became silent, and Very lights began to soar into the flushed, darkening sky. Once again I lay down to sleep, determined this time not to open my eyes before dawn, when I should be a new man. I took a mouthful of water, then immediately recollected a tin of beer I had in my pack. All the day it had been tempting me, but I couldn't drink it in front of George, Frank and Phillimore. But now Phillimore had just set off on a tour of the sentries, and Peter and George were curled up in their blankets. I listened stealthily. No sound. They must be asleep. Quietly I unfastened my pack, took out the tin of beer, and tried to open it with my nail-scissors. No use, the point was rounded and would not pierce the tin.

I went quietly to the nearest pile of equipment, Frank's, piled by his trench, and softly drew his bayonet from its scabbard. Putting the tin down on the sand, I pushed the bayonet into it. It hissed, and beer creamed up round the bayonet. Like lightning I got my lips to the opening before the beer ran away down the side.

'Good health, sir,' came Frank's voice from his blankets. I crept away guiltily. Share that tin I could not.

Again I lay down and closed my eyes. Footsteps. Burgess's runner again.

'Captain's compliments, sir, and will you prepare your platoon to move off, and come over yourself to Company H.Q.'

So we didn't sleep that night. At midnight, in stealthy silence, the platoon was loading all its belongings onto two three-tonners. I did not know where we were going. but understood we were being put in to re-inforce a position where the line had been weakened by the German attack.

The entire company was loading silently in the moonlight. There was movement in the company's lines. Flares and Very lights floated continuously in an immense circle round us. To our left, a German machine-gunner fired burst after burst of tracer, dots of fire that sprayed along the horizon quite slowly, in an undulating jet like water from a hose.

At last I took my two trucks forward and we fell into our place in the company column. Then we moved off to the left, in a direction I did not much care for, as it seemed to bring us across the fire of the Jerry machine-gunner. Now we could hear the distant patter of his gun above the throb of our engines, and the glowing dotted spray of his fire came wavering across our path. We went on, and could soon see that he was firing short. Probably he was not firing at us anyway. That seemed to be the way of things: projectiles flipped about us so casually in battle that one could never be sure where, or if, they were aimed.

A mile or so further we halted. Burgess got out of the truck and stood in talk with someone. I had fallen asleep, but woke to the chill night as soon as my driver switched off his engine. I climbed down. Burgess hurried towards me. 'Get the men's coats off, equipment on battledress. Every rifle loaded and safety-catch applied. Jerry is trying to break through.'

He went off for orders. We, the platoon commanders, waited for him at the head of the convoy, our pockets full of grenades. I put an extra round in my pistol, which was loaded with five. We waited, the three platoon commanders (Dewitt, myself, and a sergeant who was commanding the remnant of Ted Carrick's platoon) and our three runners: two little groups of three, each group huddled for warmth in the lee of the leading vehicle. It was very cold. My unshaven chin and cheeks felt the cold more than if I had been normally washed and shaved.

As we waited, somewhere perhaps two hundred yards from us, but out of sight, an officer's voice rang out.

'Number one gun: five rounds gunfire—fire!'

Then came a formidable explosion, a sudden glare, and the woof-woofing whistle of a shell: and a second or two later, from over the horizon, a second vivid glare and a distant but impressive bang.

This firing continued for about half-an-hour. I supposed the gunners were working on a fixed line, possibly on some gap in the minefields which ringed us. Finally I sent Frank back for my great-coat and his own, and Dewitt and Conlon did the same. Having draped my coat round me, I lay down on the sand, head on my respirator, and went to sleep.

Burgess was gone over an hour. When he came back, he said it was all, apparently, a false alarm. But at any rate the alarm had so far interfered with the programme that it was now impossible for us to occupy the new position to which we had been moving. We should therefore return to the position we had left.

Thus the grey light of dawn saw us unloading our trucks and crawling back into our trenches, with no change in the situation except the loss of another night's sleep, and with our stores to dig in and camouflage again.

This task kept us busy till nine o'clock, when the Q.M.S. appeared with half-a-pint of tea and one sausage per man. I was much too thirsty to eat more than half my sausage.

Shortly after breakfast I found three of the men opening up a reserve can of water. I therefore got the men together and explained the situation, and instructed section commanders to be vigilant. Any section commander whose water reserves were depleted would be arrested.

Chapter Thirty-Four

The battle in our rear continued during the morning, but again we were not involved, apart from casual ricochets which came in amongst us. At tiffin-time I went over to Company H.Q. and found the C.M.S. distributing tins of fruit, part of the Naafi consignment, which I had brought out with the rations at the initial withdrawal. I took back with me enough for one tin between two for all my men. A runner followed me back to say that the tins were, of course, to be issued on payment only. (Six piastres a tin.) This order, at such a time, annoyed me: few of my men had any money left. I ignored the instruction and issued the fruit. It was pineapple: the juice was very refreshing.

Soon after this Burgess came up in his truck and took Dewitt and me to reconnoitre new positions, into which we were to move during the night. This news depressed me, since it meant a further night without sleep, the fifth. I found myself very exhausted, more so than Dewitt, who had more stamina. Thirst added to my troubles: I felt suffocated. From time to time, unobserved, I opened my mouth and breathed fully in, so that the air cooled my tongue and throat. This gave me a temporary relief, but made me drier in the end.

We went off well to the South, into C. company's area, where we all left the truck and went to look for Major Garrick, C. company's Commander.

Burgess left Dewitt and me outside somebody's tent, and dived in. We both immediately sat down on the ground, and I fell asleep. Dewitt woke me. Burgess was coming out again. Somewhere to our right a machine-gun rattled, and we saw the sand kicked up near our empty truck. 'There's a Jerry tank over there,' remarked Garrick as he led us off to another tent.

There was a subaltern in the second tent, who seemed to have been asleep. It was Ellis, one of C. company's subalterns. Dewitt asked him *sotto voce,* if he had any water.

'Water? That's a question, isn't it?' ruminated Ellis. He did not look thirsty to me. After some hesitation, he turned and unscrewed, in the obscurity of the tent, a two-gallon container, and gave us half-a-pint each. I took it with animal gratitude, yet with hatred because he had hesitated. What right had he to a two-gallon container, anyway, if all the water was now the property of Battalion? However————

Dewitt and I got up on the back of Garrick's own truck, he and Burgess in front, and we drove off. I now saw two or three tanks lying hull down on the horizon. Occasionally they opened fire, but not specifically at us. They were sweeping the entire area, unenthusiastically, with machine-gun fire. The guns sounded like Besa's: the rate of fire was much more rapid than that of a Bren—a Bren would stutter a burst of five rounds while one of these tank guns crackled out a dozen or so. Garrick's truck bounced horribly. Dewitt and I had lost all elasticity through tiredness. We jarred up and down on the boards. I observed, and it did not soothe me, that the woodwork of the truck was riven and perforated by bullets. There was a petrol can (Jerry pattern) with three holes through it. Occasionally Garrick stopped the truck and he and Burgess scanned the desert through their glasses. I began to feel faint, and wondered why, till I remembered that the only food I had had for over twenty-four hours was half a sausage—for I had been unable to eat at tiffin.

We dropped Dewitt in what was to be his position, moved on nearly a quarter of a mile, along a minefield tripwire, and stopped for me to get down. This would be my platoon area. I was foggy about the exact disposition of the enemy, but since he was more or less all around, I dismissed as academic any pre-occupations about which was my front. Burgess and Garrick shot away somewhere else, leaving me on the vasty desert, with the sun dropping to the horizon casting my shadow far behind me. I determined each section position, took pickets out of the minefield and stood them up in the sand, and marked out arcs of fire with stones. I

317

was meticulous, determined that there should be no mistakes, and knowing that I should have to find and dig this position during the night. As I worked, paced off, marked out, and took bearings, the colonel roared up in his Bren-carrier and asked was I all right. I said I was. He said he would not stop, since it would draw fire on me: and he jolted off.

Burgess, when he returned, was to take us back to Battalion H.Q. for dinner and some final instructions. I was worried because my platoon had not, so far as I knew, been instructed to load. Had I been myself, I should have realised that Phillimore, instructed by the C.S.M., would see to the loading: but I was so dazed by tiredness and hunger that I couldn't realise the possibility of a thing being done unless I saw to it myself.

The sun had actually set and the face of the desert was dark when Burgess picked up Dewitt and me and set out for Battalion H.Q. He had not been in this part of the new area before, and he lost his way. We could not help him. For two hours we blundered miserably about the desert, continually returning to where fifteen Valentine tanks lay in a line along a little escarpment. Sometimes we ran into Tank Corps men or Gunners, who never knew where anything was except their immediate H.Q. (in which they were like the infantry). My faintness increased. I cursed Burgess in my heart, and the desert and the war and the whole business. Why the hell (I asked myself) couldn't we have fought it out in our original positions, from the very first day—the positions we'd spent so long digging?

At last, more by luck than by navigation, we found Batt. H.Q., and after waiting till after ten, had dinner—cold potatoes and bully, followed by tinned fruit. My stomach craved tea, but there was none. However Dewitt and I persuaded the mess waiter to bring us each a gin and lime.

As soon as I got into the truck which was to take me back to my platoon area, I fell into a dead sleep, from which I had to be shaken awake when we reached the end of the journey. It was after midnight. The platoon had already loaded their two trucks, and were lying on the ground nearby, fast asleep in their greatcoats. I couldn't even see a sentry, so woke Phillimore and played hell. Soon after, we moved off again, and by very slow stages, with innumerable halts, made our way to the area we had reconnoitred. Here I pulled out my own two trucks from the company convoy and began unloading as fast as the men could work. It was only an hour to dawn, and I felt confident that if the three-tonners remained in sight after dawn in this position, they would be blown to hell. As soon as digging implements were unloaded, I took a skeleton section to each position and got the digging started. My anxiety was relieved a little when from each section I could hear the clink and scrape of shovels. Now to get platoon H.Q. dug in. Phillimore I had left in charge of the two three-tonners, which he was unloading into an old vehicle pit. That left Frank, George, Kenrick with his two-inch mortar, and myself in H.Q. I took them to the position I had marked and set them digging. There was no time for elaboration: each man had to have a hole in the ground. I couldn't expect George, in the short time, to dig for me as well as for himself, so I took a pick and slogged into the ground. Of course there was hard rock underneath. After the various slit trenches I had dug and occupied in the last week, I was determined to have length in this one, so I dug it about the size of a grave. George disapproved, but I over-ruled him, saying that *I* meant to be in the trench this time as well as he. I dug worse than ever, with frequent pauses. Both George and Frank were working better than I was. But they kept stopping to lick their lips, and occasionally were mouth breathing, as I was. The sky was already greying towards dawn. Phillimore, having sent away his empty three-tonners, came to platoon H.Q., and joined Peter in the digging.

Corporal Drake came up, asked to be excused for leaving his section, and said could the men have a mouthful of water to wet their tongues. I answered, had they none in their water-bottles?

Phillimore, hearing this, said they couldn't have any in their water-bottles, because no water was issued yesterday.

This surprised me. I questioned Phillimore, but he stuck

to his point, and was supported by the others. Some blunder. I issued a quarter of a pint per man, on my own responsibility.

They all talked, if they talked at all, about water. We understood now that water has a taste of its own, a clear, sharp, delicious power to soak into the parched walls of the throat.

There was rock under the sand everywhere. But section commanders did miracles with their men, and all Light Machine Guns were in good, well-sunk positions. Kenrick and his mate Stark were in the section post nearest me. I was glad of this, for Kenrick was my best gunner, and I would be able to control his fire from my own trench.

My own pit was not deep. George, for reasons obscure to me, had started another one a few feet away. He thought, no doubt, to find easier digging. Hence instead of one good pit, we had two poor ones, neither more than a foot deep. I found this state of affairs when I returned from supervising the sections.

Dawn came. A ridge, beyond the minefield wire, lay in front of us. It was a disconcerting ridge, a low fake crest, only a hundred yards from the wire, so that visibility, from my front sections, was less than a hundred and fifty yards. I hurried down to spy at this crest from the forward gun-pits, and was not happy. The depth of the dead ground might be anything up to twelve feet. The crest might cover a considerable enemy advance.

The Bren gunners were in very good heart, wishing only for two things—water, and some German infantry to shoot at. I showed them where Dewitt's platoon lay, on our right, so that they could support him if necessary.

I did not pass on to them the information that there were no mines in the minefield in front. After all, presumably the enemy didn't know that.

So far dawn had not brought us under fire.

Breakfast—bully and biscuits—was a parched meal. One could hardly masticate the dry stuff. After breakfast Burgess came over and went round the sections with me. He had a message to all troops from the commander of the Eighth

Army, a message about our own valour and grim determination, and his confidence that we should continue to do as we were doing. Nobody could really feel that so heroic a composition was addressed to him, so we all took rather an academic view of the General's exhortation. Burgess also said that the —— Armoured Division and the —— Brigade were coming to our relief at great speed. We dwelt much on the —— Armoured Division.

Going round with Burgess, I seemed to step back from my platoon and see them from a spectator's viewpoint. Burgess asked them were they all right: would their guns fire? Meanwhile I looked back at them and saw with wonder the effect of six days' unceasing work, of no washing and no shaving, of fatigue, hunger and thirst. Around their mouths was matted stubble and caked sand. Their eyes and ears were crusted with sand, their nostrils rimmed with it. Sand made their white cheeks yellow. Their eyes, dark with tiredness, stared from sandy, gummy eyelashes. They worked or stood, shovel in hand, steel helmet thrown on the sand, stained battledress tunic buttoned close for the desert chill: their dry lips flaking. I was proud of them, of their work and resolution.

'Any complaints?' Burgess grinned.

'Only water, sir,' said Herring.

At the next section we found Marlowe mopping his face and neck with a bit of damp sponge.

'You've got something there' said Burgess. 'How do you keep it moist? Dip it in your water-bottle?'

Marlowe straightened up wearily and showed teeth through sandy black stubble in a grin. 'To tell you the truth, sir, it's piss. I piss on the bit of sponge and dab my face with it when I need it.'

Burgess laughed. 'You're a dirty old man.'

'How else can we keep going?' asked Marlowe.

'They had their water yesterday, of course, Mr. Carr?' Burgess asked me.

'No sir.'

'They must have had.'

'They didn't. No water was issued while I was reconnoitring this position.'

'Are you sure of that, Mr. Carr? The C.S.M. reported an issue.'

'It didn't reach this platoon, sir.'

Burgess returned to Company H.Q., from where he sent a runner a few minutes later instructing me to issue a double ration. I said nothing about the quarter of a pint I had issued before dawn.

I went to platoon H.Q., to find my pint mug, to measure out a double ration for each man. The rumour of water was already round the platoon. Frank, George, Phillimore and Kenrick stopped digging and watched me, like cows watching a picnic-party, as I took my mug out of my pack. Their faces were uncivilised. Stubble hid the colour of their lips, except for Frank, who did not shave and was quite beardless. His mouth was black-purple, the skin of his lips glossy and cracked. His smooth face was much less disguised by sand, and revealed black hollows of tiredness round his eyes.

All were grinning at the prospect of water. Phillimore helped me to roll a forty-four gallon container into position, and I unscrewed the bung. Clear water splashed heavily into the mug, from which I poured it into their water-bottles. They drank, sitting gratefully on the sand, pausing a long time to enjoy each mouthful.

As we sat there, tranquil, we were suddenly machine-gunned.

The stutter of the gun had just that open, smacking sound which I had heard often on the range at home when I was marking in the butts, the open bark of a gun which is pointed towards you. The bullets zip-zapped between and over our heads.

We flattened out immediately. I rolled into my long trench, which, being only a foot deep, did not seem to offer much protection, and as I lay face downwards I felt very exposed, especially my bottom and legs. I was extremely frightened. The bullets continued to zip-snip through the air. Judging by the bursts, there were two guns, each firing in the blanks between the other's bursts. It sounded like a furious conversation. Then came an explosion, fairly close. A bomb or shell.

'For God's sake' I said to myself, 'pull yourself together, you are not even touched, you daft bastard.'

My bitter abuse had remarkably little effect on myself. I continued to shiver. Another explosion shook the earth and showered pebbles on me. I lay prone: to dig, I had taken off shirt, tunic and helmet, and these now lay up on the surface a few yards away. The climbing sun beat on my naked shoulders, sweat started from my skin, and the flies immediately covered me.

Shame forced my head up at last. Everybody had gone to earth.

Phillimore's steel-helmeted head rose slowly from his trench. Frank's head came up a minute later. A rending explosion just behind us sent all our heads down again. When the stones and bits of metal had stopped falling we came up once more.

'What do you think about it, Phillimore?'

'Humph, I don't like it much, sir.'

'What are the big bangs? Mortar?'

'Aye, I reckon he has a mortar up with him, sir. Six inch, it sounds like.'

'Can we do any good from Drake's position here? Kenrick's gun?'

'Not a chance, sir. He's over two thousand yards away, using heavy machine-guns.'

'H'm. But we can't let him keep our heads down. His infantry will be walking in on us. I'm going into Kenrick's pit.'

'I should hang on a minute, sir, till things settle down a bit.'

In a pause between the firing we now heard a new sound, like the rapid snipping whir of a lawn mower, but louder.

'That's a tank, sir, that rapid fire.'

Another bomb burst with a rending scream. Down we went.

Something new again—explosive bullets. They chased each

323

other across with a twang and a whine, then burst over our heads and round about.

'Bastards' said John Phillimore.

'Can you see what he's up to, sergeant?'

'No movement, sir. He's firing indirect, from behind a crest. There must be a tank or two behind there as well.'

The thought that the enemy gunners could not see us restored some of my courage. I got up out of my trench, went over to where my shirt was, and put it on—outside my trousers, like a nightshirt. Then I put on my steel helmet, and twirled the cylinder of my pistol. Bullets were still snipping like a barber's shears, but I realised with interest that they were not hitting me, and felt convinced they never would. I walked about, rather more rapidly than I need because of an illogical feeling that I was less likely to stop a bullet if I were brisk than if I dawdled. Frank was staring up at me from his trench with awe and wonder. I was much exhilarated, though in my heart I knew I wasn't such a very fine fellow. From time to time I may kid others, but I don't really kid myself.

Mortar bombs burst in the vicinity now and again, but I could not take them very seriously, seeing that no blood had been drawn yet. I ignored them, like fireworks. Phillimore came out of his trench, and started putting our water-tins below ground.

Having checked the angle of Kenrick's mortar, I left platoon H.Q. in Phillimore's hands and went down to one of the forward sections, Herring's. Here I would be able to cover the crest beyond the minefield, and also Dewitt's left flank. I thoroughly enjoyed walking across the platoon area and hearing the zip and whine of invisible bullets in the air round me. I laughed inwardly, congratulating myself. This, then, was to be under fire. This was the real thing, and I was in it.

The gun-pit in Herring's position was just over three feet deep, and quite long. Barrow and Simpson, the gun team, made room for me. I got down into the trench, and made myself comfortable at one end. Sitting down, I had my head just above ground level.

From this forward position I could see much better into a shallow depression half-right. There I could make out the turrets of two German tanks, nearly a mile away. They were stationary for so long that I thought they must have been immobilised, but this was not the case: they moved later. It was these tanks which were putting over a lot of Besa fire in various parts of our front. From time to time they turned their guns our way, and we heard the lead swish past.

I thought that some time during the day those tanks would put down a storm of fire on my platoon, to keep our heads down whilst their infantry came over the crest just in front of me. So long as we were ready for this, however, I considered we should be able to destroy such an attack with our guns before it passed the minefield.

As I slipped down into the trench, a single bullet twanged very low, near my ear. Somewhere over by the tanks, or in them, a sniper was trying to pick off the odd man. He was evidently in a position to bring his fire low over our heads. I got down quickly.

'He's there, sir' said Barrow.

A line of scrub ran along the low slope to the right of the tanks. At one point in this scrub there seemed some slight disturbance. I watched it. The sniper fired a few more rounds, but one could not feel at all sure that the fire was coming from that spot. Still, it seemed worth while to make sure.

The Light Machine Gun had been lying on its side, so as not to draw fire. Barrow half-stood in the trench and pulled the gun on to its bipod; snapped back the butt-strap, and slid his shoulder to the butt.

'Change lever to automatic.' He pushed the lever forward with his thumb.

'Put your sights to three hundred. No, make it four hundred.'

'Four hundred it is, sir.'

'Get on to that patch of scrub. Plumb in the centre of the aperture.'

He aimed. 'On, sir.'

'Foresight dead central?'

'One burst of five. When you like.'

Two seconds' pause, then off she went: 'Uh—uh—uh—uh—uh.'

'Check your aim.'

'Gone off right a bit, sir.'

'O.K. That burst was low. Put your sights up a hundred. This time I want three bursts. One in the centre, one just left, and one just right. Check your aim each time. When you like.'

The scrub took our fire without sign of movement. Probably there was nobody there. No matter, it helped to hearten the platoon.

It was hot and pleasant in the trench. The three of us took it in turns to observe for twenty minutes each, with our heads above the surface. The sniper returned to his job later, but did not seem able to hit us. I looked across to Herring's slit-trench, and saw the old chap—the only visible figure on the terrain—sitting up on the edge of the trench, smoking his pipe.

I wished I had my pipe. Instead I smoked a dozen of Barrow's Camel Brand.

For lack of anything better to do, at one time we put the sights of the Bren Gun up to a thousand and fired off a magazine at the nearest tank. It couldn't hurt them—unless a lucky round got through his visor. Even two-pounder shells bounced off tanks at more than four hundred yards. However, he flattered us to the extent of returning our fire with the quick snippersnippersnippersnip of his Besa. Barrow was delighted. 'He don't like it, sir. The fat bugger don't like it.'

Thirst, heat, sleep. Most of the men had not had that water. I had, thank God. In the intervals when not observing, I got snug in the trench and solicitously inhaled all the smoke from a cigarette. That and the heat put me into a coma.

At midday it was very hot. The battle continued, but in the trenches was peace and quiet. The noise didn't concern us much.

Then German artillery registered our position. Suddenly,

with a scream and a roar, a shell burst in the platoon area, and I saw another towards Dewitt's platoon. After that they seemed to fall like rain. I could not see across from one section position to another, because the air was filled with flying sand and stones, a sort of tattered rough curtain of smoking yellow which was continually being rent and jerked into new rags by fresh explosions. The noise was very great. All about us the desert belched instant craters, thick yellow clumps of solid smoke which stood up, then fell in fragments, thumping down on the edge of the trench. The blue was blotted out. I could only see the minefield by rare glimpses. I turned all eyes to watching forward, lest an attack should come in under cover of the barrage. Then I returned to see if all was well at platoon H.Q. Walking under shell-fire was not very different from walking under the fire of small-arms. I felt equally positive that nothing would hit me. It seemed that the noise had very little to do with me. Also there was a lull in the intensity of the shelling as I went over, and no near misses.

At H.Q. I heard somebody shouting. The sound came from Drake's section: when I got there, I found that the gun team was knocked out, both Kenrick and Stark having been wounded by an explosive bullet which had struck the gun. Kenrick was covered in blood which seemed to be flowing from his shoulder, while Stark was bleeding from his left arm. Kenrick also had a lot of blood on his face, though I could see no facial injury. Both were alarmed at the sight of so much of their own blood. One man, unfortunately, had lost his nerve, and was flat down in the bottom of his pit: and none of his section would put their heads up. This made me angry and anxious, since, with the gun team out and the rest of the section hiding their heads, a third of my platoon was out of battle.

'Sir, we're wounded!' shouted Kenrick and Stark, afraid I hadn't seen their condition.

'All right, hang on, I'm going to get you out' I yelled back, and dashed over to Phillimore's trench.

The shell fire intensified: the noise became deafening.

At H.Q., while Phillimore was calm, George and Frank

bawled at me—Frank especially—'There's two men wounded there, sir; there's two men *wounded*————' I shouted an answer which didn't seem to be understood. The shells were making a hell of a row. The air round us seemed to be cracking and flapping like a curtain. Shards of shrapnel wailed as they went past. I heard Frank shouting again—'There's two men wounded there sir and nobody's man enough to ————' Then he jumped out of his pit, ran like hell, crouching, over to Drake's position, holding his water-bottle containing what was left of the water I had issued him before the battle: and he put the bottle to Kenrick's lips. When I saw this I felt ashamed for not thinking of water for them.

When Frank was back in his trench, Phillimore jumped up onto the surface, ran over, and picked up Kenrick out of his gun-pit: then vanished into the smoke and sand, running towards Company H.Q. with Kenrick over his shoulder. Stark, who was less severely wounded, jumped out of the trench at the same time and ran with him.

The Light Machine Gun stood there by the empty pit, with no one to fire it. I looked down at George and Frank, who were now in the same pit. 'Can you two lads man the gun if I bring it over?'

They obviously didn't like the idea—why, I don't know, unless they feared it would draw fire on them. 'We can *man* it, sir' said George, 'but it's no use here. There's no field of fire.'

This was true—I verified it by getting down into the pit. I couldn't trust the gun to any of Drake's section however. I decided to take the gun over to the forward left-hand section, but when I picked up the gun in one hand and a box of full magazines in the other, I couldn't carry the weight. Shells were coming down hell-for-leather. I staggered back with the gun and magazines, from Drake's position to platoon H.Q. Phillimore came running back through the smoke and jumped into his pit.

'I want somebody to help me with the ammo', I said, putting down gun and box. The three of them looked at me dumbly, not liking it. A shell split with a crack a few feet away, and the blast knocked me down. I was neither surprised nor alarmed. It seemed a perfectly natural thing to happen. I sprang up again, intent on the gun problem. Frank was looking at me with fascinated eyes. 'Come on, lads, come on' I said impatiently, 'I can't carry the whole bloody issue myself.'

George, with a look of great annoyance and anxiety, shot up out of his trench, grabbed the gun, and ran head down towards the far section. I followed him with the ammo. The going was pretty thick. Every second came one of those deafening detonations somewhere near us. Great ragged slices of metal, twisted and hideous-edged, lay on the desert to remind us what projectiles were thrumming and wailing round us after every shell. I saw a horrible fragment, weighing perhaps six or seven pounds, its edges wickedly riven. It was a foot long and three or four inches wide. I imagined such a missile hitting me in the face. The air was full of such stuff, whining and droning all round. But we were not hit.

No attack against our position came in that day. The fighting had been to our right. In the evening, when a little sniping was the only activity, and the Jerry tanks were still in their position, Burgess came over and said that Jerry appeared to be closing down for the night. The attack had been heavy, but the brigade 'box' still stood. C. Company had been over-run by tanks, two platoons had been knocked out, and Major Garrick was dead.

I still watched the German tanks, expecting them to withdraw into the main German lines, till I gradually realised that they were, in fact, in German ground now. The Brigade box was indented in what had been C. Company's position. The Germans had moved forward there and occupied the forward areas which, that morning, had belonged to C. Coy.

Burgess was cheerful. The ---th Armoured Division was fighting its way through from the South-East, and tomorrow it would take the Germans in the rear.

I asked what were the German forces attacking us. Burgess said, two armoured divisions, one Italian (the Ariete) and one German (the 15th). The conception of our Infantry Brigade being attacked by two armoured divisions made me reflective. Two divisions meant, I supposed, about three hundred tanks. We had fifteen, I understood.

Those fifteen of ours couldn't play any very significant part, since they were Valentines mounting two-pounder guns, whereas Jerry fitted his Mark IV's with six-pounders, and could knock out our tanks, without coming within their range. Hence their pre-occupation was mainly to keep out of the way—'until they could surprise him.'

I scratched my head and hoped the ---th Armoured Division was not too far away.

I issued water to the men as soon as evening had lulled the battle. They were almost crazy with thirst. Marlowe, to whom I praised Herring's coolness, said, 'He's the best man you've got in the platoon, sir. Do you know what he did during the afternoon, when he'd not had any water for two days?'

I said I didn't. I hoped he'd drawn on his section reserve.

'Not him, sir. He *would not touch a drop* of that water after you'd said nobody was to have it. He pissed into his mess tin and added three sterilising tablets, and drank it.'

There had been no food all day. When evening, a very beautiful evening, closed down on the desert, I went over to H.Q. to ask Burgess about a meal. He said a hot meal was coming up from B. echelon, and pointed over to the East. I had no idea where B. echelon now was, but stayed hopefully scanning the east till the darkness made it useless. Burgess, saying the cook's truck must have got lost, sent me back to issue biscuits and bully. Long after I learned that the Q.M.S., with the cook and the cook's truck, had run into the German lines in the dark, and while we waited, a party of German soldiers was eating our dinner.

I had to fix up a patrol to contact adjoining platoons during the night; and section sentries. Apart from this, the order was rest. Burgess said that this time we could depend on staying the night in the same position, and we were to make the most of it. After the stimulus of the day's excitement we were remarkably tired. I found it hard to walk straight. I went round the sections detailing the night's orders, and passing down a new message of encouragement, that a supply column, led by General Lawson, was on its way out to us, and was expected to break through the enemy's lines in the morning. The men were very pleased with themselves, glad because of this message, and stupid from lack of sleep.

As I returned to platoon H.Q., the German Very lights were once again soaring into the sky around us. They were very near now, and the ring around the brigade position was unbroken. I grinned at them, and did not find the situation at all odd. It was like living on a small island: the lights marked the edge of the unknown, incalculable sea. But the social construction of the island community was perfectly stable and dependable. Relying on that structure, I was going to have a good night's sleep. I had brought a bottle of gin over from company H.Q.: taking a mouthful, neat, of the scent tasting stuff, I wrapped myself in my greatcoat, and went to my trench.

George was fast asleep in it. I woke him and told him to get out. He did so, looking at me as if I had destroyed his faith in Man, but I was not moved. I lay down in the grave-like hole, head on my respirator, and was immediately unconscious.

Chapter Thirty-Five

I was awakened by Burgess's batman, some time in the cold, still night.

'There are two trucks coming to your platoon area shortly, sir. Will you have everything ready to load on them and have your platoon ready to move?'

'Eh? Eh?'

'Will you get your platoon ready to move, sir, there are two trucks coming.'

'Oh Jesus Christ Almighty!'

I lay in the grave-pit too paralysed with fatigue, horror and disappointment even to get up. So we couldn't have our sleep!

At last I dragged myself out of the hole where I had been more comfortable than on swansdown, and peered down into Phillimore's pit. He and Frank were both fast asleep in that one narrow little slit-trench, their limbs and bodies indistinguishably intertwined, and so hard asleep that they might have been anaesthetised. I pulled, pushed, shook and shouted at Phillimore, but he only grunted. He would not wake, was determined not to. I could read mad resolution in his inertia—'let the Jerries come, I don't give a monkey's f--k'. At last I dragged him out of sleep, like a whelk from its shell. As he disentangled himself from Frank, the latter opened his eyes anxiously, then shut them again with a shudder.

'Come on now, John Phillimore, for Christ's sake wake up, we're moving again. How long's it going to take you to have everything ready for loading?'

'Oh—Ah—Oh—AH:—not long.'

'Right. Go down to the dump in the old vehicle pit now and start getting the stuff ready to go on. I'm going round the sections. I shall be responsible for all section arms, ammo and men, so don't worry about that side of it. I shall send you two men from each section to form a loading party, and when the trucks come, I'll send one to you, and take the other myself for section stuff. That clear?'

'Yes sir.'

'You will take Frank or George with you, I don't mind which: before you go, leave your own kit ready packed, and see that mine is packed also. No noise.'

'Very good sir.'

One's feet were painful and sore, hobbling round the sections.

The trucks were a long time coming, and when they did come, there were six of them issued instead of two. I judged they had all come to me by mistake, and therefore I sent four away to the other two platoons. It was rather worrying, because a desert mist had sprung up, and it was very easy to get lost.

At last I had my trucks loaded, my men all on—sitting on top of the baggage—and we formed up in the Company Convoy and moved slowly off. When we had gone a quarter of a mile, the Germans on the other side of the minefield heard our engines, and began to pump shells into the darkness. We were not hit. Then an aeroplane flew over and dropped a couple of flares which lit us up like limelight: returning, the same plane bombed us, without accuracy.

Almost at the break of dawn we unloaded our trucks into yet another disused vehicle-pit, and I chased the sections off to occupy a platoon position which I'd never seen before, but which—amazingly enough—*was already dug for us*. But it was a bad bit of digging. My platoon H.Q., into which Phillimore, Frank, George and I tumbled together with our day's rations of bully, milk, sugar, tea, water, sausages, and biscuits, was a hole five feet square and two feet deep. No protection whatever from tanks, and not much from shells. I couldn't see much, except to the north, when I stood up. Most of the desert was dead ground. But over the minefield I glimpsed, in the morning light, a patch of desert quite close to us, which was crawling with guns, tanks and vehicles. We could also see a few slit-trenches on the German side.

No sooner was daylight strong enough than everything

broke loose. Shells, bullets and bombs came over very thickly.

Muffled in our greatcoats we sat facing each other, our backs against the wall of our pit, our feet intermingled in the middle. A good deal of miscellaneous kit had been slung into the pit, including some jerrycans full of petrol, and a bale of camouflage net. In the little space left we cooked our breakfast in a sand-tin soaked in petrol. The tea was insipid: I had rationed it too strictly: George drowned it in tinned milk to make up for the shortage of tea. Then we cooked the sausages in their tin and opened it with a knife. Nobody spoke much. Frank slept now and then, for very short snatches. His anxiety, more than the noise, made me realise that the shelling was much heavier than the previous day. With it was a sense of exposure, for in the wide square hole we occupied there was a risk that a shell might fall in with us. Frank was very agitated.

When the shells came very close, one was aware of the formidable sound of splitting metal. Debris, stones and metal flew constantly into our pit. We kept our steel helmets on. We seemed to be midway between our own guns and the Germans'. Both sides thundered across us.

I fell asleep, and was awakened by Phillimore. 'Stukas, sir.' Half a dozen German planes were coming down out of the sun. They roared over the platoon, then their machine-guns blazed. They seemed to be attacking our artillery. Others followed them. We felt as if we had been tumbled into a basin and put out for the great birds to peck at. Phillimore and I tugged a camouflage net over the trench. Under it we were soon breathlessly hot, and ticks ran all over us from the net. I wriggled out of my greatcoat.

Up to now the artillery of both sides had mainly been exchanging shots over our heads. Now came a change. The Germans were dropping their shells short, onto our position. I suggested to Phillimore in a whisper, as we peered over the edge, that the Germans had shortened range. He nodded.

And our guns were no longer replying.

Now the shelling became indescribably heavy. We knew in our hearts that such shelling could not be explained as shorts or overs. It was an aimed barrage.

It shook our nerves, made our hearts thump, and gave us no rest. Right and left, before and behind, the air was incessantly split by explosions. The screaming, cracking and rending of projectiles made one unbroken roar.

Frank turned as white as paper, shut his eyes, put his hands over his ears, and pressed himself back in his corner. '*I don't like this,* sir.' At every near miss he cringed, and even whimpered. Phillimore's face was very serious. He pushed out his underlip when the shells came very close, and shook his head. It was a cruel bombardment.

A colossal '*crack*'! seemed to lift the earth itself. Metal whistled into our pit, biting into the earth. Phillimore prodded with his boot a piece of hot shrapnel as big as his hand, and shook his head.

'I can't stand this, sir,' said Frank.

I looked at him. 'Come, this won't do, son. You mustn't get a shake on, you know. All this noise doesn't mean a thing. Lie back and forget it. You will make yourself ill if you worry, and you don't want to go sick, do you?'

He tried to lie back and relax. The bombardment continued. His face was twitching with horror. I poured him out a good measure of gin, diluted it with grape fruit juice from a tin I had. It did him good. 'God, that stuff puts life into you, sir,' he said, flushed again, but calmer.

'Good boy', I said. 'Now see if you can get a few minutes' sleep'.

I was in some physical terror myself, but it had only infected one side of my personality: because at heart I did not entirely believe in the reality of what was happening. Other things that had happened even years earlier in my life were real: I believed them, they fitted me and shaped me. For instance, the fear, when I was very small, that my father would beat me for running behind a motor-lorry and stealing a ride; the time when I had a toy bow and arrow, and shot the arrow into the eye of the girl next door; my mother combing my hair with a small-tooth comb, and looking for any lice falling on a sheet spread on the table: the Mason Pearson hairbrush with a patch where the bristles were worn off: the twopence I had every Saturday, and the whipped cream walnut I used to buy: Joey's arm round my shoulders: the sun-pattern of the school window across my desk at four o'clock, when we stood up to sing 'The Day Thou Gavest, Lord, is Ended'; all those things happened to a real me in a real world which I didn't make and was more of my choosing. But since then I had led life after life, each one more chosen and more consciously willed by myself, and each one *less real*. The intensest of them all was the life with Elizabeth, but it was not at all real as those early days had been: it was fluid, I, I, I could change it and modify it, but the earlier realities were deeper in me, fixed, immovable, not to be changed in the least by all the different elements I later chose to swim in.

And this battering of explosives in the desert was so improbable and unlikely that I (that personality which had known reality and remembered it) simply did not believe. It couldn't be so, it was preposterous, reality was not like this. You couldn't take it seriously. It was outrageous, romantic, illusory. It was an illusion.

Yes, I *was* very afraid that a shell would drop right in with us and lift us all up in a fountain of blood and bone and stone. But what saved me was the imbecile certainty that it couldn't happen. Thank God the Unconscious is stronger than logic: its fictions are the only facts we really believe. I was too well conditioned to believe in anything except the usual. My reasonable terror couldn't get down to the foundations of my being. At bottom, I didn't believe the show was real.

Just consider: I have been able to walk through shell fire: yet I have never had the courage to dive off the ten feet platform in a swimming bath.

Frank slept for a few minutes. Phillimore and I bobbed about for a few minutes, trying to see what was happening. 'I can't understand it, sir' said Phillimore.

'Neither can I.'

The silence of our own guns was puzzling.

George, having eaten his breakfast, needed to empty his bowels. It was not safe to go above ground. Frank, waking, advised him to use the empty sausage tin. This raised a

336

quantitative problem, since the sausage-tin was quite small. 'What shall I do, sir?' asked George.

I reflected. The four of us were crowded, legs bent double, into a space not much greater than that between the legs of an inverted dining-table. The proposition that George should endeavour to defecate, within this compass, into a small tin can, was not enticing. On the other hand, either here or nowhere must George function: he could not go up into the barrage. But George himself was very reluctant to perform a manoeuvre so complex, difficult and personal, within so intimate a circle. The spirit was unwilling, but the flesh was strong. Then again, this was not an isolated case: the need could, in fact would, occur to any of us—Frank, e.g., thought he might—in short, the contingency demanded a general ruling—nay—I myself———

Just then, before any conclusion had been reached, Phillimore drew my attention to several tanks on the horizon to our right: they appeared to be moving in single file into the brigade box. We watched them disappear behind a low crest.

'What's happening?' said Phillimore softly.

'I don't know. I don't know. There was no opposition.'

'Were they ours?'

'They could have been, I suppose.'

'The –th Armoured Division?'

'Possibly. What did you think of them?'

'I dunno', said Phillimore slowly, 'they looked like Jerries to me.'

'I thought so too,' I admitted. My heart felt tightened.

We sat down again, and looked at each other. Frank and George scanned our faces anxiously, looking from one to the other.

'What's on, sir?' asked Frank.

I grinned, rubbing my bristly chin. 'That's a question, son. Some tanks have come in.'

'What's wrong with our artillery?' asked George.

'Dunno, lad—I reckon the gunners know what they're at.

It now occurred to all four of us simultaneously that the German barrage had also stopped, as if a tap had been turned

337

off. Only occasionally, from quite a distance, we heard the crash and whistle of a gun. This altered George's situation, but it also meant other things.

'Somebody's wrapped up,' said Phillimore. I nodded. 'Nothing we can do, except wait and see.'

We did this for some time, half dozing in the hot sun. The unnatural quietness round us continued, but for distant noises. George reflected on his physical needs, and from time to time made statements on his condition and the dependability of his resistance. Finally we decided it was safe to go aloft, but before he went, I stood up to look.

When I got up and looked over the edge, I saw a German armoured car parked about twenty-five yards away. The head and shoulders of a man projected out of a trapdoor on the top. He held a pair of fieldglasses to his eyes, and was looking all round him.

'God love me,' I said faintly. 'Phillimore, look at this.'

Phillimore looked, and froze.

The man on the car had not seen us. He was cool and unhurried.

The car was a big thing with a kind of deck on it, and a rail, reminding me of a launch.

'I'll have that bugger' said Phillimore, bringing his rifle to his shoulder. I picked up Kenrick's rifle. Drake's voice came from one of the sections.

'Sir! *Sir!* There's a Jerry armoured car!'

The car was now turning round and bouncing gently away from us. The noise of its engine presumably prevented the observer from hearing Drake's voice. Phillimore opened and closed his bolt and fired. At the shot the observer ducked and turned round, looking for us. He ordered the car round, and cruised in a circle. Phillimore snapped his bolt again. The range was now about a hundred yards, the target bouncing. I was trying to get a round up in Kenrick's rifle —it was dry, and jammed. I jerked the bolt open, the round sprang out over my shoulder. I slammed home the bolt with all my force, snapped down the lever, took the first pressure and (accidentally) the second as well, and put the bullet

clean through a jerrycan of petrol. At the same time Phillimore fired again. The car went off to the right.

'He'll come back with half-a-dozen tanks' said Frank appre-
hensively.

Phillimore held up his hand. 'Listen.'

From beyond the crest we could hear a distant, grating
roar, like the sound of a cement-mixer, and every now and
then the high speed crackle of Besa guns.

'Tanks busy over there.'

'Where's the anti-tank rifle?' I asked.

'With Herring's section, sir. But you can't stop tanks with
that.'

I shouted to Herring's section. 'Bowers! Can you hear
me?'

'Yes sir.'

'I want you to come over here with your anti-tank rifle
and ammunition. Right away.'

'Coming sir.'

With Bowers in with us we were very crowded.

Ten minutes of hot silence, but for the noises beyond the
crest, and more tank sounds to the rear. Then Phillimore
said 'here they come.'

I was lounging in the bottom of the pit. 'What?' I asked.

'Tanks, sir.'

'How many?'

'Two—and here's another. Three.'

'Oh.'

We lay quiet, listening to the distant roar and clank and
clatter of the approaching tanks. The two boys were watching my face. Their fixed eyes were drilling down under my
expression, searching for some confident certainty in my
heart. They had no straw of their own to cling to, but if I
had any real certainty of salvation, they would cling to that.
In my heart I had nothing to offer them. I was not much
afraid, but I was absolutely ignorant of what was likely to
happen, and I was not now (in one sense) interested. Too
much of me had detached itself and become a spectator.

The reality was too strong for me, too solid and deadly:
I could not accept it. I suppose I was so afraid that I had lost

the power to admit reality. If I can find any words at all to correspond to my state of mind then, they are 'things can't be as bad as they seem.'

I could see the evidence, but I couldn't draw the conclusion. To the boys, the reasoning was simple: —'Tanks are attacking us: we can't touch them: they will slaughter us: I shall be dead in half-an-hour.'

My process of reasoning was: —'Tanks are attacking us: we can't touch them: they would slaughter me in our position: but I can't draw that conclusion.'

I wouldn't finish the sequence: the last term remained blank.

'They're splitting up, sir. One's going off to the right, another to the left, and one in the middle coming down towards us. Ah—you bugger. Here's the armoured car again, sir.'

'Ah', I said, making my hands a pillow for my head. 'Are they in range?'

'Thousand yards, sir, but coming on fast.'

'Yes. I hear them.'

'We can't do anything against these things, sir,' said Frank, 'they'll mince us up.'

'By Christ, sir, I wish we were in our slit trenches instead of this hole,' said Phillimore.

The sound of the approach continued.

'This is—*bloody awful*, sir. We're *trapped,* in here,' said George.

'Steady. We've not started yet.'

'But he's got Mark *14's* out there.'

'Um.'

'Bloody Wars!' said Phillimore gravely.

'What?'

'There's something coming up behind us. A tank.'

'In range?'

'No.'

'Oh Christ!' said Frank, covering his eyes.

'Steady. Everybody will now drink some gin.'

We drank up the remaining half-bottle. Then I got up and looked round. The boys followed my example.

The armoured car was running well into range. Behind it was a tank. There was another tank out to the right. It had stopped, while a third tank moved quickly round on our left. Behind, on the crest, two more tanks were visible.

I beckoned Bowers, and we set up the anti-tank rifle on the edge of the pit. There were some boxes of Bren ammunition on which Bowers knelt to brace himself.

We could hear, principally, the left-hand tank grinding into position: there were also unexplained noises in our rear, and suddenly a long burst of machine-gun fire quite close to us.

'Oh God I don't like this, sir. I don't wanna be mangled up by them bloody tanks. They can get into a hole like this,' said Frank.

George broke in: —'Mark 14's he's got out there, sir. We can't do a thing.'

I settled in the pit again. 'O.K. Bowers?'

'He's coming up into the sights sir.'

'Good enough. No hurry. I want———'

'He's up, sir!'

'Who? The car commander?'

'Yes, he's standing up, head, shoulders, chest———'

'Hang on.' I got up and looked. There he was, not more than three hundred yards away. I flicked the sight-lever.

'Shoot him in the belly.'

'Yes sir.'

I left it to him and shouted 'Section commanders will control their own fire and will fire on all tanks and other targets as soon as in range. Herring?'

'Very good sir.'

'Drake?'

'Yes sir.'

'King?'

'Yes sir.' ———

King's answer was drowned by the roar of Bowers's anti-tank rifle. I swung back to look at the armoured car. The observer was hanging by his hips from the turret, and in a second, as I watched, he slid out and rolled from the jolting vehicle onto the desert. Bowers jerked open the bolt, slammed it home, and fired again, and again. The car pulled out to the left, trying to turn and get away, and then stopped.

As it stopped, the tank on the left opened fire with its Besa. A stream of bullets, like water sprayed from a pipe, whanged into the top of the pit. The bullets twanged in the air, following each other so closely that they produced the familiar lawn-mower sound. A couple of bullets hit the anti-tank rifle and screamed off sideways. Sand and stone shot into the pit. We dropped, crammed together, into the bottom. As we huddled there, we heard the tank on the right move forward to close in on us.

'I don't wanna be mashed up by them buggers' said Frank. 'If it was infantry I wouldn't mind. Oh God I don't wanna be mashed up.'

'Easy, old son' I said, 'we're only starting now. We'll show the buggers a thing or two.'

The tanks were weaving in. I popped up, with Phillimore, and watched them. Now the one on the right, having come within two hundred yards, stopped, and immediately opened up with its Besa. I saw the strike of the bullets along the wall of the pit. They'd seen us all right. The left tank was coming in now.

But suddenly Drake's Bren gun roared, chattered, snarled, bared her teeth in burst after burst, and was followed straight away by Herring's gun and King's. There they blazed from each angle of our position, all the fire I had, unleashed, set loose, invincible, screaming at our great enemies. God in Heaven, it was good to hear them. God it was good. *Were* we beaten, then? *Were* we broken? *Had* the tanks silenced us? Had they? By God, hear those guns, burst after burst after burst—hear that savage, incessant, intolerant chattering, chattering—hear them now, hear them—tanks eh? tanks. Even tanks don't like it to rain lead—again, again, again, all three guns outbraying each other, hammering the air, with a combined roar like three pneumatic drills, or all the riveting-machines in a shipyard. And the tanks answering with their wicked crackle—backwards and forwards lashed the storm of lead, while Phillimore fired

342

regularly and steadily on a target behind us, and Bowers blazed off round after round from his anti-tank rifle.

We were transformed. The platoon was fighting. 'We'll stop the buggers, sir, we'll *stop* 'em'. We were taking lunatic risks, sticking our heads up into the torrent of lead that whipped about our pit. We laughed, infected by the monotonous iron laughter of the Brens.

Frank suddenly saw the boxes of Bren magazines in the pit. 'Look at these sir. The Brens are going to need these.'

'Yes. Too late now.'

'I'll take them out to the sections, sir.'

'You won't.'

'I will, sir—you give the word, and I'll get this ammo across to the guns.'

If I'd said yes, he would have been dead as surely as if I'd shot him myself. 'No, Frank. You are not going.'

What difference would it have made? In my heart I knew the tanks wouldn't stop for Light Machine Guns.

'John Phillimore, if you keep your head up there, you'll stop a bullet.'

Phillimore, his eye bright but his face sober, watched the desert. The fire went on. But the tanks were still crawling in.

'You can't stop 'em, sir,' said Phillimore. 'Brens won't stop 'em.'

'Rifle-bombers?'

'There they go' he said, shaking his head. We watched the grenades burst, short of the tanks. 'Two-pounders can't stop these things, sir. You'll never tell me that grenades will.'

King's gun had stopped firing. 'A gun-team out' suggested Phillimore.

'Or the gun.'

'Where's our artillery?'

All three tanks, approaching us, now opened heavy fire. We flattened in the bottom of the pit, trying to get down into the earth. They were now so close that the least ridge in the ground permitted them to fire down into our pits. They fired without remission, all the time edging closer, one at a time. Our own guns were all suddenly silent. There was only the roar of the tanks' guns and the sound of their tracks clanking as they came in.

'No bloody good, sir. No bloody good' muttered Phillimore.

As I squeezed down into the sand, my knees soaked in cool petrol from the holed jerrycan, I saw what the end would be. They would pull up till they could fire down into us. A couple of bursts would do it, and leave us piled in the bottom of the pit, silent, face down among the junk and tins and camouflage nets.

From right, then left, came the clank of the tracks, the jolt of heavy metal, the whir of engines.

'They can get their tracks in here, sir,' said Phillimore.

'They'll mash us up. They won't take prisoners here,' said Frank.

'Easy does it. John, let's have a suggestion.'

Phillimore's face was grey, his eyes desperate. 'I dunno. Our artillery could have done the trick, but they've packed in, I reckon.'

'So has Jerry.' The tanks had suddenly ceased fire.

We looked over the top. The tanks were coming right in on us, like great cars pulling into a park. Phillimore pushed his safety-catch forward. But there was not a man to be seen.

Phillimore dropped back into the pit: looked at me, and then at the ground, wildly. I could feel the others eyeing first me, then him. At last he raised his eyes above my head and said, 'Oh God, send the --th Armoured Division.'

'Sir, look!'

A number of British soldiers, about a platoon, were moving down the crest to our rear. They carried no rifles and were not taking cover. Their hands were raised.

'Jerry's all over us, sir,' said Phillimore.

'Um.'

From behind these men came a German motor-cyclist, and steered towards us, at about fast running speed, bouncing and zig-zagging. His rifle was slung on his back. As he rode, his feet sprawled out one after the other in giant strides, treading the sand to keep his balance and correct the swerves and skids of his rear wheel. We could almost see the concentration of his face.

'That's one bugger I'll have' said Phillimore, sliding his rifle over the edge.

We could hear the engine beating, sometimes revving up on loose stone. We could even see the quick nervous adjustment of the rider's hand on the twist-grip. Phillimore steadied himself and stopped breathing. Then he fired.

The motor-cyclist stood up, the machine came forward under him and rolled easily on its side, where the spinning rear wheel caught up his foot. There was a sudden jerk, both machine and man spinning half round in the sand, then the engine stopped.

Some German vehicles were coming forward over the crest. The tanks were circling our position. Their speed was astonishing: as if steam-rollers should move at thirty miles an hour. There was a German carrier approaching our position, now perhaps a hundred yards away. A soldier standing on the front of it was waving to us. As he came near, his voice reached us————

'———— Kaput ————'

I took out and primed a bakelite grenade. Then Herring's Bren, long silent, opened fire on the German.

For about ten seconds the Germans pumped lead at us. The tanks swerved in and blazed down into the positions. The German carrier had a Besa gun too. Then they stopped, suddenly. I looked up, and found myself facing the German carrier, which was about forty yards away. Its Besa gun pointed square in my face. The same German, unharmed by our fire, stood up clear in front.

'Kommen Sie her, Kamarad. You Kaput, for you the war is over.'

'You'll have to go up, sir,' said Phillimore.

I nodded impatiently, and stood up on the edge of the pit.

Chapter Thirty-Six

Six feet of elevation made a difference to what I saw. The place was alive with Germans. Their vehicles were crawling all over in what had been dead ground from the pit. Beyond the tanks were infantry, all working smoothly in their sections.

I felt very naked to bullets, but nobody was firing. I held up my hands, realising however what would happen to me if Herring's gun fired again. (He told me later that his gun was knocked out in the final fusillade.)

Phillimore was shouting to all the platoon. 'Throw away your bolts and magazines. Break all weapons'. There was a pick in the pit, with which he knocked Frank's tommy-gun to pieces. Meanwhile, as my men came out of their trenches, holding up their hands, a company of Germans was occupying the position.

My men were all smiling or laughing, partly, I suppose, so that the Germans would not shoot them, partly as a nervous reaction. Everything had become completely unreal again. It was like a play. Frank came to me with my greatcoat.

'Here's your coat and Glengarry, sir' he smiled, 'I've put two tins of bully in your coat pocket.'

'Thank you, Frank,' I said absently. I was looking for the cork of my water-bottle. The Germans were beside us, watching: an officer was coming towards me. 'Let's have a drink.'

I tipped up a two-gallon container, then passed it to Frank. Phillimore was strapping his pack on his shoulders, George had vanished. The platoon area was as busy as Piccadilly Circus: people were strolling or hurrying in all directions. The tanks were moving off to the left. The German Officer told me to follow him, and went off without looking back. I continued my vain search for the cork. Frank stood in the pit, scrambling amidst junk, looking for his own water-bottle.

Then a German N.C.O. came up and requested us to move over somewhere else. He called us 'Kamarads', and smiled. Frank climbed out of the pit and suddenly turned to me, as if deciding to say something that was on his mind.

'Sir, take your pips off and come with Sergeant Phillimore and George and me. You'll be happier with us than if you go as an officer.'

He stood waiting for my answer, looking at me with great kindness. I was not surprised. Everything was unreal, even kindness and the evidences of affection. Yet there was a solid, half-unexpected reality in this: something reciprocal. I had cast my bread upon the waters, and it had really come back.

'I can't, Frank. I'm still under military law. Besides—it's *me, myself*, kid—I haven't the guts.'

He half-turned away, a wry sadness mingling in his smile, and we left the pit together. 'I do understand, sir. It just couldn't be done.'

Phillimore joined us: we walked across the sand. Suddenly a machine-gun chattered, and bullets whipped round us. Startled, we fell over each other into the nearest slit-trench. But it was not big enough, and the three of us, jammed in side by side, could not get our heads under cover.

Everybody had scattered. Near us, a section of Germans were flat on the ground behind a Light Machine Gun. Though they were exposed, they made no attempt to turn us out of our trench. All the Germans were much excited. It was like seeing behind the scenes in a theatre. We had seen the fighting from the front, now we saw it from the back. This was how it was done.

From the moment of my capture I had been in a condition like stupor. Things were not real to me. I was incapable of considering the loss of my platoon position as an incident in the larger battle. I had no thought of the future, I was quite careless what happened to me. (Frank's bringing me my greatcoat had seemed fantastic—I felt neither interest in, nor responsibility for, the future of my body.) But one intense realisation now pierced through my mental paralysis. Burgess, with the remnant of the company, was counter-attacking.

Where he had been, or what had been happening in his vicinity, God knows. Since the preceding night I had not known where Company H.Q. was. I suppose he had been in some fighting, and been driven out of his position. Falling back towards my platoon, he saw it over-run by the enemy, and no doubt determined immediately to counter-attack.

The company came on in extended order, just as on training, keeping their distances carefully, at a steady double over the low crest just in front of us. The Germans were very tense and watchful behind their weapons: some were grinning excitedly.

From this little patch of desert, a sense of death and helplessness flooded in a great invisible wave which implicated even the sun and the sky.

I could see each individual section of the attacking platoons. Their bayonets were fixed, their rifles at the high port. They kept their alignment: they couldn't have done much better on Salisbury Plain. Burgess, pistol in hand, was running in front of them. Running with one leg stiff; he must have been wounded already. Serious faces. They could see Death running to meet them. The L.M.G.'s had run out to the flanks, they were firing all the time, keeping Jerry's head down. Burgess half-turned—only seventy yards from me—shouted 'Charge'. Down came the bayonets to the 'on guard', I even heard the involuntary cry of the men as they sprang forward to the last assault. Simultaneously the German guns roared, in less than ten seconds I saw half the company fall. Death struck them on the run, they bowled headlong like schoolboys stumbling in a race, they fell with the crash of their helmets, equipment and rifles. Whether all who fell were hit I don't know. Yet the others ran right on, faster than ever, full into the German fire. Burgess still ran. He was only twenty yards away now. He could feel his men still at his back. But now the situation changed very quickly. Because of the unremitting German fire, there simply were not enough men left to charge. Apart from six or seven men

348

who were still running towards Burgess, the men were either lying on the ground, or—in one or two cases—a man was standing firing his rifle at the machine-guns. While some of the Germans continued to fire, others jumped up on their feet and shouted to our men to surrender, calling 'Kamarad.' Burgess stopped, glanced back at the few men with him, turned to the enemy again, and aimed his pistol at a German soldier standing near me. The German brought his rifle to the shoulder: Burgess fired twice, the German once. Burgess fell flat on his back. Later I saw that the bullet had entered his face between the nose and the upper lip.

Some of the Germans went on shooting at our men as they lay on the ground. They killed several who were shouting for mercy. This seemed due to excitement and fear, since other Germans were at the same time calling our men to surrender. There was an oldish man from Dewitt's platoon who—I cannot understand why—had his rifle strapped across his shoulders. He got up to surrender, coming forward with his hands high up in the air, trembling, and smiling at the Germans to make them understand he was surrendering. They made signs to him to throw away his rifle, but he did not realise what they wanted, and still came on. One of them instantly shot him.

We got out of our slit-trench, and the wounded and prisoners from the counter-attack were brought in, and joined us. The Germans were exhilarated, grasping each other's hands. An efficient German sergeant came to us and ordered the men to get into three ranks. Then an officer took him off to some other task, and we returned to our listless disorder.

I looked round for Phillimore and Frank: they seemed to have melted into the fog of unreality. At last I saw Frank. A German soldier was shouting at him, signing, and pointing to his bayonet-scabbard. Vaguely I wondered why. The scabbard was not very bright. It still held the bayonet which had opened my last tin of beer. Then it struck me that probably the German wanted Frank to remove the bayonet. I moved over to interpret. However, the German pointed to a wagon about twenty yards away, and Frank went towards it.

'Oy! George!' shouted the German, apparently supposing all Englishmen to be called after their King. Frank looked round; the German signed him to run. Frank turned and trotted away towards the wagon. Before I had at all realised what was happening, the German raised his rifle and shot him in the back of the head. That was how Frank died.

I went to the body. A German—not the one who had killed him—came with me, and stood by while I looked through his pockets. He was flat on his face. His steel helmet, pushed by the fall onto the back of his head, concealed the wound. When I lifted him, I saw that his forehead was burst out by the outward passage of the bullet. His eyes were open. There was sand over the blood on his face. In his pockets I found his A.B. 64 and two letters he had had from his mother, and also one he had written but not sent: and two ten-piastre notes. I was dumb and bewildered: here was his flesh, solid and real to my touch, and his clothes, yet I could not say anything more to him, ever: could not tell him I was sorry I had not saved him after all. The same hands, the same limbs, yet he wasn't there. Touching meant nothing.

When I stood up, the German held out his hand for the papers. I shook my head and put them in my pocket. He said something in German and tapped his rifle. I took out the papers again and showed him the letters, to persuade him they were personal. He took the A.B. 64, then glanced quickly to where the other Germans were standing. Nobody was looking: he gave me the book back.

Later they took us on wagons into a German laager. It was evening when I got there. I had lost the greatcoat and Glengarry which Frank had brought me: this depressed me exceedingly. All I had was my steel helmet and my pipe, which was broken: a pair of scissors which I had bought long ago in Helston: two old letters from Elizabeth: and Frank's papers. I was dressed in shirt, shorts, socks, puttees and boots, and had nothing else whatever. Nothing to put on in the evening, or when it grew cold in the night. I had lost sight of Phillimore, George, Herring, Marlowe, Drake, King, Bowers, Kenrick—in fact of all my platoon, and did not know my fellow-prisoners. Many of them were officers. There was some attempt at separating officers from men. Most of the others had water-bottles, some had packs with tins of food in them. Many had greatcoats, all had some kit or other. I sat on the sand, leaning against a German truck. When I thought of the dead men lying on the sand, at times I deeply wished I were dead with them. But the thought of the cold night closing down on their bodies was awful.

I had had no food since breakfast. A captain opened a tin of pineapple slices and divided them amongst those near him. I had half a slice. The Germans said they would try to give us food, but at sunset they told us they could not. Nor could they give us water. We went to sleep on the sand. It was very cold, the sand became dewy and chill, and the cold pierced my thin shirt and shorts. I pillowed my head on my steel helmet. The cold did not keep me awake.

During the night we were awakened by a loud scream. Two officers sleeping near me had been run over by a tank. One died almost immediately. The other, whose legs were crushed up to his hips, was taken away on a stretcher.

We still had no food during the next day, but a German soldier who was getting his water-bottle filled at a water-tank nearby allowed me to drink it all. He said, in a mixture of languages, that I would have done the same for him if he had been a prisoner.

The Germans were all very confident of driving the British out of Egypt. They told us what a good time they meant to have in Alexandria and Cairo. They felt sure of winning the war, and spoke contemptuously of the Russians.

There was much traffic and activity in the German box all the day, and a great deal of captured British transport was brought in. I saw an armoured car, distinguished by some flag or marking which I cannot remember, in which, I was told, was Field-Marshal Rommel.

During the afternoon the German box came under heavy shelling. There was some confusion. I was on a little slope nearby, looking for an empty Chianti bottle in which I might be able to get some water. A German N.C.O. called me back to rejoin the other prisoners, and we were ordered to march. We went through the German box, to an area where tanks were forming up. This area was being heavily shelled and machine-gunned from British positions along a slope to our left. We and our German guards marched straight into this area, while at the same time two German tanks moved forward and crossed the area, putting us between themselves and the British guns. At the time our impression was that the Germans were deliberately using us as a screen for their tanks. But the British could not see who we were at that distance, and they continued to fire. As soon as we came into the open, we ran as hard as we could. Many who had kit or packs with them threw the stuff away, to run better. The German guards were as frightened as we were. The distance covered under fire was more than half a mile, and we ran all the time, as hard as we could. Eleven men were killed. A man running in front of me had his head blown off.

That evening we were taken in lorries towards the west, in a great convoy, the officers only. By now we were indescribably hungry and thirsty. A German Lieutenant talked to us before we went, and laughed when we told him we should still win the war. The last thing he told us was that we should be taken to Italy, and that the Italian word for food was 'mangiare'.

Two sentries rode in the lorry with us. The journey was a bad one, lasting all through the night and the next day. In the morning we reached Tmimi, where we were given water and a piece of bread each. Later also we were given a little of the German 'tinned bread', which was rather like malt bread wrapped in tinfoil.

Then we reached, near Tmimi, a patch of grassland by the sea, where there were hundreds of prisoners. More arrived from time to time, in big Italian trucks with trailers. We got down from our truck for the first time and joined the other prisoners. Our guards now were Italians.

The place stank strongly of human excreta. When any of the prisoners wished to urinate or defecate, they had to go a little way into the reedy grass. They could not go far because the sentries ordered them back. The air was full of flies. They swarmed on our faces, hands and knees, on every bit of exposed skin, and they buzzed in our ears. They clustered in black blots on the bandages of the wounded, marking where blood or pus had soaked through. An Italian soldier, at a table, was issuing to each prisoner a small tin of cooked beef, about half the size of a tin of bully, and a hard biscuit. There was plenty of water. Groups of prisoners were standing round water-tins, drinking: the difficulty was finding a vessel to drink from. I used one of the beef tins, though the fat floating on the water made it unpleasant. I drank four or five pints of water.

One of the prisoners who had come in my truck had a tin of marmalade, and gave me some to put on my biscuit. The flies came down on it so thickly that I had to wave the biscuit vigorously and bite it, so to speak, on the move, in order to avoid eating flies. They settled on the corners of my mouth where a trace of marmalade adhered. They sucked so hard at the skin that they almost seemed to sting. My fingers were sticky with marmalade, and whenever my hand was still, the flies covered it. They also buzzed in black clouds over the human dung in the grass.

There were officers and men in the compound. I went amongst the men, and found some, just brought in, unconscious from thirst. They lay flat and still, grey-faced, open-mouthed, black-lipped. Their friends were splashing them with water, and moistening their lips.

At last I came across some of my own men. Marlowe was fighting his way to the water-cart to get water in his steel helmet—for although there was plenty of water, the water-cart was the sole source of it for the men, and hundreds of men desperately thirsty could hardly be supplied quickly enough. Herring was in a bad state, his mouth gaping and his tongue perceptibly swollen. Marlowe brought him water. The Italian guards were giving lemons to some of the men.

Next I met George Collinson, who told me that they had marched many miles since being captured, always without food or water, though the Germans did not take from them any water they had when captured. Many men had fallen during the march, and been left lying on the sand; probably they were picked up later by German trucks.

Phillimore was in the next batch of prisoners. When he had had a drink, he told me that Corporal King had died of thirst and exhaustion during the last long march, and that Bowers had been killed by the R.A.F. when they machine-gunned an enemy area which was full of prisoners. He knew that Frank was dead. He did not complain of the Germans. They had given no food nor water to the prisoners, but they obviously had not enough even for themselves, since British counter-attacks had cut their supply-lines. 'But', said Philli-more, shaking his head, 'this will leave its mark on us'.

Marlowe, when I next saw him, was recovering his composure—he was grumbling again. 'Sir, this is a fine way for a man to spend his f——g life, isn't it? Have you ever heard of Class Distinction, sir? I'll tell you what it means, it means Vickers-Armstrong booking a profit to look like a loss, and Churchill lighting a new cigar, and the "Times" explaining Liberty and Democracy, and me sitting on my arse in Libya splashing a fainting man with water out of my steel helmet. It's a very fine thing if only you're in the right class—that's highly important, sir, because one class gets the sugar and the other class gets the shit.'

Chapter Thirty-Seven

We began to anticipate spending the night in this filthy and detestable place, but in the evening the officer-prisoners were ordered onto one of the six-wheeler Italian lorries, and we were taken along the Libyan coast road to Derna. On this trip I looked for a second time through my papers, and destroyed all traces of my unit, home address, postmarks and so on. I also destroyed Frank's A.B.64.

The road was a spectacular descent down the escarpment into Derna. There were many breath-taking hairpin bends as the road wound down the cliff face into the beautiful ravine from which Derna looks out on the Mediterranean. At times—our driver being erratic—we feared the transport would leave the road and roll down the precipice.

Derna itself was not unlike Mersah Matruh, but not desolate. Native children looked at us—with momentary interest only—as the lorry roared through the narrow streets: and then returned to their marbles and mimic wars, rightly judging the grown-up games to be less interesting and more childish. While we, playing our game under compulsion, went on to our prison, from which, unlike the children, we would not be released at bed-time: for ours was a very stupid game.

Italian and German soldiers, talking outside buildings which had been taken over for military purposes, glanced up as we passed.

The building to which we were taken might have been the town gaol. Through two clumsy wooden gates, ten feet high and twined thickly with barbed wire, we entered our cage, and the gates were bolted and locked behind us. For the first time in my life I was locked inside a prison. We were in a small courtyard perhaps twenty-five feet square, around which our stone prison was built.

We formed up in threes in this courtyard, and an English-speaking Italian told us to surrender all the papers in our pockets to him. He promised they would all be returned after scrutiny. He would not, he said, submit us to the indignity of being searched: but should any officer be found to have withheld papers, he would be punished.

Extremely tired, we stood waiting till he had collected the papers: then we were put in a long, narrow stone room, which perhaps had been a stable. The uneven floor was of bricks and earth. A sentry stood at the door with fixed bayonet. Those of us who had a blanket or a groundsheet laid it down on the floor and prepared to sleep. But first, since there was water, it was possible to wash. I tore out the inside of my steel helmet and made it suitable for holding water: the man next to me allowed me to share his razor, soap and towel. So I had my first wash for eight days.

I was depressed and despondent almost beyond endurance. To be crowded thus into this dark, narrow stone stable with no lighting, only two windows, and just enough room to be side by side on the mud floor, and to have a sentry at the door to keep us in, made me feel frantic, as if I were suffocating. I was terrified to think how long they might keep us in this same stable.

I felt with absolute certainty that I should go mad if I were kept in the place many days. Now I realise that I should have got used to it.

When I had washed, I wanted to go to the latrine. The sentry only permitted one of us to go at a time, and there was a queue, which I joined. Eventually my turn came, but the latrine, which was of the continental type, a squatting-place over a hole in the floor, was piled up with ordures to a height of a foot or more. It was revolting and humiliating.

I asked the interpreter if we should be given a blanket, and showed him that I had nothing. He promised blankets. Another officer asked for food, and said he had had only one small tin of meat and a biscuit since he was captured. The interpreter replied that a tin of meat and a biscuit was a day's ration for an Italian soldier, and we could not expect to get more than he did.

I lay down in the clammy darkness, my limbs stretched on the earth, and rested my head on my steel helmet. The man next to me spread his greatcoat so that it covered both of us.

Two Italians came in with candles, and by the smoky light they gave each of us a straw mat to lie on, and a thin, rough blanket. They also distributed biscuits, and a tin of beef between every two men. My companion agreed we should save ours for the morning.

During the night I had a vivid nightmare. I was once more in the pit where we were captured, but all was pitch black. I could hear the tanks coming in, but could not see a thing, and had a sense of utter disaster. I did not know where my men were, but knew that the moment was fatal and we should all be wiped out. In the darkness I could hear the tanks clanking and grinding almost on top of us. I stretched my arms forward into the black night, blundered and dragged myself forward till I fell into a section position, and there I gripped somebody in the dark, somebody who was asleep and would not wake. I shook him, struck him, even tried to get my teeth in him to wake him, screaming at him 'what section is this—quick, what section is this?' A babble of voices and people moving in the dark, people pushing me back and saying 'it's all right—you're quite all right now, go back to sleep, there's nothing to worry about, you're safe, everything's all right.' I dropped back to sleep, unconvinced.

The next morning I was taken, with about a dozen other officers, to a little village about forty miles or more to the west. As we left Derna, the road drew steadily inland—a tarmac road with a good smooth surface but a treacherous broken edge—till it met the escarpment, and wound up again in great loops to regain the high ground from which we had descended into Derna. All along the north coast of Africa runs this escarpment, the true edge of the continent, but at its foot is a strip of land just above sea level, sometimes three or four miles wide, sometimes merely a beach. A green and fertile margin of land, extending twenty miles or more inland, runs all round the Jebel from Derna to

Benghasi, but south of this begins the true desert, where you could no more have a settled habitation than you could build a house on the sea—indeed, it is often called the Sand Sea. The coast road we went along was the work of Fascist Italy: given the slightest opportunity—a bridge, a gradient, a junction—it became spectacular. It wound up from the beach, always turning to ascend yet higher, with a gradient just as steep as a good engine would climb, till it crested the cliff and afterwards ran monotonously along the edge of the plateau, out of sight of the sea.

The country was pleasant, wooded—though with no great trees—and sometimes the road crossed inviting little river-gorges and ravines. I was reminded of the road leading from Sheffield to Ashopton, above the Rivelin Dams. Then came corn land, set with model farmhouses in plaster and stucco, very new but not very beautiful: every one exactly like every other one: round arched porches and big shuttered windows. Political slogans were painted on the plain walls of each of these farmhouses—'Mussolini ha sempre raggione', or 'Viva il Duce'.

At last we reached Giovanni Berta, a model village made by grouping together a number of such model houses. It looked about as real as a Walt Disney set for Snow-White. Then we left the village and went by lanes amongst the square cornfields to one of the farmhouses. This was used by the Axis Intelligence.

One by one we were taken in for interview. At last my turn came, and I entered a typical Intelligence office, with desks, tables, phone, stacks of documents, and the walls plastered with maps.

'Good afternoon' said a young Italian officer, standing up politely behind his table, 'have a seat, will you?'

He wore a beautiful blue-grey uniform, smooth and fine, with shining silver buttons and stars. He was very clean and very comfortable. His tie was ironed smooth, his shirt and collar were laundry-fresh. His hair was well-brushed, glossy and tidy. His hands and finger-nails were very clean. His knee-boots were super-polished. His face was young, friendly, reserved, alert, and sensitive. He had an air of composure and control.

I glanced down at my shorts, creased, stained and sandy: my filthy shirt wrinkled like a rag round my shoulders: my cracked boots. My lank hair fell over my forehead, and I had no comb.

I put down on the floor my steel helmet containing a half-chewed biscuit, and sat down. He offered, and I took, a cigarette.

'I'm afraid you haven't been very comfortable on the way down,' he said.

'One didn't expect much comfort.'

He nodded. 'Things are disorganised up in the front areas —you understand. We shall look after you better now you're back here, though frankly you won't be really settled till you get across to Italy.'

'Italy?'

'Yes.' He paused, smiling at me. 'Now I want you to give me some particulars, Mr. Carr, relating to your parents and relatives. We like to take the earliest opportunity of notifying the Red Cross Organisation of your capture, to save your people any unnecessary anxiety.'

'Thank you.'

He pulled a paper towards him and prepared to note my answers.

'Date of capture, Mr. Carr?'

'I'm afraid you must get that from your own records.'

He looked up and smiled. 'Do you know the date of your capture?'

'Yes.'

'You prefer not to tell me?'

'Yes.'

'You will realise, of course, that we can easily ascertain it by reference to the records of the fighting units?'

'No doubt, but I'm not going to help you to do it.'

'Well, well. At all events you'll give me your name.'

'Apparently you already know it. Michael Carr.'

'Rank?'

'Lieutenant.'

'Number?'

'477573.'

'Unit?'

'No.'

'No. Why not? I ought to make it clear that this information in no way concerns the military forces. It is purely for your benefit, and will go direct to Geneva.'

'Thank you.'

He grinned, mischief breaking through the solemnity of his eyes.

'Perhaps you will reconsider giving me the name of your unit?'

'No.'

'Look here, old man, you needn't be so much on your guard. I know I'm in the enemy's uniform, but I'm acting in good faith. I'm only trying to help you.' He took from the table a map, glanced at it, and pushed it over to me, with a pencil on it. 'Will you indicate on the map whereabouts you were captured?'

The map showed the Gazala-Hacheim dispositions in detail, but my own knowledge was insufficient to check its accuracy. In any case I did not look at it closely.

'No,' I said.

He smiled patiently. 'I'm sorry. You make things so much harder for yourself. However, if you will not——.' He turned again to his writing-pad and read out the details I had given him. 'Very good. Age, please?'

'No.'

Now he laughed openly. 'What earthly use could the German forces make of your age? At any rate you will tell me the date of your commission?'

'No.'

He put down his pen and looked at me. 'You know, this is very comical. Tobruk will not fall because you tell me when you were commissioned.'

'Don't let me waste your time. I am not allowed to answer your questions. It doesn't concern me whether my replies would or would not be useful to you. I have my orders.'

'Well, well. At least you will complete this form which,

as you can see, is a Red Cross Document and has nothing whatever to do with the Axis forces.' He gave me a cyclostyled paper.

Out of the many details demanded on the form, I filled in my number, rank and name, and left the others. He tried me with them patiently, one at a time: what was my civil occupation before enlistment: or was I a regular soldier: what was my home address: my mother's maiden name.

'No', I said. 'No, and again no. The matter is closed.'

He pressed his fingers together and leaned back in his chair, looking at me as if he could find the answers in my eyes. A German Captain came in now, and the two exchanged a few words in German. The captain glanced at me out of his eye-corners and went out, smiling off-hand. The Italian returned to me.

'My superior officer says he knows your unit, in any case.'

I laughed briefly, tiring of the whole situation. 'I daresay.' He observed the bitterness of my attitude.

'You are sorry you are a prisoner?'

'Very sorry.'

'I'm sorry for you. But it might have been worse.' He paused. 'You could have been dead.'

'Yes.'

He got up. The interview was over. He gave me some cigarettes to take with me. He seemed half-embarrassed. 'Don't please think of me just as an enemy. I wish you good luck. And I hope you will soon be back amongst your friends, and the war over.'

'Thank you. I understand. Goodbye.'

'Goodbye.'

Away we went to another of the model farmhouses, this time evidently a troops' billet. They were oldish men there, perhaps some class of reservists, typical peasants, and they were very kind to us. I began to feel ill as the cool evening came on. One tin of beef per day might be enough for an Italian soldier but it certainly wouldn't support me. We spent the evening at the back of the farmhouse watching the soldiers play skittles, and talking to them by signs and approximations. You could hardly call these places farmhouses in the British sense. There was no agricultural or rural air about them: they were like buildings in a barracks: impersonal, bleak, uniform. They were as unhomelike as the waiting-rooms of 'bus stations. And though the fields all round were covered with brown, stirring oats which whispered all day in the breeze, you felt doubtful whether they would ever be harvested.

'Latrino?' said the Italians, and indicated the fields—'nelle campagne'. There was no sanitation and no bathroom, so far as we could observe. Adjoining the house was a building without a roof—no doubt intended originally for dairy or cowshed. Its concrete floor was dotted all over with piles of human dung, each with its scrap or two of paper. The smell was beastly: the flies were as bad as at Tmimi.

The Italian soldiers observed that I was ill, and broke up their game of skittles to set up beds for us all. The beds, made up of a groundsheet and an iron frame, sagged in the middle, but as I had not lain down in a bed for nine days, I was most grateful. At first I could not sleep, and did not wish to, preferring to lie awake and enjoy the sense of being supported off the ground.

From where I lay, I could see on the wall a coloured chart showing the uniforms of the British forces, with their badges of rank—so that the Italians would know their enemies. The Italians were studying the chart, like children round an interesting picture at school, and identifying our ranks. They picked out my two pips on the diagram: I was a 'tenente'.

Just as we were about to go to sleep, one of the Italians bustled in with much glee and gave us three sweets each. If we had known the price of sweets in Italy we should have appreciated this even more than we did. The Italians watched us eat, grinning to show their goodwill. I was the 'malato', they were specially kind to me. At about half-past ten—this time I had actually fallen asleep—they came in again with a bowl of hot macaroni and peas and meat, all stewed together. We had as much as we could eat.

In the morning they brought us ersatz coffee, black and sweet, and later found us some cards with which we played solo whist, while the flies bit us. There was no breakfast.

The Italians did not eat till just before mid-day. Then we had macaroni soup and a mug of wine.

During the afternoon we sat on the veranda, flipping away the flies, and looking across the fields of moving oats to some distant blue hills. Any cultivated country was beautiful and strange after the desert. In the evening a truck took us to Barce, where there was a prisoner-of-war 'cage', containing four or five hundred officers.

I was at Barce six or seven deadly days. Five hundred animals, newly caged, brooding on the change, brooding on the days when they were free to walk in any direction. Whatever we talked about (if we talked) one thought lay underneath all the time, a thought you couldn't put into words, an animal pain, the pain of being caged. There was nothing at all to do at Barce, but nobody wanted to do anything except to lie on his bed or walk up and down the narrow compound, thinking.

There was a padre in the cage at Barce, who happened to have a copy of the 'Oxford Book of English Verse' with him, and lent me it. I found it impossible to read poetry. I was beyond that kind of comfort. The dry printed words didn't mean a thing, they only strained my eyes and made my head ache. It wasn't consolation I wanted, it was my freedom. The last verse of the 'Queen's Marie' was the only thing I read twice, because it brought Frank Shaw to my mind—

> 'O little did my mother ken
> The day she cradled me,
> The lands I was to travel in
> Or the death I was to die'.

Chapter Thirty-Eight

After Barce, Benghasi.

We entered the city through an arched gate which might have been pre-Fascist. Perhaps if I had seen Cairo or Alexandria I should have been disappointed in Benghasi itself—in fact I saw the city with the same sense of wonder and romance as I had experienced at X——. I had no preconceptions. I could not demand of Benghasi that it should fulfil my expectations. What I felt was just what any schoolboy might have felt, reading his dull history about the campaigns in North Africa, if the pages faded away and the yellow walls of Benghasi rose around him.

The city is at sea-level, on the flat land between the sea and the escarpment, and is surrounded by salt marshes. Native huts and shops are on the outskirts, but the Fascist-Imperial facade predominates in the centre, with a cardboard dignity. Occasional buildings showed wide bomb-scars when we went through, though I could not be sure where Arab squalor ended and war-ravage began. I did not see any shopping centre, or much evidence of the usual life of a city, but of course we were merely being rushed along a main road. There was an open, rather beautiful tree-lined road near the railway station. I had been told to look out for the cathedral, and thought I glimpsed it.

From the main road our truck turned, and we went by a stony lane through Arab slums and bleak waste lands to an empty warehouse. We were put in the warehouse, and a sentry stood at the door to keep us in.

I sat down silently on a bed in a corner of the warehouse, and considered things: the rest of the Immortals, the action of men. All over the face of the world I saw that most men were busy, busier than usual, much busier than any idle, slothful savage, to whom they must feel superior. They were bristling with energy, making a great effort, a sustained effort which left them little time to sleep, less to think, none at all to live: they were busy sweeping all the young men into warehouses like this one, or into barbed wire pens, or into graves: and they were busy with the women and children and old people too, they were destroying them with powerful chemicals and explosives. This was the aim of the effort, the sweating multifarious work which men were doing night and day all over the surface of the earth. And surely if they had only been completely idle, only failed in every single effort, only stayed in bed from morning till night, they would have done better than all this labour: if only they did nothing at all, it would be better than doing ill. But no: such was their devotion to the duty of hate and killing that they would deny themselves rest, food, holidays, sunshine, love—they would give up the light of their own lives so long as they could be causing evil to others: so long as they could deprive parents of their children and lovers of their loves, so long as they could put millions of young men into prisons where their precious years could drop away from them dead and unused, where they could neither live their lives nor earn their food, but had to be maintained by their gaolers, alive if buried. And yet, this social system, which had visibly made one-half of the world the gaolers, if not the murderers, of the other half, and which was visibly, obviously, far blacker than the Dark Ages, was said to be an enlightened one, a civilization of temperance, wisdom, progress, thrift, foresight—all the mercantile virtues. God above, could debauchery, folly, reaction, extravagance and blindness do worse? No, because their very nature would make them fail in their ends, but the Virtues coldly saw their road clear all the way to HELL.

By the blood of those I loved who have died, by the years of my own life which have been taken from me, I swear I shall never again from humility acquiesce in the martyrdom of man, never again believe in the cunning sophistication of the world, its vulgar ignorant self-certainty, its cant and its sly admissions. I have seen the wise old world at its work: Folly and Falseness like two foul doctors poisoning their patient. The Worldly Wisdom which engendered the war was just this: Self-Interest, deliberate blindness, gay ignorance that climbs to fortune treading on its neighbour's face: and all the quackery and political-economic mumbo-jumbo which is necessary to mask and justify these things. From now on till I die I shall not cease to smash my fist into the vacant, grinning face of our cant civilization, never cease from crying 'UNCLEAN!', never cease from pointing to the blood and bones of murdered men.

Chapter Thirty-Nine

Men are perishable goods: warehoused at Benghasi some of us developed dysentery.

I had pains in the abdomen when we came to Benghasi. Though the warehouse was not particularly cold, I lay shivering on my bed, massaging my abdomen sometimes to ease the sharp pains. My head ached. There were no blankets. I got up to borrow somebody's greatcoat: I trailed my limbs across the floor like a distempered puppy. There was another issue of tins of beef, but I couldn't eat. As we could have expected, Benghasi was a breeding place for millions of mosquitoes. There were flies from dawn to dusk and mosquitoes from dusk to dawn.

In the morning I was much worse. I could not swallow, my headache was acute, and though I was still able to walk, the effort brought on waves of nausea. I asked a British M.O. amongst the prisoners for quinine or aspirin, and he gave me some tablets.

I had to use the latrine frequently. It was necessary to ask the sentry's permission, and he accompanied me to the latrine each time and stood by. I was long past worrying about that—it would have made no difference to me if the whole of the Young Women's Christian Association had been watching. As usual the latrine was a squatting-place with no raised seat, a trench dug in the ground, only a foot or so deep, with a wooden floor built over it and holes cut in the wood. Many prisoners had used it. The trench was full of ordures, and the boards were broken and fallen in. One squatted on the edge. It was a horrible place, black and buzzing with flies. The act of evacuation, which I performed over a dozen times during the morning, so exhausted me that I came near to fainting: I was afraid of falling into the disgusting trench. I had attacks of vomiting also when I went to the latrine: I became so weak that I clung, trembling, to a nearby railing for as long as half an hour. In the afternoon the Italians took me off to hospital.

In the ambulance I suffered considerably from nausea and the sharp, sickening abdominal pains. The driver took the vehicle very slowly over the cobbly roads so as not to shake me. My intestines worked convulsively: I thought we should never reach the hospital.

When at last we stopped inside the gates, I crawled down and said 'Latrino', and once again was led to one of the universal squatting-places. I foresaw a difficulty about toilet-paper, but it was not in my power to hesitate.

Having finished, for the moment, I tried to explain to the not very intelligent young Italian standing by that I wanted paper. I thought the need would have been obvious, but apparently it was not. I did not know the Italian for 'paper', and however lacking in dignity my position (squatting in the knees-full-bend position in a smelly latrine, balancing on my toes, holding my shirt clear of all contacts), I could not proceed to the last humiliation of demonstrating to him by dumb show what I wanted. I tried him with French, German, English and Latin, gazing up at him anxiously from under my eyebrows. Evidently the situation seemed comic to him, and he laughed—not maliciously, but because he couldn't help it. I peeped sombrely up at him, like an exhausted frog, and—dubiously admitting to myself the remoteness of the Egyptian Empire both in time and space—tried him with 'papyrus', which I later Italianized to 'papyro'. Perhaps 'papyro' *does* mean something in Italian, something funny. He shook with laughter. He dared not meet my eye, but looked away in polite embarrassment and snorted with laughter. It was an impossible situation.

At last another Italian came, understood, and gave me some paper, whereon the one who had been laughing became conscience-stricken and gave me the envelopes off his letters from home.

The Italian doctor and nurses were very kind. They examined me, made cooing noises expressive of commiseration, and put me in a soft, springy bed with clean sheets and blankets and a white pillow. There they brought me hot sweet milk flavoured with coffee, and asked me if I wanted anything. I only wanted to slip into unconsciousness, and soon did so: and was roused by a pleasant white-clad orderly, who gave me a pair of pyjamas, and helped me to undress. After this activity I had to go to the latrine again. I returned to my bed quite exhausted, and dropped helplessly on it, face down, without strength to get in and pull the sheets over me. As I lay thus, the orderly came in again, turned down my pyjama trousers, and stuck a needle in my bottom. Surprised and pained, I asked pourquoi. He pointed to his heart.

'Pour le coeur.'

'Ai-je donc le coeur faible?'

'Oui.'

Apparently a camphor injection.

The first two or three days in hospital were heaven itself, though during the nights Benghasi was usually raided by British bombers, and as there was an anti-aircraft battery near my window, I was at first somewhat shattered by the noise. I had the room to myself, and a sentry stationed at the door day and night for me alone. It gave me a sense of importance. Sometimes I could hear through the barred windows the voices of children playing on the beach, which was not far away. And I grew familiar with the song 'Lili Marlene' which all the German and Italian troops used to sing. It was a nostalgic tune with a kindly, if insensitive, swing.

The third day I was joined in my room by two more British officers, both slightly wounded. We talked about England: as I recovered, our conversation dwelt more and more on civilized food. There was nothing but talking, or thinking, or sleeping all the long hot day. Sometimes we played 'Battleships', David's game, which needs only paper and pencil. The two newcomers played at this game hour after hour: tired of it, fell silent till the sheer monotony of silence was unbearable, and started playing again.

Every day we talked more about food—food in England. Here we did not get enough to eat, it was not English fare, it did not have the dear, good savour. We planned enormous meals when we got back—when we felt our feet on our own land again. The longing for England grieved in me like a wound. My belly craved English food, my eyes craved and yearned for English pavements, my ears longed for the sound of English traffic: the shops, the advertisements printed in English, the cinemas, the English half-heard phrases of conversation as passers went by chattering. My nostrils thirsted for English savours. I was one incarnate longing for England. We prepared a menu of all the things we would eat when we got back—we canvassed restaurants in London, considered the Savoy and the Coq d'Or. Our menu included a kipper, two fried eggs and a rasher of bacon, steak, mushrooms, kidneys, beefsteak pudding, roast chicken, potatoes baked, mashed and fried, brussels sprouts, porridge with cream and brown sugar, rice pudding, currant pudding, apple tart with cream—and a list of drinks that began with Bass and champagne and ended with tea.

We had not lost hope of rescue at that stage. The battle at Tobruk ought to turn in our favour. So far as we knew, the 8th Army had more tanks, guns and aircraft than Rommel, and there was a reasonable chance that the Germans would be thrown back and the British once again occupy Benghasi.

We could not escape from the hospital. Our window was barred, and when one of us left the room to use the latrine, a sentry accompanied him. In any case they had our clothes, and one wouldn't get far in pyjamas. One day, when we were all convalescent and able to walk, they took us for an hour into a lounge or recreation room, very bare and rather dirty, but having one or two chairs and a table. We saw there—with a wry pain and amusement—that the walls were decorated with large, bright pictures of Snow White and the Seven Dwarfs, drawn apparently by British soldiers during one of the Allied occupations. 'Bashful' was fastening up his trousers, and in the background was a small box latrine. One felt less alone, facing this evidence that the room had sounded with British voices and British laughter, and feet that had walked in England had trodden this floor before we came there.

We all left the hospital together, in the same ambulance, and returned to the warehouse: after that I lost sight of the other two, who were flown over to Italy the following day, while I was sent on to a camp further along the North African coast, near Syrte. There I stayed for two months, and was eventually taken to Tripoli.

The camp at Syrte held, in addition to some medical officers and myself, nine thousand troops, British, African and Indian, all of whom came in a terrible condition of hunger and thirst after I had arrived there. Tobruk had fallen.

The fall of Tobruk was the end of our hopes of rescue. The Italian sentries were jubilant. They said 'Dopo Tobruk, Mersah: dopo Mersah, Alessandria: dopo Alessandria, Cairo.'

The camp was an earthly hell. For food, day after day, week after week, month after month, we ate the tiny allowance of rice stew, the third of a pound of bread, and the half-cup of ersatz coffee which was all the Italians gave us. Once when we had an orange we ate the skin as well. We soaked our bread in water to make it seem bigger. It is the truth that we lived, each week, on no more food than a healthy man eats in a day. Every day I watched the men grow thinner. The medical officers talked about the deficiency diseases which would soon break out. Very soon came the first cases of beri-beri, and malnutrition sores broke out, particularly on the men's legs. I was not affected by actual disease, though I became very thin. Each night I lay down to sleep with a raging, sickening hunger inside me. But it was terrible to look into the men's compound. They were starving to death.

And even at night they had no rest, because the camp was crawling with lice and fleas. We were all covered with vermin. In the evening, when you walked about the compound, the fleas jumped onto you from the ground in dozens. And there was always a foul smell because the Italians had not provided latrines, but merely dug trenches inside the men's compound, covering them over when full: so that in time almost all the ground actually surrounding the men's tents had been dug out, and the reek of decaying excreta came up through the soil. The tents were inadequate to shelter the men during the cold nights: the men slept on the ground, and had only one blanket each: and the flies and mosquitoes were worse than I have ever known them. When I had been there a fortnight, two men died of dysentery, and after that, day by day, the death-roll began to increase. There were no hospital facilities. The British doctors did all in their power, but they had few drugs, and men were dying as they walked about. You could see them lying by the wire, too sick to move. Their comrades carried them out of the tent in the morning, and back at night .

Some men were in that camp, a so-called transit camp, over five months. Many came in and never went out again.

Some of the men were employed by the Italians, loading trucks: they got an extra ration of bread for this. There were cases where prisoners were struck, or beaten, or tortured. A device I saw at the camp was to tie a man's wrists to his ankles and leave him in the sun for the day. A prisoner was struck on the back by a sentry who used the butt of his rifle and inflicted a gash which demanded medical attention. One evening two men were shot and killed—not trying to escape, but shot as they walked about within the wire, by a sentry outside. Also the doctors told me that some men who had tried to escape were punished thus: the Italians twisted their arms up behind their backs, and strung them up to a beam by their wrists, so that their toes were just touching the ground.

We were none of us in touch with home. I had not heard from Elizabeth since I left England. At Barce we had sent off an official card whose message 'I am a prisoner of the Italians: I am well treated', etc., was already printed. During the remainder of my five months in North Africa I was allowed to write three more letters—so were the men. We handed them in, but never received any reply or acknowledgment. We did not know what news of us had got home. I guessed we had been reported missing, at least.

The summer went over us, at Syrte and then Tripoli, and the short autumn followed, but all that it meant to us was that we grew thinner. It was worst when we went to bed: a frightening ebullience and lightness under the ribs and in the belly. The men were worse than we. Outside the barbed wire the sentries walked and watched. Inside, the weight of hunger day by day broke down the prisoners.

A group of men began to dig a tunnel out of their compound. It was discovered, and they were punished.

At the beginning of November, rumours—which were always sweeping the camp—took a new note. The British, driven back in July to El Alamein, near Alexandria, had launched an offensive. Rumour said it had failed: then contradicted itself, saying the offensive was progressing in the south: then in the north. Suddenly we were hearing that the 8th Army were attacking with twelve hundred tanks— they were breaking through—they were surrounding the German formations—they had moved forward from Alamein —they were held at Mersah—no, they were at Sollum—they were moving up to Bardia—there was a column striking from the south-east towards Tobruk—

Tobruk had fallen!

—they were still coming on—they had passed Tmimi—they were at Derna—the German divisions were running like hell for Benghasi—*the 8th Army had taken Benghasi and was still coming on.*

At this point a rumour came in so fantastic that I waited two days before at least even I was convinced.

Three divisions of American and British troops, with tanks, had landed in the west, in French North Africa, at Algiers, Oran, Mogador, Casablanca: and were driving hell-for-leather east towards Tunisia—*towards Tripoli!*

Chapter Forty

All prisoners in North Africa were sent across to Italy. We came across about the middle of November, disappointed, excited and pleased: disappointed because we had had absurd hopes of rescue; excited, because our transfer to Italy proved that the Axis feared the desert thrusts: pleased, because we might get more food in Italy —it was said that prisoners in Italy had a parcel every week from the Red Cross. And above all, from Italy we might get in touch with home.

I was taken on a small German merchantman at Tripoli, with about thirty other officers. At the quayside we saw five hundred British troops who had been captured with us, waiting to go on the same ship. They seemed, by the dust and sweat on them, to have marched some miles, and they were very thin, ill and dirty. All were bearded. They wore the same shorts and shirts as they had on when captured six months before, but these were mostly in tatters. More than half the men were barefoot. A few, who evidently had no clothing left at all, held a filthy blanket round them. Many were trembling with fever. Their thinness was such that their faces had lost individuality: all looked alike, and all like skulls. Cheek bones and jaws were prominent. Their eyes were large and bright, and stared out of their faces like the eyes of animals. One of the men shouted my name as I went past. I looked quickly but could not see a face I recognised, till one waved his arm, and I saw it was George Collinson.

All of us, men and officers alike, were put in the forward hold of the ship. When the men came on we saw several who were too sick to walk, and had to be carried aboard. George came past, and grinned at me with black lips.

'How are you, sir?'

'O.K. You?'

He shrugged and smiled again.

'These buggers have got it coming to 'em.'

'Better on the other side, they say.'

'Yeah. Hope so. See you in Blighty, sir.'

Later, when we were all in the hold, we heard that many of the sick men had asked to be taken into hospital in Tripoli, but had been refused. Two of them were in continuously fainting condition. Between fifty and sixty had dysentery: even on the quayside they had been unable to control their bowels. Some were passing blood.

The legs of all the men were remarkably thin, some had dwindled from the knee down to little more than the thickness of a man's wrist: thus the knee-joint and the ankle were thicker than the calf of the leg, like the legs of rickety children. Many had extensive starvation-sores on the legs, half-hidden by dirty bandages.

The noon sun was sweltering the ship when we went on, but in spite of this we were all ordered into the forward hold, and the sailors proceeded to close and batten down the hatches. On this the senior officer amongst us, an RAMC captain, forced his way back on deck and protested to the commander of the escort and to the Italian commandant on the ship. The latter refused any concessions, drew his pistol, and ordered our man to return below deck. There was some argument, and a further threat that if we were insubordinate we should be deprived of our bread ration. Finally the hatches were battened down on us.

No opportunity had been allowed for any of us to go to latrines. As there was no ventilation, the heat and the stench in the hold became overpowering. I got myself in a corner, my feet on the iron floor, my head and shoulders on the timbered bulkhead. Since there were no receptacles in the hold, the men with dysentery had to relieve their bowels on the floor. Many of them were also lying on the floor, too weak to stand. Urine, and the liquid motions usual in dysentery, soon covered the floor.

We knew from the pitch of the ship that we had put to sea. After some hours a door into a well-deck was opened, and we officers were taken out of the hold and put in another, smaller one, separated from the men's hold by a partition. Conditions in our hold were better: the men continued as before.

On the second day of the crossing, the Italians permitted two men at a time to go up on deck for latrine purposes. There was no latrine: defecation was performed over the ship's side—one wedged oneself in the rail. For the men who could not walk this privilege was worthless. Two men became dangerously ill, and were moved to the forecastle. Every night the hatches were battened down on us as before, but we officers were given two buckets for sanitary purposes during the night.

Two days out, a further privilege was granted to officers and men alike: three of us at a time were allowed on deck for a breath of air.

The officers' hold was covered in grease and black dust. No blankets were provided for any of us, but we were luckier than the men since we found in a corner of our hold some filthy pieces of timber, hatches, etc., and we slept on these instead of on the iron floor. It was very cold at night. One did not like to think of the men, in their thin, ragged khaki drill, lying on the iron: apart from the filth there.

In comparison with the men we had a luxury cruise, each with his own plank to sleep on. We were cheered by finding amongst us two RAF men who had been shot down within the last forty-eight hours before leaving Tripoli— one near Tunis, and the other, operating from the Libyan side, west of Ajedabia. Nothing would stop us now, they said. Rommel was finished, the Axis North African adventure was over.

The crossing took six days. Each day the smell in our hold became worse. for, in addition to the reek from our two buckets, a stench came from the men's hold, through the partition, such as I have never smelt before. It was far beastlier and more unutterably sickening than any pigsty smell. And if it were so to us, in a different hold, it was not hard to realise what the men's hold must be like.

Twice during the voyage we contrived to approach the

commandant for some alleviation of conditions. We had only bad language and threats.

Once the hatches were fastened down and the wedges driven home—as was done every night—we were in total darkness and completely without air for twelve hours. We were also battened down at any time during the day when there was an alarm, and this meant twice or thrice most days, as there was much activity in the waters between Tunisia and Italy. Whilst all the Italians and Germans of the ship and escort had life-jackets, we had none: moreover, since we were tightly battened down at every alarm, we should probably have drowned in our holds if the ship had gone down.

When we had been three days at sea, the Italians did a curious thing.

Our hold was opened, and an Italian officer called us out by name, one at a time, reading from an alphabetical list. I was second. I went out. The door was closed behind me, and the Italian put a revolver to my back. Guarded on either side by a couple of N.C.O.s, I went forward into a little cabin, a place about twelve feet square, and there they tied a bandage round my eyes, took off my shirt, and tied my hands behind my back with a piece of wire. Next they tied my legs together, knees and ankles: all the time the pistol was at my back. I was greatly alarmed.

They then pulled me face downwards over a table and beat me across the back and shoulders, using something hard, rough and heavy—I guessed thick, narrow-gauge hose piping. When they had finished, though I was not bleeding, I was in an indescribable emotional condition—humiliation, insult, outrage, and uncontrollable anger.

On the fifth day we put into port, Tampoli, in Sicily. An Italian doctor came aboard here, and the holds were cleaned out for the first time since leaving Tripoli. While in port, thirty prisoners at a time were allowed on deck. I looked for George, but he was not on deck at the same time as I.

Nearly two days later we reached Naples, and our stinking white cargo, after passing the Isle of Capri, was unloaded at the foot of Vesuvius. Photographers crowded round us on the quayside and at the station. I daresay they 'featured' us in the press as prisoners newly taken in the British November thrust from Alamein: they would draw attention to our rags and our thinness, and say this was the condition of the British fighting troops. Christ, how disgusting: but the Press is always disgusting.

Our prison camp was not far from Naples. It was a primitive place: the drains were inadequate, the water supply was always failing, there was no heating, the food was poor and scarce, and we slept in wooden huts, on beds made of three planks and a trestle. The best thing was that we had Red Cross food parcels every week, sometimes Canadian ones with plenty of dairy produce in them, and this addition to our diet transformed us completely. Within a week the change was visible. We had at last the one blessing we had dreamed of for six months—we were not hungry.

We were clean, too. Every fortnight we had a hot shower. True, all the huts and beds were alive with bugs, but after North Africa that was beneath our notice.

Every week we were allowed to write home a letter and a post-card. At last we began to hope that our letters would be answered. We heard that letters took about a month in transit, each way.

And now once again the days and the weeks and months fell imperceptibly on us, and our tiny compound, sixty yards by forty, which at one time held two hundred caged men, held also the invisible dead weight of all our wasted hours.

Chapter Forty-One

This is the notice, in approximate English, which hung over the barbed wire of our prison, close by the gate.

EXTRACT FROM THE DUTIES OF THE SENTRIES AT THE BARBED WIRE

The sentries at the boundaries of the camp must see that no prisoner of war goes near or stops near the barbed wire.

The minimum distance allowed is one metre from the wiring.

The sentries are not allowed to speak: all warnings to P.O.W. must be given without talking.

The sentries must forbid at all cost that the P.O.W. trespass the limits of the enclosed camp. In case of need they must intervene at once and with the most of energy, making also use of their weapons. IN THIS CASE THEY MUST SHOOT TO KILL, AS NO P.O.W. MUST ESCAPE ALIVE.

The sentries must see that from sunset to sunrise no P.O.W. looks out of the windows or keeps the shades open. All infractions must at once be reported to the duty officer.

Should the sentries hear any suspicious noise during the night they must immediately give the alarm using the recognised signals. In this case they are at once to flood-light the camp.

*   *   *   *

How to draw a moral from it all I do not know. But I know this: that I am very, very tired of the talk and the bitterness and the life we lead that is no life: it is a long time since my heart has been at rest. I am tired of the sneers at our 'enemies', and of their respectful hostility or

simple callousness to us. There is a time to have done wit
the responses of the nursery. I do not 'believe' in the war
—in this or any other.

I do not hate the Italians, the Germans or the Japanese.
I hate many of the things they have done, and I hate many
of the things we have done.

The war-emotions are frivolous. A grown man cannot
take them seriously. The war is as ridiculous as Sweeney
Todd, the Demon Barber. It is not related to the true feel
ings of real people. Only the sufferings are real. The cause
for which we suffer are contemptible and ridiculous.

I had been four months in Italy before the letter arrived,
the letter which meant for me the worst of it was over.

It was an Air-Mail letter card, and I stood with it in m
hand, trembling, and feeling light and empty—and tear
forcing themselves in my eyes. 'Posta di Prigionieri di guera'
—'Kriegsgefangenenpost'. The postmark was 'Helston, Cornwall: 11.30 a.m.' God, the barbed wire itself seemed to melt
away from round me as that hand stretched in for me. And
there I stood looking at the letter: seeing Elizabeth's writing: knowing that when I broke the censor's sealing-strip
I should have her with me again: knowing that the period
of separation was over.

33